A FAMILIAR CARESS

"I want to make love to you, Abbie."

"You certainly don't need to tell me first. Just come and hold me."

Zeke grinned, and as he approached her she wondered why there was an urgency about him, as though someone had told him that this was to be their last time together. He came closer and embraced her, his muscular arms encircling her tiny form. She rested her head against his broad chest that bore the scars of wounds and battles. She ran her fingers over the hard muscle of his arms, her skin looking so very white against his Indian coloring, even though she was tanned from living on the plains of Colorado for so many years. He kissed her hair and she turned her face up to him. His lips then hungrily met her mouth. Abbie did not understand why he was being so urgent, why he was not quite as gentle as he usually was. But as always, she felt lost beneath his broad strength, overwhelmed by his commanding nature, wanting to please the master of her heart and body. . . .

SAVAGE DESTINY

#6

MEET THE NEW DAWN

F. ROSANNE BITTNER

ZEBRA BOOKS

KENSINGTON PUBLISHING CORP.

ZEBRA BOOKS

are published by

Kensington Publishing Corp.
475 Park Avenue South
New York, NY 10016

Copyright © 1986 by F. Rosanne Bittner

First printing: April 1986

Printed in the United States of America

To Will Henry, a great author of books about the American West, who has been an inspiration in all my writing, and who has graciously afforded me support and friendship.

Each novel in this series contains occasional reference to historical characters, locations, and events that actually existed and occurred during the time period of each story. All such reference is based on factual printed matter available to the public. However, the primary characters in this series are purely fictitious and a product of the author's imagination. Any resemblance of the author's fictitious characters to actual persons, living or dead, or of the author's fictitious events to any events that may have occurred at that time and of which the author is unaware, is purely coincidental.

The major portions of this novel take place in present-day Colorado, Kansas, Oklahoma, Nebraska, Wyoming, and South Dakota. Fort Laramie is in southeast Wyoming; Fort Lyon is in southeast Colorado; Fort Robinson is in extreme northwest Nebraska; the reservation for the Southern Cheyenne is in northern Oklahoma per the Medicine Lodge Treaty of 1867; the Sioux/Northern Cheyenne reservation mapped out in a treaty with Red Cloud in 1869 encompasses most of the western half of South Dakota, from the Missouri River west to the Wyoming border.

This novel covers the years 1869 through 1886, during which most of the Indian wars were fought—the last days of freedom and an end to the old ways for the American Indian.

Acknowledgements: Various publications by Will Henry and Dee Brown; the Universities of Nebraska and Oklahoma; and the St. Stephen's Indian Foundation, Wyoming. Most of the facts pertinent to this story were derived from *The Southern Cheyenne*, by Donald J. Berthrong; and *Life of George Bent*, by George E. Hyde. All historical fact in this story was derived from publications available to the public.

Into this land I came
To place my hand in yours,
My man, my love, my life.
You held me close
Through pain and hardship,
Death and turmoil.
We were one in each other
And with the land,
Our spirits so blended
That even in death
We could not be parted;
For how can death take away love . . .
Or memories . . .
Or that kindred spirit that tells us
We will always be together.
I reach up to the heavens . . .
        And again, you take my hand.

                    Author

Prologue

In the West, the turbulent years following the Civil War were painful growing years—painful not only for the settlers, who faced tragedy at every turn; but also for the Indians, whose very life blood was being drawn from their bodies by the slaughter of the buffalo, incoming railroads, floods of miners, and settlers who put up fences. Their gradual demise was aided by deceitful traders, who handed bottles of cheap, sugared whiskey to the red man in return for valuable robes, and who took advantage of ignorance and desperateness, feeding the vengeful fires in the hearts of the Indians. The trail of deceit and misunderstanding that led to the end of the Indian way of life is a long one, and to this day there are many who still do not understand the Indian, and why he fought so desperately, why he committed some acts against settlers that were, to whites, despicable. Yet stories of equally despicable acts committed against the Indians by soldiers, miners, and buffalo hunters are seldom told, so that in the end, the history books give a distorted view of what really happened.

There were a few whites, like Agent Edward Wynkoop, who defended the Indians, explaining over and over that treaties should not be broken, that Indian villages should not be attacked without provocation, that all Indians should not be punished for what just a few of them did. But government and men in power didn't want to hear the Indian's side. They would prefer the Indian did not exist at all, for it would make the taking of their lands so much easier, and would relieve

13

their consciences. But the Indian did exist, and land-hungry railroad magnates, miners, and settlers dreaming of a new life had to find a way to either get along with the red man or exterminate him. The latter seemed simplest.

And so various soldier campaigns began, with unnecessary attacks on peaceful villages; the destruction of badly needed robes, food, supplies, ammunition, and horses; mutilation of women and children; constant pursuing and harassment of the Indians. These operations only caused more trouble, for the Indian was proud; his riding and fighting abilities magnificent; his spirit reckless and determined.

This story accents the last days of the fighting Cheyenne, under some of their greatest leaders: Dull Knife, Little Robe, Roman Nose, Bull Bear, Gray Beard, Tall Bull, and Medicine Wolf. Through 1867 they were chased and harassed by General Custer and Major General Hancock. The Cheyenne did not want the reservation life handed to them. They wanted what they considered their land—the plains of Kansas and Nebraska. They wreaked havoc upon the railroads, attacking work stations and tearing up tracks; brought terror to the settlers, burning ranches and stealing horses, murdering men and women alike. Eastern papers like the *Harper's Weekly* raged with headlines that told of horrible things the Indians did, but never told why, never explained the terrible fear and desperation the Indians felt at the loss of their precious freedom. Pride and strength were being destroyed by constant running, the introduction of rotten whiskey, and by white man's diseases.

Once pushed onto the new reservation land in 1867, there was a brief period of relative peace, until treaty provisions were once again ignored, promises broken, and the restless, unhappy Cheyenne exploded onto the plains again, raiding and murdering, not knowing how else to fight the puzzling whites who insisted on keeping them confined, who insisted on taking away their children and putting them into strange schools, who insisted that the Indian farm rather than hunt, who insisted that a way of life that was purely logical to the Indian was the wrong way. Misunderstanding piled upon misunderstanding, and again the Indians were hunted, with orders that

14

they be killed on sight.

Many Cheyenne headed north to join relatives who were already living among the Sioux. More and more settlers poured into the plains, the railroads continued to advance, buffalo continued to be slaughtered by the thousands that would lead to millions. Many Cheyenne still remembered the horror of the slaughter of their loved ones while camped peacefully at Sand Creek in 1864: soldiers mutilating women and babies beyond recognition, parts of bodies cut off or cut out, scalps taken, skulls smashed. The horror was reawakened in 1868, when another peaceful village camped on the Washita was similarly attacked and destroyed and a valued leader, Black Kettle, was killed. Again the Cheyenne made war, and again they were pursued and harassed to a place in northeast Colorado called Summit Springs, where a pitiful battle took place, leaving many warriors, women, and children dead, and an entire village burned, along with all food and supplies. A few of the survivors struggled north to join the Sioux but, for all practical purposes, the battle at Summit Springs in the summer of 1869 ended Cheyenne occupation of the land between the Platte and Arkansas Rivers, comprising most of Kansas and Nebraska.

The Cheyenne began surrendering themselves to Lt. Col. Anderson D. Nelson and to their new reservation in Oklahoma. They were starving and beaten. They had little choice, and bore little resemblance to the once-proud and mighty Cheyenne nation. Reservation life began under the Society of Friends, who were Quakers appointed by President Ulysses S. Grant to work among the Indians and help "civilize" the red man.

The old ways were ended, except for the few Northern Cheyenne who lived among the Sioux and continued their own hopeless fighting in Montana and the Dakotas. The Sioux had won a temporary victory over the soldiers and the United States government. Forts along the Powder River were closed and burned. The Sioux and Northern Cheyenne, under the great leader, Red Cloud, enjoyed the taste of revenge, thinking the white man would not come back to their land, for the red man had planted fear in their hearts. But citizens and congress

15

were screaming. Something had to be done. There was gold in the hills of Montana, and Red Cloud could not be allowed to interfere with white men wanting that gold. The treaty signed by Red Cloud, promising that whites could not enter his lands, would be drastically changed by the time it was signed in Washington. Again, the Indian would be deceived. The lands he so desperately fought for, spilled blood to keep, would not belong to him after all.

Through this turbulence one family clung together, a family familiar with both sides of the story. They were the Monroes: Zeke, a half-breed Cheyenne; Abbie, his white wife; and their several mixed-blood children. As the land felt the pain of change, so did the Monroes. But one thing did not change, and that was the great love shared between Zeke and his Abbie-girl. . . .

"As I rode down the trail, I could see written across the boundless western sky the signs of doom for the Indians of the vast plains; and, even more tragic, there seemed to be nothing—nothing that could save them from oblivion."

Father Pierre Jean DeSmet, a Roman Catholic missionary who worked among the Indians for fifty years, known as "Black Robe" to the Red Men that he loved.

from *The Wind River Rendezvous*
Vol. IX, Mar/Apr 1979 No. 2

Chapter One

The sky awoke in brilliant pink on a quiet morning in May, 1869, casting a peaceful glow on the ranch below. It lay there in the rich green that comes when the ground is still wet with melted winter snows, the Arkansas River dancing along the southern border of the eight hundred acres that belonged to Zeke and Abigail Monroe. Zeke raised some of the finest horses in Colorado, mostly Appaloosas; Abigail went about the many chores expected of a woman on a ranch in the 1800s.

The sun had not actually risen yet, but Zeke was already outside herding a feisty stallion into a corral while riding his own horse the way he always did. A small, flat saddle made of buffalo hide and stuffed with animal hair sat atop a colorful Indian blanket, for Zeke was himself half Indian, his mother's Cheyenne blood flowing through his veins. He looked all Indian, from his shiny black hair, which hung nearly to his waist—sometimes loose, sometimes braided—to his very dark skin and the fringed, buckskin clothing he preferred to the white man's uncomfortable pants and shirts. His feet were covered with beaded moccasins rather than boots. At his waist alongside a six-gun hung a knife, a rather infamous knife, which in Zeke Monroe's hands was much more deadly than the gun. For all his forty-nine years he was a strong, handsome man who did not show his age. He was over six feet tall, lean, and hard-muscled; a man very familiar with violence and hard living, whose body bore scars from old wounds and participation in the torturous teenage Indian Sun Dance Ritual.

He dismounted and closed the gate to the corral, which had higher fencing than any of the others, designed to keep the stallion from jumping it and going after the Thoroughbred that was also a part of the herd. Keeping the Appaloosas and Thoroughbreds separated was not always easy, for the mares didn't seem to be too particular which stallion became their mate; neither were the stallions particular about which of the many available mares became their love object. Only Zeke's constant watch let him know which mares were ready to mate, and they were corralled alone with the proper stallions at the right time. But during grazing on the open grasslands, nothing much could be done; there were a lot of mixed bloods in the herd, good enough in themselves, but not as good as the full bloods. Zeke Monroe was good with horses, and determined to raise only the best.

He moved back onto his mount with an animallike grace. A horse beneath him was as familiar and easily maneuvered as his own two feet. "Relax *Kehilan*," he told the Appaloosa stallion with a laugh. "I will bring you a woman soon. I understand your frustration, my friend." He laughed again and rode to the barn, dismounting and going inside where a man was shoveling feed into troughs for several horses that were separated into stalls.

"I finally got him into the corral," Zeke spoke to his son-in-law, walking and picking up a shovel himself. "A man plays hell trying to control that one when he's got a woman on his mind."

The other man laughed. "No different from his owner, I guess," he joked. He was as tall as Zeke and nearly as broad, a very dark, handsome man of thirty-four, twelve years older than his wife, Zeke's daughter Margaret. Morgan Brown was a mulatto, and no better match could have been made for Margaret Monroe, who had suffered some traumatic experiences because of her very Indian looks. Her unhappy, confused life had been straightened out when Morgan Brown stepped in to simply love her for what she was, understanding himself the tortured life of having two bloods. And therein lay the deep friendship he had built with Margaret's father, for Zeke Monroe could well attest to some of the miseries that came to a man of two worlds. He had learned some bitter lessons when being raised in Tennessee by his white father and a white stepmother. The young white girl he had married and their baby son had been brutally murdered by whites for running off with a half-breed. Revenge against the men who had committed the crime constituted Zeke Monroe's own first murders, after which he had fled west to find his Cheyenne mother. He lived among his Indian relatives for years before meeting another white woman, who forced him back into the white man's world simply because he loved her so much that he could not live without her. His Abbie—the reason he ran this ranch and had settled into one place.

"Speaking of women and mating, when is my first grandchild due?" Zeke asked, walking over and dumping some feed into another trough.

"Not for a good six months, I'm afraid. You think Abbie can wait that long to hold another baby in her arms?" Morgan asked.

Zeke laughed. "I suppose she'll have to. But my guess is once it's born my poor daughter will have a hell of a time getting her hands on her own child. Abbie will take full charge." He smiled, but an old, tiny ache was reawakened in his heart at the memory of how hard his Abbie had wept after the operation in Denver that guaranteed there would be no more children. After seven of them and too many brushes with death in childbirth, the operation had been necessary. That had been eleven years ago, when Abbie was only twenty-eight.

He stopped shoveling and faced his son-in-law. "I'm happy for you, Morgan, and for Margaret too. For a while there I thought my wayward daughter was lost forever. And the thought of a grandchild really makes us happy."

Morgan nodded. "Margaret is a good wife. And being raised by Abbie, I have no doubt she'll be a good mother." He looked around the barn and breathed deeply. "And I like it here, Zeke. I've never regretted the little deal we made. I didn't just invest in a ranch. I invested in a good woman, a family, and a home. We intend to stay right here and be a part of the ranch as long as you want it that way."

"Forever then," Zeke told him. "When I'm gone you can pretty much take over. The place is just as much yours now as

21

anybody's. Without your savings to restock the herd after that Comanche raid, I'd have lost everything."

"Well that's long paid back, so we're even, and I'm staying here because I love Margaret and love this place, not because anybody owes me anything anymore."

Zeke scooped up another shovelful of feed. "Well I'll need you to look after things for a while when Abbie and I take LeeAnn up to Julesberg to catch that train east. I'm not sure how long it will take us."

"No problem."

Zeke carried the feed to another trough and dumped it in. He stood there a moment, his heart heavy over the thought of sending LeeAnn off to a school in New York. He'd never seen cities like New York. St. Louis and Denver were probably the biggest cities he'd ever seen, but it mattered little to him. He hated cities of any kind. The people in them had little use for Indians, and he had little use for whites who had come west to gobble up the land and its resources with little regard for the red man who inhabited the plains and mountains and whose lives were sustained by the land. LeeAnn was one of his children who had no Indian characteristics, probably the least of any of the others. She was certainly a contrast to her father, with white-blond hair and beautiful blue eyes, apparently inheriting the genes of Abbie's older sister and Abbie's mother, both now dead.

LeeAnn had only been thirteen when the Monroe ranch was raided by Comanches and she was snatched away. Zeke had fought savagely to stop her abduction and had suffered severe wounds. There had simply been too many for even a skillful, hard-fighting man like Zeke to subdue, and he would never get over the guilt he felt for being unable to stop the Comanches that day. They had stolen nearly his entire herd, but that mattered little in comparison to the fact that they had snatched his daughter, and in spite of his wounds he was soon going after the raiders in search of LeeAnn. That had been almost five years ago. He had searched for months, risking his life to finally save her from the hands of Comancheros in a one-man rage that left eight men dead. The horror of her captivity had left a lasting impression on LeeAnn's mind. Now eighteen, she wanted nothing more than to forget—to leave the wild, lawless land that frightened her and go east where there was civilization, where she needn't fear outlaws and Indians, even though her own father was part Indian.

But what hurt Zeke was that he knew deep inside she would deny her Indian blood once she got away from Colorado. In spite of how much she might love her own father, she would not admit to her heritage, and she would deny the people who were dying now on wretched reservations because of the greed of the very people the girl would be mixing with. But he would put aside his personal hurt. He knew what she had suffered, and he wanted his daughter to be happy. If going to college in the East would help, then she should go, he supposed. He couldn't expect all of his children to be exactly the way he wanted them. He turned to walk back to a bag of feed when his son Jeremy walked in. The boy was seventeen, the fourth child, and another one who was all white in nature and looks.

"Where have you been?" Zeke asked in an irritated voice. "We could use your help."

The boy shoved his hands into the pockets of his cotton pants. He didn't wear buckskins like his father. For that matter, he had nothing in common with Zeke. "I overslept. I was up late reading," Jeremy told him. "And I had to ask mother something this morning before I came out here." The boy swallowed nervously. He was never quite sure how to talk to his father, for they were worlds apart in spirit and nature. Jeremy couldn't be like Wolf's Blood, the firstborn, the son who was all Indian and of whom his father was very proud. He supposed Zeke was proud of him also, but not in the same way, and Jeremy had never felt he could truly please his father.

"And what was so important to make you late for chores?" Zeke asked, setting the shovel aside and folding his arms.

The boy took a deep breath. "I . . . I'd like to go to Julesberg with you and Mother, when you take LeeAnn, Father. And I think I'd like to stay."

Zeke frowned. "Stay? What for?"

"I don't know for sure. I just want to see some of the world, Father, like LeeAnn will get to do. Maybe I can find a job there—maybe for the railroad, even. I've wanted to learn more

23

about trains and all." Zeke continued to frown as he listened, and Jeremy shifted nervously. "I know what the railroad is doing to the Indian," he added. "But it's coming whether the Indians want it to come or not, Father. It's part of a whole new civilization coming west, and I want to be a part of the excitement. I've never liked being here on the ranch all the time. You know that. I want to do some more exploring, get some more schooling. You know I like reading and learning. I could maybe get a real important job some day."

Zeke glanced at Morgan, who shrugged and went back to his work. Then he took some tobacco and paper from a pouch he wore on his belt, holding the paper in one hand and pouring the tobacco into it with the other. "Running this ranch is an important job, Jeremy," he told his son. He licked the paper and sealed it. "That's what you might be doing some day, you know. Who knows if your brother will come back to this life?" His heart ached at the words. Wolf's Blood was a treasured son. The boy had been Indian from the beginning, and now lived in the North with his Cheyenne uncle, Swift Arrow, where he lived and warred against soldiers and miners in Red Cloud's fight for the Black Hills and the Powder River country. How he missed his son! He lit his cigarette.

"You know what I mean, Father. And you have Morgan now, and Jason is eleven already and helps a lot. You don't really need me all that much. You thought you needed Wolf's Blood too, but you let him go north to live with the Indians—to make war and be wild. Why is that any different from me? You knew it was his nature to live like that, so you let him go because you understood that part of him. You're more Indian than white. You want to live just like Wolf's Blood, and you would if it weren't for mother. Now I'm asking you to understand me— my side! I want to go to Julesberg and maybe get a job for the railroad. I'm seventeen and old enough to try. You always understood Wolf's Blood—always let him be his own man. Can't you do the same for me?"

Zeke took a deep drag on the cigarette, studying his handsome but slightly built son, whose hair and eyes were a medium brown, and whose skin was tanned but bore none of the darkness of an Indian. Jeremy was so different from Wolf's

Blood, who would not even take a white name. Zeke felt he had somehow failed Jeremy, perhaps expected too much of him. Jeremy had never been able to ride and shoot well, had never been interested in the things Zeke thought were important. They had never been close in the way that Zeke and Wolf's Blood had been. And he knew that if he let Jeremy go, the boy would never return to the ranch.

"What did your mother say?" he asked.

The boy sighed. "She's not real happy about it, just because she doesn't want to see me go away. But she said it's my decision and that you let Wolf's Blood make his own decisions when he was my age and I should have the same right. But she said it's up to you in the end."

Zeke nodded. "She did, did she? Then I guess it's up to me to be the good guy or the villain. But since it probably wouldn't do any good to tell you that you can't go, I won't. You're old enough that you'll ride off and do what you damned well please anyway, so why should there be hard feelings over my telling you not to go?"

The boy grinned a quick, bright smile. "Thank you, Father! And you watch and see. I'll be a real successful man some day."

Zeke's dark eyes ran over this son of his. Their ideas of what success was vastly differed. "I hope you find what you're looking for, Jeremy. I guess it was never here, was it? Maybe some day you'll find out it was here all along."

"I don't know. But I won't ever know if I don't go away, will I?"

"I suppose not. Now go out and fill the water trough for *Kehilan*, will you? He's got himself worked up this morning and probably needs a drink by now. And pour the water through the fence posts. Don't go inside. You know how ornery he can get."

"Yes sir." The boy hesitated. "I'm sorry, Father, if you're disappointed in me."

Zeke sighed deeply, reaching out and grasping the boy's shoulder. "I'm not disappointed, Jeremy. No two people can be alike. Not even a father and his son. You're all different and you all have different dreams. Don't worry about it."

"But you and Wolf's Blood are just alike."

Zeke threw down the cigarette stub onto the dirt floor of the barn and stepped on it firmly. "In most ways. But even Wolf's Blood and I have our differences. Go on now."

The boy nodded, tears in his eyes, then turned and ran out. Zeke watched after him. Why should he tell Jeremy the real reason he would like him to stay? He might need him more than ever in a few years, maybe sooner. And if he went away now, maybe he would never see his son again. Jeremy didn't know about the pain he suffered. No one knew, not even Abbie. It had irritated him endlessly through the past winter, attacking his back and joints relentlessly. It had been difficult to mask it, but he had done so. At first he attributed it to a long, hard life and old wounds. But now he suspected it was more than that. With the coming of spring and warmer weather, the pain had lessened again, but he knew deep inside it would return every winter to claim him more fiercely each time, and that some day it would render him helpless, perhaps kill him. He didn't need a doctor to tell him so, but he'd see one in Julesberg anyway, if he could get away with it without Abbie knowing. Maybe a doctor could at least give him something for the pain. Outwardly he was still healthy, strong, and sure, as he forced himself to work at the same rigorous pace he had always followed. His body was rock-hard and muscular, and he was glad that so far he'd been able to keep the pain a secret from Abbie, who had suffered enough over the years. He did not intend to burden her with this unless it was absolutely necessary. And why should he use it as a tool to keep his excited young son from going after his own dreams?

"I'll tell you who you're really in the same spirit with," Morgan spoke up to Zeke, interrupting the man's thoughts.

Zeke looked over at the man and picked up his shovel again. "Who's that?" he asked.

"*Kehilan,*" his son-in-law answered. The spirited stallion's name was Cheyenne, meaning *Drinker of the Wind.* The horse whinnied outside, prancing around the corral restlessly. "You and that horse are one and the same—both wild and restless as the wind. That's why you're the only one who can ride him. You understand each other."

Zeke grinned and scooped up more feed. "Maybe so,

26

Morgan." He walked to another trough, his heart heavy with the thought of Jeremy leaving. If only Wolf's Blood would come home. He was sure even the pain that plagued his body would be better if he had his eldest son with him. Having the boy gone was like having a piece of his heart removed. But at least he had his Abbie, the ranch was doing well, and their first grandchild would be born, in the *Moon When the Wolves Run Together*.

"That's the last of the special feed," he told Morgan. "It's been sitting a while and I wanted to use it up. There's some beautiful spring grass out there. This will be a good year for grazing. All we need is a little rain now and then."

Abbie folded the handmade quilt and carefully laid it across the foot of the bed. Then she walked around it, running her hand along the smooth finish of the brass bars at the foot and head of the grand bed that nearly filled the small bedroom of the cabin. It was the most beautiful thing her husband had ever bought her. He had picked it up at Fort Lyon, where settlers who had decided to go on to California had traded it for supplies. The bed had been a sweet gift of luxury for his white woman, in appreciation for the twenty-four years she had loved him, had stuck by him through hardships the average woman could never bear. In addition to the common tragedies of living in a lawless, untamed land, Abigail Monroe had accepted the difficulties that come to a white woman willing to proudly marry a half-breed. For a good share of those years she had put up with the "Indian" side of her man—the side that sometimes took him into another world she could not fully share. In their first years they had actually lived in a tipi, sometimes among the Cheyenne. She had been accepted as one of them and had learned to love them as her family, for she had lost all those dear to her on her journey west with her father when only fifteen. Zeke Monroe had been the scout for that fateful journey, and she knew the moment she set eyes on him who she wanted to share her life with.

She smiled at the thought of it. She had never minded the bed of robes they shared most of their married life, nor those first few years living among the Cheyenne. But Zeke knew a white woman could not wander the plains forever. A white woman should settle in one place. And so he had abandoned his Indian ways for her and settled into ranching. But a part of him remained Indian: his fighting spirit; his need to sometimes ride off alone and free; his religion; the way he dressed. But the way of life his People had once known was ending, and a little bit of Zeke was dying with them. It could not be helped. He had seen most of the Cheyenne close to him die—his mother, stepfather, and two brothers. The only Indian brother left was Swift Arrow, who lived among the Sioux in the North and with whom their oldest son now also lived. If only Wolf's Blood would come home, she knew how it would gladden her husband's heart, especially now that Jeremy would be leaving them at Julesberg.

She sat down on the edge of the bed, glancing at the bed of robes that was still kept, now in the corner of the room. There had been mornings when she would awaken to find Zeke sleeping there rather than in the brass bed, for the white man's bed was too soft for his hard-muscled body. Still, when they first retired at night, it was always together in the brass bed, for she could not go to sleep without the closeness of her man. Their marriage still enjoyed the same sweet passions they had delighted in when first they fell in love so many years ago. Being one with his woman was important to Zeke Monroe, a source of strength for him. It was the same for Abbie. What woman would mind giving pleasure to a man like Zeke or receiving the pleasures he gave her in return?

The results of their great passion had been seven children, all different, some very Indian, others showing no Indian likeness or spirit. There were six now, little Lillian having died four years ago at the age of eight. The loss still tore at Abbie's heart in the night. Not many women ever fully recovered from the death of a child. Her heart was made heavier by the fact that soon there would only be two children under their own roof. Wolf's Blood, the wild, oldest son, made war in the North. Margaret was married, although she and Morgan at least lived in a cabin nearby. LeeAnn and Jeremy were leaving. That left only Ellen, fifteen, and Jason, eleven. It was difficult to accept the fact that any of them were old enough to leave the nest, and she dreaded the day when Jason, her "baby," would also go. But the boy loved the ranch, loved helping with the horses. Perhaps Jason would stay around. She prayed that he would. Ellen, of course, would one day marry. And when a woman married, she had to go with her man, just as Abbie had done. She had come to this land from Tennessee, and had never seen Tennessee again.

She called out to LeeAnn, who was in the outer room clearing the table. The girl came through the door. Although a beautiful young woman, Abbie saw only a blond-haired little girl. She rose and went to a small trunk that sat against the wall. "Come here, LeeAnn."

The girl came closer and knelt down in front of the trunk beside her mother. Abbie slowly opened the trunk, and a slightly musty smell emerged. She rummaged amid the special things inside: her own father's old fiddle; marbles that had belonged to her little brother, who had died on the trip west. They all had died on that trip—her father, brother, and sister. Her mother was already dead, back in Tennessee, and Abbie had been left alone. But Zeke had been there. Her Zeke. She held up a leather belt with eagle feathers on it.

"This was a gift from an old Cheyenne priest, LeeAnn, in honor of the fact that I had killed three Crow Indians with my own gun—not all at the same time of course!" She laughed lightly. "I killed one when your father's life was threatened while he was rescuing me from outlaws when we first met, and I killed one when the wagon train was being attacked and one when your father and I were being chased by renegades the day we rode into Zeke's Cheyenne village for the first time." She sighed. "What a long time ago it all was. I once cut a bullet out of Zeke, LeeAnn. And he saved my life once when he had to cut an arrow out of me and burn out the infection." She met her daughter's eyes. "Have I told you all these things before?"

The girl smiled patiently. "Yes. But you've never shown me everything in the trunk, Mother."

Abbie proceeded to rummage through old souvenirs: a blanket and knife from Runs Slowly, father of a little Indian girl Abbie had saved from drowning; a bow and two arrows

29

from Falling Rock, a good friend, who had also given her the gifts for saving the little girl; a jeweled music box Zeke had bought for her in Santa Fe; her father's fiddle; her brother's marbles; some jewelry that had been her mother's. LeeAnn watched her, studying her mother's well-preserved, dark beauty. The long, thick reddish-brown hair was scooped away from her lovely face and gathered into a comb at the crown of her head, the back of it hanging long and loose. Whenever she spoke of her early days with Zeke Monroe, Abigail's face had a way of glowing—lighting up like the young girl that she was when she met LeeAnn's father. She pulled out a leather pouch then, carefully opening it and taking out five turquoise stones, round and smooth, of various sizes.

"I don't think I ever showed you these," she said, a near whisper to her voice. "They're crying stones. Zeke gave them to me."

LeeAnn touched the stones held out in the palm of her mother's hand. "Crying stones?"

"When a little girl on the wagon train was bit by a rattler, Zeke buried her in mud, then sat with the child all night, singing Indian chants and praying for her. He gave her these, and told her that when she felt like crying, she should cling tightly to them and the stones would cry for her. She did what he told her, but she couldn't hold the stones because she was buried. So Zeke laid them in front of her and told her to concentrate very hard on the stones. Soon they began to sweat, and the moisture on them was salty."

LeeAnn stared at the stones, hardly able to believe the story. But her mother never lied to her.

"I'm sure part of his intention was just to take the little girl's mind off her pain and fear," Abbie went on. "But the fact remains that the stones did seem to be crying for her. Everyone was astonished. But I wasn't really very surprised. Zeke has a great inner strength, LeeAnn. It comes from that spirit world he can draw on, a world his Indian side knows. These stones are a part of that great spirit. That special inner strength he has, has given him the courage and fortitude to overcome many obstacles that could have meant death for him. That's why he carries many scars, but no wound has killed him. And you know yourself, from the night he saved you from the Comancheros, what a skilled and brave man he is."

The girl's eyes teared. "Why are you telling me all this now, Mother?"

Abbie closed her hand around the stones. "Because I know that when you leave us at Julesberg and go east, it will be a long, long time before you come back again—perhaps so long that one of us will be gone when you return."

"Mother, don't talk that way!"

"I feel I must," Abbie told her, taking her hand. "I don't mean to frighten you or spoil the wonderful things ahead of you, LeeAnn. But part of the reason I am reminding you of the kind of man your father is, is because I don't want you to be ashamed that he is part Indian, or that you yourself carry Indian blood. I know that you will deny that blood, and it breaks your father's heart—and mine. Sometimes I wrap my hand around these stones, hoping they will take some of the tears from my heart. But it doesn't always work. I have too many tears for the stones to take."

"Mother, stop it!" the girl whispered, turning her eyes away.

Abbie squeezed her hand. "LeeAnn, my love and prayers will go with you. And I want you to find all the things you think you want. But I will tell you now that no matter how much you might turn away from your heritage, it will always be there. Your father and I will always love you and you will always have a home here, if you ever want to come back. We both understand why you have to go—the fear you still carry and the memories of those terrible weeks with the Comancheros. If your father and I could die a hundred times over to change the past for you, we would do it. But there is another reason you must go, and that is simply that you do not seem to fit in out here—at least you think you don't. But you do. You are a Monroe, LeeAnn, no matter how hard you might try to ignore that fact. And part of you is Cheyenne. They are our friends, our family, even though so much has changed and some of them make war now. They're desperate, hurting."

"I know that," the girl said quietly, picking up the leather belt with the eagle feathers on it. "But I can't go running to some reservation to volunteer my services, Mother. It simply

31

isn't in me. Nor is it in me to stay here and marry some . . . ranch hand."

Abbie swallowed back an urge to scold the girl. She reminded her so much of her own sister, after whom LeeAnn was named. She, too, had been blond and pretty, and she, too, had considered herself worthy of better things than their father could offer them and had searched for a man of wealth and prominence. But that search had led to a violent death for her sister. Abbie could only pray that her daughter would not be so terribly duped because of her ignorance of the outside world. And she could not be angry with the girl for wanting something different, for LeeAnn Monroe had experienced a traumatic and frightening event at the tender age of thirteen, and it had left its mark.

"I'm not asking you to do anything that is against your nature or your desires, LeeAnn," Abbie replied. "I am only asking you to always remember your father and how he risked his life for you. And to remember your heritage. Blood cannot be denied, LeeAnn. Always remember that we love you just as you are. So should anyone else who comes into your life. Don't go off and pretend you are something other than LeeAnn Monroe."

The girl sighed. "I honestly don't know right now what I will do, Mother. It will just be fun going someplace new, going to school." She finally met the woman's eyes. "I'll write often, I promise." She swallowed. "I love you, Mother. I can't imagine that there is anyone in the whole world as strong and wonderful as you are. Look at all you've been through out here, and still you endure. I wish I could be as strong as you. I don't know how you do it."

"I have Zeke," was the simple reply. She took two of the stones and handed them out. "Here. You keep a couple of these with you. Use them in the way your father said to use them. And remember him when you do. You have the sweater I knitted for you. We set a little aside to buy you some more clothes in Julesberg. We'll get there a day or two early so we'll have some time together to shop."

The girl's eyes teared again and she suddenly hugged her mother tightly. "Thank you, Mother. I know it hasn't been

32

easy to come up with the money."

"It was worth it," the woman answered, patting her shoulder. "We'll manage just fine. With Morgan's financial help your father is back on his feet again and has already paid him back, with a tidy savings ahead for you and any other children who might want further schooling."

"But what about you. You've always wanted to make the house bigger, get some nice furniture and . . ."

Abbie waved her off. "Why have a bigger house now, when half the children are leaving us? I'll have only Ellen and Jason, and they both sleep in a loft that once held all seven of you. What little furniture we have is sufficient." She looked at the brass bed. "And I have my fine bed."

The door to the kitchen—also considered the main room of the small cabin—opened then, and Zeke's voice boomed out. "I have that rabbit cleaned and ready for you, Abbie-girl."

Abbie closed the trunk and both of them went out of the bedroom. Zeke stood at the table, laying a skinned rabbit on a piece of burlap, the huge, infamous blade still in his hand. The Indians called his knife "great medicine." His enemies never lived long enough to call it anything. Many men had suffered a dire fate by Zeke Monroe's blade—any who threatened him or his family—beginning with the men back in Tennessee who raped and murdered his first wife. Zeke had long ago lost count of how many had met their deaths by the knife, a huge blade embedded into the jawbone of a buffalo, which served as the handle. It was old, but it did its job. LeeAnn knew firsthand. She had witnessed his one-man rampage against the Comancheros who held her captive. He had actually frightened her that night, for although she had heard many tales about her own father, she had never seen in such explicit detail and reality just how he could wield a knife against his enemies.

She stared at him now, and he stared back, realizing that soon she would be gone—his LeeAnn. Never would he forgive himself for being unable to stop the Comanches from tearing the screaming girl from his arms. LeeAnn walked up to him then, hugging him around the middle.

"I love you, Father," she told the man. Then she pulled away. "I'm going up to the loft to finish my packing."

She hurried up the ladder to the loft, and Abbie walked closer to her husband. "She'll be all right, Zeke. And so will Jeremy. They may stray from home, but they're still Monroes." She walked over to the hearth. "Do you want some coffee?"

"Not right now. I have some chores to finish," he said quietly.

She turned to see him looking up at the loft. What a handsome man he still was! But something was bothering him—something more than Jeremy and LeeAnn leaving. She could not say just what, and knew he would not tell her until he was good and ready. That's the way he was. There was no sense questioning him too much. But she suspected part of the problem, and had made up her mind to try to do something about it.

"Have some coffee anyway, Zeke. Surely you can spare another minute or two. I want to talk to you about something."

He met her eyes and finally grinned a little. "What are you cooking up now, woman?"

She came to the table and sat down. "Please sit down just for a minute."

He chuckled and shook his head, sitting down at the end of the table. "What is it, Abbie?"

She set the cup down. "I think that if we're going all the way up to Julesberg, we might as well keep going—to Fort Laramie. Why don't we go see Dan and Bonnie? And hopefully Joshua. I haven't seen him since he was a baby." He frowned, and she reached out and took a hand. "Zeke, if we go to Fort Laramie, you could go on from there—into Powder River country. You could look for Wolf's Blood and make sure he's all right. You could find Swift Arrow and have a good visit with him. You haven't seen your brother in years, and it's been almost three years since Wolf's Blood left home to go back north. My God, Zeke, everyone knows how you love that boy. And I know better than most. You need to see him, talk to him, make sure he's all right. I know it would be too dangerous for me to go along, things being the way they are now with the Sioux, but at least I would know if he's all right. You can ride right into the midst of them. You're Indian."

34

He leaned toward her, rubbing the back of her hand with his thumb. "Abbie you come up with some of the damnedest ideas. To tell you the truth, I'd considered that a time or two, but I wasn't sure what you'd think of it."

"You should have known I wouldn't care. I'll worry about you. There is a different spirit among the Indians now. It would be impossible for me to go. But you know them, and you're Cheyenne. You shouldn't have any trouble." She squeezed his hand. "And knowing you, you'll spend a few days there once you find them, and you should. It would give you a chance to be Indian again. I know the ranch gets to you sometimes—the settledness of it, the routine schedules. We could both get away and visit with people we care about. Morgan and Margaret can take care of things here. We'll leave Ellen and Jason here, too. And after we leave Julesberg, it will be just you and me."

Their eyes held, and her blood felt warmer at the look he gave her. "It's been a long time since it's been just you and me, Abbie-girl, out under the open skies," he told her with a wink.

She smiled and actually blushed some, and he laughed lightly. He leaned forward then, meeting her lips in a sweet kiss, loving her more for the way she always understood him. It would be good for both of them to take a trip, and he would like nothing better than to ride into the villages of the Sioux and Northern Cheyenne and find his brother and son. The fact that they were literally at war with the miners and settlers in the Dakotas and Montana mattered little to him, for he was Indian like they were and did not fear them.

Abbie knew that she would lose her Tennessee man for a while when they reached Fort Laramie and he left her to ride into Indian territory. But she was used to that other side of him—the side that sometimes called him away. He stood up then, coming around and putting his hands on her waist, suddenly grabbing up his small wife and pulling her close, embracing her in powerful arms and holding her there so that her feet were off the floor. She laughed lightly as he nuzzled her neck.

"Zeke, LeeAnn is up in the loft, and Margaret will be here any minute."

"So? Do they think their parents don't do these things anymore?" He leaned back slightly, and she studied the dark, handsome face, the deep dark eyes that never failed to literally hypnotize her to his command. "I'll say one thing for that brass bed," he said with a handsome grin, "I don't like it much for sleeping, but it's damned comfortable for other things." She reddened and he quickly met her lips then, in a long, hungry kiss.

They would go north to see his only living white brother, Dan, who was an officer in the western army stationed at Fort Laramie. And he would find his only living Indian brother, Swift Arrow. But most important, he would find his son, his precious son, Wolf's Blood. He was tempted to tell her the real reason he needed to see Wolf's Blood again, the real reason he hoped that maybe the boy would come home with him. But he would not burden her with that. Besides, the pain was better now that the weather was warmer.

Chapter Two

Steam billowed in white clouds from the monstrous Union Pacific engine, where it sat waiting for passengers to board the several cars it pulled. More people than usual crowded the station, for this was a special day. It was May 10, 1869, and excitement penetrated the air as all waited for the telegraph message to come through.

Zeke and Abbie stood with their son and daughter on the platform, the older man's commanding appearance in bleached, beaded buckskins drawing stares from others. Men wondered if he might be dangerous; women simply were curious over the wild but handsome look about him. The thin scar down his left cheek detracted little from his rugged good looks; rather it told of a well-used man, one familiar with violence and hard living. But Colorado was becoming settled and civilized now. In the towns, men wearing buckskins were not often seen anymore, instead keeping to the more remote areas and around the army forts.

Zeke was determined that LeeAnn and Jeremy would remember him for what he was and somehow remember their own heritage and not be ashamed. His moccasins were brightly beaded, his fringed leggings and deerskin shirt painted in colorful designs. He wore a long necklace of small turquoise stones, and a wide bone choker necklace that graced his muscular throat. His black hair was plaited into a thick braid down his back, with colorful beads wound into it and a hair ornament decorated with a tiny bell at the side.

The stares came not just because of his own appearance, but because a beautiful white woman stood beside him, wearing a lovely green day dress and cape, a puff bonnet sitting daintily on her head and tied under her chin, adorning thick, reddish-brown hair that was braided and looped behind her ears. Why was the Indian man standing with a white woman, and a young blond girl and white boy? Abbie ignored the stares. She was used to them by now.

The announcement came then, as a man ran out of the station's telegraph office. "It's done!" he shouted. "They drove the last spike!"

The crowd broke into cheers, hats flying into the air, people hugging. The black engine bellowed out more steam and the engineer began wildly clanging the bell. In an open area near the station a band began playing and somewhere in the distance firecrackers were set off, causing horses to whinny and rear, some bolting away.

"By God, there's no stopping us now!" one man yelled to another. "First the Atlantic and the Pacific—next the world!"

"I'd like to be in Promontory City right now!" another laughed. "I'll bet it's wild today!"

"The whole country will be wild today! I heard they've got parades planned in all the big cities. And Wall Street is closing for the day!"

Zeke and Abbie just looked at each other, unsmiling. Completion of the Transcontinental Railroad meant more than just the uniting of a country. It meant the end of a people already being quickly forgotten, kicked by the wayside in the name of progress. It meant the demise of the Indian, just one more symbol of the red man's final days.

"If I had known what was going on today, I'd have picked a different time to be here," Zeke grumbled.

Abbie touched his arm and squeezed it gently. "I'm sorry, Zeke." She swallowed back her own tears. "Here we are saying good-bye to our daughter, and now this."

He sighed and patted her hand. "Well, that's what we get for living so far from civilization. There are things going on we don't even know about."

LeeAnn touched her mother's shoulder. "I should get on the

train, Mother," she told the woman. Her eyes were watery, and the two women suddenly hugged, hard and long.

"LeeAnn, are you sure—"

"I have to go, Mother. Aunt Bonnie told you what a good school it is, and it's just for girls. There will be someone waiting for me at the station in New York. I'll be fine."

The crowd continued cheering, oblivious to the sad parting that was taking place. Jeremy shook his father's hand, and could not hide the excitement in his own eyes, despite the sadness of this final parting from the only life he'd ever known. As soon as they had arrived at Julesberg, he'd run off to talk with railroad people, and in no time at all had gotten himself a job loading and unloading baggage cars. They even allowed him to stay with this particular train all the way to New York, so he could watch over his sister.

The boy was ecstatic over his new "career," as he called it, and Zeke knew that once the parting was done, it would be a long time before he saw Jeremy Monroe again—maybe never. Their eyes met and Zeke kept hold of the boy's hand. "I've taught you truth and honesty and hard work, Jeremy," he told his son. "Don't forget those things."

"You know I won't, Father."

"You just remember that some of the men in the railroad business are far from truthful and honest. It's easy to get caught up in a hunger for power, Jeremy."

"Father, all I'm doing is loading baggage cars!"

Zeke kept a firm hold of his hand. "You're a bright boy. You won't be doing just that for long. You have energy and a desire to grow. Just remember your roots, Jeremy."

Their eyes held, both of them wanting to say things they could not express. Their worlds were simply too far apart, yet they were father and son. The boy swallowed. "I . . . do love you, Father. I just can't be what you want me to be."

Zeke's eyes teared. "I love you, too, Jeremy."

They suddenly hugged. "I hope you find Wolf's Blood," the boy said quietly. "Tell my brother I think of him often. I'm sorry we could never be close."

Zeke hugged him tightly, unable to speak. In the next moment mother and father were trading children and Zeke was

39

hugging LeeAnn, who wept openly now. Then Jeremy picked up LeeAnn's baggage and his own small carpetbag, quickly turning away and boarding the train with his arms loaded. LeeAnn clung to her father's hands for one last moment.

"I'll regret to my dying day the fact that I couldn't keep those Comanches from taking you, LeeAnn," the man told her, his voice husky with sorrow.

"Oh, Father, I've never seen anyone fight so savagely! What more could you have done? And you came after me and got me back. I wish you wouldn't think about it so much. I'm all right now. I'll be even better when I get to New York and start a new life."

The man nodded. "I won't see either of you again, will I?"

"Father, don't be silly!"

"I won't. Once you get a taste of cities and the fine life— once Jeremy gets involved in moving up in the white man's world—neither of you will come back."

"Of course we will! It might not be right away, Father, but we'll be back."

But you won't come back in time! he wanted to shout at her. They had walked around in rain the night before, and all night his elbows and finger joints had ached fiercely. The damned, unknown disease that plagued him was determined not to go away.

"All aboard!" a conductor called out. "North Platte, Grand Island, Omaha, Council Bluffs, Iowa City, Chicago! All aboard!"

There was a last hug from LeeAnn before the girl turned then and ran to the train. Jeremy grasped her hand and helped her aboard, and both turned and waved once more. The train began to slowly move out, and Zeke and Abbie walked rapidly alongside it for a short way, waving. Abbie was blowing kisses, her eyes so full of tears that she couldn't really see her son and daughter very well. The train moved faster then, and they stopped walking. LeeAnn and Jeremy leaned farther out, waving more, until they were two small dots in the distance. Abbie put a hand on her husband's arm.

"They'll be back," she tried to assure him, hoping to convince herself at the same time.

He looked down at her with tragic eyes. "I don't think so, Abbie—not for a good long time." He breathed deeply. "Why has it always been so hard for me to tell him I love him? It's always been so easy for me to tell Wolf's Blood."

"Wolf's Blood is just like you and Jeremy isn't. Wolf's Blood refused to even take a white name, and Jeremy in turn would rather forget that he has an Indian name. Perhaps you resented him—just a little—because I almost died when he was born. Who knows why these things happen, Zeke?"

He saw her struggling to keep her own composure and knew she was only trying to make him feel better. People around them were still cheering and celebrating the completion of the Transcontinental Railroad, yet neither of them could hear the screaming and laughter. They stood in their own world, seeing only each other. Her own mother's heart was bleeding. A moment ago two of her precious children were with her, now they were gone, for months, maybe longer.

She took his hand. "Let's go back to the hotel and rest. We still have to head for Fort Laramie tomorrow. Maybe you'll be able to find Wolf's Blood, Zeke. You'll feel better when you see him. You're always happier when you've seen him. Maybe he'll come back with you."

He sighed deeply and took her arm, leading her through the crowd. "The boy is as wild as the wolves he's named after. I don't know if I can ever get him to come home again."

Abbie started awake, her first thoughts of LeeAnn and Jeremy. Her chest felt tight from worry, and the exhausted sleep she had fallen into had been a restless one. She had a terrible feeling that it was not just the recent departure of her children that had brought on this odd feeling of dread. She rubbed at her eyes. The room was dark. Apparently the afternoon nap she had intended to take had turned into something longer than that, for she had cried herself to sleep, and that always exhausted her. It was apparently early evening. She turned to see if Zeke had also slept, but he was not there.

She frowned, getting out of bed then and putting on her

41

robe. Abbie went to the window and looked out. Lamps were lit in the street below, and it was raining again. Where could Zeke have gone? He had been acting so strange lately, as though he was disturbed about something more than the children. But she didn't know what it was and knew he was too stubborn to tell her anything that might upset her more, so it would be useless to ask. Whatever was bothering him, he would tell her in his own time. But it worried her. She heard footsteps outside the door then, and someone turned a key. The door opened and Zeke walked inside. She stood up, watching him carefully.

"Where were you?"

He turned so she could not see his eyes, closing the door. "I went to have a couple of drinks. I needed a good shot of whiskey after seeing two children off and hearing that news about the damned railroad. You were sleeping so well I didn't want to disturb you." He put on a smile and turned to face her. He would not tell her he had been to see a doctor. "Feeling better?" he asked her.

She wanted to question him. He didn't usually go into taverns in civilized places, where his Indian looks and quick temper usually brought trouble. But he must have gone. Where else would he go in a town where he knew no one?

"A little," she answered. She looked toward the window. "I see it's raining. I hope it quits before we leave in the morning. What time is it anyway?"

"About eight." He walked to a chair and began removing his weapons belt and the big knife attached to it. His long, shiny black hair was still twisted into one thick braid at his back, beads wound into it. A beaded headband circled his forehead, and in the dimly lit room he looked more handsome than usual. "I thought we'd go out for a nice supper, if we can find a decent place that will allow me inside." The words were spoken bitterly and he met her eyes. "I'm sorry, Abbie, for not always being able to take you to the right places, for the children—all of it."

She watched him closely. Yes, something was wrong. "I thought we agreed you weren't going to talk like that anymore. I've been your woman for twenty-four years and never regretted one moment of it. I love you, Zeke Monroe, and I

42

wish you would tell me what is bothering you."

He hesitated as he removed his buckskin shirt. "Just the kids leaving, that's all. I'll change into white man's clothing. At least that will give us a better chance of getting in someplace decent." He turned to face her, his broad, muscular chest denying his years. She saw him as she saw him when she was only fifteen and he came to offer his services as scout for her father's wagon train. He was the same handsome, dark, mysterious man she had seen then, and she loved him and wanted him as much now as ever.

His dark eyes roved over her lovely curves beneath the soft flannel gown she wore. Always he had been able to bring excitement to her blood, stirring desires in private places only Zeke Monroe had touched and explored at her consent. "I want to make love to you, Abbie."

Her eyebrows arched and she smiled lightly. "You certainly don't need to tell me first. Just come and hold me."

He grinned, and as he approached her she wondered why there was an urgency about him, as though someone had told him he must do this quickly or never get the chance again. He came closer and embraced her, his muscular arms encircling her tiny form. She rested her head against the broad chest that bore the scars of wounds and battles. She ran her fingers over the hard muscle of his arms, her skin looking so very white against his Indian coloring even though she was tanned from living on the plains of Colorado for so many years. He kissed her hair and she turned her face up to him. His lips met her mouth then, tenderly but almost urgently. He seemed to be trembling. She reached around his neck and returned the kiss. Whatever was bothering him, if this helped, then Abbie was glad.

He picked her up and carried her to the bed, laying her down on it, then quickly removed his leggings and moccasins, then the loincloth that hid his most manly part. He was a grand specimen of man, seeming to only improve with age. And, after all, they had been together for twenty-four years, ever since that first time he took her as a fifteen-year-old girl who was alone and afraid and who wanted only one man to make a woman of her. In those years their bodies had become attuned

43

to each other so much that each seemed to be able to read the other's every need, each knowing just what excited the other the most. All the years and all the children had not lessened the excitement of these moments, for their love had endured war and separation, death and heartache. They had been through too much to let anything ever come between them now. Four years ago he had almost given it all up, when a wealthy Englishman who had bought land next to their own had fallen in love with Abbie and had offered her the world on a silver platter. Because he had always felt guilty about what she had given up to live in this reckless land with him, Zeke had been tempted to ride out of her life and leave her to the Englishman, letting her live her last years in peace and luxury. But she would have none of it. She wanted no other man but her Zeke, and had turned down wealth and comfort to stay with the only man she truly loved.

She lay back and let him unbutton her gown and pull it off her shoulders and down past her breasts, revealing their full fruits. He liked undressing her, and she liked letting him, never failing to redden slightly in spite of the many times they had done this. He leaned over and gently tasted the sweet nipples as he pushed the gown farther down, running a hand over her stomach, soft from many children but still flat. Hard work and a tendency to be too thin all her life kept her slender still, in spite of her thirty-nine years and the many children. The gown came off, and his gentle fingers found that secret place that made her breathing quicken, as his lips moved up and over her throat, lingering there a moment before meeting her own lips. He kissed her hungrily then, urgently, groaning with the want of her.

He would not tell her where he had been—what the doctor had told him. Arthritis. He had never heard of such a thing. The doctor had said it could cripple him some day, maybe in two years, maybe in ten. He couldn't say for sure. He could only give Zeke something to take when the pain was unbearable. Somehow he would hide the medicine from his Abbie. He would not tell her he had this strange disease that brought such fiery pain to his back and joints. He would fight it until there was no longer any way left to fight. When that

44

happened, he would find a way to die with honor. Somehow he must die fighting, or in some other way that was honorable. Zeke Monroe would not die lying crippled in a bed! Never! Honorable warriors did not die lying flat and helpless like women!

He would not think about it now; he could manage. Cold, the doctor had said. Cold and dampness made it worse. His back ached just a little now, probably from the cool rain that was falling. But at least this was May, and Colorado was usually dry. Winter was far away.

His wife's breathing quickened and she whimpered his name as the lovely explosion rippled through her insides at his touch. Yes. He could still make love. He could still excite her. He was still a man. He moved on top of her, entering her almost savagely. This hated disease would not stop him from being a man to this woman who had sacrificed so much for him. He would continue to be one with her, continue to love and protect her to his dying day!

Abbie did not fully understand why he was being so urgent, why he was not quite as gentle as he usually was. Perhaps he was simply distraught over the children after all. Whatever the reason, he apparently needed her badly. She arched up to him, giving, giving, taking her own pleasure in return, for never did he do this to her without bringing her sweet ecstasy that always seemed new, as though each time were the first time. Always she felt lost beneath his broad strength, overwhelmed by his commanding nature, wanting to please the master of her heart and body.

It had taken a long time for her to be able to do this again, after she had been kidnapped, raped, and tortured six years ago, while Zeke was away because of the Civil War. That was another reason he suffered from guilt. Always he had been her protector and provider. Many times he had risked his life for his woman. But that one time he had not been able to help her, and his rage at what she had suffered had been mighty indeed. He and Wolf's Blood had sought the men who had abused her, among them Zeke's bitter enemy, Winston Garvey, a wealthy but notoriously criminal Colorado businessman, and an Indian hater. Garvey and the men who'd had a part in Abbie's rape all

45

suffered terrible deaths under the blade of Zeke Monroe's wicked knife. No one but Zeke and Wolf's Blood knew what had happened to those men, or where the bodies were. And it was only Zeke's gentle love and care that had brought Abbie back from near death after that—and his tender understanding and gentle coaxing that had enabled her to again give herself to a man in love and desire, after months of patient, loving waiting on Zeke's part.

That was over now. They were one again, for nothing could truly separate them. And now he vowed that this thing called arthritis would not separate them either. And if the end came sooner than he wanted, he would always be with her in spirit. They were too close for even death to part them. But for now they were alive! Alive and well and he loved her! He pushed himself deep inside of her, wanting to touch not just her body but her soul. He came down on her, moving his hands beneath her and grasping her hips, pushing up while he whispered sweet Indian love words into her ear. Her slender white thighs were parted willingly, her beautiful eyes closed in ecstasy, her breathing coming in whimpers and groans as he ravaged her. This woman was his whole world, his reason for abandoning his Indian ways to live in one place so he could provide for her. She needed his love more than ever, and he would show her more love in the time he had left than he had ever shown her. Besides, he felt good this night—strong as ever. The doctor had said there might be several years left. He would think positively. He would keep the secret to himself and simply love her—totally, reverently, making her as happy as he could possibly make her. They would go to Fort Laramie. He would find Wolf's Blood and perhaps be able to convince the boy to return with them. Then they would go home, to their little ranch on the Arkansas, on the green plains of Colorado with the Rockies outlining the horizon.

His life poured into her then. Thank God the disease could not stop him from this! He would be a man to her to the very end, of that he was determined. He was glad that several years ago in Denver she had had the operation that kept her from getting pregnant. Now he was free of the worry that she would have more children at a time when he didn't know how much

46

longer he could provide for her.

He relaxed beside her, still half on top of her, their damp skin touching beneath the blankets, her face buried in his neck.

"Zeke Monroe, do you really expect me to get up now and go out to eat? You've worn me out."

He grinned and kissed her nose, moving down and kissing her breasts. "Want me to go get something and bring it back?"

"Would you? We have such a long ride ahead of us yet. I just want to lie here and not get up."

"Whatever my woman wishes." He kissed her lightly then. "Don't worry about LeeAnn and Jeremy. It's useless to worry about something we can't do anything about. They're Monroes—strong and independent. They'll be all right. And Bonnie did tell us it was a good school when she wrote us. She wouldn't have gone to all that trouble making arrangements if she didn't think it was best for LeeAnn. Maybe they'll both be happier being away for a while."

She sighed. "I suppose. It's just so hard to let go, Zeke—so hard to realize your children aren't babies any more. I want them with me, where I can protect them and be a mother to them."

He got up and started dressing. "You lost your own mother at an early age and you did all right."

"But I found you. I had my Zeke."

A pain shot through his heart at the remark. "One thing you don't realize, Abigail Monroe, is that you have survived on your own strength. You think it's because you have me, but it isn't. You're a strong woman who will always survive, with or without me."

"Well I much prefer it be with you, so don't go getting in any fights out there on the street when you get us something to eat," she replied, pulling the blankets over her naked body. "You do have a way of getting into trouble in civilized places. People look at you and think you're going to take their scalps. If half those women knew what you're like in bed, they'd not be so afraid of you. But luckily I'm the only one who knows what you're really like. You don't need to go proving it to any other woman."

He laughed lightly, determined to forget about his doctor visit. "You sure you don't want me to prove it to a few of them?"

"I'd rather they thought you might take their scalps."

He pulled on his shirt and strapped on his weapons belt again. "Whatever you wish." He walked to the door. "Keep this thing locked while I'm gone. I won't be long." He turned and met her eyes, still full of her, still warm from their recent lovemaking. "I love you, Abbie-girl. Sometimes that's the best I can offer you, but if it was worth money, you'd be rich."

She smiled softly. "I am rich. Your love is all I've ever asked for in the first place. I told you that when I was fifteen. I meant it then, and I still do. Now go get something to eat. You've made me very hungry, Mister Monroe."

He gave her a wink and left, closing the door softly behind him. She breathed deeply, revelling in the remains of sweet ecstasy, curling herself into the soft sheets. Apparently it was only the children after all that had upset him. She prayed again that he would be able to find their wild Indian son. That would not be easy.

The plains rolled ahead of them like motionless waves in an ocean. It seemed with every huge swelling of land they climbed, another always lay ahead on an endless horizon, a sea of green and yellow. There was a time when such land would have been unmarked by civilization, but every now and then they spotted a crude house or a soddy, fences, and cattle. Once they would have seen thick herds of buffalo that might stretch for miles. Now there were only smaller herds, scattered here and there. They crested one hill and spotted what at first appeared to be a huge black hole in the distance, then realized it was buffalo grazing. Zeke reined his horse to a halt and watched, Abbie moving her mare up beside him.

"It all looks so peaceful," she told him.

"For a little longer it will be," he answered, sighing deeply. "I remember the days when my brothers and I would ride as far as we could go, hunting, just having fun. It was so good then, Abbie. I never felt so free and happy as those first years after I found my mother and learned I had three Cheyenne brothers. Now look what's left. Just Swift Arrow—at least we think he's alive. Gentle Woman, Deer Slayer, Red Eagle, Yellow Moon, little Laughing Boy, Black Elk, Blue Bird Woman, young Bucking Horse, your good friend Tall Grass Woman, her husband and son. All gone. And why, Abbie? All because of white settlement—white man's diseases, white man's whiskey, white man's lust for land, white man's brutality. You can't ride across these plains and run into great migrating tribes anymore, only smaller villages, full of the renegades, the ones who refuse reservation life, the ones who still cling to the old ways."

"Don't torture yourself, Zeke. Let's just get to the fort. It's only a day away now. Then you can see about riding into Sioux land and finding Wolf's Blood."

There was the sharp report of a rifle then, an unusually loud boom that cracked the crisp air and made the horses whinny and move nervously. A huge cow in the distance slumped to the ground, and the rest of the herd started running.

"Goddamned buffalo hunters!" Zeke growled. Three more shots were fired in quick succession, and three more of the animals went down as they ran, one stumbling forward and rolling head over heels. Zeke reached out and grasped Abbie's arm. "Get down!" he ordered. "Those bullets are whizzing by us too close. Wherever those sons of bitches are, they might have seen you."

They were quickly off their horses, Zeke leading Abbie and the animals down the hill a short way to a washout. Abbie ducked down inside it while Zeke coaxed the horses down, speaking to them in Cheyenne, using his expertise to get the animals on their sides. He crouched down in the washout beside Abbie then. Several more shots had been fired, and at least ten buffalo lay dead or dying below.

"Don't make a move until I can see how many there are," he warned Abbie.

They waited several minutes, then four men moved out from a ridge just below them, heading for the buffalo. Zeke and Abbie watched quietly for several minutes as the men rode up to the carcasses and dismounted, then began to deftly and expertly skin off the hides.

"What a stinking waste!" Zeke growled under his breath.

"Oh, Zeke," Abbie whispered, turning away. If anything would quickly destroy the Indian and force those left onto reservations, it was this. The buffalo was their lifeblood, every part of the animal used in some way. These men would take only the precious hide, perhaps some of the meat to sell to the railroad, then leave everything else to rot.

Zeke carefully removed his Winchester .44 rifle from its boot on the side of his Appaloosa gelding. He always preferred to ride *Kehilan*, but at times like this he needed a horse more subdued and easier to control, so he had chosen a sturdy gelding for the trip, putting Abbie on a roan mare. The horses LeeAnn and Jeremy had ridden had been sold at Julesberg. He was glad now that he had not brought them along.

"A sixth sense tells me there were more than four down there, Abbie-girl," he said quietly. "Is your pa's old Spencer loaded?"

"Yes."

"Slip it out."

She looked at him with worried eyes. He knew that she was thinking about the terrible ordeal she had suffered six years ago. "Not this time, Abbie," he assured her. "You know better than to worry when I'm with you."

She tried to smile for him, but he saw the fear there and it tore at his guts. He'd shoot her himself if necessary to keep anything like that from happening to her again. He braced himself against the side of the wash so he could see above them as well as below. He was almost certain they'd been spotted, for they had been in a position from which they could be seen without being able to see the hide hunters. There was a long moment of quiet while the men below went about their dastardly business, and Zeke was sure it was only a diversion. The hunters wanted the man and woman to think there were only the four of them and no more.

A moment later he got his answer. Three horses came thundering down toward them from above, showering them with dust and small rocks as they stirred the hillside. Zeke stood up and took aim, firing once, slamming open and closed the lever of the rifle and firing again. Two men came rolling down the hillside, one lying dead close to Abbie, another rolling past them, while their horses ran on and kept going. The third man was on them by then. He swung a clublike instrument at Zeke, knocking him sideways. Abbie screamed, clinging desperately to the reins of their own two horses, which had lurched to their feet by then. Zeke's wicked blade was out and he squirmed to his feet as the hunter raised the club again. Zeke ducked under the man's horse, rolling between its legs and coming up on the other side to sink his blade into the man's hip, pulling him from the horse as he screamed with the horrible pain of the huge knife ripping into him.

Abbie gasped and backed up, still holding onto the horses as Zeke and the hunter tumbled into the wash. An enraged Zeke Monroe was feeling his Indian blood now, and in spite of the dizzy pain the club brought to his head, he managed to roll on top of the hunter and in a quick flash his infamous knife found its mark in the man's heart. He ripped downward with the blade and Abbie turned away, feeling faint. She had seen him use the knife before in her defense, but was sure she would never get used to the extent of her husband's brutality in times like these.

In the next moment he was grabbing her back down. "The other four are coming!" he told her. "You've shot three Crow Indians with that old Spencer, Abbie-girl, and plenty of deer. See what you can do with buffalo hunters. I need your help."

"The horses!"

"Let go of them! They'll come back!"

She released the reins and the two mounts ran off. Zeke retracted the lever of his rifle again, and Abbie took aim with her father's old rifle, her hands shaking.

"You take the one on your left, if you can, Abbie. Let them get a little closer first."

The thundering hooves of the oncoming hunters seemed to rumble through her very bones. These men were after more than hides this day, and she'd be damned if they'd get it. The seconds it took them to come closer seemed more like hours,

51

and then she was pulling the trigger. The man on their left was thrown backward off his mount, blood exploding at his right shoulder. Zeke's rifle fired at almost the same time, once, then again. Two more went down. The last man stared wide-eyed, hardly able to believe that he and six cohorts, all experienced plainsmen, had been felled by one man and a small woman. He turned his horse sharply, its hooves digging into the loose soil, and made an attempt to escape. But in the next instant a big blade landed with a thud in his back. He cried out and slumped forward, falling from his horse several yards farther down the hill.

"Stay down!" Zeke told Abbie, as he slowly emerged from the wash, his keen eyes and ears alert for any others that might be about. But the open plain was suddenly deadly quiet again, except for a soft wind and the very distant rumbling of the still-running buffalo herd. Zeke ran up the hill to check the other side of it. No one was about. He moved back down, kicking at bodies for survivors. The one Abbie had shot groaned. Zeke looked at her, his dark eyes wild and savage. "Turn around!" he ordered. Their eyes held, then she turned away, covering her ears. A shot was fired.

A moment later he was behind her, putting a firm arm around her. "I told you it wouldn't happen this time. And you don't have to worry now that you killed a man, Abbie-girl. You only wounded him in self-defense. I killed him." He kissed her hair. "I'll get my knife and get the horses back. You sit here and breathe easy. Everything will be all right. We'll ride hard for Fort Laramie and tell Dan about this, and you can get some rest."

She turned to look up at him. An ugly black welt was making itself visible on his left cheek where the hunter had hit him. "Zeke, you're hurt."

He wished that was all that was wrong with him. Wounds from battle he could handle. It was the secret pain he could do nothing about. He was only grateful that he could still manage himself in times of peril. His skills and strength had remained intact.

"You know how hardheaded I am," he told her with a forced grin. "By the way, woman, that was fine shooting. In the old

52

days a Cheyenne priest would have given you another eagle feather for that belt you keep. I guess you're right about the old Spencer. I keep wanting to put it away but you keep saying it's just as good as any new rifle I could get you."

The tears came then, and she half collapsed against his chest, crying quietly. She had been with Zeke Monroe. Why had she even considered being afraid.

Chapter Three

Abbie held the yarn in her fingers to keep it from getting tangled, while her sister-in-law, Bonnie Monroe, knitted rapidly, talking just about as fast as she worked. There was much visiting to be done, years to catch up on. She would enjoy her stay here at Fort Laramie, and to no surprise of her own, Zeke had already ridden into Indian country to search for their son, even though they had arrived only the day before. She did not blame him. She only prayed he would find the boy healthy and in one piece.

"And isn't Joshua handsome!" Bonnie was saying. "I'm so proud of him, Abbie. He walks so well, and he's so intelligent. He's going off to college in another year. I'll always be grateful to you for the day you and Zeke brought him to me."

Abbie forced a smile. "And I'll always be glad we thought to bring him," she replied. "We couldn't have chosen a better woman to be a mother to him."

Bonnie went on talking about the boy, but Abbie's mind was not totally on the conversation. Bonnie had no idea what kind of memories seeing young Joshua brought to Abbie's tortured mind. Joshua was the half-breed son of Zeke's sister-in-law, Yellow Moon, and the prominent, wealthy Winston Garvey. That much Dan and Bonnie knew. Zeke had rescued his sister-in-law from sexual slavery at the hands of Garvey, over fifteen years ago down in Santa Fe. The woman had later given birth to Joshua, called Crooked Foot by the Indians because he was born with a clubfoot. Yellow Moon was killed when soldiers raided her village, and Abbie and Zeke had taken the crippled baby to Bonnie at Fort Laramie. At that time, Bonnie was married to a preacher, Rodney Lewis, and was herself a missionary and nurse, her father a doctor. She was a good friend, a deep kinship having developed between herself and Zeke after he had saved her from outlaws who had captured her to sell in Mexico. Bonnie, herself barren, agreed to take the baby, and the boy had been sent east several times for special operations. They renamed him Joshua Lewis, and now at fifteen, the boy walked quite well with a brace. He was a handsome boy, with sandy hair and hazel eyes, rather slender in build. He knew only that he'd been "found abandoned" by Zeke and Abbie and that they had brought him to Bonnie. He did not know he was half Indian, nor did he know that his real father was Winston Garvey.

That knowledge had brought much suffering to Abbie six years ago. Garvey had discovered that he had a half-breed son. He was a notorious Indian hater, for purely selfish reasons, and to discover he had a son walking around with Indian blood made him furious. Through his own investigating, he realized it was the Monroes who knew the boy's whereabouts and identity. While Zeke was away in the Civil War, Garvey had arranged for Abbie's abduction. But Abigail was a fighter and a stubborn woman. Torture would not make her reveal where Joshua was. She refused to tell, for she knew Winston Garvey would surely have the boy killed, and she would rather die than be responsible for the death of a child. So Garvey had resorted to breaking her pride—rape. Still she would not tell, even when he sent in two of his men to horrify and shame her. She believed in Zeke—believed he would come for her, find her. And he had. Now only she and Zeke and Wolf's Blood knew the secret—knew how Winston Garvey and two of his men had mysteriously disappeared. If Zeke Monroe's knife could talk, it could tell too. But the story it would tell would be a horrible one indeed, for Winston Garvey had learned the terrible things Zeke Monroe could do with that knife in revenge.

Garvey's son Charles inherited his father's wealth. He was an even worse Indian hater than Winston had been. He had ridden with Chivington in the horrible raid on Black Kettle's Cheyenne village at Sand Creek in 1864. Wolf's Blood had been there that day. The young girl he loved and intended to marry had been killed. And Wolf's Blood had sunk a lance into Charles Garvey's leg, leaving the young man badly crippled for life. Charles had not even known it was Wolf's Blood; he did not know the secret link between himself and the Monroes, or that he had a half brother who was part Indian. They could only pray that Garvey would never find out, for he, too, would try to have Joshua killed. For now, Charles Garvey knew only that his father had disappeared during an Indian raid and had never been found. He was declared officially dead, and Charles Garvey, a wicked, scheming, power-hungry young man, came into his father's wealth, shedding few tears over the man's death.

And so their lives seemed to be continually moving in and out of the lives of the Garveys, and of Bonnie Lewis. Her preacher husband was killed by Indians, and she had later married Zeke's white brother, Dan Monroe, a colonel in the western army stationed at Fort Laramie. Dan had lost his own first wife to death. Their twelve-year-old daughter Jennifer, an exceedingly beautiful child, lived with her father and Bonnie at the fort. Dan's first marriage had never been a truly happy one, nor had Bonnie's. But now they were both radiant with their newfound love. Both had been lonely, Dan needing a woman and Bonnie needing a man. The marriage had been for somewhat practical purposes, as many marriages in this lawless land were: Joshua needed a father, and Jennifer needed a mother. But the practicality had swiftly turned to true love, and anyone could tell how devoted each was to the other.

Joshua came in then, carrying some supplies. Every time Abbie looked at him, her heart ached with a mixture of remembered torture and extreme pride that she had been strong and had not told the boy's identity. He was a fine young man, and some day when the time was right, Bonnie would tell him his true identity. But even then, neither Joshua nor Bonnie nor Dan would ever know what Abbie had suffered to keep that information hidden.

"Dan is coming!" the boy said excitedly. "He probably

found those men Zeke killed. I wish I could have seen it. I've heard so many stories about Zeke, I'd sure like to see him in action!"

Abbie and Bonnie looked at each other and laughed lightly. Both had seen in vivid detail what Zeke was like in action. Joshua put down the supplies and limped to the doorway. Dan rode up to the log house, which was whitewashed and had flowers planted around it. It was a spacious home, with one large kitchen and social room, two bedrooms, and a loft. It was a cheery house, with checkered curtains and braided rugs on the hardwood floor.

Dan came ambling in then. He and Zeke both shared the tall, broad build of their white father. But the resemblance ended there. Dan's hair was a thick, curly blond, his eyes a handsome blue. He was more even-tempered than his half-Indian brother, but their smile and the way they walked were very much alike. As a youth, Dan had come west to find Zeke, after Zeke had fled Tennessee many years earlier. Dan landed himself in the Army, and after saving an officer in the Mexican War, he also landed himself a commission, had moved up in rank ever since, and was now a colonel. He looked wonderful in blue uniform, although during the Civil War he had traded that uniform for a gray one and had suffered a terrible wound at Shiloh that had almost ended his life. If not for Zeke's finding him and getting him help, he would be dead for certain. The two men were close, in spite of their difference in blood and beliefs.

"Did you find the buffalo hunters?" Joshua asked excitedly. "Were they all dead?"

Dan looked at Abbie, his eyebrows arched. He well knew the kind of fighting man his older, half-Indian brother was. "Are you sure you're all right, Abbie? That was quite a mess Zeke left back there. It must have been terrible for you."

She sighed deeply and watched the yarn unwind from between her fingers. "It was. But I knew Zeke could handle it. I've seen worse, Dan, you know that." How could she tell him that her worst fear was that the men would get hold of her and she would suffer again as she had at the hands of Winston Garvey? She knew that was what had given Zeke the extra strength and courage he'd had that day. He would not let that

58

happen to her again.

Dan looked at Joshua. "Yes, they were all dead. We buried them right there." He was not about to tell the boy how they'd found some of them—ripped open by Zeke Monroe's knife. He looked at Abbie again. "Well, I don't suppose we have to worry about that husband of yours riding into Indian country, do we? I'd worry more about the Indians who might try to harm him."

They all laughed lightly, and Abbie's heart felt tight again with the fear that he would not find Wolf's Blood. He must find the boy. It was so important to him.

The only sound was the wind, high on that ridge where Zeke sat on his grand Appaloosa. It blew hard that day, rushing through the tall ponderosa pines in a near-constant moan, so loud that the noises from the Sioux village below could not be heard from his high perch. In turn, the Indians below were not aware of his presence.

He only watched for a while, wanting to impress the sight in his mind: the huge settlement of tipis, their buffalo-skin walls painted with symbols representing the character of the warrior and his family who lived inside. Blue smoke curled lazily through the bunched poles at the top of the conical-shaped dwellings.

He took in the sight: dogs and children running about, a large herd of fat ponies grazing hearby, hides pegged out on the ground to dry. If he didn't know better, he'd have thought he was a young boy again, living in the days when the Indian was free and happy. But the peace and prosperity these Sioux were enjoying could only be temporary—of that he was certain. They had won a battle, but they would lose the war.

He wore his finest Cheyenne regalia, a grand specimen of Indian sitting there in bleached buckskins decorated with beads and tiny bells. His long black hair hung loose and flowing, with just a tiny braid at one side that was beaded and adorned with an ornament made of buffalo hair and beads, and still another tiny bell. Now he was Lone Eagle, not Zeke Monroe. All his life he had been torn between the two worlds, and he felt battered and beaten on the inside. On the outside his handsome looks were overshadowed by the many scars on his back, arms, and chest, as well as the thin scar on his left cheek, which showed him to be familiar with violence and hard living. That's the way it was for half-breeds. But the hard life and his forty-nine years had only kept him strong, and he was determined to keep that strength and use it against the disease the doctor had told him he had.

He breathed deeply of the air, liking the smell of the pines. Zeke had not been this far north in many years, and felt strong today. Thanks to an understanding wife, when he needed to be "Indian" he could be, and that was all he was now—Indian. Perhaps this would be the last time he could get a taste of the old life. Views such as what he watched below were fast disappearing.

He started down, making his way quietly over fallen pine needles and flowering larkspur. A white-tailed deer skittered off to his left. As he came closer, he grasped the handle of his knife. He could not be sure what kind of a reception he would get from the restless Indians below, who would be feeling high on their recent victory in their battle over the Powder River country. If his son and brother were among them, he could be sure of his safety.

Someone below called out, and several men gathered then, eyeing the intruder warily, wondering if the approaching stranger was a lead scout for soldiers. Zeke made the slashing sign with his hands, signifying Cheyenne. "I come alone," he assured them. He dismounted then, leading his horse by the reins as he walked closer to the suspicious Sioux. "I am Lone Eagle," he told them, in the best he could remember of the Sioux tongue. He repeated it in Cheyenne, for the Sioux and Cheyenne were so mixed by now that most understood both tongues. "I come from the South. I seek my brother, Swift Arrow, and my son, Wolf's Blood. Are they among you?"

One of the men stepped forward, frowning. "Swift Arrow and Wolf's Blood are much together," he told Zeke in the Sioux tongue. "Like father and son. Good warriors. Swift Arrow honored Dog Soldier. One called Wolf's Blood much help in fighting, but cannot be Dog Soldier because of his white blood." The man looked Zeke over challengingly. "You also have white blood?"

Zeke gripped the knife again and nodded. "I do. Where are my brother and my son?"

The Sioux tossed his head. "They hunt. They come soon." He grinned a little, stepping back. "What kind of man is this half-blood who comes to our camp?" Another warrior next to him laughed lightly, then tipped a whiskey bottle to his lips. Zeke watched them all carefully, realizing that the drinking helped these restless men forget that their days were surely numbered. It saddened him, for they didn't even realize that the whiskey would only hasten their demise.

"As good a man as anyone here," he answered. "I bear the scars of the Sun Dance Ritual. I lived among my people for many years." He towered over most of the Sioux around him, for he carried the tall, broad physique of his white father.

The first Indian pounded his chest. "I am the best with the arrows," he bragged.

Zeke drew his knife and held it out. "And I am the best with this. Perhaps you have heard of Lone Eagle. Some call me Cheyenne Zeke. But then maybe you are too young to have heard of me."

"I know of you," an older warrior spoke up. The man stood to the side. He looked at the young man who seemed to want to challenge Zeke. "This man's knife is great medicine. Swift Arrow is his brother. He has told me much about this half-breed. He is not like other white bellies. His blood is Indian. And his knife makes men tremble. You would be foolish to challenge this man, Red Leaf."

The one called Red Leaf studied Zeke. He was young, full of fire from recent victories, proud of his skills and always glad to show them off. "Then we will play a game," he said. "I will shoot my arrow at a small target, then remove it. If you can throw this knife of yours and hit the same place where my arrow hits, you are welcome in our camp. If not, you can leave—on foot, white belly. We will keep your fine horse!"

Zeke looked around the village. If Swift Arrow were here, there would be no trouble. But these young warriors were itching for a challenge and he knew he would be wise to cooperate. He had no desire to harm Red Leaf for he reminded Zeke of his own son. He felt an eagerness of his own, suddenly feeling as though he were back in old times, when life like this was common to him. He nodded. "I accept your challenge, Red Leaf!"

Red Leaf and the others grinned broadly, one of them taking the reins to Zeke's horse while the rest led him to an open area. Others came to watch then, dogs barking, women peeking shyly at the newcomer. One older but exceedingly beautiful woman began walking alongside them but some distance away. She eyed Zeke seductively, annoying him with her beauty, for he was feeling very Indian this day and enjoying it. She deliberately lifted her tunic, showing more of her legs as she ran up to a large pine and stopped, peering around the trunk at Zeke as he and the other men stopped. Zeke glanced over at her again, and she smiled.

"That one is Sweet Grass," Red Leaf told Zeke with a laugh. "She lose her man when soldiers shoot him down. Since then she sleeps with any Sioux man who needs a woman, as long as he brings her meat. Your own son has been sleeping with that one. He looks happy in the mornings." They all laughed, and Zeke looked over at the woman again. He grinned to himself. There was no doubt that if Wolf's Blood had been sleeping with that one, he had learned all he needed to know about women.

Red Leaf ran to a tree roughly twenty yards distant. He whipped out a knife and gouged a small white spot into the trunk, then ran back to where the others stood. Zeke folded his arms and waited while the young man took an arrow from his quiver, which a friend carried for him. "Do you know of anyone who can hit such a small target with his arrow?" Red Leaf asked Zeke.

Zeke shook his head. "There are many who could come close. Even I could come close. But to hit that very spot would be difficult for me with an arrow, but not with my knife. First you must prove you can do it with the arrow."

Red Leaf grinned and nodded, placing the arrow in his bow and bending the handmade, perfectly balanced bow outward.

There was a long, quiet moment while he held the bow steady before releasing the arrow. Then a soft whirring sound was heard as it arched slightly and landed with a thud, its head sitting perfectly in the tiny spot Red Leaf had gouged out as a target.

The man and his friends whooped and cheered and Red Leaf pushed at Zeke. "I like your fine horse!" he laughed. He started to go to the tree to remove his arrow.

"Wait!" Zeke called out. "Leave it where it is."

Red Leaf turned and frowned, his bronze arms glistening in the morning sun. "But is is your turn, white belly," he teased.

Zeke nodded. "Step away."

The Indian moved aside, watching Zeke curiously as he pulled out the huge blade. Taking no time to stop and gauge his aim, he tossed the knife. It zipped through the air faster than the eye could watch. There was a cracking sound and a pinging thud, and Red Leaf's arrow shaft was suddenly split, still vibrating. The knife hung against the arrowhead, and the force of the throw had literally pushed the arrowhead down slightly when it met the same target.

There were gasps and excited utterings among the Sioux, as Red Leaf and the others moved closer to inspect the target. Zeke's knife had split right through the shaft.

It was then that several warriors came riding in, three of them dragging carcasses of deer behind them. Several in the village ran to greet them, followed by Red Leaf and the men with him, and for the next few minutes there was general commotion. From what Zeke could catch of the rapid Sioux tongue, there was first talk of a good hunt, then jabber about the new visitor who had split Red Leaf's arrow with his knife. Moments later a welcome sight greeted Zeke, as his son was now walking toward him. Their arrival had been one of such commotion that Zeke couldn't even be sure who was among those who had come in.

"Father!" the boy exclaimed. "They told the truth. It is you!"

Zeke's heart tightened. His son had actually grown more! He was no shorter and just as broad and muscular as his father.

Zeke felt as though he was looking at himself, for there was barely any difference except for the lines of age in the father's face. Wolf's Blood! How he loved this son. How he had missed him. Memories flashed in Zeke's mind of a small boy who used to ride with him every morning, racing against the wind, declaring that some day he would be a great warrior. Now he was one. And though Zeke knew the days of such freedom were numbered, he would not deny his son the chance to be the Indian he wanted to be.

They clasped hands, wanting to embrace but unable to show such emotion in front of the other braves.

"What brings you here, Father, so far from home!" the boy asked, tears in his eyes. "Is everything all right? Is Mother sick?"

Zeke smiled softly. How could he tell the boy it was he who was sick, not Abbie. "Your mother is fine," he answered. "I just . . . missed you, Wolf's Blood. We had to take LeeAnn to Julesberg, so we decided to keep coming north and see Dan and Bonnie; and I decided to come and find my son. Abbie is waiting for me at Fort Laramie."

The boy frowned. "Why did my sister go to Julesberg?"

They released hands. "She got on a train to go to New York. She's going to school there."

"School! LeeAnn has gone east to the place of the white man?"

"You know how she feels, Wolf's Blood," he told the young man. "She's eighteen now, old enough to go find whatever it is she's looking for. She's never been really happy out here. Of all the children, I guess you and LeeAnn were the least alike. I have much to tell you, Wolf's Blood."

Red Leaf was coming then with Zeke's knife, which he handed to Zeke stiffly. "I not call you white belly now. You are Lone Eagle."

Wolf's Blood laughed. "I could have told you, Red Leaf! No one challenges my father and wins! He is no white belly." He sobered somewhat. "Just as I have shown that I also am no white belly! I have many white men's scalps to prove it!"

They all let out war whoops, some raising weapons, certain

now that since Red Cloud had led them against the whites and they had won their war for the Black Hills, there would be no more problems from the soldiers and miners. Another familiar face approached then. He had waited for the more important reunion between father and son before coming forward. Zeke caught the man's eyes, and while the others whooped and yelped the two men appproached one another. Zeke put out his hand. "Swift Arrow!"

"It has been many years, my brother," the man replied, grasping Zeke's wrist firmly. "I miss the old days," Swift Arrow said quietly.

"And our mother," Zeke answered.

"All of it," Swift Arrow told him. "So much is gone." The man's jaw flexed in deep emotion. "Come to my dwelling. You and I and Wolf's Blood will talk. I am glad you have come. It is good you dressed and behaved as a Cheyenne, or they would have killed you. There are no longer any good feelings among my people for the whites."

Zeke shoved his knife back into its sheath. "I'm well aware of that. Things are bad in the south, too. Black Kettle was killed at the Washita, and they try to keep the People on a hot and worthless reservation in Oklahoma."

"I have heard all of this. Some have managed to come to us for refuge. But we also are always running and hiding. For now things are good. We have beaten back the soldiers and miners, burned their forts, signed a new treaty. But if it is like the other treaties, the white man will find a way to break it. For now we will be happy with this victory." He stepped back and eyed his half brother. "You look as fit as ever, Zeke; but I see pain in your eyes, and I wonder what has brought you here. It is more than just missing your brother and you son. Come. We will go and rest and talk." He called out to Wolf's Blood to come to his tipi. Wolf's Blood in turn called to a gray, menacing-looking wolf. The animal came running, jumping up onto the young man and growling in delight as Wolf's Blood hugged him and buried his face in the thick fur. The animal was the boy's pet, found as a wild pup and simply called Wolf. Wolf's Blood was the only person who could toy freely with the animal without fear of being attacked. Others stayed away from him. The animal then began following Wolf's Blood toward his uncle's tipi.

Wolf's Blood turned before entering, motioning to Sweet Grass. "Come! My father is here, and we are all hungry. Cook some venison for us."

She smiled seductively. She liked Wolf's Blood. He was young and hard and eager in bed. Of all the braves she slept with, he was her favorite. She hurried to her own tipi to get some of the smoked venison she had made up from a deer Wolf's Blood had brought her a few days earlier. She would prepare a worthy meal for her lover, and for his fine-looking father.

Charles Garvey leaned back in the leather chair, putting his feet up on his desk. He liked his fine office in Washington, D.C. He was an accomplished journalist but also studying to be an attorney, and was now a fast-rising apprentice in a prominent law firm. He had moved up more quickly than others, but then money could buy a man a lot of things.

He rubbed at his thigh, cursing again the young Indian who had stabbed him at Sand Creek. Never had he dreamed a man could suffer so much pain, and for a while it was feared his leg would have to be removed. But it had finally healed to the point where he could at least walk with a cane. The pain he suffered would always plague him, and it only fed his determination to do all he could to annihilate the Indians from any lands they still held. But it would have to be done cleverly, legally. His father had taught him that much more could be accomplished through twisting the law and through bribes than could be accomplished any other way. Already he had had a hand in convincing the railroads that they could provide food for their workers for free by hiring buffalo hunters. Three things could be thus accomplished: The workers would be fed, the railroads would get built, and the Indians would die of hunger. It was really quite simple. Now the hides were becoming more valuable back east, and Garvey had invested in a factory that treated the hides and transformed them into all kinds of valuable outer wear, quite fashionable now. He had also invested in the huge, long-range rifles that were used to hunt buffalo from a safe distance, and had hired hunters himself. He wanted only the best. The job must be done right—and swiftly. The next ten years were bound to bring near extinction to the great, ugly beasts of the plains, solving a lot of problems for white progress.

He grinned and lowered his feet, having to take his hands and literally lift the bad leg to the floor. He winced with pain as he did so. "Cussed red filth!" he swore. He turned to his desk then, picking up a quill pen and continuing to write. Every week he contributed a column to several eastern newspapers, telling of his own life in the west and his experiences fighting Indians, explaining what worthless, ignorant savages they were and how important it was that they be given absolutely no sympathy. Of course he neglected to mention that he had never committed a brave act in his life, or that the attack on the Cheyenne at Sand Creek had been brutal and uncalled-for, that women and children had been mutilated, their insides cut out, their heads bashed into nothingness. He did not mention that time and again the Indians had tried to live up to treaty obligations, only to have those treaties broken by the government, by soldiers, by settlers and miners who wanted more and more Indian land. There was no attempt made to help the whites understand the Indian side, the Indian spirit, the Indian culture. Besides, his readers did not want to hear those things. They wanted only to read exciting things, about the great wars between brave white soldiers and savage, wild Indians. So he would give them what they wanted. After all, he was his father's son. Indians had obviously done in his father, although the man had never been found after that night the Garvey ranch was raided. Not that the boy cared. After all, that made everything belong to him now. But to say that Indians had killed his father only gave him more credibility. And, they had already killed his mother, before his very eyes, when first he came west with her many years ago. He had never forgotten that. But somehow his mind had blanked out the fact that on that fateful day his own mother had offered her little boy to the Indians in exchange for her life. They had not taken her up on the offer, but had killed her instead. That was all that Charles Garvey remembered, and it was enough to instill the hatred for Indians that his father had nutured over the years.

"So, your daughter goes east to live among the white eyes," Swift Arrow said to Zeke.

Zeke finished chewing a piece of tender venison. "I'll miss her very much. And I have the terrible feeling that I'll not see her again, Swift Arrow. She doesn't want anything to do with her Indian blood. I fear she'll never come back."

A fire at the center of the tipi crackled and popped, and Sweet Grass watched from the shadows.

"You know better than any man that blood cannot be denied forever," Swift Arrow told his brother. "All your life you have wrestled with two bloods. You could not deny either one." He wiped at his mouth and leaned back, and Zeke rubbed at his eyes.

"Sometimes I can hardly stand the guilt of how my family has suffered, Swift Arrow. Maybe I should have gone back east myself when I married Abbie."

"If you had not lived here among your People, you would have been only half a man," Swift Arrow reminded him. "Abbie knew this. She wanted her man whole and happy."

Zeke stared at the flames. "She sacrificed so much to stay out here with me. And she suffered the most, Swift Arrow." He met his brother's eyes and knew what the man was thinking. He, too, loved Abbie, secretly, quietly. Zeke knew that was the reason Swift Arrow had come north so many years ago to live among the Sioux—to be away from the woman who belonged to his half brother, for to be near her brought great pain. He had objected vehemently when Zeke first brought his frightened, young wife to the Cheyenne, saying that a white woman would only bring them bad luck, for Swift Arrow had never had any use for whites. But Abbie soon proved her worth. She was not like other white women. She was strong and brave and willing to work and learn. And when Zeke had been forced to go away for many weeks, Swift Arrow had watched over her, and to his own surprise had found himself falling in love with her.

"She is well?" Swift Arrow asked his brother quietly, thinking himself of the story Wolf's Blood had told him about Abbie's abduction and rape.

"Considering all she has been through, she's fine. She still weeps for Lillian," Zeke answered. "It's never easy for a woman to bury that which has come from her womb."

Swift Arrow nodded, while Wolf's Blood only sat and listened quietly, petting Wolf and waiting for his turn to talk. Something was bothering his father, and it worried him.

"It took her a long time to get over what Garvey did to her," Zeke went on, poking at the fire then with a stick.

"And Margaret?" Swift Arrow asked, thinking it best to change the subject not just for Zeke but for himself, as the thought of men hurting Abbie brought a hot rage to his own heart.

"Margaret is as dark and beautiful as ever—all Indian like Wolf's Blood. I'm sure Wolf's Blood has told you the fine man she's married to—Morgan Brown." He leaned back and rolled and lit a cigarette. "I like Morgan. He's a mulatto, so he understands the hardships mixed bloods suffer, understands some of the problems Margaret had. He's a strong, tall, very handsome man. And you know how beautiful Margaret always was. They make a damned handsome couple, and their children will be beautiful. I trust Morgan completely. He helped me get back on my feet after the Comanches stole my horses. We work the ranch together now. And Margaret is pregnant. She's due in about six months."

Wolf's Blood and Swift Arrow both smiled warmly. "Father, why did you not tell me sooner!"

Zeke grinned. "Just thought I'd save it. Abbie's trying to get used to the thought of being called grandmother. She certainly doesn't look like one. She's as young looking and beautiful as ever."

He met Swift Arrow's eyes again and saw the love there. "I

wish I could see her," the man admitted. "But if I go near whites, I will be arrested. And this country is no longer safe for white women. There was a time when you could have brought her among us and she would not have been harmed. But there is too much hatred now. Our people have lost too much, their own women raped and butchered by soldiers and miners. I do not like what we do, and yet we have no choice. We will fight to the end."

"I'll give her your love, Swift Arrow, and tell her you are well. She talks about you often, worries about you, prays for you. She loves you like a brother."

Their eyes held and Swift Arrow's teared. "Of course. Like a brother. And she is my sister in spirit. I think of her often also." He took a deep breath. "And what about the rest of the children? Your son Jeremy?"

Zeke puffed the cigarette quietly, his eyes sad. "Jeremy is gone, too. He came with us to Julesberg and got himself a job loading baggage cars for the railroad—said he wanted to work for the railroad and learn all he could, maybe get into the business end of it some day. He's always been fascinated by trains, and he never liked ranching. He's seventeen—old enough to know what he wants, I guess, or at least to find out."

Wolf's Blood frowned, rubbing Wolf's fur. "My brother was always the smart one with books. But it is strange that he would work for the iron horse, hated enemy of the Indian. It makes me feel like he is not my brother."

The remark brought a heaviness to Zeke's heart. "He has to go his own way, Wolf's Blood, just like you did." He stared at the flames of the fire, taking another drag on his cigarette. All was quiet for a moment until Wolf's Blood spoke up again with a frown.

"Father, what is wrong? What is the real reason you came here? It was a dangerous thing to do."

Zeke met the boy's eyes. "You know I'd walk through fire to see you again. I just wanted to find my son. And I . . . I hoped maybe you'd come back with me, Wolf's Blood. It's torture for us never knowing how you are, and I miss having you around. Now with Jeremy and LeeAnn gone, Lillian dead, it's hard on

70

your mother. Here you're always in danger, and a worry to both of us. Abbie doesn't need anything more to worry about. And it worries Dan, too. He has nightmares about going out on a campaign and shooting down his own nephew." Zeke threw the remainder of his cigarette into the fire.

The boy shook his head. "No. Here I am free, Father. I can live the way I really want to live. And you say Morgan helps you at the ranch, and Jason is getting older now. You do not need me."

Their eyes held, and there was an alarming sadness in his father's. "I miss you, Wolf's Blood."

The boy's eyes teared. He cherished his father above all things, but his experience at Sand Creek had left a terrible bitterness in his heart that only raiding and killing could help sweeten. "I miss you too, Father," he said quietly. "Surely you know this. You are my life. But I need to be here. I am not saying it will be forever. But I love it here!"

Zeke forced back the urge to beg, to tell his son he had a crippling disease, that he feared dying without ever seeing his precious firstborn again. But he would not use that as a tool to manipulate his son's life. And he understood full well the boy's need to be Indian.

Their eyes held and Zeke reached out and grasped the boy's wrist. "Well then, I'm glad that I at least found you well and happy. Your mother will be glad for that much. You could at least try to find a way to get word to us more often, Wolf's Blood."

The boy nodded. "I will try. And tell my mother . . . tell her I love her . . . and I miss her also."

Zeke nodded, forcing a smile. "Well, since you don't think you can come back with me, then I will stay here a few days— be an Indian again. This might be my last chance at living the old way. I want to hunt buffalo, Wolf's Blood, and I'll show these Sioux what a Cheyenne can do in the shooting and wrestling games, right?"

The boy smiled through tears. "Yes, my father. You can show them a thing or two. I have told them many stories about my great warrior father and his knife that is great medicine."

Zeke smiled, and Sweet Grass came near him then, bending close to offer him more meat, the side slit of her dress falling away and exposing her leg all the way to her bare hip. Zeke took in the sight and Wolf's Blood laughed.

"She likes you, Father. You had better not tell Mother about Sweet Grass."

Zeke grinned and rolled another cigarette, finding her beauty difficult to ignore. "I see you have learned about women, my son, and what a pleasure they can be."

The boy laughed, understanding more than ever the pleasure his own father must find in his mother, for their love was strong and good, and his mother was beautiful. "Sweet Grass enjoys all men," he answered. He turned to Swift Arrow. "My uncle can also tell you so."

Swift Arrow's handsome dark eyes moved over the woman. "All a man has to do is be a good hunter and bring her plenty of meat," he answered.

They all laughed together, and Zeke rose, lighting his cigarette. "I'm going out to get the rest of my gear." He glanced at Sweet Grass. "And it would be easier on me, Wolf's Blood, if you slept with Sweet Grass in her own tipi. I'll share this one with Swift Arrow."

They laughed even harder, and Zeke left. Wolf's Blood started to rise, but Swift Arrow grasped his arm, forcing him back down. "Something is wrong, my nephew!" he told the young man.

Wolf's Blood frowned. "What do you mean?"

"There is another reason he wants you to go back with him. There is something he is not telling you. I am sure of it. There is fear in his eyes I have never seen before. Your father fears nothing—nothing! Yet I see it there; it is something he cannot stop, something he cannot control."

Wolf's Blood frowned. "I do not know what you speak of."

"You watch him, Wolf's Blood. You are close. You will see it, too. I love you, my nephew. I would miss you painfully if you left, for I am a lonely man. But the father is more important than the uncle. And your father needs you, for more than helping on the ranch, for more than just missing you. You must find out what it is that frightens him and why it is that he

72

wants so badly for you to return with him."

Wolf's Blood's heart tightened. Perhaps his uncle was right. He would watch his father for the next few days. They were one in spirit. If something was wrong that Zeke was not telling him, he would know, and he would make his father tell him before they parted.

Chapter Four

The days that followed were good ones, rich with shared stories of great hunting and warring against enemy tribes. There was feasting and celebrating, drumming and dancing, and even Zeke, who normally stayed away from excessive amounts of whiskey, drank his share of the firewater. That was when Wolf's Blood knew for certain something was deeply wrong, for Zeke seemed to want to be constantly drunk. Surely it was more than the joy of being with Indians and living that life he seldom shared anymore. It was as though he were making an effort to be happy and pretend nothing was wrong.

Women stretched and cleaned hides, hung meat in strips to dry, carved useful instruments out of buffalo bones, and made new clothing for their husbands and children. It was one of the last great periods of plenty that these Indians would know, and it was good. Zeke won his share of wrestling matches and all the wrist wrestling, basking in secret joy that he was still strong. He would fight this ridiculous disease. He would never be crippled!

But in the wee hours of the night he knew the disease would not go away, and that the coming winter would bring back the dreaded pain. Even in this warm weather, there were hints of it, and after a day of wrist wrestling, his right arm throbbed with it. He should have known better, but he didn't care. He'd had something to prove to himself, and he'd done it. How he would cover the pain the next day when they went on the buffalo hunt, he didn't know. But he would do it.

The morning dawned to find him sitting near a freshly stirred fire, holding his arm over the flames to absorb the warmth. Swift Arrow watched him quietly, allowing Zeke to think he was still asleep. Zeke flexed his arm, wincing as he did so, then flexed his fingers, beads of perspiration on his forehead. He moved the arm up and down then, breathing deeply. Swift Arrow suddenly sat up and stretched, and Zeke put his arm down quickly, picking up a piece of rabbit and putting it in a black frying pan that he set on the fire.

"You are getting lazy, my brother," he told Swift Arrow. "Already I am up and have breakfast started. This easy life you have now that Red Cloud has won this land is making you soft," he teased.

Swift Arrow grinned. "There is a time for making war, and a time for peace," he answered. His smile faded. "And there is a time to be silent, and a time to speak out."

Zeke cast a look at him, meeting his brother's knowing eyes. "You have something to speak up about?"

"No, my brother. But you do. I was watching you." Zeke simply scowled and turned the meat. "Something is wrong, Lone Eagle," Swift Arrow went on. "You need not tell me. But you should tell Wolf's Blood. You are in pain."

Zeke set the pan down. "I'm fine." He rose then, pulling on a buckskin shirt. "I'm going to get my gear ready for the hunt."

"You are a fool to go on the hunt if you are in pain. It is dangerous."

Zeke whirled, looking angry. "I have hunted buffalo all my life! I know whether or not I'm able!" He stalked out and Swift Arrow sighed, his heart heavy.

Nothing more was said. They rode out, following the instructions of Heavy Foot, their leader for the hunt. It was vital that the hunt be organized and that each man did as he was told, or it would be a failure and someone might be badly hurt or killed. When the time was right Zeke rode down his own beast, his surefooted Appaloosa, steady and dependable and unafraid of the great beast it charged. The village had been moved to this place where the buffalo had been found, and it

76

had taken only a few hours to ride out and stalk one of the last few great herds left. Zeke's heart beat excitedly as he came close, the large, white eyes of the great cow beside him rolling up to look sidelong at the man and horse that chased her.

Zeke readied his lance. He would do this the old way. He would not use a gun. He could do all the things he'd done in the old days, including lancing a buffalo. He aimed the spear, then flung it. But at the last moment pain shot through his elbow and shoulder, and the lance did not land right, nor with enough force. The cow rumbled on, the spear sticking out of her side but doing little damage. Zeke cursed it vehemently and charged forward again. He pulled out his knife, and as he approached the buffalo he let go of the reins, riding the horse with only the strength of his legs holding him on. He came closer, horse and man understanding one another, and as soon as they were side by side with the buffalo, Zeke leaped off the horse onto the other animal's back. He would prove his manhood in the very ultimate sense. Few ever tried such a dangerous venture. He clung to the cow's thick shag and began stabbing at it—the neck, the heart, the throat, hanging on for dear life as his huge blade found its mark over and over until the buffalo began to finally stumble. It went down hard then, its legs folding, and Zeke went flying off, tumbling for several feet, the buffalo tumbling beside him. If it had landed on top of him, he knew he would surely be dead. But *Maheo* was with him this day. Both man and beast finally came to a stop, several feet from each other.

Zeke got to his feet, panting and grinning. He was covered with scrapes and dirt and buffalo dung, but he didn't even care. This was a great feat! He laughed, ignoring the pain in his arms and back. He raised his arms and gave out a belting war whoop, just as Wolf's Blood came thundering up on his own horse, his young dark eyes angry.

"Father! Why did you do such a thing!"

"Because I wanted to!" Zeke answered with a grin.

Wolf's Blood just stared at him. It was true his father would find much honor and attention that night, and what he had done made the boy very proud. But he had also seen Zeke miss with the lance, something unusual for his father. And there were all the other things—the whiskey, the wildness. He watched Zeke kneel down to rip open the buffalo's hide so he could gut it right away. He laid the knife at the animal's throat and started to slice downward, but he only went about a foot when he stopped and suddenly dropped the knife. The man said nothing and did not look up at his son. He flexed his hand and picked up the knife again, forcing it the rest of the way down the animal's middle, but with much effort. This, too, was unlike Zeke, who would normally rip through the hide with ease. The knife was as sharp and useful as it had ever been. Zeke Monroe did not let a knife get dull. There must be another answer. His father suddenly did not have the strength to slice the hide, or he was in some kind of pain.

Wolf's Blood threw his leg over his mount and slid off, kneeling beside his father, who suddenly looked weary. He reached out and grasped Zeke's wrist. "Stop, Father. I want to know what is wrong—the truth."

Zeke just looked at him, then turned away and started gutting out the buffalo carcass. "Nothing is wrong, nothing being a few years younger wouldn't cure. I'm just getting older and a little lonely, that's all. Don't pay any attention to my asking you to come back, Wolf's Blood. This is the good life right here. You enjoy it for as long as you can have it. When you're ready we'll be at the ranch, and you'll always be welcome."

The boy rose, watching Zeke continue to gut out the carcass, seeing that the act took great effort. The man was trying to make it look as though there were no problems. "I guess I proved to your friends today that I'm no white belly," Zeke told him, holding up the heart of the animal. "Let them call me that now! I've made more war and killed more men than any of them."

Wolf's Blood smiled, but his heart was heavy. His father was lying when he said that nothing was wrong. But whatever it was, he didn't want Wolf's Blood to know about it, and the boy would respect that. He only nodded to his father. "You have," he said quietly. "You are a better warrior than any of them. And I have never seen a man ride a buffalo. You will be a most honored man tonight. But you had better be careful of Sweet Grass. She will want to please the great warrior who was brave

78

enough to mount the buffalo."

Zeke looked up at him and grinned. "I'm feeling pretty good about this myself. You'd better not let her catch me alone."

Three days later Zeke Monroe packed his gear, including many gifts from others in honor of the man who had ridden the back of a buffalo. Zeke joked with Wolf's Blood and Swift Arrow that he'd better not tell Abbie about what he'd done, or she'd chide him to no end for performing such a foolish and careless act.

"White women do not understand such things," Swift Arrow agreed. "But then Abbie is different. She would understand better than you think. If she did not understand, she would not even have wanted you to come here, knowing you would stay and be Indian again."

Zeke glanced at Sweet Grass, who smiled seductively. He sobered and looked back at Swift Arrow. "You're right. I was blessed with a good woman, even if she is white." He met his son's eyes then, seeing tears in them. They had already embraced inside Swift Arrow's tipi before coming outside. Nothing had been said about the day Zeke had trouble opening up the buffalo's belly, and he had seemed fine since then. He had said nothing more about Wolf's Blood returning with him, and now he gave the boy a supportive smile, even though his own eyes were wet with tears. "It is good here for you, Wolf's Blood. Enjoy it, son, while you can. I am glad there are still places where an Indian can live like an Indian. I have enjoyed being here and am sad to leave. Yet I miss your mother and will be happy to take her back home and be with my kindred spirits—my horses. I will pray for you, Wolf's Blood. And you know your mother does, even though it's to her own God. But then our Gods are probably the same after all."

Wolf's Blood nodded. He put a hand on his father's arm. "I still ride every morning, father—and think of you. We are together, even when apart, just as you have always said we would be."

Zeke swallowed, wanting to beg the boy to come. But his pride would not let him. He pulled away and quickly eased up onto his Appaloosa, turning the horse and looking down at his brother and son. "May you always ride the free wind," he said, his voice husky with emotion, "as all Indians once were able to do." He kicked the horse's sides then. If he had to leave, it must be done quickly. He galloped through the camp and into *Paha-Sapa,* the Black Hills.

A mist hung in the meadow, partially shrouding the lone man who rode there. Zeke was taking his time returning to Fort Laramie. He needed these last days alone, to wrestle with his sorrow over leaving Wolf's Blood behind, and his fear and anger at the disease that interrupted his life now. He had too much to do. He loved his Abbie too much to consider leaving her through death. The thought of leaving her alone was torture. He thanked his God for Morgan and Margaret, and the knowledge that the ranch would keep going and Abbie would at least always have a home and protection.

But being with Wolf's Blood again had made it harder. He had wanted to see the boy, yet doing so had made it all the more difficult. To see him and leave him behind tore at his guts, yet how could he ask the boy to come back when he was so happy being right where he was? Memories of early days with a young Wolf's Blood plagued him in the night. He could hear the boy's voice, see him riding beside him. But Wolf's Blood was a grown man now, with his own life to lead. And it was the very life his father had hoped he could have, so how could he take him away from it?

He breathed deeply of the early morning air. The overnight fog and dampness had left a dull ache in his back and hips that riding didn't help. But he refused to let this thing change anything about the way he lived. One thing was sure—he would ride a horse until his last breath. He was as natural on a horse as on his own two feet. Men came from miles around to ask Zeke Monroe to doctor their horses or to train an especially ornery steed. He had a way with horses that few men enjoyed, and his own stock were some of the best in Colorado.

Birds began breaking into song as he headed for a distant butte, and an owl gave its last hoot. The sun was just beginning to peek over the trees behind him, and the moon still hung in the sky, faded by the mist. Flowers bloomed abundantly in the meadow, surrounded on all sides by hills black with pine. The morning was already warm; it would be a hot day. Zeke wondered how long it would take white men to finally invade this beautiful land and destroy it, as they surely would one day. The Sioux had won, but only for the moment.

He heard a sound then, a strange birdcall that did not fit in with the others. He frowned, reining his horse to a halt and studying the thick forest all around him, seeing nothing. He moved his mount forward again, and again came the call. He halted a second time, wondering if he should find cover.

"Pave-voonao!" someone hailed then in Cheyenne, a morning greeting.

Zeke turned his horse to look behind him, his hand cautiously on his rifle. A gray wolf came bounding out of the trees then, running hard toward Zeke, but alone and not growling. Then a lone man on a painted Appaloosa appeared from the trees, holding up his rifle. "You move slowly, my father!" he shouted. "I waited two days and still caught up with you! Perhaps it was because you were hoping I would come!"

The voice echoed across the meadow in the morning mist, and Zeke's eyes teared. Wolf's Blood! Did he dare believe the boy had come because he'd decided to go home with him after all? Wolf ran in circles around Zeke's horse then, as Wolf's Blood galloped forward, his horse's mane and tail flying, as well as his own long hair. The young man galloped past Zeke, laughing, then circled back.

"Once we raced every morning," he told his father with a daring grin. "Have you forgotten?"

Their eyes held. He would not ask—not yet. "Hell no, I've not forgotten," Zeke replied. He kicked at his horse and charged off with Wolf's Blood galloping after him, catching up and riding side by side toward the butte. Hooves thundered and horses breathed in loud, rhythmic pants, as father and son charged toward their destination, reining their horses when they reached the hill, Zeke's horse a nose in front of Wolf's Blood's. For years father and son had both wondered if each

81

was just letting the other win, or if he was really trying. They still wondered.

Wolf's Blood let out a war whoop and dismounted. "We will let the horses rest and enjoy this morning," he told his father. "I love the mornings." He met his father's eyes. "I had forgotten how much I loved racing you in the mornings until you came to see me. And then I thought to myself how good those days were, just as my life here has been good. On the ranch I am just as free. You have given me this time—this freedom. Now I will give some of my time to my father."

They both breathed heavily, and Zeke dismounted slowly, his horse tossing its head and snorting, its nostrils still flaring. Zeke approached his son. "You're coming home with me?" he asked cautiously.

Wolf's Blood's smile faded. "I am—not because I know you want me to come, but because I myself want to come. I miss the ranch, the horses, my mother. But you also owe me the truth, Father. That is all I ask of you."

"The truth about what?"

The boy sobered more. "You know what. You do not have to ask. Our spirits are too close, my father. Swift Arrow said he saw a fear in your eyes the first day you came to us—something he had never seen before. And then he told me he saw you in pain one morning, but you denied it. I watched you drink—something you seldom do—and I saw you that day you killed the buffalo, Father, saw you miss with the lance, saw you drop the knife. You do not have a fool for a son, Lone Eagle. And when you rode the buffalo, that was a desperate thing you did, as though a final good-bye to wild daring. If you had not done that, I might have ignored the rest. But that was not you, my father, and I want to know what is wrong."

Zeke sighed and walked a few feet away, taking out his tobacco pouch and rolling a cigarette. His horse walked slowly over next to him, shaking his head again and bending down to nibble at some grass. Zeke sealed and lit the cigarette, watching his horse eat as he spoke.

"I have . . . pain, Wolf's Blood. No one knows, except a doctor I saw in Julesberg. He gave it a name . . . called it arthritis . . . the crippling kind, he said. I've not told Abbie,

82

and I don't intend to—not until there is absolutely no choice. If I'm lucky I'll—" He stopped and cleared his throat, flexing his hands. "Last winter it was pretty bad. It's always worse in the cold, or on cool, rainy days. It's in my back . . . my joints. Sometimes I feel fine for a long time, and then it comes back."

Wolf's Blood frowned, looking the man over. He seemed as strong and powerful as ever. "You look well, Father."

Zeke finally turned to face him. "But I don't always feel well. On the outside I seem normal. I can still fight, ride and shoot, defend my family, work the ranch. But it's all done in pain, Wolf's Blood. No one knows how glad I am to have Morgan there."

The boy's eyes brimmed with tears. "Are you . . . dying?"

Zeke sighed and reached up to pet his horse's neck, turning away from his son as he checked the animal's bridle. "In a sense. The disease is crippling, I'm told. It does kill, eventually. I don't know if I have two years or ten, Wolf's Blood. I only know I'll not let it get to the point that I'm helplessly bedridden. I'll find a way to die honorably first."

A tear trickled down Wolf's Blood's cheek. "You . . . cannot die! You are my father! You are Lone Eagle—strong and brave. You can fight many men at once and win. You are known all over this land for your skill with the knife. Men fear you! Mother needs you. You cannot die!"

Zeke swallowed back his own tears. How he hated hurting this son! "I am just a man, Wolf's Blood," he said in a husky voice. "How I've survived this long, after all the fights and dangers I've been through, I'll never know. But those are things I can handle. This . . . pain inside of me . . . is something I can't fight . . . something I can't do anything about. All the skill and bravery in the world won't help it. If I could cut it out with my knife, I would. But I can't and I fear I will be defeated from within rather than without. When the time is right, perhaps you can help me find an honorable way to die."

The young man's shoulders jerked as he struggled against tears, and Zeke turned to face him, coming closer and putting his hands on the boy's shoulders.

"Wolf's Blood, it isn't something that's going to happen tomorrow. And I'm forty-nine years old. That's old out here in this land. It's not as though I'm going to die next week, or die before my time. But the fact remains that I know what is happening, and I wanted to see you once more."

Wolf's Blood swallowed hard. "I would die in your place if I could."

Their eyes held, and Zeke's heart tightened with love. "Yes, I think you would," he said quietly. They embraced, and Zeke could feel his son trembling. "I'm not really dying, Wolf's Blood," he told the boy. "For when I look at you, I know that I live on."

The boy pulled away, wiping angrily at unwanted tears. "I am glad now that I decided to come. Swift Arrow and I talked for a long time. He agreed I should come after all, even though it will be lonely for him."

Zeke swallowed back his own tears. "Just remember that your mother must never know."

"She is wise. You will not fool her forever."

"Then I must fool her for as long as possible."

Wolf's Blood nodded, trying to smile. "Perhaps we can . . . ride every morning again . . . like we used to do. Remember how mother sometimes got angry . . . to wake up and see us both already gone?" His chest heaved with deep breaths in an effort not to break down. "She used to say . . . you were like the wind . . . that she could never hold you for long . . . or me."

Zeke forced a smile. "I remember."

The boy shook his head. "What will she do . . . without you?"

"Don't worry about my Abbie-girl. She's stronger than even she knows. And she'll have you and the other children. And I'll always be with her—and you—even in death. You know that. The spirit is a strong thing, Wolf's Blood."

The boy sucked in his breath and turned away, deftly mounting his saddlehorse. "We will go to her now," was all he said before riding off. Zeke watched after him.

"*Nemehotatse,*" he said quietly. Yes, he loved this son more than anything, except perhaps his Abbie. How did a man measure love? It was impossible.

They approached the fort carefully, Wolf's Blood wary now of any man in a blue uniform. He had killed such men himself. His chin was held high and proudly now as they entered the fort, for he was still rich with the recent Sioux victory, and he could see the scowls on the faces of some of the men. The wind blew his long black hair to the side. His face was painted with red and yellow stripes, his chest and arms scarred like his father's from the Sun Dance ritual. He wore only leggings and no shirt, for the morning was warm, and his dark skin glistened with moisture from his own body. He rode the Appaloosa stallion his father had given him when he first returned north three years earlier, and Zeke rode beside him now. It was difficult to tell which was father and which was son, for no two men could look more alike, except that Wolf's Blood's face didn't carry the lines of age his father's did.

A few men watched nervously, some seemingly prepared to shoot down both of them if necessary. The soldier who had let them in did so because he'd been told these two could arrive any day. He ran to get his superior officer as Zeke and Wolf's Blood headed for Dan and Bonnie's log house. Wolf, whose dark eyes watched carefully followed behind, the animal's lips slightly curled and his hair bristling on his back in a protective pose. He didn't like white men any more than his master did. Some of the horses pranced and whinnied nervously at the presence of the animal, and a soldier called out to them, pointing a rifle at Wolf.

"You'd best get that animal out of here, boy!" the man ordered. "He's scarin' the horses."

Wolf's Blood turned his horse, resting his hand on a six-gun shoved into the sash he wore at his waist. "Do not hurt him! He is mine. He will harm no one."

Another soldier standing to the side rubbed his chin nervously. "Seems to me you're outnumbered, boy. We don't know why you're here, but this isn't exactly a good time for a stinking Indian to come riding into this fort. Like as not, we could kill you and the wolf, and you'd sure as hell not be missed by anybody. So why don't you get that flea-infested horse killer out of here before we take care of him for you."

Wolf's Blood started to remove the gun, but Zeke had turned his horse also and was beside him by then. He put a hand out, pushing against his son's wrist. "Don't do it," he said quietly. "Please, son. It's what they want."

"Then they can have what they want—gladly!" the boy hissed. "If they harm Wolf—"

"That's enough!" Zeke growled. He rode his horse forward a few feet, glaring at the two men who had made the threats. "I will tell you how it will be," he spoke up loudly to them, his own appearance as Indian as his son's. "If either of you harms my son or his pet, you will both die." He whipped out his huge knife. "I might die, too, but you can bet I won't go down until I see your guts greeting the sun!" He grinned wickedly. "Which one of you wants to see if I can do it!"

They both swallowed and stepped back slightly, and by then Dan was running over to the confrontation. "What's wrong here?" he asked angrily, facing the two soldiers.

"Those men seem to think my wolf and I should be dead," Wolf's Blood sneered in reply.

"Sir, that man threatened to kill us both!" the first soldier told Dan. "He waved a knife at us!"

Dan looked up at Zeke and half grinned, then looked back at the men. "I can tell you this. He'd have done it if you harmed that boy or the wolf. This man is my half brother, and the boy is his son—my nephew! And if you knew this man's reputation with a knife, you'd be on your knees thanking God right now that you're still alive after threatening the boy! He'd have ripped your hide from here to kingdom-come if you'd hurt either one of them, even if he was full of bullet holes himself. Now get back to your proper business or I'll have you punished for being troublemakers!" He looked around at the rest of them as the two soldiers eyed Zeke sullenly. "I might remind all of you that we are temporarily at peace with the Sioux and Cheyenne and are under a treaty! It's small incidents like this that can start a whole war! These two men are my guests and will be leaving soon. If any Indians are going to be harmed, it will be at my orders, not at your own free will. Now all of you go on about your business!"

Zeke shoved his knife into its sheath, and Dan turned to look up at both of them, grinning and shaking his head. "You two!" He eyed Wolf's Blood. How strange it was that he had so savagely fought painted Indians himself, and here sat one who was his nephew. The boy's shoulder still bore the deep scar from a severe wound he had suffered three years earlier. Dan and Bonnie had seen to the wound themselves, which was received in a battle between Dan and his troops and Sioux Indians. By chance, Dan had recognized Wolf's Blood and had seen to the boy's care. But ever since, he feared being the one responsible for the boy's death, for although he had convinced Wolf's Blood to go home when he was healed, he knew the boy would come back, and he had.

"You going back with your father this time?" he asked his nephew. "For good?"

Wolf's Blood eyed the other soldiers with a sly sneer. "We will see." He had promised his father to keep the disease a secret, and only to say he was coming home to appease his parents and because he was ready to stop making war, but when he set eyes on the soldiers he was not so sure he could stop fighting.

Dan found the boy's resemblance to his father incredible. "Try, Wolf's Blood. Your parents want you to be safe," he told his nephew.

The boy's wild eyes kept scanning the soldiers: "And where is it safe in this land for an Indian?" he shot back. Everywhere we turn there are whites who scorn us and shoot us for no reason!"

"Wolf's Blood, calm down," Zeke told the boy. "You're talking to your uncle. Dan has always helped you."

The boy sighed, meeting his uncle's eyes. "I am sorry, Uncle. But white men like you are few."

"Come to the house, Wolf's Blood." He looked at the gray, menacing animal beside the boy. "Is he safe?"

"He will do whatever I tell him. He will lie quietly and sleep, or he will tear a man's guts out—whichever I prefer."

Dan frowned. "I have a twelve-year-old daughter at the house."

Wolf's Blood grinned. "She is safe from the wolf—and me—

if that's what you are thinking."

"I was thinking no such thing. I'm only thinking she might try to pet the wolf."

"That would be a mistake. No one can touch him but me. But if I order my wolf to lie in a corner and bother no one, he will do so. Do not worry. Just tell your daughter not to go near him." He grinned in a friendlier way then. "Let us go to the house. I will meet this cousin I have never known."

"She's the prettiest thing this side of the Mississippi," Zeke told his son with a smile. "Except maybe for your own sister LeeAnn." He turned to Dan. "We'll be on our way soon and out of your hair. I know having us here makes things difficult for you."

"Don't worry about it. Come on."

They trotted their horses alongside Dan, who walked quickly to the house then, where Abbie was coming out the door and down the steps, her eyes brimming with tears of happiness.

"Wolf's Blood!"

The boy swung a leg over his mount and jumped down. He wondered if his mother ever changed. She was still beautiful, and her face hardly showed her age. "I am glad to see you, Mother." He walked up and let her embrace him, always annoyed that white women needed to show their affection so readily, always embarrassed that she showed hers openly in front of others. But this was his mother, and only he and his father knew how she had suffered at the hands of Winston Garvey. If she wanted to hug him openly, he would let her. He knew deep inside that she wished he'd be a little less Indian, but she had given him that freedom, had told him at an early age that if he would rather ride than sit and read and learn, he was free to do so. He had always been the wild one—the restless one.

She leaned back and looked up at her tall, broad son. "Wolf's Blood, my heart is so happy! I never expected to actually see you. How long will you stay? Please say you will stay a day or two. Dan won't let the soldiers harm you."

He studied her beautiful face, this mother who had loved

him and put up with his wild nature—this mother who was the strongest and bravest woman he knew. "I am going home—to the ranch," he told her.

Her smile faded, not out of disappointment, for the words brought her great joy; but it was a total surprise and it made her wonder. She frowned slightly.

"To visit?" she asked.

He searched her eyes. She was too damned wise. "To stay— for as long as my restless spirit can bear it."

She looked from her son to his father, suspicion in her eyes. Wolf's Blood was as wild as the land he had just come from. Why was he going home? "But how? Why?" she asked Zeke.

The man shrugged, smiling nonchalantly. "Ask him. I didn't force him or even suggest it in the first place. But I'm goddamned glad he came riding after me. Maybe he just wants to come home and keep you stirred up again all the time. You know how his antics exasperate you sometimes. I think he misses seeing you get mad, Abbie-girl."

She smiled, but still felt something was not right. Still, why question it for now? Her son was coming home with them! She turned back to Wolf's Blood, looking him over again.

"You know I am close to Father," he told her. "Seeing him again just made me realize I have missed him more than I thought. He told me Jeremy left, and that your heart is heavy because of that, and also because LeeAnn is gone. So I decided to come home for a while so you'll be a little happier."

A tear slipped down her face and she ran a hand over his muscular arm. "What can I say, Wolf's Blood, but thank you? And seeing you is . . . it's like seeing Zeke when I first met him," she told him in a shaking voice. "You look well, Wolf's Blood. Is everything all right? Is Swift Arrow all right? And don't you have a wife yet?"

The boy grinned. "My uncle is fine, and thinks of you often. And I do not have a wife yet." He thought about Sweet Grass, but decided not to mention her. "I have been too busy fighting soldiers to think about taking a wife." He glanced at Dan, who frowned.

"I'm afraid your stay can't be long, Wolf's Blood," the man

89

told him. "It makes things rather awkward for me, although if it were fully up to me you could stay as long as you want. I hate to see any of you leave. It seems like every time I see Zeke and Abbie, it's years before I see them again."

Wolf's Blood looked back at his mother. "I will not cause trouble here, my mother, for your sake. But we should leave soon."

"In the morning," Zeke told him. He looked at Dan. "Brother, why don't you and I do some visiting tonight? Like you say, it might be a while before we see each other again." Inwardly he wondered if he would ever see Dan again.

Dan grinned. "I have some fine whiskey that makes the talking go on forever," he answered.

Zeke laughed and dismounted, and then Bonnie was herding them all inside, telling them she had a grand meal planned for them. There was much commotion and visiting, and Wolf's Blood squatted with his legs crossed Indian style in front of the hearth, sitting on the floor and ordering his wolf to lie down near him. He watched his relatives jabber, listening as his mother shot question after question to Zeke about his trip. How long did he spend at the village? Did he hunt with them? Did he see anyone she knew? How was Swift Arrow? That question was asked with deep concern.

Bonnie was bringing a young girl close to Wolf's Blood then. The girl's beauty moved him. Her hair was a gentle red, her skin fair and smooth, her eyes as green as grass. She was graceful and slender, yet something about her told him she was strong and true. She smiled bashfully when they came closer, and Wolf's Blood rose then, towering over her. She shied back a little, against her mother.

"Wolf's Blood, this is Dan's daughter by his first wife—Jennifer. She's twelve now. She wants to meet her Indian cousin. Jennifer, this is Wolf's Blood."

The girl nodded. "How do you do, Mister Wolf's Blood."

Wolf's Blood laughed lightly. "You do not need to say mister," he told her. "And I am glad to meet you, Jennifer."

"You can call me Jenny." She studied the tall, almost frightening looking young man before her. She thought him the most handsome man she had ever seen, even though he was her cousin and an Indian. She felt a secret pride that she was related to him—to be able to say that she personally knew and was related to a Cheyenne warrior. Bonnie patted the girl's shoulder and turned.

"I'll let you two talk," she told the girl. She went back to meal preparations, and Jennifer stared at Wolf's Blood.

"Does that come off?" she asked.

"What?" he replied with a grin.

"The paint—on your face."

He knelt down. She was as pretty as a flower. "Sure it comes off. It's made from plants, some from real blood."

Her eyes widened. "People blood?"

He laughed again, his grin bright and handsome. "No, not people blood. Animal blood. You want to touch it?"

She swallowed and reached out, lightly touching his cheek. She pulled her finger away, and some of the paint was on it. She met his dark eyes. "Have you . . . killed white people?"

He sobered. "Some. Mostly soldiers and miners."

She stepped back a little, studying his weapons, meeting his eyes again. "The men at the fort say the Indians kill women and little children, too. And they do bad things to them. Have you killed women and children?"

He rose again. "No," he replied. "But some of the warriors have, and I do not blame them. Do the soldiers tell you what the white men do to Indian women and children? If you knew everything about it, you would see why we fight, and why sometimes women and children die also. There is much hatred in the hearts of the Indian for what the whites have done to them. Do not be so ready to say the Indian is all wrong and the soldiers are right. I was at Sand Creek! I saw what the soldiers can do! They killed the girl I was going to marry."

He plunked down again beside his wolf, scowling, and she hesitantly sat down near him. "I'm sorry, Wolf's Blood, about the girl. I didn't mean that you are bad. I was just wondering. Besides, I like you. I think it's fun having an Indian for a cousin. Wait till I tell all my friends. They won't believe me."

He smiled again and removed a coup feather from where it

was tied into his long, flowing hair. He handed it to her. "You can show them this. I earned it by touching my enemy." She took it carefully, noticing how dark his hand was next to hers. "And I will give you my old war shield. I need a new one. My mother will make me one. You can have mine. Then your friends will believe you."

"You truly mean it? You will give me your war shield?"

He nodded, reaching over and petting his wolf. She eyed the animal. "Can I pet him?"

"No," he answered quickly, reaching out and grabbing her hand as she started to reach for the animal. Wolf snarled but didn't move. "Only I can touch him. But he will not harm you if you stay away. He stays wherever I tell him to stay."

"But he looks so soft. I do wish I could touch him." She sighed and pulled her hand back. "I am going to a special school in Denver in a couple more years," she told him proudly. "Have you ever been to Denver?"

His smile faded again. "I have been there. I do not like big cities and all those people. And when I was there I got in trouble, and so did my father. Whenever we go to cities it seems we get into trouble, but we don't try. Others start the trouble—white man who scorn us. I do not understand why any man would want to live in a place like that."

"Oh, but it's fun. There is so much to do."

"There is much to do in the mountains also. A man can sit and think and know who he is. He can be one with the animals and the earth. He can hunt and know that he is a man. He can ride and breathe the wind and feel the sun on his back, taste the mountain waters. He doesn't worry about a fancy house and silly furniture, or worry about anything he owns. The Indian believes that only God owns the land, and that the earth and the animals are put here to sustain us, and to be shared by all. The white man knows nothing of how to share. He wants to own everything himself, each man fighting the other to have the most. It is all silly and useless. You own something, then you die and someone else own it. So what does it matter?"

"I never thought of it that way." She sighed, puckering her lips, and he thought about how pretty she was. Some day this girl would be a beautiful woman. It was too bad she was so young, and his cousin besides. But then it didn't much matter. He had no use for white women anyway, except his mother and Bonnie Monroe. When he married, it would be an Indian girl. He thought of Sweet Grass and missed her, but she was not the kind he would ever marry. He would marry a young, innocent thing that could be all his. He would be her first and only man. Sweet Grass had taught him the intimacies of women, and he did not mind the learning. Some day he would have a wife and children. Maybe that would make it easier to stay in one place with his father. He would have to think about it, for he knew how badly Zeke wanted him to stay at the ranch. It would not be easy, but he would try.

"How old are you?" Jennifer was asking.

"I am twenty-two summers," he replied.

"I am twelve," she told him.

"I know. Your father told me."

She looked at the wolf again. "Can't I please try to pet him? Surely if you sit right here he will let me."

"I don't know. If he hurts you, your father will be angry with me. I do not want to displease him, or to see you hurt."

"Please, Wolf's Blood. Let me try. You can hold him."

He frowned and sighed. "All right. But move slowly."

She reached toward the animal and he started to snarl again. Wolf's Blood pet the animal soothingly, talking to him in the Cheyenne tongue. The animal's lips stopped curling, and to Wolf's Blood's surprise, the girl's hand touched Wolf's head and the animal made no move against her. She grinned happily and began petting him more, burying her fingers in the deep, thick fur.

"See? He let me!" she said proudly. "Oh, Wolf's Blood, he's so beautiful!" She looked up at him with her wide, provocative green eyes. "Do you think we will ever see each other again after you go back to your home in Colorado?"

He frowned, irritated that he should find a cousin so pretty, let alone the fact that she was white. "No," he answered. "You will go to Denver and become a fine lady and marry a fancy white man, I think. I will go help my father, and one day I will probably make war again because it is in my blood. Besides, we are just cousins. It matters little if we see each other again." He suddenly stood up, ordering Wolf to follow him. He quickly left, and Jennifer watched after him, utterly fascinated and very sad. He was probably right. She would never see him again after this visit. But she knew she would always remember her Indian warrior cousin, and would treasure the feather and the war shield forever.

Chapter Five

The sky was black but brilliant with so many stars that they seemed to run together. Abbie breathed deeply of the night air.

"Remember when we used to sleep like this every night—on our way to your mother's village?" she asked Zeke.

He turned on his side, resting his head in his hand and putting his other hand to her face. "How could I forget my young and beautiful Abbie and the good times we had under the stars?" he teased, moving his hand down over her breasts. "The best part is you've hardly changed."

She laughed lightly. "That's because you see me every day. If you saw me just once the way I was then you'd see the difference."

He leaned down and kissed her lips lightly. "I'd see no difference."

She reached around his neck and pressed her cheek against his own. "I hate to tell you, my husband, but there is a vast difference between fifteen and thirty-nine, especially after seven children."

"Then you must not look in the mirror very often," he answered, kissing her neck. They were both still dressed but warm under the blankets and buffalo robe that covered them where they lay near their campfire. He moved his hand to her stomach and pressed it lightly. "Wolf's Blood is far off. He said he wanted to camp by himself tonight. I think he knew I wanted to be alone with you."

"Zeke Monroe, you aren't suggesting—"

He silenced her words with a hungry kiss. "I most certainly am," he told her, moving his lips to her neck. "How long has it been since we made love in the open—under the stars? We'll be home soon, Abbie-girl, and back to the everyday business of running a ranch. Tonight feels like old times. I like the feeling. It seems like the years are going by too quickly."

"And you seem to want to do this more often lately, my loving husband. Sometimes I think you're hiding something from me. You wouldn't by any chance have had a last fling with some loose squaw while you were in Swift Arrow's camp, would you? I know how you get when that Indian blood comes to the surface."

He laughed and pulled her close. How could he ever tell her the real reason he wanted as much of her as he could get? "You know me better. I'm just happy, that's all. My son is coming home with me, LeeAnn and Jeremy are off doing what they think will make them happy, Margaret is finally settled and with child, the ranch is back in order, and we're together. I've seen Swift Arrow and Dan, and they're both well. And here we are under the stars on the Colorado plains, just you and me, like when we were first together. And I'm remembering that first night I took you—a scared little girl, afraid and alone."

She looked up at him, the broad shoulders hovering over her in the moonlight. How she had wanted him that first night he took her! The pain had not mattered. His being a half-breed Indian had not mattered. She had loved him from the moment she set eyes on him, and then she had lost her whole family on that fateful trip. He became her friend, her protector, then her lover. They had been together ever since, through hardships that would destroy the average person. But they were both strong, and totally in love. That love had been tested to the very thinnest breaking point, but could not be shattered.

"I love you, Zeke Monroe."

He met her lips again, the long black hair falling around her face and shoulders. For the next several minutes the brilliant stars shone down on two people who were only a speck on the Colorado plains. There was no one to see the clothing tossed aside, no one to hear her soft whimpers and his urgent groans but the crickets and the nighthawks. It was as though no one existed at that moment but the two of them. There was no civilization, no railroads, no cities, no war. On such a night one could imagine what it once was like when the only things that existed on these plains were wild things, untouched lands, a people who lived and hunted free. The waters were clean again, the prairies and plains unbroken by farmer's plows. The mountains had not yet been conquered, gold had not been discovered, and men like Zeke Monroe were the only ones who had explored the vast wilderness of the West.

She tried to reason why his lovemaking was more urgent and more often of late. Not that she minded, for being one with him was always a joy. And it all seemed better than ever these last few weeks, probably because they had been over the highest mountains and had made it through the lowest pits of hell and were still together. The last three years had been peaceful and prosperous, so prosperous that they could afford to send a daughter to college in the East. She knew that living the white man's way had always been hard for him, for it was against his nature. But he had done it—for her—and for that she loved him even more. Why he was suddenly more amorous than usual didn't matter. He was apparently happy. It was good to see him smile more, for there had been little smiling ever since her abduction and rape. It was time to forget those things; forget LeeAnn's abduction by the Comanches; forget the problems Margaret had had because she looked so Indian. She was glad Wolf's Blood was coming with them, for whenever the boy was around, Zeke was always in a better mood.

Their passion filled the night, so much so that they overslept in the morning, waking only when Wolf's Blood suddenly appeared on his horse. Zeke jumped awake and grabbed his knife beside him. Abbie gasped, pulling the blankets close around her neck to hide her bare shoulders. Wolf's Blood only laughed.

"You are losing your instincts, Father!" he joked. "See what I have learned from my Indian friends? I could have had you that time."

Zeke grinned and shoved his knife back into its sheath. "Go collect some wood or buffalo chips for a better fire, Wolf's Blood," he told the boy. "And take your time."

The boy nodded with a knowing look. "You should be careful doing such things out here. It can be dangerous for a man to have his attention taken from what is around him."

Zeke threw a clod of dirt at him and the boy laughed, riding off again. Abbie's face was crimson.

"Oh, Zeke, he knows! I should have been up and dressed."

He only laughed and turned to kiss her before getting up to put his clothes on. "Don't be silly. Of course he knows. So what? Is he supposed to think we never make love anymore? Why do you think he rode off last night?"

"It's still embarrassing. Get me some canteen water. I've got to wash a little."

He laughed again, walking to his gear wearing only his loincloth, a wonderful specimen of man in the morning sunlight. He stretched, ignoring the irritating dull pain in his back and elbows from the night air. "Abbie, he's twenty-two years old. When I found him, he'd been living with a widowed squaw who was very accommodating—and damned pretty, I might add."

"Zeke, he's a boy! My son!"

He walked to her with the canteen, shaking his head. "He's been a man for a long time—longer than most and you know it. And he's not ignorant of women. Now hurry up and wash and dress so we can eat something and be on our way. Margaret will be glad to see him, won't she?"

"Oh, yes! And I can't wait until the baby comes! Oh, Zeke, I'll have a baby to care for again! It's been so long!"

Her eyes teared and he knelt down beside her. He was well aware of how hard it had been on her to have the operation and know she would never have another child. She was only twenty-eight then, but already had seven children and had lost an eighth. He knew if she could have done it, she'd have kept right on having more, but he would not allow it.

"Something tells me Margaret will have a time getting her hands on her own child," he told her, kissing her cheek.

A tear slipped down her face. "Zeke, I do so wish I could have had one more. Just one more."

"It would always have been just one more. And there I'd be with ten kids and no mother, because it would have killed you.

Now get dressed and don't start fretting over that again." He kissed her lightly and began taking things from his parfleche to make breakfast.

She watched him lovingly, wondering at how sad he must feel inside that the time he had spent with Swift Arrow and the Sioux and Northern Cheyenne on the Powder River was probably the last time he would live like a true Indian. He had hardly talked about it, and she knew that was probably because it hurt too much. She wondered about the widowed squaw, Sweet Grass. She knew how "accommodating" such women could be to a guest, especially if that guest were her lover's father. What warm-blooded Indian squaw wouldn't want to test a handsome Indian man whose knife was great medicine?

But no. She knew him too well; knew how powerfully he loved only his Abbie. If someone told him he must cut off his own legs with his own hatchet to save her, he'd do it. If he had slept with the woman, she would know, for it was not his nature to be unfaithful. All she knew was that Zeke Monroe seemed unusually happy, and that was good; but he also seemed to have resigned himself to something, and she didn't know what.

An eagle flew overhead then, and they both looked up at it.

"*Voaxáae!*" Zeke said softly. "*Epevae!*" He watched it disappear into the horizon, then looked at her, a sudden alarming sadness in his eyes. The eagle was his sign, his personal spirit representative. His Indian name was Lone Eagle. And apparently in this one he had seen some kind of omen.

"Zeke?" her heart tightened. "What is it, Zeke? What are you not telling me?"

Their eyes held. Then he suddenly smiled for her. "I am sorry. For a moment when I saw the eagle, I thought about the People and what they have lost. I sometimes wonder if the eagle, too, will one day lose his freedom."

He mounted his horse then, bareback. He had not even put a bridle on the animal yet. He grasped the mane in his hands. "Wolf's Blood and I will ride for a while. I need to ride. We will keep in a circle not far so do not be afraid. You dress. We will be back soon. Then we will go home. I am anxious to get there now." He gave her a wink and kicked the horse's sides, riding off at a gallop, nothing to keep him on the horse but his own strength and riding skills.

She watched him ride away, then lay back down for a moment, studying a puffy white cloud in the deep blue sky. "Don't take him from me," she prayed. "Not now. Not ever. Not my Zeke."

The eagle circled back and called out, then disappeared again. She felt a tightness in her chest. Eagles were rarely seen out here over the plains. They were more likely to be seen in higher country. Why had this one come by—alone? Alone. Lone Eagle! She felt an odd chill.

In November of 1869, Margaret presented her parents with a grandson, Ezekiel Morgan, named after his grandfather, and dubbed "Little Zeke." A second grandson, Nathan Daniel, was born in January, 1871, to Abbie's great joy. In the spring of 1871 the first letter came from Jeremy, after an absence of nearly two years. They had received one short note after his arrival in New York—that he was fine and was going to stay with the railroad. LeeAnn had written several times at first, extolling the wonders of the East, raving over the school. But then the letters became fewer, and soon only occasional, usually to ask for more money and nothing else. It saddened both of them. The latest letter mentioned only that she soon be through with school and was going to Washington, D.C., where she was being placed in the employment of a law firm as a secretary. LeeAnn promised that soon she would need no more money, as she would be making her own.

It was obvious to both Zeke and Abbie that the girl had no intentions of returning home any time soon, and it saddened them. But she was apparently happy, and that was what was important.

Always when a letter came, the family gathered in the main house, now occupied by Zeke and Abbie, Ellen, now seventeen, and Jason, now thirteen. Margaret, Morgan, and their two sons lived in a cabin nearby. Wolf's Blood did not like the confines of a house, choosing to stay in a tipi Abbie helped him make with hides from buffalo and elk that he and Zeke had hunted. Abbie had enjoyed tanning and preparing the skins and sewing them together, for it reminded her of her first years with Zeke when they lived among the Cheyenne. Zeke's own mother had taught her such things, and it had been a long time since she was able to use such knowledge again.

They all gathered now to hear Abbie read the letter from their long-lost brother, the return address bearing the mark of Abilene, Kansas. Mail was always an exciting thing, for it did not come regularly and had to be picked up at Fort Lyon, which was a three-day ride from the ranch. Thus, its delivery was confined to once a month, when Zeke went to the fort for supplies.

Margaret held Nathan sleeping in her arms and Morgan bounced Little Zeke on his knee, while Abbie opened and read the letter.

    Dear Family,

    I am writing this from Abilene, Kansas. You would not believe how wild this town is. Since the Kansas-Pacific tracks reached Abilene, practically all the cattle bound for the East from Texas are herded here to the trains. The drovers pour in, ready for drinks and women, and there are plenty of both for any man.

    I work for the Kansas-Pacific now, managing the station here in Abilene. I hope to move up even more. There is much money to be made working for the railroad, and the railroad grows more every year. Eventually the K-P will go all the way through Kansas and into Colorado, probably all the way to Denver by 1880. There is so much happening in this country, and I love being a part of it.

    I never saw anything like New York City and never will again. I wish you could all see it—buildings so tall they're like mountains. I would like to see Wolf's Blood in such a place. He would not believe it. People in the East know almost nothing about Indians—only what

*they read in newspapers. You would not believe the
exaggerated stories they tell. I have to laugh sometimes. And there are little paper books all over with
stories about the West, all of them so silly. . . .*

Abbie stopped reading for a moment and looked around
the table. "Well, it seems we have lost a son to the glitter of
civilization."

"He is a fool!" Wolf's Blood scowled. "I would like to take
him to that useless land in Oklahoma where they have put
our People—his People, too! I would like to show him what
the railroad is doing to them—show him their sad faces and
lonely eyes! He pretends he does not even know them!"

"He's your brother, Wolf's Blood," Abbie reminded him.

The boy rose. "He is not my brother! He has deserted us
for no reason. LeeAnn had a reason. She had bad memories.
But Jeremy is just selfish. He is just making fun of me when
he says he would like to see me in New York. He thinks less
of me because I choose to be Indian!" He walked to the door.
"I do not want to hear any more of this letter from a brother
who deserts his father when he—"

Zeke shot him a warning look, and Wolf's Blood caught
himself just in time.

"When he knows he is needed on the ranch," he quickly
finished.

"Morgan, you, and Jason are good help," she told him,
frowning with curiosity, sure the boy had intended to say
something else.

"When Jeremy left he did not know if I would even come,
and Jason was younger. Father needed him then but he left
anyway. Then he takes all this time to tell you how he is
doing, and brags about a life he knows father would hate,
and brags about the railroad—enemy of the Cheyenne! You
think you may never see him again. Well, I hope we never see
him again, because if I see him, I will put my hands around
his throat and choke some sense into him!"

He stormed out, Abbie standing there in surprise at the
outburst. Again she felt the gnawing feeling that there was
something happening she didn't know about, little realizing

102

that Wolf's Blood's anger stemmed from the fact that if Jeremy did not return in time, Zeke would never see his second son again. The strange disease that clawed at his father had given him a bad time that winter, and there were many times Zeke had taken the pain medicine the doctor had given him, which Wolf's Blood kept hidden in the tipi for his father. It angered Wolf's Blood that Jeremy was off taking part in things that were destroying the Indian, while his own father needed him.

Zeke lit a cigarette and stretched his long legs, tilting his chair back. "Finish the letter, Abbie," he said quietly. "Don't mind Wolf's Blood. He's feeling ornery again. I think I'll take him back with me to Fort Lyon next week when I pick up the supplies they couldn't provide. There's a wagon train full of supplies due in from St. Louis in a few days and I want to be one of the first ones there. The trip would be good for Wolf's Blood—keep him occupied." He looked at his son-in-law. "Unless you'd rather go, Morgan. I just went, but they didn't have everything I need," Zeke told the man. "Maybe you get tired of staying here while I go."

The man shrugged. "Makes no difference. Wolf's Blood needs to go and he's better off with you. And you know what you need. I hate to leave the babies right now."

Zeke grinned at Little Zeke, a beautiful boy with large brown eyes, creamy brown skin, and a brilliant smile. It felt good to have grandsons—to know something of himself would live far into the future. He wished Wolf's Blood would marry and have sons. The babies were a real joy, especially to Abbie. Zeke looked at his son-in-law. "Have I ever thanked you for all your help—what you've done for Margaret?"

Morgan laughed lightly. "About a million times. But you forget it works both ways. I was looking for a home and family and I found one. There aren't many men I hold in real high esteem, Zeke, but you're one of them.

Zeke puffed the cigarette, leaving it in the corner of his mouth. "The feeling is mutual and you know it," he answered. He looked at Abbie. "Let's hear the rest the Jeremy's letter."

Margaret took hold of her husband's hand. Nothing was

more important to her than her husband and her father. To have them get along so well warmed her heart, for there was a time when she thought she had no one. But her father had come for her in Denver and would not leave until she came back with him. He had not hated her and cast her out for what she had done during that terrible, confused time in her life when she had turned to prostitution. He had simply patiently loved her, perhaps because he understood so well what it was like to have mixed blood but to look all Indian and so be cruelly branded.

The road back to the real Margaret had been difficult, but then Morgan Brown had come along, a man who loved her simply for who she was, a man who recognized the inner beauty as well as the obvious outer beauty. He was a man of mixed blood himself, his mother black, his father a wealthy plantation owner who had never even known about the boy, having sold the mother before he was ever born. Now she had a good husband, and was near her father, too.

"He says his goal is to end up in management," Abbie was saying, "with an office in Denver, and that he's under the supervision of a very prominent railroad man who likes him and is working to help him advance. And he wants to know how all of us are doing—if Margaret has had a baby yet and if we've heard from Wolf's Blood."

"How nice of him to ask," Margaret said rather sarcastically.

Abbie's eyes teared. "He's still your brother, Margaret—and my son. He's doing what makes him happy. He can't help it if it is something no one else in the family cares about. It's the same for LeeAnn. They are your brother and sister, and we will always love them."

Margaret sighed. "Is that all of it?"

Abbie folded the letter. "Yes. I'll answer it right away and Zeke can take the letter to Fort Lyon when he goes. Someone there will get it to Abilene."

Zeke got up, rather slowly Abbie thought, as though something hurt him. "Come on out to the barn, Morgan," he told Margaret's husband. "I have something to show you."

Morgan rose, and Zeke gave Abbie a quick kiss, assuring

her he would be right back. Both men left and Abbie looked at Margaret. "Do you notice anything different about your father?" she asked her daughter.

Margaret frowned. "Something. But I'm not sure what. Sometimes I think perhaps he's in pain but doesn't say anything. I've caught him wincing when he chops wood or pitches hay—sometimes even when he rides."

Their eyes held. "He's keeping something from me, Margaret. And it frightens me."

"Father never keeps anything from you. If it's important enough, he'll tell you, Mother. It's probably just old wounds. You know that old bullet wound in his side bothers him sometimes. It always has. But it's never stopped him."

Abbie sighed and slipped her son's letter into her apron pocket. "Perhaps." She thought about the wound—the one he'd received saving her life. She in turn had saved his by removing the bullet herself, a mere fifteen-year-old girl then, frightened to death that the man she loved would die. He had lived, but the wound had always bothered him. It upset her that she didn't really know what she was doing when she removed the bullet. Abbie had always worried that she'd done something terrible to him. Now she found herself hoping it was the old wound and nothing more that bothered him.

Outside Zeke led Morgan to the barn, both men almost equal in build. They went inside, and Zeke took out his knife, grabbing up a bag of feed and slashing open the top. Morgan Brown had heard many tales of the things Zeke Monroe had done with the knife, and he swore to never be considered the man's enemy.

"I have something important to talk to you about, Morgan," he spoke up, slashing open another bag of feed as though he simply needed something to do with the knife. He shoved the bags aside in a standing position and put the knife back in its sheath. "We'll use those two in the morning." He sighed and looked at Morgan. "I've done just about everything in my lifetime, Morgan. I've hunted, trapped, scouted, lived with the Indians, lived in Tennessee, got mixed up in the Civil War, fought Indians and Comancheros

105

and outlaws. I've lived on this piece of land with Abbie for nearly twenty-five years now—watched it grow from a few horses and a tipi to nearly a thousand acres, outbuildings, two houses, and quite a big herd." He turned and leaned against a large, square support post. "If I told you all the things Abbie and I have been through, we'd be up all night."

"I've heard a lot of stories from Margaret. I have a pretty good idea.

Zeke grinned sadly. "Well let's just say we've done and seen it all. I've tried to be a good husband to Abbie. Lord knows she's put up with a lot living with a man who'd rather be Indian. But she's never demanded that I abandon any of my Indian ways. The few that I did abandon I did willingly— for her. Now something has ... come up ... unexpectedly." He grabbed a pitchfork and began stabbing at some hay. "I want to be sure to set some money aside, Morgan, a tidy bundle that will see that Abbie lives decently even after I'm gone."

Morgan's eyebrows went up. "Gone? Where might you be going?"

Zeke met his eyes. "I have a crippling disease, Morgan. Wolf's Blood is the only other one who knows, and I want it to stay that way. Do you understand?"

Morgan frowned, his dark eyes showing their concern. "Of course. But when did all of this come about?"

"It's bothered me for a long time. Two years ago I saw a doctor in Julesberg. He called it arthritis—said it sounded to him like the kind that slowly cripples a man so that eventually he can't get out of bed. I do not intend to let it get that bad, if you get my meaning. I'll find a more honorable way to die."

Morgan's eyes teared. "Zeke, I'm sorry. Are you sure?"

The man grinned sadly. "Oh, yes, I'm sure. Last winter I was better, but this winter has been worse again, reminding me that this thing is not going to go away like I'd hoped it would. The doctor told me it wouldn't, but that sometimes it goes away some, then comes back." He sighed and leaned on the pitchfork. "I'm telling you because I'll need your help. I need to know you intend to always stay here on the ranch—

take care of it. I won't always be here to do it, and Wolf's Blood is as dependable as the wind. It would comfort me to know that someone else loves it as much as I do and will keep it going when I'm gone."

"You know I will. I love Margaret, and I'm happy here. Meeting Margaret in that brothel was the luckiest day of my life."

Zeke nodded. "I just need to be sure. Another reason is that I might have to do something more to get some money set aside. That school of LeeAnn's drained me pretty good, and the ranch isn't enough to sustain such a big family and have anything left over to set aside. I may have to go off and do something extra, and I need to know you'll be here to keep the place going. I've taught you a lot about horses, diseases to watch for, the best way to break them, the best markets, all of it. I think you could run this place by yourself once in a while if you had to. You've already done it for short periods of time."

Morgan frowned. "What are you thinking of doing?"

Zeke rubbed at his neck. "That's the hard part. But I think it's best and the pay is good." He sighed and kept hold of the pitchfork. "It's over for the Cheyenne, Morgan. Most of them are on that stinking reservation. Abbie and I have been there, and it kills me to see it. Yet the preservation of what is left of the race is all important, and it's useless for the young renegades among them to continue to make war and run and hide. To do so can only mean the loss of more precious lives. The best way I can help them now is to make them see that they should go to the reservation. There was a time when I'd have fought just as savagely as some of them are still doing. And if I thought they could win, I'd tell them to keep on fighting. But they can't win and they're dying like flies, and the more they make war, the less the government will give them in the end to keep them alive. I know the plains of Colorado and Kansas and Nebraska like the back of my hand. The Army needs good scouts. I'm thinking of obliging them—to help my people, not destroy them. The pay is good. Once I swore I'd never scout for the enemy of my people, but now their enemy is banishment and hunger.

107

They must get to the reservation and do all they can to survive."

Morgan ran a hand through his dark hair. "What will Wolf's Blood think of that?"

"I think he'll understand when I'm through talking to him. We're very close. I'd like to get him to help me—for his mother's sake. Some of his pay can go into the kitty also. The hardest part will be explaining it to Abbie without her suspecting some secret motive." He threw some hay into a stall and a horse's tail swished. "Another reason I'm considering it is because scouting would get me out there and keep me active. In a way I'd be living similar to the way I used to live. I'd be riding the plains, tracking, living out of doors. I want to live that way, even though it's more painful for me. I want to feel free, Morgan, to feel like a Cheyenne again, to be as active as I can be for as long as possible. Somehow I feel that if I can stay active, I'll put this damned disease off even longer. I refuse to sit down and wait for it to take over. Scouting will take my mind off things and keep me moving. I intend to talk to the commanding officer at Fort Lyon the next time I go. Being able to use Dan's name as a brother won't hurt."

Morgan sighed and put out his hand, and Zeke took it. "Good luck, Zeke. I won't say anything to Margaret, and I'll pray for you. I'm damned sorry. But you won't have to worry about the ranch. I'll do a good job for you, and little Jason is turning into quite a man now. He'll be a big help."

Zeke grinned, squeezing Morgan's hand in return. "He's a fine son. I'm proud of Jason. He's our little 'Yellow Hawk.' All the children have Indian names. But Wolf's Blood refused a Christain name when Abbie gave them to the rest of the children." He released Morgan's hand. "Abbie was always afraid that if they weren't duly christened with Christian names, someone would come and take them from her because they were part Indian. I doubt that would have happened, but it made her feel better. What I really hate to see is what they're doing down on that reservation—taking children away from their parents and putting them in strict schools, cutting their hair, making them wear uncomfortable white man's clothing, robbing them of their freedom and heritage, and torturing the hearts of their mothers and fathers. The white man thinks he can make the Indian live just like he does—overnight. But it won't happen. It might not even happen in the next hundred years, Morgan. Mark my words. The Indian culture is so entirely different from the white man's that I doubt the two will ever truly be as one."

"You're probably right there." His eyes saddened. "Good luck, Zeke. You'll make a hell of a scout."

Zeke turned away. "Yeah," he replied quietly. He picked up the pitchfork. "You might as well go back before Abbie and Margaret suspect something. Just tell them I showed you a new brand of feed."

Morgan put a hand on Zeke's shoulder, thinking how strong and solid it was. It was difficult to believe there could be anything wrong with the man. "I'll do that."

He turned and left, and Zeke took the pitchfork and stabbed at a stack of hay, over and over again, becoming vicious in the stabs, wishing the hay were soldiers and settlers and trains and cities and all the things that had destroyed his people. Most of all he wished it was the hated disease that plagued his joints. If only he could stomp it out this easily. He rammed the pitchfork again, then grasped it tightly, closing his eyes and struggling not to weep. He wondered if he would ever see Jeremy or LeeAnn again. And how would he tell Abbie about scouting for the Army? It wasn't what he wanted, but it was necessary. He only hoped the scouting expeditions would not take him away for too long at a time. More than anything, he wanted to be with his Abbie-girl as much as possible, while he was still strong and virile. She had always hated it when he went away, and she would certainly argue about the scouting. But other than raising horses, it was what he knew best.

Chapter Six

They rode into Fort Lyon side by side. Here they were not questioned, for Zeke Monroe was known in these parts. Smatterings of Cheyenne were a common sight, although most of them were hundreds of miles away now. Each time Zeke came here he heard more stories of scattered raids by those refusing to succumb to reservation life, as well as more and more talk of untold slaughter of buffalo. The year before, developments in the tanning process made the buffalo hides of any season commercially workable, and the slaughter of massive herds became a year-round business. The introduction of more long-range guns made the job even easier, and up to twenty thousand hunters now roamed the plains and prairies. The slaughter was only enhanced by the need of railroad workers for food, and men were hired by the railroad to do nothing but hunt buffalo to keep the crews supplied with meat. Whether the kill was for food or for the hide, other valuable parts were left behind to rot in the sun, and every buffalo killed was one more tragedy for the Indian, whose very life depended on the animal. Thus, a more subtle way had been found to wipe out the Indian and make those remaining more dependent on the government reservation life to survive. Even there they were cheated by swindling traders, crooked reservation agents, and men in power—men like Charles Garvey, whose wicked pen was doing its dirty work in more and more eastern newspapers.

Wolf's Blood and Zeke were quiet as they rode in, both lost

in thought and angry over passing dead buffalo carcasses on their three-day ride from the ranch. Both could see the chapters closing on an old way of life, and they rode into the fort with heavy hearts. They halted in the middle of the courtyard, where a few passing settlers stared at the "wild Indians," and there was the general commotion that always accompanied a busy army outpost/supply station. Fort Lyon was on the Santa Fe Trail, a major route from St. Louis to New Mexico.

"I'll go talk to the commanding officer," Zeke told his son. "You go on to the supply store with the list."

The boy met his father's eyes. "Are you sure you want to do this, Father?"

Zeke studied the sadness in his eyes. "I don't think I have any choice. You saw those carcasses, Wolf's Blood. The Cheyenne can't survive the old way anymore. The same thing will happen to the Sioux and Cheyenne in the North. And look how many died last year from whooping cough. We have to preserve what's left. Shall I tell them you will ride with me sometimes?"

The boy grasped the reins of his horse firmly, his jaw flexing in a mixture of anger and resignation. "Only because I want to be with you. What does Mother say?"

Zeke cleared his throat. "I'm afraid I haven't told her yet. I'm still trying to get up the courage."

The boy laughed lightly and rode off to the supply store, while Zeke headed for the command post. He dismounted and tied his horse, going inside where he was greeted by a young lieutenant who demanded that he state his business. The lieutenant moved aside then, fascinated by the menacing-looking Indian who claimed he was there to scout for the Army. The man ushered Zeke into an inner office, where a lieutenant-colonel sat writing something. He looked up when he saw Zeke, his greenhorn eyes surprised and wide with curiosity. He appeared to be on the defensive as he rose, putting out his hand carefully. "I'm Lieutenant-Colonel Petersen. They tell me you've come volunteering to scout for the Army. Monroe, is it? You don't look like a man who would have a white name."

Zeke shook the man's hand. "Zeke Monroe. My father was white, my mother Cheyenne. I own a ranch west of here, about a three-day ride. I've been around these parts all my life, lived with the Cheyenne for years before marrying." He watched the soldier's eyes carefully. "My wife is white. We have several children and a large herd of horses, mostly Appaloosa. I've sold horses here at the fort many times."

The soldier's eyes scanned the dark half-breed before him, curious about the white woman. Had she been a captive? Just how wild and untrustworthy was this man? "Well, I'm new here, Monroe, or I'm sure I'd have known about you. You own a ranch, you say? I didn't think Indians or half-breeds could own land."

Zeke bristled. "It's in my wife's name, if that's what you mean."

The soldier caught the irritation in Zeke's voice. "And how did you come upon a white wife?" he asked.

Zeke just stared at him a moment. It was none of the man's business, but he knew what Petersen was thinking. "I met Abbie almost twenty-six years ago. I was a scout for her wagon train going to Oregon. She lost her family. She's from Tennessee also. Things just happened, that's all. She's my willing wife if that's what you're wondering."

Petersen nodded. "I see. And if you have a ranch and all, why are you volunteering as a scout?"

"My reasons are personal, except to say that I need the extra money. I can find a track in places no other man could find it. And I speak Cheyenne, Sioux, and Arapaho, and even a little Comanche and Apache. I know the Indian, know his ways. I have many friends among those at Camp Supply in Oklahoma."

"So why would you want to help us hunt down the renegades?"

Zeke sighed, taking out paper and tobacco and rolling himself a cigarette. "There was a time, Lieutenant-Colonel Petersen, when I would have joined those renegades. But I've seen the signs. It's a useless fight, and I love my people. Their only hope of survival is to get themselves onto the reservations, much as I personally hate the thought of it. The white man is

113

destroying a beautiful people, a precious culture. They'll regret it some day, but that's not my problem now. My problem is to help preserve what is left. But I won't be any part of unwarranted raids on peaceful villages. If I get mixed up in something like that, I'll take the Indian side. I know all about Sand Creek and the Washita. That's no way to make the Indians come to terms. The white man has a way of doing the very thing that will make the Indian retaliate the most. Maybe I can help in that department also."

He lit and took a drag on the cigarette, while Petersen studied him. "Well, Mr. Monroe, the problems are many. Big Jake, Red Moon, and some of the other chiefs around Camp Supply are having trouble keeping their young warriors from joining the Kiowa and Comanche raids into Texas. And most of the Cheyenne on the reservation are being very stubborn about learning to farm and about sending their children to school. Several of the ones who belong at Camp Supply are in the north with the Sioux, like Bull Bear and Medicine Arrows. And we're having a devil of a time with whiskey traders and gunrunners. We expect trouble this spring, when it's rumored Bull Bear and Medicine Arrows will start south to report to Camp Supply. They'll be coming right through Nebraska and Kansas, and the settlers are going to be very uneasy. Those in the north, of course, are reeling with their victory over the Powder River country, and none of them—especially the Cheyenne—seem inclined to report to the agencies set up through that latest treaty. They roam wild and unrestrained, and rumors of the freedom they enjoy just keep the more restless ones in the south stirred up. Not only is Red Cloud looked to as a leader for freedom, but there are others stirring up trouble in the North—one called Sitting Bull, and another leader very intimate with the Northern Cheyenne, Crazy Horse, an Oglala Sioux. So you see, we certainly are far from a settled peace. If you are going to volunteer as a scout, you'll get mixed up in some pretty heavy work, and you may get involved in very difficult decisions."

"I am well aware of everything that is going on. My own son, Wolf's Blood, rode with the northern Sioux for several years, fought with Red Cloud. He is home with me now, and I ask that

114

he joins me in scouting. We are very close. He will do what I tell him and will cause no trouble."

Petersen frowned. "How old is he?"

"He is twenty-four."

The man shook his head. "The young ones are not very dependable."

"My son is. I told you he will cooperate. It is important to me that he can sometimes come along. It will be good for him. He gets restless on the ranch."

Petersen leaned forward, reaching for a folder and a pen. "And how old are you?"

"I am fifty-one."

The soldier's eyebrows shot up and he studied Zeke again, noticing the scar on his left cheek. "You certainly don't look your age, Mr. Monroe. And you look like a strong man."

"I can hold my own. I have been in many dangerous situations and have the scars to prove it. I am sitting here, so that tells you I have lost no battles. I am skilled with the rifle, but my greatest skill is with the knife. You can ask around the fort about me. Some of the other scouts know me as Cheyenne Zeke; the Indians know me as Lone Eagle. All know of my reputation with the knife, and few men challenge me with it."

The soldier studied him again. He was a huge man, sprawled into the chair as though it did not fit him, his whole countenance that of someone not to be messed with. "Yes, I am sure you tell the truth there," he said a bit under his breath. "I will have to meet your son, then talk to some of the men around here who know you. Your eyes show truth and trustworthiness. I generally go on my own suspicions, but I'd still like to talk to a few men. When you agree to scout for the Army, Mr. Monroe, you have to follow orders. You don't look like a man accustomed to following orders."

Their eyes met. "I can follow orders if they are sensible and fair. But there are times when the soldier must listen to the scout if he wants to save his hide. Many massacres of soldiers could have been avoided if they had listened to those who know the signs."

Petersen grinned. "I'm aware of that. I am a man who listens. But you wouldn't necessarily work for me, Monroe.

You would simply go where you're needed and work under that commander. By the way, do you drink whiskey? Does you son?"

"Doesn't every man—to some extent? I don't overdo it. I drink very seldom, Mr. Petersen. I am well aware of what whiskey is doing to the Indians. My own brother is dead because of whiskey. My son also drinks very little."

"Yes, well, the firewater has it effects, and all bad. Drunken brawls within the reservations have started small wars between the Indians themselves. Another problem is ancient hatreds, making it difficult for some tribes to live near each other on the reservations. It's an impossible mess any way you look at it."

Zeke smoked quietly for a moment. "There'd be no mess if the white man hadn't come out here in the first place," he answered.

"Progress cannot be stopped, Mr. Monroe," the man replied, while writing something on a piece of paper. "I'll get in touch with you, Monroe. If you're so well known around here, someone will know how to find you and tell you when and where to report, right?"

"That's fine. I'm picking up some supplies today, then heading home."

"Who will watch over the ranch for you? And what about your wife?" the soldier asked, both men rising.

"I have a son-in-law who can run the place as good as I can. And a son at home, as well as two strong daughters. And my wife knows as much about it as anyone."

"But what does she think of you being gone for scouting?"

Zeke left the cigarette at the corner of his mouth and walked toward the door. "She'll understand," he answered, hoping he was right. "The need for money has taken me away other times."

Petersen smiled. "She must be quite a woman."

Zeke met his eyes, standing in the open doorway. "She is. There aren't many like her. She's a survivor—has been out here for years and has been through things that would make the white women back east faint dead away."

Petersen studied the grand physique of the wild-looking man in the doorway. "Yes, I'm sure she has." He nodded a good-

116

bye. "Thank you for the offer, Monroe. Stop back with your son before you leave, will you?"

Zeke hesitated. "I forgot to mention I have a white brother up at Fort Laramie. He's a colonel up there—Dan Monroe. You check me out through him if you want."

Petersen's face brightened. "I'll do that. That's good news, Monroe. That will make a big difference. Any Indian brothers, by the way?"

"Only one left—Swift Arrow. He lives in the North with the Sioux. He is a Dog Soldier."

Petersen rubbed his chin. "You're quite a mixture then, aren't you?"

Zeke felt the ache of living in two worlds again. "Yes, Lieutenant-Colonel. I am quite a mixture."

He walked out into the sunshine and untied his mount, walking it over to the supply store and going inside to find Wolf's Blood waiting nervously at a counter with a list for the storekeeper to study. A very young and very shapely Indian girl with hair hanging nearly to her waist was on a ladder putting canned food on a shelf. Zeke grinned when he saw that Wolf's Blood was closely eyeing the slender legs revealed by the slit in the girl's tunic. But he also noticed that Wolf's Blood was slyly watching the storekeeper, who was also eyeing the legs. A can slipped and fell, and in an instant the storekeeper slammed down a sack of flour on the counter and walked over to the ladder, picking up a switch on the way. He suddenly lashed the girl across the calves of her legs, so hard that a faint line of blood quickly appeared. The girl jumped at the pain and nearly lost her hold on the ladder. Wolf's Blood bolted toward the counter, but Zeke grabbed his arm. The girl looked at Wolf's Blood, her heart racing at his hard handsomeness and at the way he had started to her defense. She was not sure if he was Cheyenne, but supposed he must be, for that was nearly the only kind of Indian seen at Fort Lyon.

"Don't act in haste," Zeke was saying quietly to his son. "Indians get hung very easily in these parts."

"He had no right to hurt her!" Wolf's Blood hissed.

The storekeeper eyed them. "You got a problem, kid?"

Zeke jerked at Wolf's Blood again as the boy made for the

117

man. "You always go around beating helpless girls?" Zeke asked the man before Wolf's Blood could say anything.

The storekeeper grinned and eyed her again. The girl was struggling against tears, and stayed on the ladder to finish arranging the cans. "That little Apache piece belongs to me—paid for proper," the man replied. "She's my property and a man would be best not to mess with her. I bought her off a whiskey dealer." He grinned more at the sudden possessive look on young Wolf's Blood's face, realizing the young man had eyes for the lovely Apache girl. "I haven't got inside her yet," he said, deliberately teasing the boy. "She's a fresh one, you see. I'm trying to decide if I should do the honors, or sell her for a profit to somebody else."

"I will buy her!" Wolf's Blood said quickly.

Zeke and the girl both looked at him in surprise, the girl feeling flames in her blood.

The storekeeper just laughed. "You don't have enough, boy."

"How do you know? How much do you want?"

The storekeeper eyed the girl again, then walked over and pulled her off the ladder with a jerk, running a hand over her breasts. Wolf's Blood felt hot with rage and the girl hung her head. "Well, boy, I can get three hundred dollars for her. You got that much?"

Wolf's Blood looked up at his father and knew his answer. He looked back at the storekeeper. "I will get it. I have horses that are my own that I can sell."

The storekeeper chuckled. "That would take time. I don't know how much longer I can go without exploring that pretty thing's insides."

Wolf's Blood whipped out the huge Bowie knife his father had bought him as a gift after suffering the ordeal of the Sun Dance Ritual. "Touch her and I will kill you!" he snarled. "Even if I hang for it!"

The storekeeper backed up, looking from the boy to Zeke, who looked just as menacing as his son. "I was only going to make a suggestion, Indian," he told the boy. "You good at wrestling—Indian wrestling?"

"As good as any." Wolf's Blood lowered the knife a little but

118

kept it out.

"Well, then, stick around a couple of days. A bunch of Pawnees are coming here for some sporting games with the soldiers." He grinned, knowing the Pawnee were a hated enemy of the Cheyenne. "The Pawnee have helped the soldiers hunt down Cheyenne a time or two, you know. They're generally welcome here. We have some good games—betting games. You look like a strong young man—a scrapper. And I'll bet you don't hold no love for the Pawnee. I'll sponsor you in the wrestling games and anything else you're good at, and if you win me the three hundred bucks, the girl is yours."

Wolf's Blood looked up at his father again, who scowled at him. "Come outside and we'll discuss it," he told his son.

The boy stormed out and Zeke followed, corralling his son outside. "Wolf's Blood, you don't even know that girl," he warned him. "This is the first time you've ever even seen her."

"I don't care! You saw what he did to her—saw the look in her eyes. I want to buy her, Father. If I do not buy her, I will steal her! I cannot bear to see that white bastard touching her and hurting her! I want to take her home with us."

Zeke grinned and shook his head. "What if she doesn't want to go?"

The boy held his eyes. "You saw how she looked at me. She will go."

Zeke's eyebrows arched. "And you intend to make her your wife?"

"I don't know yet. I only know I want to get her out of there. We could take care of her, couldn't we, Father? Even if I didn't marry her? Maybe we could take her back to her people if she wants to go."

Zeke sighed. "Sure. What's one more mouth to feed? But you'd better join with me in scouting. We'll need your share of the earnings, and I want no trouble. It will be hard for you, Wolf's Blood."

"I will go. For you and for the girl. And I will take part in these games, Father. I can win! I know I can. And you could enter, too. Between the two of us, we could make enough. It would be fun, Father, fighting the Pawnee and beating them!"

The boy's eyes flashed, and Zeke felt his own excitement.

119

"It would at that," he answered. "All right, my son, we will join in the Pawnee games. Just be careful how you talk to that storekeeper."

"If he hurts her he will die!"

Zeke grinned. "Of course he will. What you have to learn is to do in a white man without being caught. Just like we did with Winston Garvey. Go easy, Wolf's Blood. We'll tell him how it must be and that we'll enter the games. And if you're going to buy the girl, you could at least find out what her name is!"

The boy grinned, his blood hot for the slender legs he had seen, the wide, innocent eyes of the virgin Apache girl he suddenly wanted for himself. "I will find out her name. We will buy her and take her home where she can be safe."

Wolf's Blood dashed back inside and Zeke shook his head. He, too, felt sorry for the girl and would probably have done the same thing if he'd had first chance—just to keep her safe. He'd seen his fill of the abuse of Indian women. He grinned to himself at the thought of the look on Abbie's face when they came riding home with more than just supplies.

LeeAnn pushed at one of the combs that helped hold up her beautifully coiffured hair, its thick blond curls gracing her exquisite face. Just the right amount of coloring accented the lids of her wide blue eyes. She had learned much about the ways of being a proper lady—how to dress and act. Not that her own mother hadn't taught her, but here in the East all the latest fashions were available; and with so many things to do and places to go, a woman had to be current with fashions and manners.

She smoothed a wrinkle in her baby blue *Dolly Varden* dress, the latest rage. The garment was named after the heroine in Charles Dickens's novel *Barnaby Rudge*, and had a blue and white flowered overskirt that was very short in front but very bunched in the back, made of chintz and accenting the plain blue silk skirt of the dress. The color only accented her creamy beauty, making her eyes look bluer, her skin softer.

She shifted on the wooden bench where she sat waiting for the lecture to begin. It was a warm, lovely day, and after the lecture someone was giving about the West, there would be a band concert, while investors and railroad people circulated among the crowd telling people all about the wonderful advantages of the American West. LeeAnn had come out of pure curiosity, for she knew probably better than any of them what the West was really like. Why she had felt drawn to the occasion, she wasn't sure, for she had spent the last two years or better trying to forget she had ever lived there. If she could just forget her family, everything would be perfect. But missing them was not enough to make her go back.

LeeAnn was secretary to an attorney now, making good money but still attending college on the side and planning to be a teacher, preferably at a university. She lived in Washington, D.C., to her a most interesting and exciting place to be. She had already met many prominent men, always introducing herself as simply LeeAnn Whittaker from New York, telling others her parents were dead and never letting on to anyone that she was really from Colorado and her father was a half-breed Indian. Why should she tell them? They would only shun her. She had come here to forget, and the only way to do that was to turn her back on the life she had once led. There was no ranch, no family. And her ordeal with the Comanches had never happened. But occasionally she would suffer the pain of guilt and sweet love at the memory of her father risking his life to save her. Still, Zeke Monroe was a part of that wild land that she wanted nothing more to do with. He fit the land. She did not. And no one she knew here in the East would ever understand or accept her if they knew.

LeeAnn turned to a girl friend who sat reading a dime novel about the West, and she grinned at the drawing of an Indian spearing a buffalo. The buffalo was drawn far out of proportion, many times taller than the Indian. Sometimes she was tempted to shock Sharon by telling her she knew firsthand about buffalo hunting and Indians—had even lived with Indians a time or two. But no. She would never tell. She was from New York. Her parents were dead.

A band marched by, and balloons danced in the wind from where they were tied to a speaker's stand.

"There are always young men interested in the West,"

Sharon spoke up, putting the book down and looking around. "We'll surely meet some of them today. Isn't this exciting, LeeAnn?"

"It's something to do. But I don't really care about any young man who has an interest in the West. I do not intend to go to that lawless land."

"It sounds wonderfully exciting to me. Just look at the picture of a buffalo in this book!" She opened the page again to the drawing and LeeAnn frowned.

"I am sure the buffalo are very big animals, Sharon, but surely you don't believe they're several heads taller than a man on a horse!"

"How do you know until you see one? They might be that big. I've seen an elephant, and an elephant is that big."

LeeAnn quelled an urge to say she knew exactly what a buffalo looked like. A young man limped up to the speaker's stand then, using a cane, while nearby a white man walked around dressed in buckskins, his face painted, a long headdress of feathers on his head. It made LeeAnn think of her father again, and she smiled at how ridiculous the white man dressed as an Indian looked. How handsome her father would look next to the ridiculous fake who stood nearby!

The young man with the cane positioned himself at the podium, and a heavyset man climbed up beside him, raising his arms and bellowing out in a loud voice for the crowd to quiet down. People stopped talking and more sat down, waiting for the speaker's next words. The majority of the crowd were men, and Sharon scanned the sea of choices eagerly, her eyes telling them that she was single and available. Several of them eyed her back and smiled, some tipping their hats. But LeeAnn stared ahead, at the young man who had limped to the podium. He was not what anyone could call handsome, nor was he ugly. He had a look of sureness and power about him, and he was watching her, an odd, hungry look to his eyes that stirred something inside of her. His eyes both frightened and fascinated her. He was obviously someone important or he wouldn't be on the speaker's stand. And he was watching her, singling her out from Sharon or any other women there. It made her feel important too.

"Ladies and gentlemen, I want to introduce you to Mr. Charles Garvey," the fat man bellowed.

LeeAnn frowned. The name was somewhat familiar, but she wasn't sure why. To ensure total secrecy, none of the Monroe children had been told the details of their mother's abduction and rape, who had done it, and why. Only Wolf's Blood knew the details. Nor had the others been told that their cousin Joshua Lewis was the half-breed son of Winston Garvey. The fewer who knew, the better, for their own safety, for Joshua's safety, and to ensure no one ever pieced things together and linked Winston Garvey's disappearance with Zeke Monroe.

"Young Mr. Garvey is here representing his real estate interests in the great territory of Colorado," the announcer went on. "His father was a senator for many years, and later a prominent businessman in Colorado, owning property not only in that territory but also in New Mexico territory. He and his representatives will gladly work with any of you interested in investing in property in the golden West—and golden is the word, folks, for it's a known fact that the gold that lies in the mountains of Colorado has only been lightly tapped. There is more, folks! Enough to enable every man here to fulfill his dreams!"

The crowd cheered, and the fat man stepped aside. Charles Garvey scanned the crowd, his dark eyes commanding attention, his wealthy power having an almost hypnotizing effect on his audience, who quickly quieted down. He looked at LeeAnn again before beginning his speech, his eyes taking in her fair beauty and full figure.

He began speaking then, his grammar excellent, his voice clear, the words well enunciated and well chosen. He carried on about the beauty of the West, the money that could be made if people settled along the railroad rights-of-way, the money that could be made just supplying gold camps, let alone the possibility of discovering gold themselves. He talked of rolling green plains and purple mountains with such eloquence that LeeAnn began missing home. He claimed that he missed it all himself so much that as soon as he was finished with his law apprenticeship here in Washington, he would go back home, even though deep inside he had no intentions of going back. He

123

liked the East, the easy living, the cities and progress. Why should he want to go back to his father's stinking ranch, to dust and cows, to rudely built towns with their dirt streets? He'd wait a few years. Let these people go and do the dirty work. Let them settle and build and civilize the West. Then he would go back. But aloud he carried on about all the benefits of looking to the setting sun, for he would make a lot of money off these people, selling them worthless land for a tidy sum, promising them gold and success.

Then came the question about Indians, and LeeAnn's heart tightened. Garvey's eyes darkened, and his hands gripped the podium more tightly. "We have virtually wiped the Indians out of the Territory of Colorado," he told them. "I rode with Chivington myself back in '64. We showed them at Sand Creek the hopelessness of trying to stay in our territory. I walk with a cane this very day because of Sand Creek!"

"You were there?" someone asked behind LeeAnn.

Garvey's eyes narrowed. "I was there. And I can tell you that after Sand Creek the Cheyenne were taken down a notch or two. Now most of them are in Indian Territory, far to the Southeast. We have a few renegades who continue to stir up trouble, but nothing that can't be handled."

"But what about Kansas, New Mexico, Nebraska?" another asked. "We have to go through those places to get to Colorado. Word is the Indians are raiding worse than ever in those places."

"Exaggerations!" Garvey told the man. "But of course there are some encounters. Until we gouge every stinking red man out of the creases of the land, there will be problems. But the more of you who come out, the better. We'll simply smother them with whites. On top of that, buffalo hunters and the railroad are doing their own good job of bringing the Indian to their knees. Buffalo are being killed by the thousands, and the Indian can't survive without the beasts. All of you would do well to support the slaughter of the buffalo—preferably until every last one of them is gone. Kill the buffalo, and you kill the Indian!"

LeeAnn felt an urge to argue, to stand up in support of the Indian. But something stopped her—an inner determination

124

to wipe out her past. Besides, she dared not stand and speak for them in a crowd like this one. How would it look, a blond-haired, blue-eyed, sophisticated young lady standing up and defending Indians? It was ridiculous.

"I can tell you people that it will not be long before the Indians will be no problem at all," Garvey went on. "I work diligently on legislation to send all Indians packing onto reservations, or have them risk being shot on sight. My own mother was killed before my eyes when I was a small boy!" The crowd mumbled, and Garvey half grinned, enjoying his power over them. "And my father, the reputable, prominent Winston Garvey, disappeared after Indians raided his ranch west of Denver. And so I tell you, I have more reason than most to wish for the extermination of the savage red man! Some of you may have read my columns in many eastern newspapers. They tell you about the Indians, their filthy habits, their cruelty to white captives . . ." His eyes moved to LeeAnn again. "What they do to white women." Their eyes held for a moment, and then he scanned the crowd again. "So do not sympathize with them, ladies and gentlemen, and do not fret at whatever the government or the railroad or anyone else does to ensure that the Indians do not bother new settlers. Rest assured, the problem will not last much longer."

He went on about real estate, gold, railroads, flourishing towns. LeeAnn listened. Some of it was right. Most of it was exaggerated. Yet she would not stand to argue with him. And in him she saw a way to truly deny her own heritage and roots. What if this man really was interested in her? He was obviously wealthy, and intending to be an attorney! What a wonderful life they could have together. She could be a Washington socialite. Surely this man had plans for more than even being an attorney. His father had been a senator. Surely the son would want to follow and get involved in politics.

The speech finally ended, and Garvey picked up his cane to slowly descend the steps. LeeAnn was grateful that two young men had stopped to converse with them. It gave her an excuse to stay nearby. She kept her eyes averted from Garvey, but felt him approaching her. Then a hand touched her arm, and she turned to see him standing beside her. Her face reddened some

125

under his dark gaze. Why did he make her feel like clay? He wasn't even handsome. But he reeked of power and sureness and importance.

"May I have the honor of knowing your name, lovely lady?" he asked her.

She smiled, and he felt on fire. She was the most beautiful thing he'd ever seen. What a ravishing wife she would make—perfect for a man of prominence. With his money and a wife like this, he would be the envy of every man in Washington.

"LeeAnn Whittaker," she answered softly.

He grinned, looking more handsome when he did so, losing some of the mysterious, threatening look he carried. "Well, LeeAnn Whittaker, are you married? Promised?"

She laughed lightly. "No. I am a secretary to a law firm, and I am finishing up my studies to be a teacher."

"Ah! An educated woman, on top of all that beauty! What man could ask for more!" he exclaimed. "I don't suppose an educated beauty like yourself would consider dinner and the theater with a poor soul like myself? This evening perhaps?"

She reddened more. "Why, I'd . . . be honored, Mr. Garvey," she replied.

He frowned. "Please call me Charles. And where shall I pick you up?"

"I live on Sixteenth Street North—the large apartment building for women only called the Virginia House."

"Yes, I know where that is." His eyes roved her body again. "And is there someone from whom I should get permission? Parents? An overseer?"

She swallowed, feeling torn inside. "I . . . have no parents. They were killed in New York when fire burned my father's clothing business. I am afraid I was raised in an orphanage, Mr. Garvey . . . I mean, Charles. Perhaps . . . perhaps that changes your mind?"

He grinned more. "Why should it? Your parents were respectable business people. Can you help it if they died? And why should a man mind about anything when a woman is as beautiful and educated as you, Miss Whittaker."

But my father is part Indian! she wanted to say. *I'm not from New York. I'm from Colorado! I know all about your west. I was*

126

captured once by Comanche Indians!

"Thank you, Charles," she said aloud. "I will be ready at seven. And I do so want to hear more about your Colorado, and what you are doing now in Washington. And I . . . I do hope you don't think me too forward—accepting your invitation so quickly. It's just that you're obviously a respected man here. If I doubted that, I would not accept."

He breathed deeply, drinking in her beauty. "I don't think you forward at all. And I would have been very frustrated and disappointed if you had not accepted. Seven then." He bowed, then straightened and donned his hat. He turned and walked off with the fat man, using the cane to support his crippled leg. She forced back renewed memories of what her own brother had told her happened at Sand Creek. Charles Garvey seemed very much the gentleman, a sophisticated, civilized man. He surely would not participate in such horrible mutilations as her father and brother had told her had been visited upon the Cheyenne. And little did she know that it was Wolf's Blood himself who had wounded Charles Garvey so badly that day that the young man would forever use the cane.

Chapter Seven

Dust billowed from the center of the courtyard of Fort Lyon, where Wolf's Blood wrestled the Pawnee favorite, while a crowd that included a mixture of soldiers and traders alike cheered their choice. The storekeeper, Matt Crenshaw, held up fistfuls of money, intending to make not only the three hundred dollars he was demanding for Sonora, his Apache slave, but much more. He'd considered enjoying the adventure of being her first man, but could not forget the look in the young Cheyenne man's eyes the day he'd threatened him with a knife. If the girl told the young man she'd been violated, Crenshaw did not doubt that the savage-looking Wolf's Blood would find a way to do him in. If not the boy then the father, who was equally threatening. This way he'd make money, and keep his skin.

Zeke watched the crowd carefully. He'd have his own turn, but had agreed only to knife throwing and wrist wrestling. The atmosphere was volatile, Pawnees and soldiers outnumbering a smattering of Cheyenne. The few Cheyenne who were present were those who had taken the easy way to avoid reservation life, and hung around the fort doing errands for soldiers and traders alike in return for whiskey. It sickened him, and he felt helpless to do anything about it. But there was still some of the old pride, even in the lazy fort Indians, and with Wolf's Blood being so good at the wrestling games, he would be the first one the Pawnee would single out if there was a confrontation. Neither did he want his son's temper to bring trouble on the lad from soldiers.

He found himself yelling and rooting along with the others, tensing up whenever it seemed the Pawnee had the upper hand, yelling at the top of his lungs whenever Wolf's Blood was in command. Finally Wolf's Blood had the Pawnee warrior pinned flat for several seconds. It irritated Zeke that the soldier who refereed seemed to wait longer than necessary to declare a win. He finally shouted that the match was over and that the Cheyenne had won. Shouts went up—some cheers, some in anger. Wolf's Blood held the Pawnee a moment longer, and Zeke knew the boy hated the rule that there could be no weapons. His son would like nothing better than to sink his blade into the Pawnee's heart then and there, but he finally jumped to his feet, putting up his arms.

Matt Crenshaw was the first to pound him on the shoulder, then shouted for others to pay up. Wolf's Blood walked up to his father, panting rapidly, his body covered with dirt, his teeth looking extra white against his grimy face. "That was the third one—and their best!" he said proudly. "I have beaten all three of them!"

"I'm proud of you, Wolf's Blood!" Zeke answered. "And you've almost paid for Sonora. In fact, you might have brought in enough just now. But I'll hold up my end and we'll go home with some money to boot. Anything over the three hundred dollars gets split fifty-fifty between myself and Crenshaw."

The boy frowned while the noisy crowd behind them made more bets. "Father, maybe you should not do the wrist wrestling. Just do the knife throwing. I don't want you to do anything to bring you pain."

Zeke grinned. "Don't worry about it. You know how I like these games."

Crenshaw approached them then, shouting that Zeke Monroe was his man against any Pawnee man who wanted to wrist wrestle or throw a knife. The crowd separated, allowing the Pawnee betters to bring in a new man—one they'd been keeping hidden. Zeke's eyebrows arched and he grinned. The opponent they introduced was Walks Tall, a huge man for a Pawnee, broad and burly and obviously very strong.

"Father, don't do it," Wolf's Blood spoke up aside to Zeke.

130

"You'd better be good," Crenshaw joked with Zeke before Zeke could reply to his son. "I don't quite have that three hundred dollars yet, Indian."

Zeke studied the big Pawnee, then glanced at his son. "You still want that girl, don't you?" Their eyes held and Zeke grasped his shoulder. "She's yours after this match." He turned to Crenshaw. "I'll break his arm," he said in a loud, cold voice.

The crowd roared at the remark, and bets flew. Wolf's Blood looked at his father with love and gratitude. Then the boy looked over at the window above the supply store. A face looked out at him—Sonora! His heart tightened and his legs felt weak. And all that was important then was that he get her out of this place and take her home.

"They want to know if you really can break his arm," Crenshaw was saying to Zeke. "They'll make bets on that alone."

Zeke stared at the Pawnee, who stared back at him, grinning. These Pawnee had long ago stolen the Sacred Arrows of the Cheyenne. A bitter hatred and constant warring had followed over many years, and now the Pawnee helped soldiers find renegade Cheyenne, attacking them once found, killing and scalping at random.

"Bet on it," Zeke told Crenshaw.

Crenshaw laughed and took more bets. Zeke continued to glare at the Pawnee. He thought of old times. He had himself once raided Pawnee villages. He thought of his Cheyenne stepfather, Deer Slayer, and of his mother, Gentle Woman. He would do this for them—for old times.

A crude table was quickly erected, consisting of a narrow piece of board, its ends supported by two huge wine barrels. Zeke and the Pawnee stood on either side of the board, which was just wide enough to permit the proper distance between their elbows. The two men grasped hands, and Zeke breathed deeply, praying to *Maheo* for strength, for he could feel great power in the Pawnee's arm. The Pawnee kept grinning, but Zeke only glared at him as he gripped the man's hand firmly, getting a feel of his hold and strength. Wolf's Blood watched fearfully, worried about his father. But Zeke had many ways in which to draw forth his uttermost strength. All he had to do was think about his Abbie being abused by Winston Garvey or about Sand Creek or about the rape and murder of his first wife back in Tennessee. There were any number of past horrors that could bring forth his anger and bring out the extra strength that only vengeance can feed. And, of course, there were the Sacred Arrows. Besides, there were no greater fighters in the West than the Cheyenne. Everyone knew that. He would not disappoint that reputation, and he would not let his son lose Sonora.

A gun was fired, and the contest began. The roar of the crowd disappeared for Zeke, as he concentrated on the grinning Pawnee. In moments both of them were basked in perspiration from the strain. The morning was warm, and the sun beat down on them as muscle pitted itself against muscle. Veins stuck out, arms vibrated with strain. There was no movement at first from either side. Then Zeke's arm started to go down, but a moment later it was Zeke who was pushing down the Pawnee's arm. It seemed to take hours just to get it halfway down, and then with a sudden surge and a growl the Pawnee's arm was all the way down except for about an inch. Again it hung there, while the Pawnee turned practically purple with strain until finally the hand touched the table.

Cheers went up from those who had bet on Zeke—and many had, for Zeke Monroe was well known around Fort Lyon. Zeke still had hold of the Pawnee's hand when he suddenly kicked aside the board and jerked the Pawnee forward, quickly turning the man and jerking his arm up savagely behind his back. The Pawnee grunted, already in pain from the wrist wrestling and the terrible strain of trying not to lose. Zeke bent upward, pushing at the arm with one hand while he grasped the Pawnee around the throat from behind with his other powerful arm. He held the man there for several seconds while the crowd cheered, waiting for all the strength to go out of the Pawnee's arm. Then he whirled the man again, and before the Pawnee knew what was going to happen, Zeke grasped the limp arm in both hands, bringing up his knee and bringing the arm down on it violently. There was a loud snap, and the Pawnee cried out and slumped to the ground, while the crowd cheered insanely.

Now it was Zeke who grinned, glaring at the Pawnee proudly. He turned to Crenshaw. "Does that make your three hundred?"

"More so! You've made a little profit for yourself, my friend!"

Zeke grasped the man's vest. "Don't call me friend, bastard. And that girl had better be untouched!"

Crenshaw swallowed. "She is, I assure you."

Zeke gave him a shove and followed the crowd to the knife throwing. Only those few ignorant of Zeke's reputation or not believing the stories they had heard about the man's "great medicine" were willing to bet against Zeke. This was one area in which Wolf's Blood knew his father would find few takers and no one to beat him. He wished the soldiers would allow an out-and-out knife fight, for his father was the best. But only knife throwing was allowed, and by the time the contests were finished, Zeke Monroe had a tidy sum in his own pocket.

The three of them walked to the supply store then, Crenshaw, Zeke and Wolf's Blood, while the rest of the crowd moved to the only drinking room at the fort and proceeded to spend their winnings on whiskey, exchanging stories about the contests.

Sonora watched from above as they approached, her heart beating wildly. The young Cheyenne man and his father had won! They were coming for her! She was not sure what they had in mind for her, and could trust only in the look of gentleness in the young man's eyes. Surely he would not bring her harm or violate her. Yet for some reason the thought did not totally frighten her, for he was exceedingly handsome, and obviously brave and strong.

There were voices below, and then the door to her room was opening. It was cool inside the stucco walls, and Wolf's Blood noticed the room was clean, almost barren, holding only a crude handmade bed and one small dresser. His heart raced when Sonora stood at the window, staring at him as he entered, her beautiful dark eyes wide and wondering. Her breasts were full beneath the soft tunic, and he could see she was breathing rapidly, as though afraid. He came all the way inside, standing a few feet from her.

133

"Do you speak English?"

She nodded. Wolf's Blood smiled, and she wondered if flames were visible on her skin.

"I won't hurt you," he assured her, reaching out. "You're going home with us. My father has a ranch about three days from here. I have brothers and sisters. My mother is white. You'll like it there. My mother is very kind."

The girl backed up a little. "I . . . belong to you," she said quietly. "You must expect . . . something. You paid money for me."

"Only because that's the only way I could get you away from Crenshaw without killing him. I did not buy you like a man buys a slave. You are not a slave. You can come home with us. And if, after a while, you choose to go back to your own people, I will take you there myself. I am not afraid to go into Apache country." His eyes roved her voluptuous form again. How he wanted to see what was beneath the tunic, touch her, lie next to her. He met her dark eyes again. What a pretty face. "But I hope . . . I hope you will want to stay . . . at the ranch," he added.

She swallowed and reached for a parfleche that lay on the bed. "All my belongings . . . are in here," she told him. "I would like . . . one day . . . to go back to my people. But I belong to you now. I will stay . . . wherever you are happy . . . for as long as you would want me to stay."

He grinned and nodded, and she picked up the parfleche and took his hand. It was warm, and she had to smile at his appearance, still covered with dust and scratches, all just to pay for her. Yes, she liked this handsome young Cheyenne very much. She would go home with him, and she would not be afraid.

He pulled at her then, half dragging her down the steps in his eagerness. Zeke waited downstairs, and when his eyes rested on her beauty again, he could not blame Wolf's Blood for wanting her; nor was he sorry that at this very moment he was suffering from pain in his shoulder caused by the wrist wrestling. It would go away. Better his own pain than what the girl would have suffered at the hands of cruel men. Wolf's Blood would not be cruel.

134

"Let's go, Father!" the boy spoke up excitedly.

"Now?" Zeke asked. "Let's at least clean up first."

"We can ride down to the river first and clean up there. I want to get her away from here, Father. I am afraid of trouble when the other men see her. And you broke the Pawnee's arm. If we stay around here, something might happen. Let's get our supplies and get home. Besides, Mother will be worried."

Zeke grinned and shook his head, motioning for them to go out ahead of him. Perhaps having the girl around would help settle down his son and make it easier for him to stay here after all. He followed them out, and Wolf's Blood was already mounted, the girl perched in front of him.

"You go on ahead," Zeke told him. "You and Sonora can be alone for a little while—get to know each other better. Wait for me by the grove of cottonwood at the river south of here. You know the place. I'll gather the rest of our things and finish packing the spare horse with supplies and be along soon."

Wolf's Blood nodded. "Thank you, Father." He turned the horse, and Sonora wondered if she would faint at the feel of the young Cheyenne's strong arms around her, her back against his broad chest, her bottom nestled between his powerful legs. Men stared as she rode proudly out of the fort in front of him on his grand Appaloosa. She belonged to Wolf's Blood now. She would go to the ranch he told her about, and see the kind white woman who was his mother. It couldn't be all bad, the way he described it. Maybe she would stay there forever.

Bonnie called Joshua into her bedroom. The night was quiet, almost too quiet, for everyone was on edge. The Sioux, haughty and high with their victory over the soldiers for the Powder River country, had grown more restless and demanding. More trouble was brewing; one Indian agent had been killed at the Red Cloud agency, and a flagpole chopped down. Dan had his orders. They would be leaving Fort Laramie and going to Fort Robinson, the new name given to the Red Cloud agency. Fort Robinson was much more the center of action now. Fort Laramie was too remote from the heart of Indian country, and for the soldiers to continue to keep control and hold the treaty, Fort Robinson was the place to be. It would be dangerous, but Bonnie would go along.

She sat down on the bed, motioning for her adopted son to sit down beside her.

"What is it, Mother?" the boy asked with concern.

Bonnie sighed. "You know we're going to Fort Robinson, Joshua," she told him. The boy nodded and she took one of his hands. "It will be dangerous, Joshua. And since you're ready to go to college anyway, I think this would be a good time to send you back east. I want you to stay there awhile. My father—your grandfather—is in Alexandria now, not far from Washington, D.C. It would be a wonderful, educational place for you to live for a while. Your grandfather has his practice going there now. You know, of course, that he returned because he was simply getting too old for life out here. He would love to have you with him, Joshua. It would warm his heart. I know he's lonely. You could live with your grandfather and get your education, and be company for him at the same time. I would feel so much better, Joshua. I'm so afraid of Father dying alone."

The boy kissed her cheek. "Then I'll go. It's a little earlier than we planned, but if it means that much to you to go now, it doesn't matter to me. But I'll worry about you, Mother."

She smiled and patted his hand. "I'll be fine." She searched the hazel eyes, keeping hold of his hand. "Joshua, if . . . if something should happen to me . . ." She sighed deeply and rose. "Joshua before you go east I think it's time you knew something about yourself—where you really came from."

The boy frowned. "You said Zeke and Abbie found me abandoned years ago, probably by settlers, because I was crippled. They brought me to you and you adopted me."

She turned to face him, rubbing her arms nervously. "It wasn't . . . exactly like that, Joshua." She came and sat back down on the bed. "I told you . . . my original friendship with Zeke was from when he'd saved me from outlaws who had attacked the stagecoach I was on, down near Santa Fe. Zeke rescued me and took me to Father in Santa Fe—saved my life."

"I know that, too."

She met his eyes again. "What you don't know is why Zeke

136

was out roaming that godforsaken land in the first place." She swallowed. "He was . . . looking for an Arapaho sister-in-law, Yellow Moon. Zeke's brother had sold her to outlaws for whiskey, then shot himself in remorse. Zeke was determined to find the woman, and her son. There are many details to his search, some of them unknown to me. But in the process he came across me, rescued me. Then he went on to search for Yellow Moon. Her little boy had been killed, and she'd been sold—to a wealthy Colorado businessman named . . . Winston Garvey."

The boy frowned. "Garvey. Why is that name familiar?"

"Probably because we read a few years back that the man disappeared after an Indian raid. No one knows what happened, but that is beside the point for now, Joshua. Zeke managed to convince Garvey to give up the woman— threatened him with his life, I don't doubt. He took Yellow Moon home, and she was given to Zeke's other brother, Swift Arrow, to care for."

"Swift Arrow rides with the Sioux now. He is the one Wolf's Blood was living with."

"Yes. Swift Arrow took her in. But . . . but Yellow Moon was already with child . . . Winston Garvey's child." She held the boy's eyes steadily until he began to see. She felt him trembling and he paled slightly.

"Me?" he asked quietly.

She nodded, squeezing his hands. "You are Zeke's nephew—the son of Yellow Moon . . . and Winston Garvey," she told him carefully. "Yellow Moon was killed by soldiers at Blue Water Creek, and Swift Arrow, being a Dog Soldier, did not want the burden of a crippled child. He gave the child to Zeke and Abbie, and they brought him to me. He was called Crooked Foot. I renamed him Joshua . . . and I have loved him as my own son ever since . . . the child I could never have."

The boy's eyes teared. "Then . . . I am part Indian!"

"Yes," she whispered.

The boy blinked and swallowed, rising from the bed. "I am part Indian!" he said again quietly. He turned to face her, and she couldn't quite read his eyes. Did he still love her? Was he angry? "Why didn't you tell me a long time ago?"

"Because I wanted to be sure you were mature enough to handle it. I always thought you had the right to know, Joshua, someday. Now that you're going east, and anything could happen out here while you're gone, I thought the time was right. You're a mature, intelligent young man."

He turned away, running a hand through his hair, then lowering it and looking at his skin. "I don't feel Indian. I don't look Indian."

"Neither do some of Zeke's children. But they are, just the same." She swallowed, her heart tight. "Do you hate me now, Joshua?"

He turned to look at her, this gentle woman who had been so good to him and had loved him like her own son. He smiled, tears in his eyes. "How can I hate my own mother? I'm just . . . so shocked." He walked over to a dresser, staring into a mirror, studying himself. "I do have high cheekbones, don't you think?"

She smiled. "Yes, you do."

He turned back to face her. "Arapaho?"

"Yes."

He frowned. "I'd rather it was Cheyenne."

"What?"

"Well, if I'm going to be part Indian, I'd rather be what Zeke is."

Her eyebrows arched. "You mean you don't care?"

The boy shrugged. "I think it's kind of exciting. I've always felt the Indians have been treated unfairly. Now I have all the more reason to do what I can to help them. That's what I intend to do, you know. I'll go east to get my education, and then I'm coming back here to do what I can to help them. Maybe I'll get into Congress or something—get some legislation passed that will benefit the Indian. Or maybe I'll be a doctor and come out here and help them like Grandfather did. I'm not really sure, except that I do like writing and journalism. Maybe I can help them that way. What do you think?"

Bonnie smiled and shook her head. "I don't know what to think. I thought you'd be angry and upset."

The boy looked into the mirror again. "There isn't really much I can do about it, is there? And it's not so bad. In fact, I could fool some people, get some of those white men to help me pass legislation in favor of the Indian, maybe get a job for some big eastern newspaper and tell people out there what's really happening—you know, from a man who's 'been there.' Then I'll surprise them all when I tell them I'm part Indian myself. There are all kinds of possibilities."

He turned back to face her, and she rose, sobering again. "Joshua, there is something else—something you must remember always. You must never say who your father is."

"Why not? In fact, if he was such a prominent businessman, maybe I have something coming to me."

"Joshua, you'd never be able to prove it—not enough to satisfy courts. You'd have only Zeke's word, and to drag him and Abbie into a court battle would only bring them a great deal of trouble. Winston Garvey's son, Charles, would make things very bad for them, and he'd fight it to the bitter end. It wouldn't be worth the terrible things Zeke and Abbie might suffer."

The boy frowned. "I have a half brother?"

"Charles Garvey. He's older than you, and the last we knew he was somewhere east himself in law apprenticeship. He's hard to keep track of. I only know that Zeke swore us to secrecy about your identity. He knows the kind of man Winston Garvey was, and that he'd have had you killed if he knew. He was an avowed Indian hater, Joshua. And if his son knew he had a half brother who was part Indian, he would do everything in his power to silence you—including having you killed. He's as wealthy and powerful as his father was, Joshua. So if you want to say you're part Indian, that's fine. But don't tell who your father was. Do you understand? Promise me, Joshua. Zeke nearly died saving my life once. And they've been through so much. I do not intend to put them through a court battle over your identity, nor do I want you killed, with perhaps harm coming also to Zeke and Abbie. Charles Garvey would do anything he could to silence them."

The boy sighed. "I need to go outside and be alone awhile, Mother. I need to let all this sink in—need to think." He walked toward the door.

"Joshua!"

He turned to face her, seeing terror and tears in her eyes. "Promise me you won't tell!"

He sighed. What good would it do? He didn't need Charles Garvey's money anyway. He'd make it on his own and prove what a half-breed could do. He'd show a few people up, be a success, and then surprise them be telling them he was part Indian. Maybe the time would come when he could tell who his real father was. But he had too much to accomplish first, and he didn't care to bring trouble to Zeke and Abbie any more than his mother did.

"I promise, " he told her.

She blinked back tears. "I love you, Joshua. I truly love you as my own."

He nodded. "I know that, Mother."

The boy walked out, and she went over to the dresser, pulling open a drawer and taking out the bone necklace Zeke had given her so many years ago after saving her from the outlaws. Yes, she had loved him then, probably still did in her own secret way. But she had Dan now, and for the first time in her life she felt fulfilled. She could never have had Zeke, for he had Abbie. She carefully replaced the necklace. Now if Joshua could accept what he was and not hate her for it, her happiness would be complete. She had finally told him the secret of his past, and a great burden had been liften from her shoulders.

Chapter Eight

Dinner around the Monroe table was quiet. Abbie was torn between wanting to be friendly to the strange Apache girl Wolf's Blood had brought home, and anger at Zeke for not conferring with her about scouting before going to Fort Lyon to offer his services. Zeke ate little, worried he would not be able to convince her his only reason was to help the Cheyenne. She was a wise, all-seeing woman, and she knew him well. The last thing he wanted was for her to know about the arthritis.

Sonora ate quietly and mannerly. She knew the ways of the whites, even though she was related to the great Chiricahua guerilla fighter, Cochise, something that made Wolf's Blood beam with pride when she told them. Here was a girl with good, strong blood, in addition to her exquisite beauty. Like Cochise, who was a cousin, she was somewhat taller than most Apaches, and she carried a grace and beauty that set her apart from the others.

"Sonora's parents worked on a ranch that helped supply the Butterfield stage stations with food and wood," Wolf's Blood told his mother as he ate. "The ranchers were also missionaries and had saved Sonora's life once. Her parents became Catholics, and lived on the ranch and helped them. That is where Sonora learned how whites live, even though she also knows the Apache ways and misses some of her other relatives."

Sonora just looked at her plate and ate slowly as he talked, feeling self-conscious at being the center of attention.

"Then Mexican bandits raided the ranch and killed everyone. They took Sonora and sold her to a whiskey trader, who brought her to Fort Lyon and resold her to the storekeeper, for a profit. Luckily none of them abused her. She is still a—"

"Wolf's Blood," Abbie spoke up quickly. "You'll embarrass Sonora—and your sister Ellen." He scowled and Abbie smiled. "We understand, my son. And we're glad. There isn't one of us here who doesn't understand the terror of what Sonora experienced. I'm glad you found her at Fort Lyon. And I'm glad she's here. She can sleep in the loft, and she can help me with the chores around this place that I never seem to be able to keep up with."

Sonora looked up at her then and smiled softly. "I will do whatever you ask of me, Mrs. Monroe."

"The name is Abbie. And I don't intend to make a slave of you, but any help is appreciated. And if you want to go home— back to Apache country—Wolf's Blood will take you, just as he promised."

Sonora looked at Wolf's Blood and they both smiled. How he warmed her heart! Why should she go home before finding out just how much this brave, young Cheyenne warrior might care for her?

Abbie watched the way they looked at each other and smiled to herself, glancing at Zeke. Both were hoping this girl would become a wife and would make their wild son a little tamer.

"I will stay here," the girl spoke up to Abbie. "It is Wolf's Blood's home, and his family is very kind. Your home is very nice, and the ranch and horses very beautiful. I think I will like it here. I owe much to Wolf's Blood—and to your husband, who helped get the money for me by fighting the wrist-wrestling contest. Did he tell you he broke a Pawnee's arm?"

Abbie's eyes widened and she gave her husband a chastising look. "No. What else have you not bothered to tell me, my husband?" she asked teasingly, losing some of her anger. Zeke Monroe did not do anything without good purpose. Perhaps she shouldn't be too angry with him for not telling her about the scouting. What worried her most was that he would be away again. She didn't like it when he was away.

Zeke cleared his throat and glanced at a smiling Morgan Brown. "Sounds like you almost got yourself in a peck of trouble," Morgan joked. "All over a pretty little Apache girl."

Zeke grinned and leaned back in his chair, taking out some tobacco and a paper and rolling himself a cigarette. "It's my son who gets me in trouble. It would have been worse if I hadn't walked in when he first spotted Sonora. He was about ready to sink his blade into that storekeeper." He lit the cigarette and Wolf's Blood grinned, while Sonora looked down shyly again. "I keep having to remind him he's not in Indian country anymore. A man can get hung real easy, especially an Indian." He took a deep drag. "There was a day when it was easy for a man to deal his own justice. I dealt plenty of my own, and I still do when I can get away with it." He glanced at Margaret. He had killed the white man who had once jilted her badly and turned her to a life of prostitution before she met Morgan Brown. No one knew it—not even Abbie. He didn't regret it—no more than he regretted killing any of the men he'd killed in revenge, especially Winston Garvey.

"Well, it seems you did almost get yourself in trouble, Mr. Monroe," Abbie spoke up. "And on top of that you come home telling me you'll be scouting for the Army. Perhaps you'd like to explain why to all of us—something you haven't bothered to do yet."

He met her eyes, and in spite of his strength and skills, his Abbie had a way of unhinging him that made Zeke angry with himself. She'd done it since the day he met her, and he'd never been able to figure out how. She watched him carefully now, too closely. He moved his eyes to Wolf's Blood, who looked from his father to his mother.

"The renegades are starving and dying, Mother," the boy spoke up. "In the North, the Sioux and Northern Cheyenne still live well, but even I know that won't last. Here it is worse. The Southern Cheyenne have no hope of survival at all if they don't settle on the reservation and stop running."

She studied him closely. "Much as I am glad you are here with us, my son, I cannot believe it is you speaking such words." She leaned back and looked from father to son. "I totally agree with the theory, and that scouts with compassion

143

are needed rather than the hated Pawnee. But may I hear a better explanation?''

Zeke took a deep drag on his cigarette. ''Two of them are sitting right here at the table—Little Zeke and Nathan. The family seems to be growing instead of getting smaller, and it's costing more every year to keep this ranch going. Prices of feed and supplies are getting ridiculous. We need the money. It took a lot of our savings to put LeeAnn through school, and Ellen and Jason might want to go, too. I want to be prepared.''

''I thought we were well ahead—''

''I said we need the money!'' Zeke snapped.

The table grew silent, and Abbie stared at him, her face crimson. It was not often anyone heard Zeke Monroe get short with his wife. Zeke sighed deeply and rose from the table, walking outside without saying a word. Abbie swallowed and set her fork down. She looked at Sonora.

''Sonora, dear, you haven't told us your age. You look very young.''

The girl raised her eyes. ''I . . . I am sixteen summers.'' The girl looked at Wolf's Blood. ''You have not told me how many summers you have seen.''

The boy was scowling. He did not like to see anger between his parents. ''Twenty-four summers,'' he answered rather curtly, his eyes on his mother. ''Mother, be patient with Father,'' he told her. ''His heart hurts for the people, that's all. And so does mine. It is a decision we both made. And it is true that we need the money.''

Abbie sighed deeply. ''I am sure it is, Wolf's Blood. But something is being left out and it frightens me.'' She rose from the table. ''The rest of you finish your meal. I'm sorry there was a little problem. I'll go talk to Zeke.''

''Perhaps . . . perhaps I should go. Perhaps he is upset that I am here,'' Sonora spoke up.

Abbie gave her a smile and came around behind her, patting her head. ''No, Sonora, it has absolutely nothing to do with you. Having you here will be a help, not a hindrance. And you apparently make Wolf's Blood happy. Don't think for one moment that you are not welcome here.'' She smoothed the girl's long black hair, then walked outside.

144

The summer night was still but for singing crickets. There was a bright moon, and a dark outline far in the distance told of mountains on the horizon, even in the darkness. Abbie strained her eyes to see, then saw the red glow of his cigarette near the corral.

She walked quickly to the spot, calling out to him quietly. He turned and she approached him, and suddenly threw down the cigarette and reached out, grabbing her close and hugging her. "I'm sorry," he said quietly.

She wrapped her arms around his waist, resting her head against the broad chest and breathing deeply of the scent of man and leather. "You're leaving something out, Zeke," she answered. "But I won't press you. I guess what upsets me is the thought of you being gone. You know how I always hate it when you're gone and I don't know what is happening to you."

"I'll make it clear it's strictly voluntary, Abbie. I won't be part of the Army. They can't give me orders or make me stay any longer than I choose. But the pay is good, and in a way I'm helping." He hugged her tightly and kissed her hair. "I don't like being away from you either. You know that." He gently pushed her away then, turning and leaning on the fencing. "Did I ever tell you about Sitting Bear, Abbie?"

"The old Kiowa chief? He's in Oklahoma on the reservation, isn't he?"

Zeke sighed. "He's dead now. He escaped from the reservation, led a raid into Texas—wanted one last great fling, maybe. He got himself arrested, and they held him shackled in a dungeon for a week. Somehow he got hold of a knife, hiding it the morning they finally took him out and put him in a wagon to go to court and be tried. He was chained to the wagon bed and they put a blanket over him, and on the way to court he sang the Kiowa death song and kept putting his head under the blanket. You know what he was doing under there?"

She frowned and put a hand on his arm. "What, Zeke?"

"He was stripping the flesh from his hands with his teeth— with his teeth, Abbie! So that he could slip his hands through the handcuffs. Finally he stood up, holding the knife and giving out a war cry, slashing at one of the guards and sending two young, healthy men tumbling out of the wagon. A

145

seventy-year-old man standing alone against five troops of cavalry. They shot him down, but he got up again, standing there with his hands gnawed to the bones, pointing a soldier's rifle at them that he didn't even know how to use. The soldiers cut him down again until finally he stayed down. One seventy-year-old man, and all the soldiers were in a panic when he stood up and threatened them. But he chose to die fighting all of them rather than go to white man's court and be hung. He wanted to die the only way an Indian can die—with honor."

She studied the handsome face in the moonlight. "That's how you intend to die, isn't it?" she asked, her heart pounding. "You think perhaps through scouting you'll find a way to die fighting."

He looked down at her, then touched her cheek with the back of his hand. How he loved her! The way she looked at him now made him think of the fifteen-year-old girl he'd claimed in the wilds of Wyoming. "That's part of it. But I don't intend to go riding away tomorrow and dying. It isn't anything like that."

She studied the dark eyes. Perhaps he was already dying—of what she couldn't be sure. He didn't want to tell her. She would not ask. And hadn't she always known it would be this way? Zeke Monroe was not a man to live to a ripe old age and be decrepit. Not Zeke. She wanted to scream and scratch at him. Her breathing came in short gasps and her eyes teared. "I couldn't live without you!" she whimpered.

He smiled sadly. "Oh yes you could. Abigail Trent Monroe is a survivor, much stronger than she knows. I'm fifty-one years old, Abbie, and these old bones are feeling the effects of years of violence—old wounds." He stepped back and held out his arms. "But look at me. You certainly don't think you're going to lose me tomorrow, do you?"

She studied him through tear-filled eyes—so tall and strong and handsome! Had he really changed in the twenty-six years she'd known him? It didn't seem so at all. "You . . . look wonderful," she sobbed.

"Well, then, what are you crying about?"

"Oh, Zeke, you know what I'm crying about!"

He forced a smile for her and pulled her close again. "Abbie, you're still just like a little girl sometimes. You snared me with those tears and you still destroy me when you cry." He gave her a squeeze. "I've got some hard riding years left, Abbie-girl." He pulled back slightly and looked down at her. "And some hard loving years." He came down to meet her mouth, tenderly, hungrily. She returned the kiss with great passion. How long would she have him? A year? Ten years? He was her life. What was life without him? He picked her up in his arms then and started walking toward the house.

"There, you see how strong I still am?" he teased. "Not that a little thing like you is much to carry. You know what I like about suppertime around here, Abbie-girl?"

She wiped at tears. "What?"

"We all work so hard it's practically bedtime when we eat. Now we can send everybody packing and make use of that brass bed you're so crazy about."

"Zeke Monroe, what are you going to do! Don't you carry me all the way inside and embarrass me!"

"I've been embarrassing you for years."

She tried to get down then, but his grip was much too powerful for her small frame. He barged through the door with her, and she put her head against his shoulder and covered her face.

"Morgan, you mind taking Ellen and Jason to your place tonight—Sonora, too, if you can fit her. I would like to be alone with my wife."

"Zeke Monroe!" came the muffled name from his shoulder.

They all laughed as he carried his wife through the curtained doorway of their bedroom. He plunked her on the brass bed and grasped her shoulders. "You stay right there, Abbie-girl, and don't you move—except maybe to get undressed," he told her softly.

Her eyes widened with exasperation. "I should punch you for doing that!"

He just grinned. "Go ahead. Get it out of your system." He stuck out his chin and she was tempted, but then started laughing.

"I'd probably break my hand and not hurt you in the least," she told him.

Their eyes held, and then he met her lips gently, holding the kiss, then moving his lips to her throat. "Go ahead and get in bed, Abbie." He nuzzled her breasts. "Who cares what anybody else thinks? All we've got is each other these last years. To hell with the rest of the world."

She smoothed the long, dark hair, so soft and shining, with only a hint of gray around his temples and forehead. "You . . . you are all right, aren't you, Zeke? I mean . . . there isn't anything seriously wrong, other than you realize you're getting older . . . and I guess we do need the money. Tell me there's nothing else wrong, Zeke!"

He leaned back and placed his hands at either side of her face, squeezing gently. "There's nothing else wrong. And I'll only go out on short patrols, I promise. You know I don't like being away from you. The longest I'll be away at a time will be a month, if I can help it, and sometimes it will only be a week or two. And sometimes Wolf's Blood will stay here. But I'll be here more than I'm gone. So relax, Abbie-girl." He kissed her cheek and walked out into the main room, where Margaret was clearing the table.

Some were still giggling, and Wolf's Blood was happy to see that his parents were no longer angry with each other. He took Sonora's hand.

"Come with me to my tipi for awhile. We will talk," he told her eagerly. She hesitated, pulling back her hand. "It is all right. I mean you no harm, Sonora. I only want to talk—to learn about the Apache ways. Just for a while. Then I will take you to Margaret's cabin."

Zeke grinned to himself, turning to poke at nearly dead coals in the potbellied heating stove. The nights were always cool on the plains, even in summer. A small fire was usually kept going. When he looked up again, Sonora was following Wolf's Blood out the door. He thought about Abbie—only fifteen when he made a woman of her, and he was twenty-five. It seemed like perhaps a month ago, not twenty-six years. He didn't really feel any different, except for the damned pain in his joints. At least it was summer again, and he enjoyed some relief. He looked at his daughter, Margaret, an Indian beauty, as lovely as Wolf's Blood was handsome. Her dark hair hung long and loose, reaching almost to the roundness of her hips. She and Morgan were happy. That was good. That gave him some relief.

These two oldest children of his were the most Indian, and closest to their parents. He wondered for a moment about LeeAnn. She had been on his mind so often. What did she look like now? What was she doing now? Should he go east and try to find her? No. What would be the use? He would only embarrass her, and that brought great pain to his heart. Again came the wave of terror that he would never see her again before he died. And perhaps he would never see Jeremy either. They heard little from either of them now, just occasional letters to verify that they were doing fine.

But then there were Ellen and Jason. They were good children, a grand mixture of Indian and white, looking mostly white. He enjoyed Jason. Jason was a good son—a hard worker, too. Jason would always be dependable.

The house was suddenly quiet, as everyone had left but Margaret. She dried her hands and walked over to her father, putting a hand on his shoulder as he closed and latched the stove door. He looked up at her, then rose. How sorry she was about the time he'd had to go to Denver to try to drag her out of a brothel. But that terrible time was over. She was home now.

"I love you, Father," she said quietly.

He kissed her forehead. "Thanks for taking everybody in for the night."

She smiled and left, and the only sound was the ticking of a mantle clock that Zeke had bought for Abbie many years ago in Santa Fe. She treasured the clock. The first time she used it, it sat on a log inside a tipi. How swiftly the years had gone by! He looked at the curtained doorway to their bedroom. How many times had he passed through it and shared her body on the bed of robes? Now it was a brass bed. They had started out with only a few personal belongings and horses they rode into his family's village. It seemed a lifetime ago, and in this land twenty-six years very often was a lifetime at that. What if the arthritis did kill him? He had already lived much longer than some men lived in this lawless land. Poor little Lillian had only lived to be seven. All his brothers but Swift Arrow and Dan were dead. All of Abbie's family was gone by the time she was fifteen. And here they still were, alive, together.

He walked through the doorway, but she was not in the brass bed. She sat on the bed of robes in the corner of the room, a furry robe pulled over her nakedness, her hair brushed out long. "This bed fits you better," she told him. "And I hope you know how utterly embarrassed I'm going to be at breakfast in the morning."

He grinned and removed his shirt. "Why? They all know we're still lovers."

"Of course they do. But we don't usually announce when we're going to make love."

He removed his leggings and moccasins, chuckling to himself. "Actually I had more chores to do. But since I was already cleaned up for supper, and since they can wait till morning, I decided to hell with it."

There was some other reason, she knew. The same reason he always made love to her more urgently now, why their lovemaking over the last couple of years had actually heightened rather than lessened, had become more beautiful and fulfilling if that were possible, for it had always been so.

He walked to the bed of robes and dropped to his knees. "Some things can wait," he added, pulling the robe away from her. The lamp was dimly lit in the room, and her full breasts looked softly enticing. She reached out and untied his loincloth, always blushing when she did something so bold, even though she'd been with this man for so long. They had done these things many times, yet there were certain moments, special moments like this one, when the passion was more intense, the need greater than normal. She lightly touched that part of him that revealed his manhood, and she wondered what her life would have been like if she had not met this man on that fateful wagon train so long ago.

His breathing quickened, and he leaned down and lightly tasted the fruits of her breasts, his long hair brushing against her nakedness, a big hand moving teasingly over her thigh and bottom, around to her stomach and that secret place that belonged only to him, as he laid her back and kissed her hungrily. He felt her passion building as he explored the moist depths of her womanhood, making her weak and willing under

150

his touch, as she had always been at the hands of Zeke Monroe. His lips left her mouth, traveling down over her throat, her breasts, her stomach, lightly brushing the love nest that belonged only to Zeke Monroe and making her whisper his name.

He moved back up then, nuzzling her breasts, moving to her lips and embracing her, pulling her close and rolling onto his back. She looked down at him, her breasts touching his chest, her long, thick hair that still showed no gray framing her face. He studied the dark eyes that still glittered like a little girl in love. This time it was she who came down to meet his lips. He grasped her hair, holding her there and searching her mouth. Then he closed his eyes, as this time she moved over him, kissing the broad chest, the flat stomach, that part of him that had branded her his woman.

"Nemehotatse," she said softly, using the Cheyenne word for "I love you." He grasped her hair again, gently pulling her back to his mouth and rolling her over, kissing her almost savagely then, moving between her still-slender legs. A moment later he was invading her, devouring her, reclaiming her, suddenly overwhelmed at the thought of the possibility she would have many more years left after he was gone. Would she live those years alone? Would she find another man eventually? She was so well preserved, still so pretty and desirable for her age. And she was such a beautiful woman in other ways—all the ways that pleased a man. Surely she would need . . . No! Not for a long time, anyway. Not for a long time! And he would make sure no other man matched him in her bed—make sure no other man would ever satisfy her in the ways Zeke Monroe could satisfy her. He would always be her first love, her favorite, her treasured one. She would hold no other man as dear, love no other man with the same passion!

They moved rhythmically, and it seemed to Abbie she could hear music—singing. It was an Indian love song the people had chanted at times around campfires. How long ago was that? She couldn't remember. She could only see their smiling faces, see the young girls dancing for the men, some throwing their blankets over their favorite man, signifying that favoritism. She breathed deeply of her husband's familiar scent, wanting

151

to remember it forever. She could see a tipi, its painted interior swirling around her—horses and buffalo, arrows and warriors. When she was with him this way, sharing not just bodies but soul and spirit, she could hear drums and war whoops. She was his captive woman and he had complete control over her, as he had always had from the first moment she set eyes on him and saw the loneliness in his own eyes.

They pushed against each other with such rhythm and emotion that when he finally finished with her they were both exhausted and perspiring. For several minutes they lay there saying nothing, only enjoying each other's arms. She kissed his chest then.

"Tell me you won't go for a while yet."

"Not for a while. There's always more to do around here in the summer. Don't worry about it, Abbie." He sighed deeply. "I've been thinking a lot again about LeeAnn. Do you think we should do anything more? Maybe I should go find her?"

Her throat tightened. How she wanted to scold LeeAnn for being so delinquent with her letters—for not coming to see them. She knew how it hurt Zeke. "I don't think so, Zeke. The fact that she uses a post office box for a return address tells us what we need to know. She doesn't want to be found, Zeke. When she is ready, she'll come home."

He kissed her hair. "I guess we can't expect every child to turn out just the way we want. At least we have Margaret and the grandchildren. And Wolf's Blood is here." He frowned. "I just remembered. Wolf's Blood took Sonora to his tipi—to talk, he claimed. That young man had better not take advantage of that pretty little thing."

Abbie smiled. "I wouldn't go over there thinking she needs rescuing, my husband. You saw how she looked at Wolf's Blood. She worships him. But I sense a very honorable young lady—and Wolf's Blood is an honorable young man. He won't take advantage of her. I sense he doesn't want to until he knows her better and he makes up his mind if he wants to make her his wife. He won't just use that one, Zeke. I'm hoping she's the answer to keeping him here and settling him even more. If they do marry, you'll have to talk him into taking a legal white name, Zeke, and doing the same for his children—establishing

152

them as having white blood so there's no worry with officials over making them go to a reservation or taking the children away and putting them in schools. I always worried about that with our own, and I was white. Wolf's Blood looks all Indian and Sonora is definitely Indian, so they'll have to be careful."

He pulled her closer. "I don't want to think about those things tonight. I just want to think about you, Mrs. Monroe. We don't take enough time to think about just each other."

"It's hard to find that kind of time."

He moved on top of her, kissing her hungrily again. "Well, we have the time tonight, and that's just what we're going to do—think about just each other and nothing else. And I am going to make love to you again before this night is over, maybe twice more. Who knows? I'm feeling very energetic tonight for an old man."

She laughed lightly. "I dare anyone to call you an old man. You'll never be old, Zeke Monroe."

Their eyes held, and she wondered if the statement held more meaning than she meant it to. She remembered the eagle again and the way he had looked at it, remembered his promise many years ago that if anything happened to him, he would always be with her in the spirit of the eagle—that he would come to her and she would know.

"Make love to me again—right now," she whispered. "I'm still full of passion, my husband. Why does it always last longer for the woman?"

He grinned. "So the man can take her twice without having to go through all the preparations again," he answered, pushing his hardness against her flat stomach.

She reddened, but she did not argue the point. For however long she had him, they would do this, for it was right and good.

"Our nation is melting away like the snow on the sides of the hills where the sun is warm, while your people are like the blades of grass in the spring when the summer is coming."

Charles Garvey threw the newspaper in the corner angrily. Imagine it! Red Cloud himself in New York, speaking to hundreds of eastern sympathizers! It was ridiculous! What peeved him most was the eloquent way the damned Indian leaders had of speaking, as though they knew just the right things to say to curious easterners who were beginning to romanticize about the stinking red men of the plains. His job was cut out for him now. He would have to hit the papers with both barrels, stepping up his own articles and balancing off this ridiculous following that was building in sympathy for the Indians.

He rose and walked to a window, looking down on the quiet street below where fancy carriages transported all sorts of important dignitaries. He liked it here in Washington, liked the feel of it, the power that hung in the air. Let Red Cloud come to New York and make his pleas for help. It would never really work. It was only a matter of time before the Indians committed more depredations that would turn the public against them again. It was easy to arrange with men like greedy whiskey traders and dishonest agents to cheat the Indians just enough to keep the anger and vengeance going. He had the money for that. Go ahead and put them on reservations, but sell the good meat and provisions for a profit, and give the Indians sugared whiskey, rotten meat, and used provisions. The only good part about the Indian sympathizers was that although they raised a cry against cheating Indians and breaking treaties, they still agreed that Indians must be given land of their own.

Charles smiled. Sure. Give them land. Little did these eastern greenhorns know that in some places out west eighty acres would not support even one family. How could they know such things if they'd never been out there? Yes, the government would give the Indians land, thousands of acres— hundreds of thousands. That sounded good to the sympathizers. Little did they know the kind of useless land that would go to the red man. Nor did they realize that some Indians couldn't survive out of their normal habitat. So much the better. Between the killing off of the buffalo and hot, mosquito-ridden reservation land, the Indian would die off quickly enough, and the government and cheating agents and traders would reap the rewards.

He sat down and thought about LeeAnn Whittaker. She was

154

a treasure: bright, easy to talk to, beautiful. Yes, beautiful. He longed to rip off those fancy clothes and gaze upon the body beneath them. At times he was tempted to do just that, for there was a wickedness in his soul when it came to women. He liked them all. But he had to pick just the right one for a wife, someone who would make him the envy of others. LeeAnn could do that for him. He must be careful with her and not frighten her off before he could marry her—and marry her he would, for he was determined that no other man would have her. The thought of invading her on their wedding night and taking her virginity gave him great pleasure. He wouldn't wait then. She would be his wife and he'd have her, whether she was afraid and hesitant or not. He'd teach her quickly about men, and then they'd have a time of it, for what man would not enjoy such a body, such beauty? And what woman would not enjoy being the wife of Charles Garvey, wealthy, a promising attorney, perhaps one day a politician.

He looked forward to taking LeeAnn to the museum this day and to an office party the next. Time. He must take his time. Perhaps a year. That would be an honorable length of time. He would bait her, tease her, make her want him, impress her with his wealth and station, which he knew was already happening. LeeAnn liked social prominence and pretty clothes. She would agree to marry him when the right time came.

He picked up pen and paper. It was time to compose another article, something outrageous that would contradict the fine picture Red Cloud posed for his eastern sympathizers. They would know about rape and torture and all the other heathen things Indians committed against white settlers. This ridiculous Indian sympathy would not continue!

Chapter Nine

The summer night was hot, with a rare humidity in the air that made breathing difficult. Abbie lay awake listening to the threatening thunder in the distance. In all the years she had been in this land, she wondered if she would ever get used to thunderstorms on the plains. They were so fierce, so sudden and terrorizing, often violent for the short time they lasted. She knew that's the way this one would be.

The thunder came closer, suddenly so loud and vibrating that the ground literally shook, and Abbie jumped and screamed, grabbing Zeke and snuggling closer. He only chuckled. "You were afraid of these storms on that wagon train, and you're still afraid of them," he joked, kissing her hair. He gently pushed her away. "I'm going out to the barn, Abbie. The horses always get nervous when it storms. I don't want any bruised-up animals."

The room lit up like daytime and she ducked her head. "Zeke, you'll be struck by lightning!"

He pulled on his buckskin leggings. "I should be so lucky as to die that easily, Abbie-girl." He pulled on his moccasins. "You'd better get dressed, just in case something should happen that I need you. I'll go get Morgan and Wolf's Blood, although I suspect they're both already up. With this storm, Wolf's Blood probably already went to the barn. I've seen some tipis literally blow away in a prairie storm." He pulled on his shirt, and Abbie was up, hurriedly pulling on a cotton dress. She could hear a dull roar as the wind picked up.

"You don't think we'll have a tornado, do you?" she asked, pulling her long hair out from the collar of the dress. "We've never had one right here, you know. There's a first time for everything."

He shook his head. "Quit worrying." He squeezed her shoulder, and they heard voices in the outer room. "Now you've got Ellen and Jason and Sonora to keep calm," he added. "That will keep your mind off the storm—maybe."

They left the room to find the three younger ones huddled at a window in the kitchen. "The lightning makes it just like daytime!" Jason exclaimed.

"It scares me," Ellen said quietly.

"Lightning great medicine of the gods," Sonora said softly.

"Comes from *Heammawihio*," Zeke added. "The Most Powerful Above." He grabbed a deerskin cape and donned a leather hat. "I'm going to go talk to the gods," he joked. He ducked out the door and disappeared into the darkness. Abbie opened the door a crack and watched him, catching glimpses of him as he stopped at the tipi and at Margaret's cabin, visible when the white lightning lit up the grounds. Then she saw him run to the barn, just as the heavens opened up and a torrential rain came down. Thunder boomed with a shattering explosion again, and she slammed the door and looked at Jason, Ellen, and Sonora, who all stared back wide-eyed.

"All of you get dressed, just in case you're needed," she told them. They scurried up to the left, giggling with fear and excitement, and Abbie went to the kitchen window, but there was really nothing to see. She sat down in a rocker then, picking up some knitting, but she only fiddled with a few stitches. Why did storms seem to bring back memories? There was a lonesomeness about the thunder, a reminder that such things went on forever but people didn't. It had stormed this way once when Zeke was first bringing her to his people, after they'd left Fort Bridger as husband and wife. They were making their way through the Rockies, and a frightening storm came. They found a cave and holed up there.

She closed her eyes and leaned back in the chair, thinking about the cave and the tender moments they had shared there,

158

making love, their marriage new. She'd been so afraid then of meeting the Cheyenne—afraid they would hate and reject her. But they hadn't. Those were good days, friendly days. It would not be so easy now for a white woman to be accepted by any Indian tribe. How sad that things had changed so much. But at least she had memories—those sweet memories—lying in that cave, only sixteen years old, starting out on a fateful journey through life that would lead her to places she'd never dreamed as a child she would go. She had left Tennessee headed for Oregon, and had ended up living among the Cheyenne on the Colorado plains, in the arms of a half-breed Indian called Lone Eagle.

Thunder boomed again, violently disturbing her thoughts, and the three younger ones came charging down the ladder. Sonora went back to the window. "Will he go to the barn, too?" she asked, looking at Abbie.

"You mean Wolf's Blood?"

The girl nodded, smiling shyly and looking down. Abbie laughed lightly. "Yes, he'll go to the barn. I'm a little worried about Margaret, alone over there in her cabin with the children. She'd probably rather be here, but it's too dangerous for her to try to run over here in that terrible rain." It seemed to pour harder then, and the wind picked up to a howl. The little cabin creaked, and the children all looked at the ceiling and walls. "Don't worry," Abbie reassured them. "You father built this cabin well. It won't fall apart." She put down the knitting and walked over to Sonora, who watched out the window again. She put a hand on the girl's shoulder. "Do you love him?"

The girl swallowed. "He is . . . a fine man . . . strong and bold. But he has not said how he feels about me." She turned to meet Abbie's eyes, her young face beautiful even when just aroused from sleep. "Yes, I love him. Sometimes when he is near me, I think my heart will burst."

Abbie smiled. "I know the feeling, Sonora. And I think Wolf's Blood has much feeling for you also. He just wants to be sure—to give you some time also. It hurt him very badly to see the girl he loved killed at Sand Creek. I think he's a little bit

159

afraid to care that much again, and yet I'm sure he already does. He lived free among the Sioux and Northern Cheyenne for a long time, Sonora. It has been hard for him to settle in one place. I think he wants to be sure he can stay in one place—sure he won't return to the fighting—before he takes a woman. The Indian cannot ride in great tribes and with families anymore. Those who fight must do so as hunted renegades. That is no life for a young wife and perhaps babies. Wolf's Blood knows that. He is a young man who makes sure of what he wants before he does it. But if he is not ready, and you wish to go back to the Apache, we will see that you get there. No one is forcing you to stay here, and I know what it is like to miss home."

The girl shook her head. "I could not be happy there—or anyplace without Wolf's Blood," she said quietly.

Abbie squeezed her shoulder, and the rain lightened, the storm fierce but short. Sonora looked out the window again. Then her eyes widened.

"The barn!" she shouted. "It is on fire!"

Abbie's heart tightened and she looked out the window to see flames licking the roof of the barn. "The lightning!" she gasped. "Zeke! Wolf's Blood!" She turned to the children. "Grab some buckets!"

Each grabbed anything relatively large that would hold water, and all four charged through the door. The thunder and lightning were already in the distance, but it still rained lightly. They hurried through the mud, the sound of whinnying horses in the distance.

"The horses!" Abbie yelled. "We've got to save them!" They were their livelihood. Her only thought was that Zeke could never bear another loss—not after the Comanches had stolen his entire herd six years ago. It had taken so long to build things back up again. Just losing the barn would be a bad enough loss. And the loft—full of feed! She slipped in the mud and fell hard on her left arm, but struggled back up, the arm throbbing. But she didn't care. She started running again, now able to see Zeke and Morgan rushing out of the barn herding six horses, shouting at them and smacking them on the rear, forcing them to run free of the barn. They ducked back inside, and then Wolf's Blood came out, herding two more of their best Appaloosas.

Sonora reached him and he grabbed her, telling her not to go inside, but she wiggled loose of him and ran in to do what she could to save more. Zeke came out then, leading *Kehilan,* his prized stallion. "Zeke!" Abbie shouted to him. "We have buckets! What can we do?"

He ran up to her. "To hell with the buckets. We'll never stop it, Abbie-girl! Take *Kehilan* up to the house and tie him. He's the most important one and he's in one of his moods. I don't want him running off!" She took the rope that was tied to his bridle. "Be careful! Don't get behind him!"

She nodded, her hair already soaked, her tears mixed with rain. "Zeke!" she said mournfully.

He squeezed her arm. "It's all right. Just do like I say. Now get going! I think we can get most of them out." He left her then and dashed back inside the barn. Morgan came out with more, to see Margaret approaching. He shouted to her to get back to the house with the babies. "There's nothing you can do! The babies are more important!" he shouted. She wanted to argue, but knew he was right.

It began raining harder, and Abbie hurried with a balking *Kehilan* toward the house. She quickly tied him to a hitching post, making sure it was a good, strong knot. She patted the horse's neck, trying to make him calm down, afraid the frightened animal would hurt himself. He whinnied and tossed his head, then unexpectedly threw himself sideways, pinning her momentarily between himself and the hitching post. Abbie gasped with pain at the jolt, and just as suddenly the horse moved away again. She struggled away from him, holding her ribs, momentarily dizzy. Breathing brought great pain, but she could not let that stop her. She must help.

She forced herself back toward the barn, finding it difficult to stand up in the slippery mud. The men had managed to get a few of the horses into a corral, but most of them had gone scurrying off. They would have to be rounded up later. The important thing was to get them out of the barn. Ellen and

Jason took more from their father's and brother's hands and led them to the corral, as Sonora came out with two more, her face and arms black from smoke. Planks could be heard falling then, and Wolf's Blood noticed part of the hem of Sonora's tunic was smouldering. He grabbed her and plunked her down in the mud, rubbing the burning dress into it.

"Do not go back in there!" he ordered.

"But I must help!" she argued.

He grasped her arms. "Do not go back!" he ordered again. His breathing was heavy from the excitement. He placed a wet cheek against her own. "I don't want anything to happen to you," he told her, his lips against her ear. He pulled back, and faint lightning lit up his face. His dark eyes looked at her lovingly, and she wondered if perhaps she really was on fire. "Stay here, Sonora. Are you hurt?"

She shook her head. In the next moment his lips were touching hers in a light kiss.

"I am glad," he told her. He dashed off then, helping lead out more horses as she got to her feet and watched.

Abbie hurried up to Zeke. "What else can I do?" she asked.

"Take these two to the corral," he shouted, leading two mares to her. "Then get back to the house. I think we got all of them but one or two. Luckily the smaller barn is all right. All the Thoroughbreds should be untouched."

She nodded, reaching up for the bridles. But then a strange look came over her face and she gasped, grabbing her side and sinking to her knees.

"Abbie!" He let go of the horses and knelt down in front of her. "What's wrong?"

"*Kehilan* . . . and I . . . had a little run-in," she gasped. "He pinned me . . . against the post. Oh, I'm sorry, Zeke! I should . . . be helping!"

"Damn!" he swore. "I never should have let you take him! That was stupid of me, as frightened as he was!" He quickly picked her up in his arms. "Everybody stay away now and let it burn!" he shouted to the others, his heart breaking a little at the words. But at least most of the horses were out. What else could be done? "Abbie's hurt! I'm taking her to the house!"

162

Wolf's Blood and Sonora ran up to them. "Mother!" the young man said in alarm. "Is it bad?"

"That damned *Kehilan* got ornery with her!" Zeke told him. "Sonora, you come with me. Wolf's Blood, go help Morgan. See if you can round up a few more of the strays and get them into a corral."

He hurried then with Abbie, followed by Sonora and Ellen, while Jason hurried to Margaret's cabin to tell her to stay with the children and not worry. Zeke carried her through the door and into the bedroom, laying her carefully on the bed. "Get a towel for her hair," he told Ellen. "Sonora, help me get these wet clothes off and get a dry gown on her."

"Zeke, I'm all right. It's just a rib, I think. It will just have to heal by itself. My arm . . . hurts more."

"Your arm?" He scowled, quickly pulling down her dress and getting it off.

"I fell. My arm hurts bad."

Sonora threw the wet clothes on the floor. "Let's just get her under the covers until I can look at her injuries," Zeke told the girl. "I'll get a gown on her later. I might have to wrap her ribs."

They covered her, and Ellen came in with a towel, wrapping it around her mother's wet hair.

"You two go on out," Zeke told both the girls. "Ellen, get some gauze ready. He stood up and removed his own clothes after the girls went out, quickly pulling on some dry buckskins and donning a cotton shirt. He sat down on the edge of the bed, while outside the heartbreaking sound of a crumbling barn could be heard.

"Oh, Zeke, the barn!" Abbie groaned.

"The hell with it! We'll build another," he said, gently picking up her left arm. It was already red and swollen. He ran a hand along the bone, and she cried out with pain, but he had no choice. He had to be sure.

"I don't think it's broken, Abbie, but it might be cracked, as red as it is. I'll wrap it. There's not much more I can do." He pulled the blankets down, feeling her ribs. A bruise was making itself visible on her left side. "Damned horse!"

"Don't blame him," she said weakly. "He was just . . . frightened. It's just that he . . . moved sideways so fast, I didn't have time to . . . get out of the way."

"It's the same with your ribs, honey. I think you have a couple of cracked ones. All I can do is wrap them. You'll stay right in this bed a few days and let Ellen and Sonora and Margaret do your work."

"But . . . the barn. There will be . . . so much to do!"

"Don't worry about it." He called out to Ellen to bring the gauze, and then began the tedious procedure of wrapping the ribs and arm. He was gentle, but it didn't seem to matter. She could not help but whimper at the pain, and it tore at his heart. It had been a long time since he'd had to see her in pain—not since . . . He put away the horrible memory of how he'd found her in the cave after Garvey and his men were finished with her. To think of it now was more than he could bear. There had been another time he'd helped her—a time when the pain had been much worse than this. She was only fifteen then, badly injured by a Crow arrow that he had to remove himself—a wound which later had to be burned out because of infection. There was still a scar on her back and near her left breast from that terrible time. It was then that he'd known he loved her too much to live without her. She seemed no different to him now. To him she was the same little Abbie.

He finished with her and covered her, bending down and kissing her forehead. "I don't suppose you planned this just to keep me around a while longer, did you?" he teased.

She forced a smile. "Of course I did," she answered.

Their eyes held and his teared. "This damned land has hurt you again, Abbie-girl. I'm sorry."

"Since when are you responsible for thunderstorms and lightning and fires?" she asked. "Don't be silly."

He bent close and kissed her lips lightly. "Try to sleep. Things will look better in the morning. I'd best go back out and get things in order. Sonora and Ellen will stay."

"How many did we lose, Zeke?" she asked.

"I'm not certain. Only four, I think. That's a hell of a lot better than when the Comanches raided."

"But the barn! The feed! Can we replace them?"

"We'll make do. But I'm glad now for the scouting job. Looks like I'll need the extra money more than I thought." He rose from the bed.

"Zeke," she called out. "I love you."

He picked up a piece of rawhide from the dresser, pulled his wet hair behind his head, and began tying the rawhide around it. "I love you, too," he answered. He walked out, and her injuries brought on a depression as the thunder still boomed far in the distance now, the rain only a light patter on the roof. There was another loud crash outside, and she struggled not to cry because the sobbing made her ribs hurt. She watched some stray lightning through the window.

"You're such . . . a savage land," she whispered. "That's how our destinies will be . . . isn't it?" She sniffed, tears running into her ears. "Savage. It's only . . . fitting."

Ellen came inside then, rushing to her mother's side. "Mother, don't cry! Are you in a lot of pain?"

"Not that much," Abbie whimpered. She looked at her daughter. "I hope . . . life is good for you, Ellen."

The girl frowned and sat down on the edge of the bed, gently removing the towel from her mother's thick, lustrous hair. "It already has been, Mother, being here with you. I like it here. I won't go away like LeeAnn did."

Abbie reached over with her good hand and patted the girl's arm. "Thank you, Ellen. Sometimes it seems . . . we have no control over our destiny. It frightens me sometimes . . . things that can't be controlled . . . like the elements . . . like tonight's storm. All of life is that way, Ellen."

The girl took her mother's hand. "And what would you change if you could, Mother?" she asked curiously.

The barn outside gave one last rumble and Abbie looked toward the doorway. "Nothing," she replied. "I wouldn't change anything, if it would mean not being with your father."

It was three days before the horses could be rounded up, three days of intense pain for Abbie. The men were gone almost constantly bringing in horses, while the women waited on Abbie and took care of the horses already there.

By the fourth day the task of picking up the debris began—a messy, tedious job. But the pile of embers had to be removed before a new barn could be built. Abbie forced herself up, insisting on doing a few things for herself at least part of the day so the women could have a little time to rest from doing household chores plus taking care of the many horses.

On the fifth day Abbie noticed Zeke seemed to have trouble lacing his buckskin shirt, finally leaving it untied and going out to work. A small fear gnawed at her, and she went outside where her rocker had been set, at her insistence, so that she could watch the clean-up procedures and get some fresh air. She sat down slowly, angered at her injuries. She should be helping, but Zeke was upset that she was doing even this much.

She watched the men work, while Ellen and Sonora fed horses and Margaret took turns between tending to the babies and filling water troughs. One thing was certain. They were a family, a hardworking, close family. Maybe LeeAnn and Jeremy did not want to be a part of it, but the others did, and she had them all with her. She had that much to be thankful for. She noticed Wolf's Blood and Sonora stealing occasional looks. The two of them had had little time together since the fire, much to Wolf's Blood's regret, she was sure. They made a beautiful couple, and she wished her son would make up his mind and take a wife. Zeke would like nothing better than for his oldest son to have sons of his own. He'd had his days of riding and making war. It was time now for other things. He was almost the same age Zeke had been when he married her. Yes, there was a time for making war, and a time for making love.

She watched Zeke saw at a piece of burned wood. Part of it was still good, and all good pieces must be saved to be used over. Their work was cut out for them. Not only would they have to travel to Fort Lyon to get supplies for a new barn, but before long they would have to go west along the river toward the mountains to find heating wood to cut for the winter supply, which would take time away from building the barn.

The structure was needed before winter, or at least a smaller building with stables; some kind of shelter for the horses that once were kept in the barn. It would be costly and time-consuming, for surely not all supplies needed would be found at Fort Lyon. Zeke would probably have to go to Pueblo. She felt sorry for him. There would be no time for scouting for a while, yet he needed the money now more than ever, and it angered her that Jeremy was not there to help. At least Zeke would be home a little longer, but she didn't want it to be this way for him. And worse than that, he'd probably go out on longer missions when he got around to scouting for the Army, just to make up for the money he'd be losing now.

She wished she could go and help him, but her arm and ribs were still much too sore to do any work. She noticed then that he had stopped sawing before the wood was cut through. He put his head back and squinted, rubbing his shoulder and elbow. He was a strong man. It was not like him to tire in the middle of cutting one piece of wood.

Her heart tightened when he appeared in pain. He flexed his hands, unaware that she was watching him. He started sawing again, then suddenly kicked the piece of wood and the saw to the ground, rubbing at his arm once more. She wanted to think he was just angry over their misfortune, but it was more than that. He was in pain. She watched him remove something from under his buckskin shirt—something tucked into the waist of his leggings. A small bottle. He uncorked it and took a swallow, then put it back.

Abbie frowned in alarm. Whiskey? It was not like her husband to drink whiskey other than on special occasions of celebration. Again she worried over what it was he was not telling her—why he sometimes hinted that she would do just fine without him, that he had lived longer than the average man in this land. Why did he say such things? He was strong, tough. Because of his Indian blood she'd always expected him to live until very old, like so many Cheyenne men. And yet she'd never been able to picture him that way.

He took a water bucket from Sonora, who was bringing it to him and the others to drink. He sunk the dipper into it and then poured it over his head to cool off. His long hair was braided to keep it away from his face. He flexed his hands again, and Sonora went on to take water to the others. Zeke picked up the piece of wood, angrily setting it back on the barrels to finish sawing it, but she could see it was done with great effort. A few minutes later he came to the house, stopping short when he saw her sitting there, as though to wonder if she'd been watching him. He could tell by her eyes that she had and he cursed the damned arthritis that had flared up again. It wasn't supposed to bother him in warm weather, but the storm had cooled things off the first three days afterward, and it had kept raining, releasing a pain in his bones that had lingered even though now it was very hot again.

He leaned down, smiling and putting his hands on either arm of the rocker. "How's my Abbie? I'd rather you stayed in bed, you know." He kissed her lightly.

"I feel pretty good today," she answered, watching him closely. "If I don't move around too much, the pain isn't too bad, except if I laugh or cough."

"Well, those ribs had better heal soon, because I miss making love to my woman." He kissed her neck and stood up. "I forgot my tobacco." He turned to go inside.

"Zeke."

He stopped, not turning around.

"What's in that bottle under your shirt? Surely you aren't drinking whiskey."

He sighed deeply. "It's just a little something for pain, Abbie—nothing to be upset about."

"What kind of pain?"

He turned and met her eyes. "Look, Abbie, I just get the aches once in a while. You know what I've been through in my lifetime. A man doesn't fight his way through life like I have without suffering the consequences. These old bones gnaw at me sometimes, that's all. So I asked a doctor at Fort Lyon if there wasn't something I could take that would make me feel better. The last few days I've worked extra hard and my bones are telling me so. That's all. I'd have given you some of the stuff when you were hurt, but I knew if you laid still the pain

168

wouldn't be too bad, and I knew you'd question me up one side and down the other wanting to know where I got the stuff."

She held his eyes. "What is it?"

"It's called laudanum. You took some when you had that operation in Denver."

She blinked back tears. "And it's only to be used in cases of extreme pain, not just for a few aching bones."

He just grinned and knelt down beside her, taking her hands. "Abbie, don't exaggerate things in your mind, all right? Let it be, Abbie. Just let it be."

She looked down at his hands. Why hadn't she put it together before? She'd noticed at other times that his knuckles were strangely swollen, like they were right now. But she'd ignored it. She had thought that surely it was just from hard work. But no. It wasn't just that. They'd never looked that way before. And besides, it seemed to come and go. She rubbed at his hands gently. Her grandmother had had a similar ailment, and had ended up a crippled old woman, bedridden and hardly able to do anything for herself. She met his eyes again. Zeke Monroe would never allow himself to be brought down to such a humiliating condition. It all made sense now. She knew the other reason for the scouting. It gave him an out. When he knew he would be so crippled he could never ride again, he'd find a way to die honorably. There was no other way for Zeke Monroe to leave this world.

He saw the knowing tears well in her eyes and leaned forward to kiss her cheek. "It's not as bad as you think, Abbie-girl. If it were, I'd tell you. Just relax and get yourself healed. Don't cry. You'll just make your ribs hurt." He squeezed her hands. "I'm okay. I'm too goddamned mean to give up anything without a hell of a fight, and you know it. So you'll just have to put up with this wild Indian for a few more years yet."

She sniffed and held his hands tightly. "Promise?"

He gave her a handsome grin. "Promise. And that includes making love to my woman, so don't do anything to slow the healing process."

She smiled through tears. "Can I . . . do anything, Zeke?

169

Can't I help you in some way?"

He patted her hand. "You can sit here and get well. And you can ignore any terrible thoughts that are going through you mind. I don't want to talk about it, Abbie. What's the use in worrying about something that hasn't happened yet? Let's just take one thing at a time—one day at a time. All right?"

She nodded. "All right." She sniffed again, her lips quivering. "I need you Zeke," she whimpered.

He grasped her chin in one hand and gave her a quick kiss. "Well here I am, so what are you crying about?" He gave her a wink and rose, going into the house for the tobacco and coming out with a cigarette in his mouth. He walked down the steps and back to his work, and she watched his long, ambling gate, the slim hips that stirred her, his animallike grace. Surely, surely there was no sickness that could truly defeat such a man. She would not think about it. She could not think about it. Not Zeke. Not her Zeke. He looked wonderful. He'd be fine. This was just a passing thing.

The night was warm, a soft breeze keeping away the mosquitoes. Sonora carried eight-month-old Nathan back to Margaret's cabin. She had been watching the baby to give Margaret some relief. Wolf's Blood came out of the tipi with Little Zeke, putting his nearly two-year-old nephew on his shoulders and joining Sonora. She knew inside he'd been watching for her so he could walk with her.

"Do you think Margaret had time to rest?" she asked him.

He laughed lightly. "I think she and Morgan did more than rest."

Sonora blushed deeply. Even in the darkness Wolf's Blood sensed she was reddening. Sometimes he'd say things to deliberately embarrass her, finding it amusing that even with her dark skin, he could see her blushing. She hoisted Nathan up to get a better hold of the boy as they walked.

"I think perhaps Margaret is very lucky," she said daringly.

"To have Morgan?" he asked. "I think so, too. Morgan is a good man. My sister did well. I am glad for her."

170

"I didn't mean just that. I meant . . . she is lucky to be able to . . . to have the man she loves. Some women . . . can only dream."

He stopped walking and she went a few steps further, then turned to face him in the moonlight. His heart pounded. Her long dark hair blew in the soft breeze, and he could see the fringes of her tunic dancing in the wind, almost inviting him to touch the soft roundness beneath the dress.

"And is that what you do?" he asked her. "Dream?"

She breathed deeply. Why not tell him? What did she have to lose? "I dream every night," she answered. "About you, Wolf's Blood." She turned and walked to Margaret's cabin, and he watched her. Why had he put it off so long? He wanted her, that was sure. In fact, he loved her. But he was afraid to love and then have what he loved taken from him. Yet could that be any worse than never having that which he wanted so badly?

He hurried up behind her then, getting to the door just as Margaret opened it. Morgan sat at the table, his muscular arms and shoulders bare. Margaret wore a robe, obviously quickly wrapped around a naked body. She reached for Nathan. "Thank you so much, Sonora," she told the girl. Wolf's Blood lifted Little Zeke down from his shoulders, and the boy ran inside to his father. Margaret looked at him and back at Sonora, then to her brother again. "Thank you both," she told them. "You'd better go get your own rest."

Sonora nodded and turned, heading back to the main house. Margaret frowned at her brother. "It's a lovely night, don't you think?"

He looked up at the sky and shrugged. "I suppose."

She looked out at Sonora. "If I were you, I'd make use of it, my brother. With your handsome looks, you need no deer tails or any other charms to have the woman you want." She took the baby inside and shut the door, and he turned to watch after Sonora, who was several yards away. His sister was right. Why waste the night? A man had to make a decision one way or the other eventually, and his body ached for a woman, but not just any woman. He had wanted Sonora since the first day he

171

saw her in the supply store. For a brief moment he thought about Jennifer. There had been other occasions he'd thought of her, but only in a curious way, for her white beauty was rare indeed. But she was a little girl and far away, and a half cousin besides. Worse than that, she was white. He had little use for white women other than his own mother and sisters and Dan's wife Bonnie. It was just that on rare occasions Jennifer's wide, green eyes would come to mind, as well as her girlish curiosity about Indians. He'd never seen hair so red nor skin quite so white. Not even LeeAnn had skin as white as Jennifer's. But then the vision left him as quickly as it had come, and he decided it was only due to the fact that two bloods ran in his veins, and there were times when the white blood would come to tease and annoy him. But he was Indian, and his passion was for Indians and Indian ways.

"Sonora!" he called out, running to catch up with her then. She stopped, turning and waiting for him. He came up to her then, just staring at her in the moonlight.

"What is it, Wolf's Blood?" she asked.

He came closer, his breathing heavy. He reached out and touched her hair. "I want . . ." He swallowed. "Stay with me tonight—in the tipi. It is the Indian way. Stay with me tonight, and you will be my wife. My mother says people need a white preacher to marry them, but you and I do not need such things. We are Indian. You need only to give yourself to me, and you are mine."

Her eyes teared, and her breathing quickened. "You want me to be your wife?"

He came closer, moving his hands to her hips and pressing her against him. "I love you, Sonora. I have loved you for a long time, but was afraid. I am not afraid anymore."

She felt weak at the manly scent of him, the closeness of the broad shoulders, the feel of his manhood pressing hard against her belly. He could feel her trembling. "I . . . I would like to be your wife, Wolf's Blood. I . . . want you for my man. But . . . it frightens me."

He kissed her hair. "Do not ever be afraid of me, Sonora. I would not hurt you." His lips found hers then, and she felt on fire, her passion so great she lost all fear. If being his woman brought pain, so be it. It would be pleasurable pain. He moved his lips to her neck and she reached up to embrace him, her breathing coming in short gasps. He picked her up in his arms and carried her inside the tipi, setting her on her feet and closing the deerskin flap over the entranceway, tying it so no one could come in unexpectedly. She stood before him, shivering, half crying, wondering how her legs still worked.

He walked around her then, eyeing her up and down as he removed his own clothing. When the loincloth came off she looked at the ground shyly and he smiled. He came closer and took her chin in his hand. "Don't be afraid of it," he told her. "All of me belongs to you, Sonora, and all of you belongs to me."

He unlaced her tunic at the shoulders and pulled her arms open so that it fell to the ground. She stood there in naked splendor, looking at him boldly as he gazed at full, firm breasts and milky brown skin.

"You are . . . the most beautiful creature I have ever seen," he told her sincerely. "You make me tremble, Sonora."

She reached out with a shaking hand and touched his chest. "And you are the most beautiful man I have ever seen."

He took her hand and led her to his bed of robes. He sat down, gently pulling her down beside him. "You are shaking. I want you to be relaxed, Sonora." He gently pushed her down onto the bed of robes. "I will relax you, and you will want me so much that it will not hurt you." He moved away for a moment, carrying over a wooden bowl. "It is a sweet-smelling oil. I have been . . . saving it. When I lived with the widowed Sioux woman in the North, she taught me the secret of oil, and how it helps a woman not be afraid." He took her arms and laid them up over her head. "Do not be afraid to let me look at you, Sonora. You are so very beautiful. I could not have a more pleasurable wife." He dipped his hands into the oil and rubbed it on his palms, then began massaging her, moving from her wrists down her arms to her throat. She gasped when his hands gently moved over the full breasts. "I will massage all of you—every muscle, every hidden place," he told her. "And then I will make you my woman."

He smiled. This was going to be the most glorious night he'd

173

ever experienced. Perhaps they would not even leave the next day. He would lie next to her all day and make love to her again and again. It had been a long time since he'd had a woman, and this one was going to be his wife.

Wolf lay at the other side of the dwelling, totally unconcerned over what his master was doing. The big gray beast yawned and turned over, curling into a new position, ignoring the gasps of pleasure and whispered words of love.

The next morning found everyone at the breakfast table but Wolf's Blood and Sonora.

"Where are they?" Abbie fussed. "Maybe Sonora stayed at Margaret's. Jason said she never slept in the loft last night."

Zeke grinned and sat down. "I wouldn't go looking for her at Margaret's, Abbie-girl. I saw our son carrying her into his tipi last night. They didn't know I was outside."

He met her surprised eyes. "But they aren't . . . I mean we need to get a preacher here. Maybe they didn't even—"

"Abbie, you know as well as I that when it comes to being in love, nobody needs a damned preacher. And yes, I'm sure they did do exactly what you're thinking. I say it's about time."

She began to redden, cursing her injuries, for she suddenly wanted her own husband. No, when it came to passion, a preacher made little difference. After all, hadn't Zeke Monroe made her his woman without a preacher? The formalities had come later, but they were already married in heart and soul and body, of that there was no doubt.

Their eyes held and she smiled, both of them remembering a night in Wyoming when a half-breed scout grasped and held a grief-stricken young girl named Abigail Trent. She had lost her family, and there had been only one way to comfort her—to love her in the only way she wanted to be loved and to put his own brand on her. He had to be her first man and show her she was not alone but that someone loved her and wanted to protect her. He'd been doing this ever since.

Abbie looked at Ellen and Jason. "I don't want anyone

174

disturbing Wolf's Blood today," she told them. "I know there is a lot of work to be done, but let him come and help when he is ready. Tell Margaret and Morgan as soon as you're through with breakfast."

Ellen giggled and picked up her fork, and Jason frowned, not totally sure what was going on. But everyone seemed happy enough, so he guessed it didn't much matter.

Chapter Ten

Settling in on the reservation in Oklahoma was no easy accomplishment for the freedom-loving Cheyenne, but during the years of 1871 and 1872 there was relative peace, with even the wayward Big Jake, Bull Bear, Red Moon, and Medicine Arrows bringing their people south to the reservation. But the Cheyenne made little effort to take up the ways of agriculture or education. Schedules, learning, plowing, and planting were all things totally foreign to the proud Cheyenne. A man must hunt or make war against his enemies. But walk behind a plow? Sit on a hard bench learning useless scribblings? It made no sense. In 1872 only eight Cheyenne children had shown up in the Quaker school on the reservation, and they were the offspring of mixed bloods, none of them full-blooded Cheyennes.

With the relative peace during the winter of '71–'72, Zeke's services were not needed to any great extent, much to Abbie's relief. It was a hard winter for them, as it was spent cutting wood, trudging around for supplies, and trying to get a barn built.

In that same winter Wolf disappeared, and Wolf's Blood knew in his heart that the animal had gone off to die, for his beloved pet, which had been found and adopted as a pup, had been acting listless and sick. Wolf's Blood spent nearly a week looking for the animal, returning without him. His heart felt great sorrow at the thought of things getting old and dying, like the Indians and like what was happening to his father. He knew

177

Wolf's death was a sign that his own life must change also. One more wild thing had gone out of it.

During that long winter Abbie could see her husband silently suffering. Every movement seemed to bring him pain, and his hands and wrists were often swollen. But he worked as much as the others, saying nothing about his own agony. Abbie could see that his affliction was obviously worse in the winter, and by spring the barn was built and her husband was noticeably better.

In May of 1872 Wolf's Blood's spirits were lifted when Sonora gave birth to a son, named Kicking Boy because he was so lively inside his mother's stomach before he was born, and continued kicking wildly after birth. Some day Wolf's Blood hoped his son would be able to go to the mountains and fast and pray until he had a vision, in that way knowing what his name should be when he became a man. Wolf's Blood had once been called Little Rock, but had shed the name when he had his own vision, and had lived with a pack of wolves in the Rockies at the age of twelve. He was the only one of Zeke's sons who had followed all the customs of the Cheyenne. He wanted his own son to do the same, but feared the boy would never get the chance. He was fiercely proud of Kicking Boy, determined to teach him everything he could about both the Cheyenne and the Apache, hoping the child would carry on the Indian ways and teach them to his own children. Like his father, Wolf's Blood feared the old ways and language would die out once reservation Indians began to slowly adjust to white man's ways and schooling.

Reservation life in Oklahoma remained precarious. With nearly all the Cheyenne nation finally in one place, the powerful force they felt in being together brought back thoughts of again being free. The buffalo hunts had been good. There were many robes dressed and readied for the whiskey and gun traders, who always found ways to illegally enter the reservation, which sprawled across thousands of acres of open land impossible to guard night and day. With whiskey and guns and the ability to gather together in council, rumors of a planned outbreak began spreading. And at the same time Kicking Boy was born, Brinton Darlington, agent on the Cheyenne reservation and respected by the Indians, died. In honor of the elderly Quaker, the Cheyenne made sure there were several days of quiet during his illness and immediately following his death.

A new agent, John D. Miles, was appointed, and not long thereafter the Kiowas began raiding anew. Many of their raids were blamed on the Cheyenne, for there was again unrest among the young warriors, and it was well known that the Kiowas were constantly after the Cheyenne to join them in the raiding. Those Cheyenne who stayed at Camp Supply according to treaty, drawing rations from the government, still refused to consider settling into white man's ways. They wanted to wait and watch their kin, the Arapaho, to see how they fared at farming, still considering such things woman's work.

A few Kiowa chiefs, such as Lone Wolf and Kicking Bird, worked hard at restraining their young men. But they had little control. The constant goading of the warring Kiowas toward the Cheyenne, calling them cowards and squaws, had its effect, and some of the younger men joined in more raiding. Still, the fighting was sporadic and could not be called an all-out war. The major portion of the Cheyenne remained on the reservation and still favored peace. But they continued to refuse to send their children to the Quaker schools, to farm, or to listen to Christain teachings—for all these things were against the Cheyenne way.

If the whites in charge of running the reservation and "educating" the Indians could have tried harder to understand Indian ways, perhaps the peace would have lasted forever. But their attitude did little to help keep the peace. In the words of one white agent, the one main obstacle to more rapid advance in Indian morals and religion was the Indians' reluctance to "acknowledge the superiority of the whites." Such attitudes could not have been more damaging when used against such a proud people as the Cheyenne and most other tribes. To the Indian the white man was not superior at all—stronger in force and weapons and numbers, perhaps, but not superior as men.

179

It was this constant spiritual and social abuse that kept the fires of hatred and misunderstanding burning and prohibited any real understanding from either side.

In late summer of 1872 a few Southern Cheyenne and a part of the Northern Cheyenne who had finally come south to the reservation, headed back north from Camp Supply to hunt buffalo. When approaching a group of buffalo hunters, one warrior laid down his gun in a sign of peace, only to be shot in cold blood. Shortly thereafter, Indians raided a settler family and killed all of them. The Cheyenne hunting party was blamed, although they vehemently denied committing the act, saying Kiowas had done it. Such confusion kept the pot constantly boiling, and by the end of 1872, the young men were becoming restless again, and control of those who opted for peace became difficult if not impossible. Slowly but surely, the relative peace that had been enjoyed was crumbling.

It was late February, 1873, when the small company of soldiers rode onto Monroe property and halted in front of the main house. Abbie stayed at the table while Zeke went to the door. Her heart felt like it was shattering, for she knew why they had come before they even spoke. A sergeant removed his hat.

"You by any chance Zeke Monroe?" he asked, already sure of the answer just by looking at the Indian in the doorway.

"I am."

"I'm Sergeant Hal Daniels, from Fort Lyon. May I come inside?"

Zeke stepped back, and Daniels came inside, walking to stand near the stove. It was cold, very cold, but there was not a lot of snow on the ground. Abbie knew Zeke had been suffering again, and she resented the sergeant's appearance, unable to give him an entirely friendly look when his eyes met hers. At first he stared in surprise, looking from her to Zeke.

"My wife, Abigail," Zeke told him.

Daniels could not hide his shock. She was beautiful—a rare sight in these parts—but more than that, she was white. He glanced up at the loft, and saw a pretty girl of perhaps eighteen

180

and a boy in his early teens looking down at him, both white.

"Our daughter and son, Ellen and Jason," Abbie told him, amused by the surprised look on the man's face. "There are more, but they aren't here at the moment."

Daniels nodded to her. "Hello, ma'am." He looked back at Zeke, wondering if he could trust the tall, powerful-looking man who was obviously more Indian than white, at least in looks. "Lieutenant-Colonel Petersen sent me, Mr. Monroe. Says he needs your services, if you've a mind."

Zeke motioned for him to sit down. "Coffee?" he asked.

"I'd appreciate it. And I'm wondering if my men can hold up in your barn. They'd not harm anything."

Zeke nodded, looking up at Jason. "Go show the sergeant's men where they can bed down, Jason. And get Wolf's Blood."

The boy nodded and climbed down to put on his coat and winter moccasins. Sergeant Daniels frowned. "Wolf's Blood?"

Zeke grinned and began rolling a cigarette, while Abbie rose to pour the coffee. "My son. This is a slow time of year and I have a son-in-law to run the place. Wolf's Blood has expressed a desire to go with me if the Army should ask. Do you know what it's all about? I'll not go along to hunt down my own people if they're going to be slaughtered."

Daniels cleared his throat. He was young and good-looking, but seemed out of place with fair skin and curly red hair and a red mustache. His eyes were bright blue. He was just under six feet, of stocky build, with a true friendliness to his eyes. Zeke had a knack for studying and deciphering people quickly, and so far he liked the sergeant.

"Nothing like that, Mr. Monroe. That's why the lieutenant thought you might like to have a hand in this one." His eyes dropped to the knife at Zeke's waist. "He . . . uh . . . he talked to a lot of men, heard a lot about your skills in fighting, especially with your knife." He cleared his throat again and Zeke took a drag on the cigarette.

"Go on," he told Daniels. Abbie set a cup of coffee in front of each man.

"Thank you, ma'am," the sergeant spoke up.

"Certainly," she replied. Her voice and manner surprised

181

him. He simply had not expected to find such a lovely, refined woman living in a log house with a half-breed Indian. He turned back to Zeke, full of personal questions he knew he dared not ask.

"Well, sir," he continued, "Petersen would like your help in digging out some whiskey traders. They're the scum of the frontier, sir, causing all sorts of trouble. The agents and soldiers just can't keep the peace as long as the illegal whiskey peddlers keep coming into the reservation. Sometimes they trade through other Indians, like the Seminoles and Delawares, claiming that because they're Indian the soldiers can't do anything about it. Some traders are more open about it, hauling whole wagonloads of whiskey out of Dodge City into Oklahoma. The reservation being so big and all, and with the Indians helping the traders, the soldiers just can't keep up with it all. Petersen was hoping maybe there was some way you could filter in—maybe go to Dodge City and offer your services to the traders, find out who the biggest dealers are, what routes they take and all, then report back to Petersen so he'd know when and where to intercept them."

Zeke smoked quietly, looking at Abbie, who frowned. "It sounds very dangerous," she warned. "Men who do such things certainly are not going to care about a human life, especially an Indian's. If they find out what Zeke is up to, they'll kill him."

Daniels ran a hand through his hair. "You're probably right, ma'am. But from all the reports my commanding officer has received about your husband, killing him is not an easy thing to do. He's a clever, skilled man. Petersen seems to think he would be good for this job and it wouldn't be all that dangerous for him."

She half grinned at her husband. "You're right about the first part. Killing him is not easy. Plenty have tried." She sighed deeply, her eyes still on her husband. "I just worry about one of them succeeding someday." She could see the excitement in his eyes and already knew he'd do it. Her biggest worry was not the danger, but rather whether he would decide this was his time to die. If Zeke Monroe did not choose to die, it was unlikely anyone could harm him. But how bad was his pain? Was he ready to give it all up? Would he use this mission as his excuse?

He gave her a wink then, taking another drag on the cigarette. "Don't worry, Abbie-girl. I'll see this one through."

Her eyes teared. He had read her thoughts, as he always seemed to do.

Ellen came down then and sat at the table, blushing slightly under the gaze of Sergeant Daniels. She was attracted to his burly shoulders and the blue uniform. He was soft-spoken and mannerly, and the way he looked at her, with great admiration and appreciation of her beauty, made her skin tingle. She smiled shyly and nodded to him.

"Refill the sergeant's cup," Abbie told her daughter. The girl gladly obeyed. Wolf's Blood came through the door then, and again Daniels' eyes widened in surprise. The younger Monroe looked even more menacing than his father, if that was possible. And the two of them held a striking resemblance. Practically the only difference was age lines in Zeke's face and the thin white scar down Zeke's left cheek. At first Wolf's Blood stared rather haughtily at the sergeant. He had never liked soldiers and never would, but he had promised his father he would help in scouting, partly because he knew the pain Zeke suffered and did not want him to be alone.

"This is my son," Zeke spoke up. "Wolf's Blood, this is Sergeant Daniels, from Fort Lyon."

Daniels put out his hand, but Wolf's Blood just stared at him.

"Shake the man's hand, Wolf's Blood. He's not an enemy at the moment. I trust him."

Wolf's Blood put out his hand, gripping Daniels's firmly as they shook, telling him by his grip what he would do if tricked. Daniels nodded to him.

"The sergeant here was sent to bring us back to the fort to see about routing out some illegal whiskey traders. What do you think?"

Wolf's Blood frowned and leaned against the wall. "I think since it is white whiskey traders, I would like the job," he answered. "It is bastards like that who destroy the Indian's strength and pride, with their rotgut whiskey that makes a man

183

weak and stupid! I would gladly wipe out any whiskey trader I could get my hands on."

Zeke grinned. "That's what I thought."

"Just remember," Daniels spoke up. "We only want to know who and where. Leave the arresting to the soldiers. They will be tried and sentenced in court."

Wolf's Blood hissed out a sarcastic laugh. "And be turned loose again to do the same thing. My father and I can make the job easier by killing them ourselves."

"Calm down, Wolf's Blood," Zeke warned. "We're scouts, not hired killers."

Daniels watched and listened in amazement, finding it easier now to believe the stories he'd heard about Zeke Monroe. Could it be true the man didn't even know how many men he'd killed? He swallowed, hoping neither the father nor the son would ever consider him an enemy. He glanced at Ellen again. He would dearly love to see more of that one, but what if he offended her father? This would take some consideration, but in studying the girl's simple beauty and fetching smile, it might be worth the risk.

"Where is the fun in just hunting and not killing?" Wolf's Blood scowled.

"It's not for fun, it's for money, Wolf's Blood," Zeke reminded him. "Now keep that in mind and do what you're told. If killing is necessary in self-defense, that's another matter."

The young man shrugged. "When do we go? And where?"

Zeke put out his cigarette. "Dodge City, I expect, to begin with," he answered.

"You have a few days to prepare," Daniels told him. "I have some other places to go. I'd like to use your barn for the night. Then I'll leave out in the morning, come back through here in about four days. Can you be ready by then?"

Zeke nodded. "I'll be ready." He looked at Abbie.

"Just like that?" she asked.

He sighed. "I can't put if off forever, Abbie-girl. Don't worry. You know we can take care of ourselves. You can put Sonora up here and dote on Kicking Boy all you want while we're gone."

She smiled. "That part I don't mind." She looked at Daniels. "How long do you think they will be gone?"

He frowned. "It's hard to say, ma'am. However long it takes them to find out what we need to know."

"Then I'll find out fast," Zeke spoke up. "I don't like being away from my home and my woman for too long at a time." He gave her a wink but her eyes were already wet with tears. How she hated to see him go away! There had been other times, but she would never get used to it, and now with him obviously ill, it would be harder. So much harder.

The marriage was a minor social event in spite of Charles Garvey's long list of invited guests. Those who came did so out of curiosity and because Garvey might be important someday, few because they actually liked Charles Garvey. Most knew him for what he was, and somewhere deep inside LeeAnn also knew. But she ignored those inner warnings. Charles was kind to her. Charles was rich. Charles held great promise, and he was very much in love with her. By marrying Charles Garvey, she would be taking her stand against Indians, and therein professing the ultimate denial of her own Indian blood. She was determined that he would never know.

How the foolish young girl thought she could keep it hidden forever, she didn't know. Sometimes the fear of his discovering her heritage kept her awake at night. Worse than that, what if he found out she'd actually once been a captive of the Comanches? She'd not been raped, but he'd never believe it. She knew he'd think the less of her just for being in their hands, even though there had been nothing she could do about it. The horror of her slavery and beatings and the constant fear of being raped still startled her awake in the night, and remained her most passionate reason for denying her own Indian blood. She wanted nothing more to do with the Indians or anything else from her past. Through her own ingenuity and her job in an attorney's office, she had even devised papers showing her as LeeAnn Whittaker, once the ward of a Catholic orphanage in New York.

Charles Garvey cared only that she was educated and

185

beautiful, and to LeeAnn's great relief, did no further checking into her past. Her college records showed her registered as LeeAnn Whittaker, as did the landlord of her apartment. It all fit, well enough at least for Charles Garvey. If the young man had the cunning wisdom of his dead father, he would have done further checking. But the son was more careless and too quick to grab what he wanted. He wanted LeeAnn, and on February 7, 1873, twenty-eight-year-old Charles Garvey married Miss LeeAnn Whittaker, twenty-one, the orphaned girl from New York. It was a grand church wedding, with all the trimmings.

LeeAnn hadn't the slightest idea she was marrying the son of her father's most bitter enemy, that her own father had killed Winston Garvey with the help of Wolf's Blood, or that Wolf's Blood had been the one who injured Charles's leg at Sand Creek. She had no idea that her husband's father was the man who had raped and hurt her mother to find the whereabouts of Joshua Lewis. Everything had been kept quiet. LeeAnn knew that her mother was abducted and suspected she'd been raped, but she was merely ten years old then, and for the safety of everyone involved, had never been told any details.

The wedding was soon over, and Charles Garvey whisked his new wife off to the fanciest hotel in Washington, D.C. She felt uneasy as soon as they walked through the doors, for her husband seemed to be in too much of a hurry.

"Tomorrow we catch a train and we'll go all the way to Florida," he told her excitedly. "Have you ever been there, darling?"

"No," she answered as he hurried her up the stairs, followed by a young man who carried their luggage.

"You'll like it, LeeAnn. It's like nothing you've ever seen— palm trees, beaches. And maybe next year I'll take you on a cruise. Would you like to see Europe?"

"Oh, yes, Charles! That would be wonderful."

"Then you shall see it. You shall go wherever you wish, my love. But of course I have my job, too. I'll be a lawyer soon, Mrs. Garvey. And we won't live in my apartment for long. The house I'm building is almost finished. You shall live in the country, away from this bedlam, in a grand mansion—the wife of Charles Garvey, prominent journalist and attorney. You shall have servants, and a nanny for our children."

Her heart pounded. Children. She hadn't even thought of that. What if one of the children was born dark, like Wolf's Blood or Margaret? It could easily happen. What if she bore a child that looked all Indian! No. That could not happen. She was so fair, and Charles was not dark. Their children would be as ordinary as any other children.

They went through a heavy door into a spacious room with a canopied bed. Everything was pink and white and plush. Charles paid the boy who brought their luggage, and suddenly the door was closing and he was locking it. It had all happened too fast. Had she done the right thing? She suddenly wished she could talk to her mother, but she stood there alone in the room with her new husband, determined not to turn into a blubbering baby.

He was at once removing her headpiece. He threw it to the floor and began unbuttoning the back of her dress.

"Charles!" she protested, bolting away. "What are you doing!"

His eyes darkened strangely. "What do you think I'm doing? I'm undressing you. You are my wife now."

She reddened. "Charles, I . . . I've never . . . been with a man. I need some time."

He frowned and began removing his own clothes. "Then take some time—about five minutes. Why don't you go into the dressing room over there and put on that nightgown I bought for you."

She put a hand to her crimson cheek. "Charles, you can see right through it."

He grinned. "Of course. I've waited almost two years to set eyes on your naked body, LeeAnn, and I'll not be turned away on my wedding night. Now go put the thing on and come to bed and let an experienced man make a woman of you. Go on, now. Be a good girl."

She just stood there staring at him as he stripped down to his underwear. He looked at her with a scowl. "What's the matter with you?"

She blinked back tears. "Charles, please be patient with me. I'm scared."

187

He snickered and came closer, grasping her arms until they began to hurt. "You are Mrs. Charles Garvey. I love you, LeeAnn. I have done you the honor of offering you myself, my fortune, my name. I might remind you that you were a mere orphan, working for a living like a commoner. I am making a lady out of you—a rich one at that. I just told you I'll take you all over the world, if you want. I'm spending a fortune on a grand house for you. The least you can do is come to my bed on our wedding night." He kissed her almost savagely. "I won't hurt you, LeeAnn. It happens to hundreds of women every day. It happened to your own mother, for God's sake, or you wouldn't be here. I've been with plenty of women in my time, and lots of them whores, so I know what I'm doing. There's nothing to be afraid of. Now go get these clothes off. I want to see you—every inch of you. Hurry up, before I rip up that pretty wedding dress. I'm sure you'd rather save it in one piece, now, wouldn't you?"

She could see by his eyes that he meant every word of it. She pulled away and walked to the dressing room, taking her bag with her. Of course her mother had done this. But she knew her father well enough to know that it surely wasn't like this—frightening and mechanical.

The next two hours were shocking and hideous. Could being raped by the Comanches have been any worse than her husband's strange sexual pleasures? She lay limp and unfeeling. She didn't dare feel anything. What was done was done. She had agreed to marry him, had agreed to turn her back on the past. There was no changing it now, and most certainly no going back. She had got what she thought she wanted and she already knew her only happiness would be during the day when she would be alone in the lovely mansion and her husband would be gone. If she was lucky she would get pregnant soon and then he'd not be able to touch her. And after that there would be a baby to love. She suddenly didn't even care if it looked Indian.

When he was finally asleep she stumbled to the dressing room and vomited.

*   *   *

188

The soldiers returned, and Abbie quickly finished packing her husband's parfleche. Inside the tipi, Wolf's Blood was saying his own good-byes to Sonora and Kicking Boy, promising to return soon, but his eyes were alive with excitement. He would be riding out alone with his father on a dangerous mission. If he were lucky, he would kill a few whiskey traders, something he would not mind.

Abbie handed Zeke the parfleche, as he buckled his weapons belt. He took the deerskin bag from her and laid it on the table, pulling her close. "I'll be all right," he told her. "You know that. So get that worried look off your face. I haven't come across a man yet I couldn't handle—or more than one at once. And Wolf's Blood will be with me. Do you really think anybody can take the two of us?"

She rested her head against his chest. "It isn't just that. Promise me you'll come back, Zeke. Tell me you aren't so sick you'll do something foolish, like get yourself killed."

He kissed her hair. "I promise. Have I ever broken one promise I've made to you?"

"No." She leaned back and looked up at him. Their lips met hungrily. The night before had been one of passion and little rest. Every time he knew he was going away it seemed he couldn't get enough of her, as though he must put a final brand on her and make her remember who she belonged to. But she didn't mind the branding. He searched her mouth now, wishing the kiss could last forever. But it could not, and he must go. "God be with you," she whispered, as his lips moved to her cheek.

"And with you," he answered. *"Nemehotatse."*

"And I love you, Zeke." She blinked back tears and pulled away reluctantly. "There are plenty of biscuits in the parfleche, some jam, and a few potatoes."

"I'll get full supplies from the Army, honey. Don't worry about that."

She nodded, and their eyes held a moment longer before he finally turned and went through the door. She followed after him, and he said a quick good-bye to the rest of the family, giving some last orders to Morgan.

Sergeant Daniels was there with his company, and he

189

nodded to Ellen, who smiled back at him. "Take care, ma'am," he told the girl.

"You, too, sergeant," she replied, reddening again.

Zeke mounted a large Appaloosa mare he favored. He preferred *Kehilan*, but there might come a time when he'd need a horse that would keep still when he wanted it to, and *Kehilan* had a mind of his own that sometimes even Zeke could not control.

Abbie watched him, her heart swelling with love. Always she adored seeing him on a horse, so much man, so sure. Wolf's Blood was already mounted.

Daniels signaled his men. "Move out!" he shouted. He turned to Zeke and Wolf's Blood. "You two ride up front with me."

They headed east then, toward Fort Lyon. Both the Monroes looked back at their wives and gave a final wave and a smile. Sonora just watched, holding Kicking Boy. Abbie waved, forcing a smile of her own. She watched until they disappeared over the eastern ridge. There was nothing to do now but wait and pray. She walked back to the cabin. There were so many changes in life, so many good-byes. She wondered how a person stood them all. Somehow most people did.

In Denver the newspaper told of the marriage of Charles Garvey, son of the now-dead Winston Garvey, prominent Colorado businessman and realtor, to Miss LeeAnn Whittaker of New York. There was no picture.

Chapter Eleven

Wolf's Blood grinned as he spun the chamber of his new Colt revolver, making sure it was fully loaded. "I will say one thing for scouting for the Army," he commented. "They are generous with their supplies. I wish I could find a way to get some of their rifles to Swift Arrow and his Northern Cheyenne."

Zeke turned a piece of meat over the fire. "You just remember what you're here for, my young warrior. Don't get your loyalties mixed up."

The boy sat on a new blanket and leaned back against a rock. "That is not always easy when I am out here free on the plains."

Zeke laughed lightly. "I know the feeling." He had to agree about the Army supplies. They had each been issued two blankets, a Spencer repeating carbine, a Colt revolver, one hundred forty rounds of rifle ammunition, thirty rounds of revolver ammunition, a lariat and picket pin, a canteen, a haversack for supplies, butcher knives, tin plates and cups, and cold rations.

Zeke had turned down the offer of saddle and bridle. Neither he nor his son used standard saddles, and he did not want to be seen using one. They would be searching out whiskey traders and didn't want to be suspected as Army spies. The guns and other supplies could easily be explained as stolen from dead soldiers. For all the renegade warring that was going on, what sneaking whiskey trader wouldn't believe he and Wolf's Blood had simply taken booty from a couple of soldiers they'd killed themselves?

"Thanks to your fine aim we will enjoy rabbit tonight," Wolf's Blood was telling his father, who turned the animal again. "But I miss Sonora's cooking. I do not know what it is she does to the food, but if I am not careful I will be fat."

Zeke sat down and rolled a cigarette. "I doubt that. You're built like me and my father before me. We aren't made to get fat even if we tried."

Wolf's Blood sobered. "Do you ever think of your white father anymore?" he asked.

Zeke sealed the cigarette and lit it, taking a puff. "Sometimes. I hated him most of my life, until I saw him that time I went back to Tennessee because of the Civil War. He was a stooped old man, and he begged me to forgive him for what I'd suffered in Tennessee—for taking me from my Cheyenne mother when I was so small. But I wasn't ready to forgive him, Wolf's Blood, even then." He sighed and puffed the cigarette again, watching the rabbit cook. "He was shot down before I'd had a chance to forgive him, and I knew then what a terrible thing it is to let a parent die without giving them any love. I could see in his dying eyes he really was sorry about my younger years in Tennessee. I finally allowed myself to realize I really did love him, and I told him so. But he died seconds later, so it wasn't much consolation for me."

He smoked quietly and Wolf's Blood studied his father. He would never let his own father die without knowing he loved him. That was why he had come home.

"I will be there, Father," he said quietly, his throat suddenly hurting. "When you die I will be with you. I know that I will. A dream has told me so."

Zeke's dark eyes met his sons over the firelight. "Then I will die happy."

Wolf's Blood looked away, pressing his lips together and breathing deeply. "I am not really . . . your first son," he spoke up. "Your first son was killed . . . back in Tennessee. You must wonder what he would have been like, if he had lived."

Zeke turned the rabbit again. "Sure I wonder. But that was

192

practically thirty-five years ago, Wolf's Blood. There isn't much to wonder about anymore, and when I see Timothy again once I walk *Ekutsihimmiyo* in death, I will be glad, just as I will be glad to be with you. You know how special you are, for I have had you all my life, and you have been everything I wanted in a son."

The boy grinned, but his eyes were watery as he faced his father again. "And you are everything a man could want in a father. I am glad we are out here alone, riding free again, even though I miss Sonora."

Zeke finished his cigarette and took the rabbit from the flames. "You are happy with Sonora then, as if I didn't know." He pushed the rabbit off the skewer onto a tin plate and began cutting it down the center to split it with his son.

"She is my life. I desire her the same as the first day I saw her. And I am hoping she is pregnant again. I tried very hard before I left her to plant a seed that will grow, for she wants another child and so do I."

Zeke laughed lightly. "Well, there's certainly a lot of pleasure in the trying, isn't there?" They both laughed and Zeke put half the rabbit onto another plate and handed it to the boy. "I'm glad you found a wife, Wolf's Blood, and glad that she pleases you. A man needs to settle sometime in his life with a good woman, have sons. But it isn't always easy to stay settled. Every once in a while the old urges to be free nip and snap at him with great annoyance. But then he looks at his woman, and she smiles and beckons him to her bed, and he says to hell with freedom. Who needs it?"

They both laughed again and bit into the rabbit, saying nothing for several seconds as they savored the fresh meat.

"You know," Zeke spoke up then, "you could search the whole earth and never find another white woman like Abbie— one who understands every corner of her man's mind."

The boy's chest tightened. "And what will she do when you are gone? You are her life."

Zeke took another small bite and chewed it. "She's still Abigail Trent, the fiesty, stubborn, strong little girl I met twenty-eight years ago. She'll survive, better than she thinks." He bit off another piece, chewing and swallowing. He thought about Anna Gale, the infamous prostitute from Denver. That was an unspoken understanding between himself and Abbie. He had been untrue to his wife only twice in their twenty-eight years, both times with Anna Gale and neither instance out of love, for he lived, ate, and breathed Abigail Trent. Other women had loved him, wanted him, but he loved and wanted only Abbie. In his few moments of weakness, he had succumbed only perhaps because he loved Abbie too much and had wanted to prove to himself he could do without her, for always he wondered at how much better his Abbie's life would have been if she had married her own kind and settled in a civilized place. She had suffered so much just to stay with him, and he had shed many tears over her suffering. But no matter what had ever pulled him away from her, he could not stay away. He could not live without being one with her as often as possible, and he missed her dearly right now. When he returned, they would make good use of the brass bed, that was sure.

He looked at Wolf's Blood again. "Let's not talk about me being gone. I feel good, in spite of the cold nights," he lied. "I promised your mother this was a simple mission from which I fully intend to return. My time has not yet come, Wolf's Blood, and this rabbit is damned good. Let's eat up and get some rest. Tomorrow we'll be in Dodge City—and you'd best do as I say. That's a good place for a young warrior like yourself to get himself hung, so don't let that temper get the better of you. Remember why we're going."

The boy nodded. "I will try. But the soldiers said it is a wild town since the railroad came through. That is where all the cattlemen take their cattle now from Texas, to meet the train going east—the train my wayward brother Jeremy helped build!" he added with bitterness.

"That railroad would have gone through with or without Jeremy," Zeke answered. "Don't blame him too much. Besides, it's the Atchison, Topeka and Santa Fe that passes through Dodge City, not the Kansas-Pacific. Jeremy works for the K.P."

"A railroad is a railroad," Wolf's Blood grumbled. "But it is not for the railroad that I blame him. It is for never coming

194

home to see you and Mother."

Zeke sighed, wondering what his son looked like now, and wondering about LeeAnn, who wrote only occasional letters with no return address. The message was very clear. If he thought she wanted to be found, he'd go and see her. But she evidently did not want him to, apparently not missing them enough to come to Colorado. And he knew with great sadness that he would never see his beautiful LeeAnn again.

"Eat up and get some rest," he told Wolf's Blood. "And remember what I told you about Dodge City."

They rode down the muddy street of Dodge City, amid stares of curiosity and distrust. Dodge City was not a big town yet, not as big as it would get in the next few years. More and more cattlemen ended their trail drives there, and the town was fast becoming one of the only landing points allowed by the state of Kansas since the discovery that most Texas cattle carried a deadly tick that killed local stock. A quarantine line, north and south, had been designated, ordering the cattlemen to keep their herds in the western part of Kansas, where there were fewer farmers. The once-booming cattle towns of Abilene, Ellsworth, and Wichita had suffered from the loss of cattle business. Still, there were enough farmers in the cattle drive areas remaining to suffer severely from crops ruined by herds of cattle and livestock lost because of the Texas tick. Now Dodge City was the stopping-off point for the great herds, and would enjoy its own boom.

Zeke and Wolf's Blood stopped in front of Wright's General Store. There were signs on the building and windows proclaiming that they sold everything from tobacco and groceries to portable houses, clothes, wagons, saddles, and the like. "You ask for it—we have it," one sign read. Zeke tied his horse and pushed his hat back, studying the signs. He looked over at Wolf's Blood, who stood beside him then.

"Well, I need some tobacco. Let's go in and see if theirs is as fine as they brag."

They started inside when a man in a suit came out, stopping to stare at the two big Indians. He looked from them back into the store, then at Zeke again. "Where do you think you're going, Indian?"

Wolf's Blood bristled, and Zeke stood near the man in the suit, looking down at him. "Inside."

"Indians aren't allowed. Get going."

Zeke just grinned, towering over the man. "You going to stop me?"

The man studied them. Zeke was not only mean looking, but wore several weapons. The man looked from him to Wolf's Blood, who had an equally threatening glare. He looked back up at Zeke. "I suppose not. I'd be a fool to try."

Zeke nodded. "You would."

The man frowned. "You don't talk like an Indian."

"Not many Indians grow up in Tennessee."

The man smiled and took a thin cigar from his pocket. "You a breed?"

"What's it to you?"

The man shrugged. "Just wondering. What are you doing in Dodge City?"

"That's my business."

The man nodded. "I suppose it is. My name's Rage. Julius Rage. I own the bank and half the town. If you're here looking for a job, I might be able to use you." He grinned slyly. "A breed has a great advantage in these parts, as I am sure you know."

Zeke's dark eyes narrowed. "In what way?"

The man just chuckled and lit the cigar. "You tell me. You understand the white man—and the Indian. You figure it out. And if you want to make some money, come see me." He walked away from the doorway and a few feet down the boardwalk, turning and looking back at them. "Who's the young one?"

"My son," Zeke replied.

Rage studied them both. "Remember what I said."

A wagon rattled past, its driver turning to stare at Zeke and Wolf's Blood. Wolf's Blood looked at his father with a frown. "What was that all about?"

"I'm not sure," Zeke answered, watching Rage walk away. "But it might be worth looking into."

"But why did he say he could give you a job when he doesn't even know you?"

Zeke turned to look at his son. "Because he knows I'm a half blood, and most half bloods are choice game for jobs that take dirty work because they'll do anything for money—or so Mr. Rage seems to think. We might have struck gold, my son. Mr. Rage is in bad need of some hired help, it seems."

He motioned the boy to go inside, where Wolf's Blood stared in wonder. This was nothing like any supply store at Fort Lyon, nor like living in the Black Hills among Indians. The inside of the store was fascinating, its hardwood floors decked with glass showcases, behind which lay jewelry and perfume. Paintings of pretty women hung on the colorfully papered walls.

Wolf's Blood followed his father up and down aisles of provisions. An assortment of ranch supplies, groceries, blankets, boots, shoes, furniture, potbellied stoves, coffee grinders, and barrels filled with square-cut crackers were on display. Bottles and bottles of "female remedies" lined the shelves, alongside health tonics for all other ailments, stomach bitters, things for pain, cod liver oil, spices, soaps, weighing scales, even amputation kits displaying numerous knives and a saw. There were handsome Stetson hats and men's suits, and a wall full of rifles and handguns. Wolf's Blood stared at a set of lady's long johns and tried to picture a woman's body inside them. More shelves displayed kerosene lamps and tilting water basins, canning jars and flatirons. The young man picked up a piece of cast iron that was shaped like a naked woman, the legs slightly spread. He stared at it and held it out to his father, who grinned.

"That's a bootjack," he told Wolf's Blood.

"A what?"

"They're used to help draw off high leather boots. Since you never wear boots, I guess you wouldn't know what it is."

"But it's shaped like a woman! It even has—"

"I know what it has," Zeke answered, taking it from his hand and putting it back. "They're usually just a piece of iron, but they can make them into any shape they want."

Wolf's Blood looked around the store. "I have never seen anything like this. Are there many such places in the East?"

Zeke walked to a glassed-in counter behind which several brands of tobacco sat. "Everyplace. This is nothing compared to some."

Wolf's Blood stared while Zeke studied the tobacco. A man came over to the counter, watching them warily as though he thought they might try to steal something.

"I don't know how you got in here, Indian, but as long as you're here, what are you after? I'll sell it to you, if your money's good."

"My money's as good as the next man's," Zeke replied coolly. "Give me a couple of pouches of that Durham smoking tobacco."

The man scowled and took out the tobacco. "Anything else?"

Zeke looked around. "How about coffee? You got any of that kind that's already ground? I want some for my wife—a good brand."

The man looked him over, then took in Wolf's Blood, who was still staring. He walked to a shelf behind him and removed a bright red can decorated around the lid with pretty designs. "This is a two-pound can of Mocha & Java Coffee," he told Zeke. "Packaged by Woolson Spice Company out of Ohio—a good brand. The coffee is good, and any squaw would like a pretty can like this to put other things into when the coffee is gone."

Zeke glared at the man. "Give me two of them," he answered, holding the man's eyes in a threatening stare. "My wife is always looking for something to keep hair combs and buttons in. You know how white women are about such things."

The man reddened, and he swallowed. "Yes," he replied, looking Zeke up and down again. This wild-looking Indian was married to a white woman? "I suppose so." He walked over and got a second can. "Now is that all?"

"It will do for now."

Zeke slapped an eagle on the counter. The storekeeper stared at the ten-dollar gold piece in surprise. "Don't worry. I didn't steal it," Zeke told him sarcastically. "And I want my change in gold coins, not those damned worthless paper certificates the

198

banks issue. I prefer the real thing."

After the storekeeper handed him his change, Zeke picked up the coffee and tobacco and walked out, with his son following. Near the doorway was a lifelike wooden Indian, standing nearly six feet tall and painted in many colors, his arms folded and his face sober, a headdress of wooden feathers falling to the floor. Wolf's Blood stared at it, reaching out to touch the wooden face. He turned to his father.

"Is this all there will be of us one day?" he asked somberly.

Zeke met his eyes and held them for a moment, then turned and walked out without replying. Wolf's Blood quickly followed. He suddenly didn't like the store and what it represented.

Zeke shoved the supplies into his parfleche and they rode farther down the street to a saloon. It was already dusk. "We'll camp outside of town by ourselves. I doubt a hotel in these parts would take us in," Zeke told Wolf's Blood. He dismounted and tied his Appaloosa, turning to Wolf's Blood, who also had dismounted and stood near him at the hitching post.

"The best place to find out what is going on is a saloon," Zeke told his son. "It's also a good place to get into trouble, so watch yourself."

They walked through the swinging doors. Several people stared, but none made a move to stop the menacing-looking Indians. Zeke strode up to the bar and ordered whiskey, and the barkeeper eyed him warily as he handed out a bottle and two glasses. "I don't want any drunk Indians in my place," the man warned. Zeke slapped more coins down to pay for the whiskey.

"I'll keep that in mind," he answered. He took the bottle and glasses and walked to a table where three men sat playing cards. "Got room for one more?" he asked. "Like all Indians, I like to gamble."

The men looked from one to the other, eyeing the huge blade on Zeke's belt and an equally big one at the younger man's side. "Indians ain't much trusted around here, mister," one of the men spoke up. "A lot of the railroad people died from Indian raids, and a lot of the settlers in these here parts. Mostly

Kiowa and Cheyenne that done the killing. What might you be?"

Zeke plunked down the bottle. "Cheyenne," he answered curtly, taking a chair. "At least half of me."

One man jumped when the bottle hit the table, and no one tried to stop him from sitting. Half-breeds were more dangerous than full-blooded Indians—or so they'd always heard. Zeke pulled out several coins and set them in front of him.

"Money's the same, whether it comes from an Indian, a white man, or a skunk," he told them. "Deal the cards." He motioned to Wolf's Blood. "The boy here will watch."

Wolf's Blood pulled up a chair beside his father, turning it backward and straddling it, putting his arms across the back and resting his chin on them to watch and listen. One of the men dealt the cards and Zeke poured shots of whiskey for himself and for his son. For the next hour they played, Zeke winning several hands but mostly staying even. He watched the men carefully, his dark eyes determining which ones might know something about running whiskey to Indians. The men in turn stole glances at the buckskin-clad Indians, their long black hair combed out loose except for a thick braid Wolf's Blood wore down his back, Zeke wearing one at the side. Both looked hard and mean but spoke good English. Wolf's Blood sported a streak of red paint under each eye.

"How come you ain't down in Oklahoma with your red-skinned brothers?" one of them asked.

Zeke leaned back, lighting a cigarette he had just rolled and giving the man a hard look. "I don't think you've even told me your name yet," he answered.

"Dole. Frank Dole."

"I am called Lone Eagle, and this is my son, Wolf's Blood. And neither of us has a taste for the stinking reservation life, sitting around like women while white men hand us our food. If a white man hands me anything, it will be money—for whatever it is he wants me to do. As Julius Rage puts it, a half-breed enjoys great advantages in these parts."

Dole looked slyly at the others, and Zeke suspected he knew something the others did not. The man's eyes were not honest;

they were blue but too pale. He sported a couple day's growth of beard and an unclean shirt, seemingly caring little for his appearance, which in Zeke's eyes meant a man who also cared little for anything else, including how he earned his money and who he associated with. Dole met Zeke's dark eyes.

"You know Rage?"

"I've met him," Zeke replied, wanting the man to think he knew the banker better than he really did.

"You . . . do business with him, do you?"

Zeke puffed his cigarette. "Just considering it at the moment."

"You do business with Julius Rage, it will be something illegal," one of the others spoke up with contempt. "Everybody in town knows half that money in his bank is got by illicit means. Trouble is, most can't pinpoint how—and most don't have the means to stop him even if they wanted to."

Dole did not reply, and the cards were dealt again. Zeke smoked quietly and Wolf's Blood shifted uncomfortably. He didn't like the smoky room and the smell of white men.

A train huffed to a stop close by, and they could hear steam hissing and a bell clanging. Zeke drank a little more whiskey, being careful not to go overboard. He did not allow Wolf's Blood to have anymore, afraid that too much whiskey would make the young man's temper flare. No one mentioned Julius Rage again. Several minutes later a group of men came inside, three of them in suits, the other three wearing plain cotton clothing but carrying rifles and wearing revolvers on gunbelts at their waists.

"We just came in on Number 409 of the Atchison, Topeka and Santa Fe!" one of them announced. "And we're here to celebrate the killing of ten bastard Indian bucks who tried to attack the train!"

The place had nearly filled up by then. Cheers went up and glasses were raised, and Zeke cast a warning look to Wolf's Blood, whose face darkened angrily. One very well-dressed railroad man looked familiar. He wore a gray pin-striped suit and tall black leather boots. A fine Stetson hat decorated his head, and he held up a rifle, his hazel eyes dancing.

"I got one myself, right in the brisket!" he told them with a

201

laugh. "Haven't shot an Indian in a long . . ." He stopped short, staring at Zeke and Wolf's Blood, his face draining of all color. Zeke stared back at Jeremy Monroe. ". . . time," Jeremy finished. His throat tightened. He could hardly believe what he was seeing. Could it truly be his father—in Dodge City? And if it was, the younger man beside him had to be his own brother, Wolf's Blood! His father glared at him. Jeremy lowered his rifle, devastated that he had stood there bragging about killing Indians, embarrassed that his own father was in the room. He wanted to go and greet the man, but he could not admit to his friends that he was part Indian. How could he turn around now and tell them his own father was sitting in the room—an Indian!

His breath suddenly would not come and he put a hand to his chest, tearing his eyes from his father.

"You sick, Monroe?" someone asked.

"Yeah. He just realized he killed an Indian. He's been around civilization too long!" one of the other men joked. "The sight of blood finally got to him. You'd better go back to your fancy office in Denver, Monroe."

Jeremy half stumbled blindly out of the saloon, as the others watched curiously. Wolf's Blood was hot with anger, realizing himself who the man was. He started to rise, but Zeke grabbed his arm. "You can't go after a man just because he killed a couple of Indians," he told the boy, trying to tell him with his eyes not to let on that the railroad man was his brother. The first thing they had to do was keep their identity hidden. He had told Wolf's Blood so over and over, warning him it would be important to stay calm. He could feel the boy trembling, and Zeke himself was overwhelmed. This was the first time he'd seen Jeremy since the boy left Julesberg four years before. But his heart was shattered at the fact that Jeremy had stood and bragged about killing an Indian.

"I'm folding for the night," he told the others at the table, anxious to get Wolf's Blood out of the saloon and see if they could find Jeremy. He threw in his cards and picked up his money. "You men are welcome to the rest of my whiskey."

"Thanks, breed," Dole answered. He watched the Indian who called himself Lone Eagle. He would have to talk to Julius

Rage about the man.

Wolf's Blood gladly followed Zeke through the doors and into the refreshing night air. They both breathed deeply and started to untie their horses. "We've got to find him," Zeke was saying.

"Father!" the voice came then, so softly Zeke could hardly detect it. He turned to see Jeremy standing at the corner of the building, looking nervous, as though afraid someone would see him talking to an Indian. Zeke wanted to walk over and plant a fist in the young man's face, but this was his son, and this just might be the last time he ever saw him. Wolf's Blood stormed past him however, his fists clenched.

"Traitor!" the boy growled, ready to pound his brother into the ground. Jeremy ducked around the corner into an alley, and Zeke charged after Wolf's Blood, grabbing him just before he reached his brother. Jeremy backed up as Zeke struggled with Wolf's Blood, no easy feat since the boy was as big as his father and twenty-six years younger.

"He's your brother!" Zeke growled, trying to keep his voice down and not attract attention. "And we can't afford to get into trouble, Wolf's Blood!"

The boy strained to get away. "He's no brother of mine! Not anymore!" he hissed.

"Goddamn it, Wolf's Blood, calm down!" Zeke ordered. "Don't you understand how important it is for me to talk to him? Think about it! I might not see him again—ever!"

Wolf's Blood's breathing was heavy, but he relaxed some. It was doubtful that he could get away from his father, but even if he could, he didn't care to hurt the man trying. Zeke cautiously released the boy.

"And think of your mother," he added. "How would she feel if she knew her sons fought and one hurt or killed the other! She could never live with that!"

"I . . . I'm sorry, Father!" Jeremy spoke up from the shadows. "My God, I'm sorry! I never dreamed I'd find you here!"

"And what if you had!" Wolf's Blood growled. "Would you pretend you do not deny you are part Indian? And would you still have looked away, embarrassed that you are related to us?"

"I . . ." Jeremy swallowed, shaking violently. "Honest to God, I'm happy to see you—both of you. I'm just . . . so surprised! What the hell are you doing in Dodge City?"

"I'm not so sure I can trust you enough anymore to tell you," Zeke answered the young man. "You're better off not knowing. What's the difference? The real question is, why haven't you come home or bothered to find out how your mother is, your sisters and brothers?"

Jeremy sighed, straightening his expensive suit. He stepped closer, his face dimly lit from the moon and from a lamp in the street. "I . . . I have no excuse, Father. I guess I thought . . . thought you wouldn't care. You never cared that much about me, anyway."

Zeke frowned. "Never cared! How could you think such a thing, especially of your mother!"

Jeremy breathed deeply. "Look at you and Wolf's Blood— two of a kind. You and I were never two of a kind, Father. Coming home would have been too hard. Once I got away, I knew what I wanted, and I'm getting it. I'm a manager now and have a fine office in Denver. I'll be getting married soon to a doctor's daughter. I just . . . my life on the ranch . . . my kinship with the Cheyenne . . . that's all behind me. My future wife doesn't even know I'm part Indian." He met his father's eyes squarely. "I'm sorry, Father. I know that hurts you, but that's the way it is. It doesn't mean that I don't think about you—and mother. I think of you all the time."

"I'll bet!" Wolf's Blood scowled. "I have killed white men just like you! What kind of a man are you, turning on your own blood! Your own kin! Our father is dying, and you—"

"Shut up, Wolf's Blood!" Zeke barked.

"Why! He should know. I hope he dies of pure guilt!"

Jeremy stared at his father. The possibility of the man dying had never entered his mind. His father was not a man that anyone could picture dead. "What is he talking about?" he asked the man.

Zeke sighed, giving Wolf's Blood a scowl before answering Jeremy. "It makes little difference at this particular time, Jeremy. I have a disease that can cripple a man, but nothing can be done about it, and I'm fine for now," he lied. "You apparently have a fine life in Denver now. My problem is no reason for you to change any of that."

"Why should he anyway?" Wolf's Blood sneered. "It is too late to change anything! To come back now would mean nothing, and his heart would not be in it! Better he stays away than to come back just as a token—just to ease his own stinking conscience!"

Jeremy removed the Stetson hat and ran a hand through his hair. "I'm sorry, Father, that you're sick. You . . . look well enough."

"It comes and goes—more here than gone of late." He studied his son's eyes, always rather cool, hard to read. "I think I can trust you enough to tell you we're here on Army business. We do some scouting for the Army, as long as it has nothing to do with hunting down Indians to kill them. I want the extra money—to set aside for your mother after I'm gone. Morgan pretty much runs the ranch for me now. At any rate, we don't want anyone here in Dodge City to know our white name, or that we're scouts. We're here to roust up some illegal whiskey traders."

Jeremy nodded. "I see." He forced a nervous smile. "Well, pity the whiskey dealers once you two get hold of them." Wolf's Blood just scowled more, and Jeremy searched desperately for something to say. "The last time I wrote you wrote back saying Margaret had a son," he said hastily. "Has she had any more?"

"Another son—born in '71. Your brother here is married, too—to an Apache girl. They have a son, Kicking Boy."

Jeremy met his brother's eyes. Wolf's Blood still glared at him as though he'd like to choke him. Jeremy had always been afraid of his warrior brother, but also in awe of him. "I'm . . . glad for you, Wolf's Blood—truly." He took a deep breath. "I don't think you ever knew how much I envied you—how much I wished I could be like you. But it just wasn't in me, Wolf's Blood. I wanted it to be—I tried to make it be there. But I had to face the fact that it wasn't, and I had to go where my own heart took me—just like you did."

"I do not care what you do with your life, my brother! But

you deserted the family!"

"And you did not?" Jeremy shot back. "You went north to live with Swift Arrow! You do not call that deserting? I stayed and helped work the ranch after you left."

"Only because you were too young to do otherwise!" Wolf's Blood shot back. "I intended to come back one day, and I have always been proud to be Indian! You intended to never come back—to never see any of your family again! And you deny your Indian blood! You even brag about shooting Indians! You are a traitor to our father! I could love you as a brother if not for that!"

Jeremy's eyes teared and he ran a hand nervously through his hair again. He looked at his father. "Don't worry about telling me you're here for the Army. It's none of my business what your actual mission is, and I won't tell anyone."

"You won't tell because you won't even admit to anyone that you know us!" Wolf's Blood growled.

Jeremy sighed, keeping his eyes on his father. "I'll be leaving on a morning train for Denver, so I'll be out of the way. How is Ellen?"

"She's fine," Zeke answered impatiently. "Look, Jeremy, do you know anything about LeeAnn? Her letters are rare now. They come from a post office box in Washington, D.C. It's obvious she also is turning her back on her past—and her family. But I worry about her nonetheless, just as I have worried about you."

Jeremy frowned. "You have?"

"Of course I have. I'm your father, whether you like that or not."

Jeremy rubbed at his eyes. His head ached fiercely. He wanted to weep, but could not. Why was his heart so cold? "I don't hear from LeeAnn anymore. The last I knew she was still in school in New York."

"In her last letter to us she was working in a law office in Washington and getting more schooling—thinking about teaching. Abbie misses her very much."

Jeremy met his eyes again, and a tear finally slipped down his cheek. "How is my mother?"

"She's well, but she misses you."

Their eyes held and the boy swallowed. "I . . . look, if you weren't on this . . . this mission of sorts, for the Army, I'd go back in that saloon with you, and I'd tell everybody who you are. I would, Father, honest. But apparently it's better that no one knows. I have a special car of my own on the train where I'll be sleeping tonight. So I guess I . . . I won't see you after tonight. But I promise to come to the ranch and see everyone—maybe next summer. I'll bring my wife so mother can meet her."

Zeke shook his head. "No. You won't. You don't want to tell your wife where you came from. Don't say things just to be saying them, Jeremy. I don't care that you're ashamed of your Indian blood. But you've hurt your mother, and she's the finest woman in Colorado. To not see her again—to not want your wife to meet her—that's what hurts the most."

Jeremy searched his eyes. "How can I explain it, Father? I do love you—all of you. But I just can't . . . can't go back." His voice broke and he hung his head. "I'm sorry. So damned sorry."

"We're all sorry . . . for a lot of things, Jeremy," Zeke told him, his own voice husky with emotion. "Even LeeAnn has a reason for what she's done. She has the memory of that Comanche raid. But you have nothing but good memories. I was never cruel to you, and your mother was good to you, taught you well—maybe too well. Those books went to your head. Wolf's Blood and I will go now. We're camping outside of town. So I guess this is good-bye—again—perhaps for the last time."

Jeremy met his eyes again. "Then please . . . let me embrace you. Please, Father."

He looked like a little boy, suddenly wanting to please his father but not knowing how. Zeke stepped closer. "Pleasing me was really a very simple thing, Jeremy. You let it be difficult. You made it into something that wasn't there at all. If you thought I expected more of you than what I got, you were wrong. We were just different, and that's the hell of it."

He embraced the boy, and Jeremy wept against the man's chest for several minutes, then pulled away. He looked at Wolf's Blood, who put out his hand in a cool expression of brotherhood, though the feeling was not there.

"You are still my brother," he told Jeremy. "Nothing you do can ever erase that. I will not think of you as I think of you now. I will think of the early days—when we were young and played together and I tried to teach you the warrior ways. You never wanted to learn. You used to make me sit down and you would read to me until I grew too restless and ran off."

Jeremy smiled through tears. "Things haven't really changed so much then, have they?" he answered. "Take care, Wolf's Blood. Don't go getting yourself in trouble."

He glanced at his father once more and tried to smile. "Good-bye," he said in a near whisper. "God be with you." The boy dashed past his father then, hurrying out into the street, disappearing toward the train station.

Wolf's Blood touched his father's arm. The man was trembling. "Are you all right, Father?" he asked.

Zeke breathed deeply. "Go back in that saloon and get us another bottle of whiskey," he said in a choked voice. "I intend to get very drunk tonight." Tears ran down his cheeks. "And don't tell your mother we've seen him."

Chapter Twelve

Zeke poured himself a cup of strong coffee, rising as he heard the big black engine, Number 409, come closer to where they were camped outside of town. The train began to gather speed as it continued on, smoke pouring from a wide stack and trailing nearly the entire length of the wooden cars that carried more people westward. Blank faces peered out the window at the two camped Indians, some pointing.

Wolf's Blood watched his father closely. Zeke had drunk a great deal of whiskey the night before, and he had wept over Jeremy and LeeAnn. Wolf's Blood wondered if he even remembered. It was a private thing. He would not mention it. And he wondered if his father had ever been really happy after his tortured boyhood in Tennessee. The only time the man seemed really content was when he was with Abbie. She seemed to bring a joy and peace to his life that no one else could bring him, not even Wolf's Blood; and although the boy had little use for most white women, he was glad his father had found his white mother all those years ago and made her his wife.

Zeke watched the train until the last car was well out of sight, wondering if Jeremy had looked out and seen them. It was difficult to tell. The nameless faces had whizzed by too quickly to know if one of them could have been his son. He sipped the coffee and turned to Wolf's Blood with tired, cold eyes.

"I think it's time to pay Mister Julius Rage a visit," he told the boy. "Stir up some breakfast, and we'll pack up our gear and go back into town."

The boy nodded. "Are you all right, Father?"

Zeke swallowed the rest of the coffee. "There comes a time in a man's life, Wolf's Blood, when there is nothing left that can hurt him anymore. He takes just so much, and then he gets calloused."

"Can I do anything?"

Zeke smiled sadly. "You're doing enough just be being here. And I don't want to talk about it anymore. Let's get going."

They quickly ate an almost silent breakfast. Wolf's Blood's heart hurt so badly for his father that he wanted to cry himself. But there was nothing that could be done, and this morning Zeke was brooding and quiet—hardening himself against the hurt of the night before. Perhaps that was good. At least he would be meaner and more alert for whatever lay ahead of them. They were soon packed and headed back to Dodge City. Wolf's Blood noticed his father grimace slightly when he mounted up, and he wore the extra warmth of a fleece-lined buckskin jacket. It was a crispy cool morning, but Wolf's Blood wore only his buckskin shirt, which Zeke would normally have done. The man was apparently in pain again, hoping the extra warmth would penetrate his bones and make him feel better. What worried Wolf's Blood was that his father's blood had to still be full of whiskey, so the pain should be dulled. If he hurt now, in spite of a night of drinking, how much must he hurt when he was sober? Each winter had been worse, this past one no different. He wondered how many winters he had left with his father.

They approached the bank building and dismounted, tying the horses and going inside, where a teller glanced up at them, his eyes widening. The man dropped a pen and swallowed, looking at them as though he thought they might be there to rob him.

"I'm looking for Julius Rage," Zeke told the man.

The teller removed a pair of spectacles. "I'll . . . get him. Wait right there, please." He hurried away and walked through a door into another room. They could hear muffled voices, and shortly after the teller returned, leaving the door open. He looked Zeke and Wolf's Blood over as though he were seeing a grizzly. "You can go in," he said nervously, hurrying back to his post behind the barred counter. Zeke's dark eyes followed the little man with contempt.

Father and son entered Rage's office, where the man stood behind a desk waiting for them. He put out his hand, but Zeke made no attempt to take it. "You mentioned yesterday you might have a good-paying job for a breed," he said coldly.

Rage's eyes glittered with anger that he'd been snubbed by an Indian, but he kept his false smile, putting his hand in a vest pocket. He nodded to Wolf's Blood. "Close the door, young man." He met Zeke's eyes again. "Unless my life is in danger."

Zeke stared back at him, looking more menacing today because of bloodshot eyes from a drinking, sleepless night. "It isn't—at the moment," he answered.

Wolf's Blood closed the door and Rage offered both of them a chair, sitting down himself. The man reminded Zeke of Winston Garvey. He didn't like him, but he'd listen. If working for this man meant possibly exposing him and routing out illegal whiskey trading, he'd play along. Rage took out a cigar, then handed the box to Zeke and Wolf's Blood.

"No thanks," Zeke told him. "I prefer cigarettes." He pulled out a tobacco pouch and began rolling one. "I was going to wait a couple of days, but the boy here is anxious to get back down to Texas. He's got a favorite whore down there that he doesn't like to be away from for long. You know how Indians like Mexican women."

Rage grinned. "I've shared my bed with a few myself. A man has to be in good shape to handle that kind."

Zeke smiled and lit his cigarette, and Wolf's Blood listened cautiously, realizing he must go along with anything his father said. "At any rate, we have a place where we hole up when we need to, where the women are free and the food is good. And when we run out of money, we venture out to see how we can make more. Beats reservation life."

Rage smirked. "I suppose it does. And might I ask just how you do make your money?"

Zeke grinned a little himself. "A man could get himself hung giving out that kind of information to a complete stranger.

Why don't you tell me what it is you have in mind?"

"Ah, but you are also a complete stranger."

"But you're white. It isn't too likely a half-breed is going to get a prominent white man in trouble. Wouldn't do me much good to go spouting off about your questionable activities when you'd just deny it, now would it?"

Rage grinned. "You're a wise man. The least you can do is tell me your name."

Zeke took a deep drag on the cigarette. "I am Lone Eagle. I don't use my white name because I don't care for my white blood. My son is Wolf's Blood."

Rage studied them closely. Two men who could handle themselves, that was certain. And the one called Lone Eagle seemed intelligent enough—maybe too intelligent. "Cheyenne?" he asked.

Zeke nodded. "And don't tell me you don't already know who we are and what we are. I'm sure your man Frank Dole has already filled you in."

Rage brushed at his fine silk suit. He was a medium-built, soft-looking man, with slick black hair and hands that looked as though he had never worked hard. He arched his eyebrows. "You are not only wise, but perceptive." Rage shifted in his chair, feeling uneasy at the way Wolf's Blood stared at him, as though he would take great joy in slowly moving a knife through his body and watching the blood trickle out. He swallowed and tried not to look at the boy, but the father's eyes didn't make him feel much better. They were piercing and discerning. Rage set his cigar in an ashtray and leaned back. "Tell me, Lone Eagle, you ever run whiskey?"

Zeke grinned. "Is there an easier way to make money?"

Rage laughed lightly. "Probably not—at least not for a man who can work with whites and Indians both." He rubbed at his chin. "You don't mind selling sugared whiskey to your kin on the reservations?"

"Whatever makes them happy. If the poor bastards have nothing better to do anymore than get drunk, who am I to stop them? And if they're foolish enough to trade valuable robes and reservation supplies for a drunken orgy, who cares? The Indians don't give a damn about what's valuable and what

212

isn't. Money means nothing to them. I've seen Indians raid supply trains and throw paper money into the wind. The only thing I care about is that I get paid well and get a case of whiskey for myself—the good stuff, not the watered down, gut-wrenching kind. Like any other Indian, I like my whiskey too, but I'm most particular about my brand and I don't drink it until I'm through with a job."

"You look like you had your share last night."

Zeke's eyes darkened. "I am also not working for anyone—yet."

Rage nodded. He moved his eyes over the man called Lone Eagle—a lean handsome man with enough scars to verify he could fight when necessary. Rage's eyes rested on the wicked-looking knife for a moment. "I take it you have no trouble killing a man when it's called for?"

Zeke grinned. "Mister, I lost count a long time ago. Man or woman—makes no difference if they're in my way. It's the same for the boy here."

Rage grinned more. He liked these two. "Can you . . . uh . . . give me some names—people you've worked for before me?"

Zeke puffed the cigarette from the corner of his mouth and shook his head. "I don't give out names—same as I'd not give out yours if somebody asked me. A man doesn't get to be my age when he runs around giving out names. Let's just say I've done a lot worse things than run whiskey."

Rage leaned forward. "The trouble with half-breeds is they can turn on a man real easy. I'd hate to say what happens to men who turn on me, Lone Eagle. In fact, that's why I'm hiring someone new. My last man tried to go running to the authorities. He regretted that, and so will you if you try to do the same."

Zeke's eyes narrowed, and he calmly removed the stub of a cigarette, putting it out. He stood up then, and Rage's chest tightened when the tall Indian leaned over the desk, suddenly whipping out the big knife and stabbing it into a large desk blotter, holding it there, his big fist wrapped around the buffalo jawbone handle.

"It works both ways, mister," he hissed. "You double-cross

213

me, or try to have me killed or not pay me, and every inch of your skin will greet the sun—inside out. When I say I'll do a job, I do it and get out."

Rage tried to act unruffled, but his face was red and covered with perspiration. He swallowed hard. "All right," he said in a husky voice. "It's a deal. We each know where the other stands. The job is yours for as long as you want to risk it. You know the backcountry between here and Oklahoma, I take it?"

Zeke straightened, jerking out the knife. "Of course I know it."

"The problem is getting the whiskey to the Indians and getting the robes and other supplies from them without being detected by the damned agents or soldiers. They're really cracking down on the whiskey traders and gunrunners."

"I can get through in places the Army never heard of."

"I hope you're right. I can get a ten to twenty-dollar robe for a few cents worth of whiskey. The whiskey comes from a warehouse in St. Louis. Comes down by the Missouri River to Kansas City—gets put on the A,T & SF and railroaded to this point, where it's unloaded. From here it goes out in wagons, under sacks of potatoes, taken by men like you. You exchange it for robes, skins, and supplies issued by the government to the reservation Indians. You bring the supplies back here, and they get shipped back to St. Louis, under various fake freighting bills. They go back to the same man who supplies the whiskey. I get the profit from the robes, he gets to resell the same government issue over and over, seldom having to order more. So he makes a tidy profit on government reservation supplies, while I make a tidy profit on the robes, and we split the expenses of shipping and paying men like you."

Zeke grinned, shoving his knife back into its sheath. "The wonders of the white man's ingenuity at getting rich never cease to amaze me," he told Rage.

Rage stood up then. "And the things men like you will do for money never cease to amaze me. Let me guess. You've even dealt in the capturing and selling of white women into Mexico. Am I right?"

Zeke grinned more. "A few never made it to their new owners, depending on how pretty they were."

214

Rage chuckled. "Just as I thought." He looked Zeke over again, a powerful man with such a mean appearance that a woman just might end up wanting to see if she could please him. "Not all of them objected, I'll guess."

Zeke tossed some of the long, loose hair behind his back. "Not many. Now how much do we get for this?"

"Five hundred dollars for every load delivered and returned."

"Each?"

"No. Both of you together."

Zeke shook his head. "Five hundred each or the deal is off."

Rage sighed. "Can't do it."

Zeke shrugged and turned. "Whatever." He looked at Wolf's Blood. "Let's go find a better source of income," he told the boy, who also rose.

"Wait!" Rage spoke up, his face reddening again with repressed anger. "Eight hundred—four hundred each. I'll give you four hundred right now, and the other four hundred when you return with the goods to be shipped back to St. Louis. You handle three or four loads right, and I'll up it to a thousand."

Zeke turned to face him. "Sounds fair. Who's the man in St. Louis? How do I know when a shipment is coming in?"

"No names, remember? And there'll be a shipment in two days from now. I have a spread east of town. The whiskey wagons are kept in a barn there. It's a big frame house, painted blue. Can't be missed in country like this. You be there in two days and bring the wagons into Dodge City. The whiskey will arrive by train, packed into crates and cushioned with straw. The crates are completely enclosed and say 'Potatoes, U.S. Government Issue.' You load them into the wagons as though they're supplies for the reservation. Several sacks of potatoes will be thrown on top. If you are stopped, you say they're extra bags that weren't crated. There hasn't been an agent or soldier yet who didn't believe that there was nothing but potatoes in the entire wagon. Sometimes the crates will be marked as something else—flour, beans, whatever. But we still carry the sacks of potatoes to make it look like just a wagon full of food. Usually a few boxes on the top near the end of the wagon really will have food, so when the soldiers open them to inspect them, they can see there really are government rations."

Zeke rolled another cigarette. "Who do I meet once I get to the reservation?"

"Peter Holbrook. He's a government man—an assistant to the new agent at Camp Supply, John Miles. He'll tell you where to meet the Indians who want to trade, and it's usually done after dark."

Zeke lit the cigarette. "Most illegal things are done after dark, aren't they? Kind of like when you sneak around enjoying another man's wife."

Rage laughed and put out his hand again, but Zeke still refused to shake it. "Sorry, Mr. Rage. Shaking hands signifies friendship. I don't make friends with the men I deal with. A man tends to trust his friends too much. We're strictly business."

Rage pulled back his hand. "You're a cautious man, Lone Eagle."

"That's why I'm still alive," Zeke answered with a nod. "I'll see you in a couple of days." He turned and left without another word.

For three months Zeke and Wolf's Blood made the deliveries. Each time it tore at their hearts to watch the Cheyenne and other tribes eagerly trade valuable goods and government issue for the cheap whiskey. There were many of them Zeke knew, but none of them even seemed to blame him for what he was doing, actually thanking their "old friend" for bringing the whiskey. Some wondered why he was doing it, for their friend and kin Lone Eagle once preached against the firewater, warning that it would turn them into weak women. But they supposed he was doing the only thing left for him to do, just as they were doing. Why should they blame him? After all, wasn't he doing them a favor? A few of them even offered him their wives and daughters for the whiskey, when they had nothing left to trade. He refused, saying only that he was required to return with actual goods and he could not accept physical services for the drink. But inside he was enraged, wanting to strangle the once proud men who would stoop so low as to trade their women for the firewater. It sickened and depressed him, for he realized how unhappy these warriors were. They were so desperate to feel good, even if just for one or two nights a week, that they would do anything to get their hands on the magic water. There was nothing else now for them to do. They had lost their pride and their fighting spirit. Only a few hung on, holding back and not going to meet the whiskey wagons. Still, even those few would not tell the Army or the primary agent how they got the whiskey and what secret routes the traders took to get to the reservation. That would be like telling on their own people.

Zeke and Wolf's Blood kept up the job long enough to prove to Julius Rage that they were trustworthy. It was not until May that Zeke made his first contact with Lieutenant-Colonel Petersen. After leaving with a shipment from Dodge City and getting into backcountry, they pulled the wagons into a remote canyon. Zeke held up while Wolf's Blood rode hard for Fort Lyon, a five-day trip even for a man riding alone. Their own mounts were always taken along as extras in case of trouble, tied to the wagons. In three days Zeke would head out again, tying one team of horses to the back of his own wagon and driving both on south. It would not be an easy feat, but somehow they had to make contact with Lieutenant-Colonel Petersen. On the last trip south Zeke had managed to fully win over the trust and friendship of Peter Holbrook, the assistant agent who helped with the whiskey trading. He got Holbrook drunk and even talked him into laughingly revealing who the source of whiskey was in St. Louis. Holbrook had been so drunk that the next day he didn't even remember what he had said to Zeke, but trusted him so well by then that he didn't bother worrying about it.

Now Wolf's Blood would ride hard to Fort Lyon to get the news to Petersen, while Zeke took his time heading south, not wanting to lose too many days and arouse suspicion. Wolf's Blood would ride fast to catch up so that the two of them would ride into the reservation together as they always did, each driving a wagon.

Zeke prayed his son would have no problems. The secret to stopping a great deal of illegal whiskey was to get the man in St.

Louis, not the middle men like Julius Rage. He knew it was most likely this was not the only whiskey the man in St. Louis supplied. Surely there were other runs being made, by other men. The answer was to kill the source, and Zeke Monroe knew who that source was—Thomas West, one of the wealthiest men in St. Louis, owner of West Enterprises, a vast supply warehouse for western outlets, the army, and Indian reservations. To stop Thomas West would be a huge step forward in cleaning up reservation cheating and illegal trading. Zeke knew it would not stop it all together. There were too many white men ready to get in on the lucrative business of dealing with the government. But it would help, nonetheless.

Now if Wolf's Blood could get to Petersen with the name, the lieutenant-colonel would take care of planting a man in West Enterprises, who would follow the next shipment bound for Camp Supply to Dodge City and watch it being loaded onto Zeke's wagons, waiting for Zeke to return with supposedly empty crates. As soon as the crates were taken to Julius Rage's barn, they would be inspected and found to contain buffalo robes and government supplies already issued once to the reservation but traded back for whiskey. Normally the illegally traded goods were packed into different boxes marked "U. S. Government" and shipped by rail back to St. Louis to be stored in a warehouse, designated for "Thomas Supplies," a nonexistent company. They were then picked up from the warehouse by West Enterprises, returned to West Enterprises, and resold to the government, while the robes were sold at a great profit to tent and clothing suppliers.

The operation was intricate, and no other drivers for Julius Rage had ever bothered to try to figure it out, or cared. Only one man had put it together, but his plan had been to try to blackmail Rage and West. Zeke was not about to be that foolish. He only wanted to get his information to Petersen and have it over with. He could only hope it wouldn't take much longer. He missed Abbie desperately, longing only to be in her arms again and be back on the ranch. His pay for this job would be very good—and badly needed. But he was playing a dangerous game, and he missed his family. There had been many nights that he had thought again about Jeremy, with a heavy heart. He would simply have to accept his fourth child and second son for what he was, and realize he would probably never see him again.

After a lonely three days of waiting in the canyon, he set out for Camp Supply, praying Wolf's Blood would show up before he reached the Oklahoma reservation.

Abbie opened the note Sergeant Daniels brought her from Lieutenant-Colonel Petersen.

"I saw your son, ma'am," he told her. Her eyes lit up, and Sonora gasped.

"Wolf's Blood! Is he all right? Why did he not come with you?" the young woman asked, her eyes tearing.

Daniels removed his hat. "He couldn't, Sonora," he answered. "I can't say what him and his pa are up to. I can only tell you their job should be finished soon—maybe in another month or so, if all goes well."

Abbie frowned. "Are they in danger?"

Daniels sighed. "Not too much, I don't think. I don't know all the details myself, ma'am. Only Petersen knows for sure. Wolf's Blood had me write that note for him—said he's not too good at writing. But he wanted to get it to you. I said I could just tell you, but he wanted it on paper—figured it would be something you could keep, I guess."

Abbie smiled through tears and opened the note.

We are fine. Father had bad pains in March, but is much better again. Do not worry. We will be home by the Moon of the Red Cherries. Miss the ranch and the whole family. Especially miss my Sonora and Kicking Boy, and Father is restless in the night missing you, my Mother.

Abbie blushed, and Daniels glanced at Ellen, who also blushed and looked down. He had called on her three times, whenever he could get away from Fort Lyon. They enjoyed each other's company, and Daniels was determined that the next time he was allowed to take her alone for a walk, he would be brave and steal a kiss.

219

We will make very good money, and this will be good for the ranch, but I think Father will wait a while before doing this again. He misses home too much, and so do I. Our love is with you, and the summer moons will find us all together again.

Abbie put down the note. "That's all there is," she told Sonora. Sonora put a hand to her stomach. She was pregnant again, although not showing yet. She would not say anything in front of Daniels and had asked the others not to tell him. She did not want to risk Wolf's Blood finding out. The news might make him in too much of a hurry to return. Perhaps he would do something careless. How she longed to see the happy look on his face when she told him!

"Thank you for letting us know you've seen Wolf's Blood," Abbie told Daniels. "Zeke wasn't with him?" she asked hopefully.

"No, ma'am. Wolf's Blood couldn't tell me where he was, and he came and left the same day, saying he had to ride hard to meet his father. That's all I know."

Abbie sighed. "I'm worried, Sergeant. Zeke isn't a well man."

Daniels twisted his hat in his hand. "One sure wouldn't know it by looking at him, ma'am. And he's a capable man, that's for sure. He'll be all right. He's got Wolf's Blood to help him."

Abbie folded the letter carefully. "Yes. Thank God for Wolf's Blood. I wish I would hear from Jeremy or LeeAnn so I could give Zeke some kind of news about them when he returns." She rose from the table, looking tired. Abigail Monroe wasn't her usual strong and spirited self when her husband was gone for long periods of time. "If you'll excuse me," she told them, "I'm going outside for a while. I'd like to be alone."

She left without another word, walking several hundred feet behind the cabin to a little grassy spot beside a stream, a special place, hidden by bushes and undergrowth, a place where she and Zeke often went to talk, sometimes even to make love when the weather was warm. It was here she had sat and wept once, sure her husband was dead. But he had come to her there, by the stream. How many times had he gone away and she had worried he would not come back? But he always had. The only difference now was that she knew it would not be long before he really wouldn't come back.

She picked a few purple irises, her favorite flower. It bloomed abundantly in this spot. She sat down beside the stream, the flowers in her hand. "Don't let this be the time," she said aloud, watching the rippling water. "Not yet, Zeke. Please not yet." Her throat hurt with a need to cry, but the tears would not come. She must pray and believe. They were the only two things that had kept her going for twenty-eight years—praying and believing. "I love you, Zeke," she shouted into the wind. Surely he would feel her words in his heart. Surely the Wind Spirit would take them to him and whisper them into his ear.

Chapter Thirteen

Bonnie opened the letter from Joshua. The nineteen-year-old boy was doing well in college now, living with his adoptive grandfather in Virginia but sometimes going into Washington D.C. for lectures and to visit museums and historical sites. He was also busy writing for an Alexandria newspaper. Bonnie sat down, eager to read the letter. With Dan gone so often now trying to keep a very tentative peace and always searching for whiskey traders and gunrunners, she was often alone and missed Joshua painfully.

The letter was full of news about college and about newspaper writing. Then her heart tightened as she read:

I have seen my brother. Of course I did not tell him who I was, so don't worry. He was at a library, giving a special lecture to teachers and the like who were considering going west to pursue their careers. His speech was very fine, until he got to telling about Indians. Mother, he exaggerates so, and his hatred for Indians is very intense. It's sad, because he is doing so much damage, ruining everything Indian sympathizers try to do. I am afraid I found myself unable to refrain from arguing with him on many points, and he became extremely angry. I am afraid, Mother, that I do not like Charles Garvey, even one little bit, even if he is my half brother. I can see in his hateful eyes that you are right. He is very powerful, and he probably would try to quiet me if I told him who I was. But I swear to you that someday I will be prominent and important myself—important enough that he won't dare try to harm me. When that day comes, I will end Charles Garvey's lies about the Indians. I will tell the truth, and I will show him up for what he is and tell him about his half-Indian brother. Someday people will know my name through my newspaper writing, and I will stop people like Charles Garvey.

I saw his new wife. She is very beautiful, with blond hair and eyes as blue as the sky. She wore the latest fashion, of course, and is very gracious and charming, but I also saw a sadness in her eyes and am sure she cannot be happy with a man like Charles Garvey, who although not ugly, mind you, is also not handsome. I think it is because there is a certain evil air about him, a coldness in his dark eyes that unnerves people. If he were a good person with kindness in his eyes, I think he would be more handsome. It is his attitude that detracts from his looks. Why a beautiful, obviously gentle woman like his wife would marry him, I cannot understand.

Bonnie took a deep breath. The thought of Joshua actually coming face-to-face with Charles Garvey—even arguing with him—made her tremble. She prayed he would have sense enough to keep his secret until the time was right.

Zeke and Wolf's Blood headed back north with another load of skins and government supplies. Zeke breathed easier now. Wolf's Blood had made it to Fort Lyon and had given the message to Lieutenant-Colonel Petersen. In return he had learned from Sergeant Daniels that the family all were well, a great relief to Zeke. It wouldn't be long now. Petersen would get word to a contact in St. Louis, who would investigate West Enterprises. The soldiers were now aware of some of the most secret routes, and also that the aide at Camp Supply, Peter Holbrook, was assisting in the illegal trading. He would also be closely watched, for there were other shipments he helped with besides those coming from Julius Rage, most of them also originating with West Enterprises and ending up there. No matter what happened now to Julius Rage, West Enterprises and Peter Holbrook would still be caught and arrested. It was good to know that there were a few things the soldiers were trying to do right, even though it concerned Indians already forced onto a reservation. The whiskey only kept tensions high, and although this plan would eliminate some of the trading, Zeke knew whiskey would still get into the hands of his brothers, who had nothing left besides the white man's firewater to bring excitement and wild freedom to their souls. But he had at least done something to help stop the rotgut drink that was killing his red brothers. The most satisfying part was that he had exposed greedy white men who were making money off government supplies and desperate red men who practically sold their souls for whiskey and guns. The whites had beaten and murdered Indians, stolen their land, forced them onto hated, barren reservations; then turned around and stole from them even more, taking valuable hides in return for killing whiskey, taking advantage of the Indians' ignorance of the white man's greedy trickery.

Zeke smiled. Now an Indian had performed his own trickery on such white men. Zeke Monroe and his son had totally won the confidence of Julius Rage, and by doing so would expose the man for what he really was.

All they needed to do now was deliver this load of goods. He was slightly ahead of schedule, due at the Rage ranch by the eighth of July. Plans were for Sergeant Daniels and a company of men to raid the ranch on the tenth of July, finding the skins and government goods in Rage's barn, all the evidence they needed. By that time Zeke and Wolf's Blood would not be around, and their identity and location would never be given to Rage. Rage would be told the two had been arrested and then killed trying to escape, and that would be the end of it. Zeke wanted no connections between Julius Rage and his own family. Things had gone so well that he and Wolf's Blood had found a couple of days to hole up on the Cimarron River, relaxing, talking about wives and family, and each dreaming

225

his own thoughts of what he would do when he got home. Their mission would be accomplished, and they would have money in their pockets.

Zeke counted his days, arriving on Rage land on the eighth of July as planned. The two big wagons clattered through the gate to Rage's thousands of acres and rattled on for the two-mile trek from the gate to the buildings. The two of them headed for the barn, where Zeke spotted Frank Dole taking a bridle from his horse. The man looked up and waved, and Zeke waved back. Dole hurriedly opened the barn doors for them, and Zeke and Wolf's Blood pulled the wagons inside, their own horses tied to the backs. Dole closed the door while Zeke and Wolf's Blood climbed down.

It was then that Julius Rage stepped out from behind several bales of hay, wielding a rifle at Zeke and Wolf's Blood. Dole latched the barn doors, turning and pointing his six-gun at the two. A man called Huston also stepped forward, pointing an ugly-looking shotgun at father and son.

Zeke and Wolf's Blood stood still, wary, surprised. What had gone wrong?

"Have a good trip, Lone Eagle?" Rage asked the man.

Zeke studied the man coldly, keeping his hands visible, glancing at Wolf's Blood quickly to warn the boy to keep quiet and let him talk. He faced Rage again, as Dole stepped closer, standing behind Zeke and Wolf's Blood.

"Best trip we've had yet," Zeke answered him. "What the hell is this all about, Rage? The goods are on the wagons, like always. I've done nothing wrong."

"Haven't you?" The man shifted nervously. He had the upper hand, but this man called Lone Eagle and his vicious-looking son were men of obvious skill. He could not take any chances. "Why did your boy ride to Fort Lyon this time around, Indian?" the man demanded.

Wolf's Blood looked surprised but kept quiet. Zeke just frowned. "Who says he did?" he asked.

Rage grinned. "Dole saw him—followed him." The man signaled for Dole to take Zeke's and Wolf's Blood's guns from their sides. "You see, Indian, just as you once told me you

226

don't make friends with the men you do business with, neither do I. Nor do I ever fully trust them. You had done a fine job for me, but that meant nothing. So I told Dole to tag alone this time—make sure all you did was go straight south and come right back. But your son there took a little side trip of his own, while you went on south with the wagons. Dole followed him— all the way to Fort Lyon. And I am very interested in hearing your explanation of why he went there."

Zeke lowered his arms carefully, as Dole took his gun and Wolf's Blood's, throwing the weapons into a corner. Their rifles were on the wagons. The only weapons they had were their knives, and for some reason Dole didn't take them. Apparently these white men didn't consider knives a weapon to worry about, not against guns. Zeke grinned inwardly. He needed no gun when he had his knife at his side.

"I don't owe you any explanations for anything," Zeke said coolly. "If you think I'm stupid enough to pass up a good deal like I'm getting here, think again. You think I've betrayed you. Well I haven't. It just so happens there is a little Mexican girl at Fort Lyon that my son gets a need for from time to time. He's young and eager. What handsome young buck his age doesn't need to get rid of his desires once in a while? I can't control something like that."

Rage scowled, eyeing Wolf's Blood. "That true?"

The boy grinned in a bitter sneer. "She is the grateful kind. Sometimes I burn for her so much that if I do not go there I think maybe I will grab the first white woman who comes along and violate her."

Rage chuckled but kept his rifle on them. "And what about the whore down in Texas? I thought that was your woman."

Wolf's Blood eyed him haughtily. "What man keeps just one woman when he is married to none?"

Rage studied them closely, still wary. "What man keeps just one woman, even when he is married?" he replied. The other men laughed, but Zeke and Wolf's Blood just glared at them. Rage sobered, backing up a little. "I think I'll make double sure you're telling the truth. Personally I don't believe you." He motioned to Dole, who had been standing behind Zeke and

227

Wolf's Blood and had quietly picked up a shovel. The man abruptly slammed the shovel into Wolf's Blood's lower back, buckling the boy's knees, then whacked the shovel across the back of his head.

Zeke whirled at the movement, grabbing the shovel and wrenching it from Dole in a fierce rage, yanking the man around in front of him as he tried to cling to the shovel handle. The movement was so fast that Huston panicked and fired the shotgun before waiting for Dole to be free of Zeke. The pellets ripped through Dole, opening up his back. Zeke pushed the man from the shovel toward Rage and Huston, part of his own side catching some of the shotgun pellets, his flesh and a side of his buckskin shirt ripped away. Blood began immediately running from his side as he ducked and rolled toward several bales of hay, crawling as fast as a centipede behind the hay. Rage and Huston immediately moved back behind hay themselves, Rage cursing at Huston for being too quick on the trigger.

"We'd have had him if you'd waited for Dole to let go, you stupid son of a bitch!" the man growled, afraid now for his own life. They had injured Lone Eagle's son, and Rage did not like the look in the father's eyes—the kind of look that told of a man who would kill before he let himself die of whatever wounds he might suffer. Rage's idea had been to lash Wolf's Blood with a bullwhip until his father told the truth. Those plans were foiled now. Both must die, and the buffalo robes and government goods had to be shipped out right away. But first they had to get out of the barn, and Lone Eagle had grabbed up a six-gun as he moved behind the hay bales. Rage had no idea how many bullets were in the gun, but Lone Eagle's ammunition belt had been removed, so he could not reload. The man still wore a knife, but what good was a knife against their guns and rifles?

"Want me to try to sneak out and get more men?" Huston asked.

"Hell no! I don't want the others knowing what's going on or what's in those wagons!" Rage hissed. "And if you try to get out, he'll kill you. Let him make the first move!"

Wolf's Blood lay on his stomach, groaning, everything a blur, his body screaming with pain.

"Come on out, Lone Eagle, or I'll blow your son's brains out!" Rage shouted. "I've got my rifle right on him!"

The only reply was silence. Wolf's Blood lay still, trying to gather his thoughts, trying to remember what had just happened.

"You'll die either way, Rage," Zeke finally answered, his voice calm and determined. On the inside he was exploding with a need for vengeance. His son lay badly injured. He had gotten Wolf's Blood into this and he would not forgive himself if the boy's injuries were irreparable. It mattered little that a great deal of flesh had been blown away from his own ribs and he was bleeding badly. The important thing was to get these men. Zeke and Wolf's Blood had to flee the ranch without either of them being killed. He could only pray that his own loss of blood would not weaken him or make him pass out before the deed was done. But one thing was certain, it had to be done and quickly too.

He let out a war whoop and stood up, running fast across the top of the bales of hay, yelling blood-curdling Indian yelps and firing the six-gun rapidly as he moved. Zeke kept ducking and moving, making himself a difficult target for Rage and Huston, neither of them a good aim and both of them in a panic. They didn't pay any attention to Wolf's Blood for the moment. The boy was surely injured badly enough that they could finish him off later. It was the father who demanded their attention at the moment. Julius Rage knew instinctively that even wounded, Lone Eagle was not a man to deal with lightly. He was a warrior at heart, and now he fought like one, cunning and devilish, using fright as just as strong a weapon as his gun.

The barn was suddenly silent again, and Rage and Huston searched the hay bales above, where they had seen Zeke running and ducking. They heard nothing now, and gripped their rifles nervously, paying no attention to Wolf's Blood at all.

"Where the hell is he?" Huston whispered angrily.

"He's up there—the loft," Rage answered. "And I counted.

He used six bullets. He's got none left, and he's hurt besides. He won't last much longer. Just keep your eyes open."

"I don't like this," Huston fumed. "Why in hell did you have Dole hit the boy? That was stupid!"

"Shut up and listen!" Rage growled.

Something fell to the right side of the loft and Huston fired off three rapid shots at the noise. At the same time a chilling scream came from behind them. In the next moment a big Indian was on top of Julius Rage from behind, knocking the man forward. The rifle fell from Rage's hands. Huston whirled to take aim at Zeke, but a strong arm grabbed him from behind, around the throat. A shining Bowie knife was slammed into his heart. Wolf's Blood moved back and threw the man's body to the floor. Meanwhile Zeke yanked Julius Rage around onto his back, just in time to see Huston falling, his chest ripped open, a wobbly Wolf's Blood standing there with a bloody knife and a grin on his face.

Rage's eyes bulged. He looked up at Zeke, who straddled him, his hand grasping Rage's hair, his big knife pressed against the man's cheek, the tip of it near Rage's eye.

"You would have been better off letting us go, my friend!" Zeke growled. "An Army prison would have been much better than what I will do to you for hurting my son!"

The first thing to go was Julius Rage's larynx, so that he could not scream. The rest was done more quickly than Zeke would have preferred, for few of his enemies died without great suffering first. But more men might come at any time. They had to get away. But he would have his vengeance first. To hell with civil courts and white man's laws. There was only one way to deal with men like Rage. The West might be becoming more civilized, but to men like Zeke, laws and courts meant nothing. He had his own laws.

He wiped his knife on Rage's fine silk suit, then shoved it back into its sheath. Wolf's Blood stood holding onto a support beam, panting with pain. Their eyes held, and the boy's fell to the mass of blood at his father's side. His eyes widened.

"Father! You are wounded!"

"No worse than you. Let's get the hell out of here. More men

230

will come any time. Can you ride?"

The boy stumbled toward his father and they supported each other as they walked to the wagons. "I am not sure," he answered.

"You may have to do some trick riding on the way out of here, Wolf's Blood. Those gunshots are sure to draw more men. We've got to bolt out of here fast and make for Fort Lyon, hole up wherever we find a good place to rest and hide. What happens here happens. They'll probably send men after us, but if we can make it to Fort Lyon we'll be all right. We had a right to kill those men."

Wolf's Blood nodded. "The pain in my back . . . it will be hard to ride," he said, his voice sounding weak.

"I'm damned sorry, Son. I didn't mean for this to happen. Everything went so smoothly. I never expected this."

They untied their own mounts, and Zeke quickly grabbed their extra supplies and rifles from the wagons. He helped a dizzy Wolf's Blood to mount up, then went to his own horse, finding it difficult to get on its back. Every muscle seemed to be giving up. The blood was draining his strength with each trickle that left his body.

"Father, you are bleeding badly," Wolf's Blood lamented. "I am afraid for you."

"I'll make it. I promised your mother I'd be back." He turned his horse and rode up to the barn doors, lifting the wooden latch and peering out carefully. Several men had gathered around the house not far away and were headed for the barn with rifles. "Men are coming," he told his son quietly. "As soon as we get through the doors, ride hard to the left, Wolf's Blood. Are you able to hang on and jump a couple of fences?"

"I . . . have no choice," the boy answered. "I am a warrior . . . and have fought with Dog Soldiers. I can . . . do it."

"We've got to ride fast and hard for a few minutes till we get to the hills south of here. You ready?"

The boy breathed deeply, his back and head reeling with black pain. "I am ready. I draw on the spirits within. Let's go, Father."

Zeke pulled open the door, shoving it aside and charging out. *"Hai! Hai!!"* he shouted to his Appaloosa, slapping his reins against the animal's neck and kicking its flanks. The dependable mount turned out in a thundering gallop, while somewhere behind him Zeke could hear shouts to stop. Wolf's Blood's mount was suddenly beside him then, both animal's manes and tails flying as behind them they could hear gunshots. Both men lay flat toward the horses' necks, leaping a fence and riding on, hanging sideways then to dodge more bullets, clinging to manes as the animals leaped yet another fence. In moments they were out of range of the guns, and sod flew as they headed for the hills to the South.

The small company of soldiers drew up in front of the Monroe house, and Morgan came running from the barn while Abbie came from her garden, dropping a hoe and walking quickly to the house. Zeke should have been back by now. She did not like the ominous presence of the soldiers. A lieutenant dismounted, asking Morgan if Mrs. Monroe was home.

Abbie came around the corner of the house, and the men stared. She wore an Indian tunic, her preference in the summer, much cooler and more comfortable than conventional white woman's clothing. Most of the fairly new recruits had seen Zeke and Wolf's Blood and had imagined the wife and mother must be Indian. They did not expect the beautiful white woman who came up on the porch.

"I am Mrs. Monroe," she told the lieutenant. "Is something wrong?"

The man removed his hat. "Ma'am, I'm Lieutenant Young, from Fort Lyon. Your husband and son are at the fort. Your son asked me to come and get you. Your husband is too sick to travel, or we'd have brought him here instead."

Her chest tightened. No! He promised this would not be the time! "What's wrong with him?"

"Well, ma'am, I don't know all the details. I wasn't told what he was supposed to be doing for Lieutenant-Colonel

232

Petersen. I only know he and your son were both wounded. Your son will be all right, though. But your husband took some buckshot on his left side, lost a lot of flesh and it got infected." Sonora was running toward them then, carrying Kicking Boy.

"How bad is it?" Abbie asked cautiously.

"It's hard to say, ma'am. The doc had to burn some of it out. He had a bad time of it."

"They did that without me there?" she asked angrily. "Someone should have come to get me sooner!"

"Your husband asked us not to, ma'am. Figured he'd be fine soon and would just come home. I think he was just wanting to spare you the worry, ma'am."

"What is it?" Sonora asked. "What is wrong?"

"It's all right, Sonora," Abbie told her, putting an arm around the girl's shoulders. "Zeke and Wolf's Blood were wounded, but they say Wolf's Blood is fine. He stayed at the fort because he didn't want to leave his father. Zeke is sick, Sonora. I'm going to him."

"I will go too!" the girl said anxiously.

"No. You're five months pregnant. The important thing is that nothing happens to Wolf's Blood's second child. And apparently Wolf's Blood is all right. I'll go alone and you help take care of the house until we return."

"But I should go—"

"No you should not." She gave the girl a reassuring hug. "Please listen to me, Sonora. Stay here and take care of yourself. If Zeke isn't better in a couple of days, I'll have Wolf's Blood come on home and I'll stay with Zeke." She looked up at the lieutenant. "Give me a few minutes to change and pack." Her eyes moved to Jason, who looked frightened. "Don't worry, Jason. Your father will be fine. Go and saddle the roan mare for me." The boy swallowed and nodded, running off toward the stables.

Abbie turned and went inside, Morgan and Margaret following. "Mother, are you all right?" Margaret asked quickly, little realizing there was more to Abbie's fear than just Zeke's wound. He intended to die fighting, and she worried

233

that he would give up and let this be the time.

"I'll be all right, as soon as I see him," she answered, going into the bedroom. She soon exited, wearing a soft green summer dress with a split skirt for riding. The braid she had worn down her back was now wound at the nape of her neck. She put on a slat bonnet to protect her face against the sun. "I know I can count on the two of you to take care of things," she told Margaret and Morgan. She looked at Ellen then. "And you." She gave her daughter a hug, then moved to Margaret to hug her also.

"Everything will be fine here," Morgan reassured her. She smiled through tears, pressing his arm.

"You're a godsend, Morgan," she answered. "Just when we thought things had gotten as bad as they could get, you came along. I knew then God was still watching out for me." She turned to Sonora, who sat at the table with Kicking Boy on her lap, tears on her cheeks. Abbie patted her head. "You're better off here, Sonora. You want a healthy child for Wolf's Blood, don't you?"

The girl nodded. "Tell him I love him. Send him home," she said quietly.

"I'll do both. But if Zeke is . . ." The words caught in her throat. "If he's dangerously ill, he probably won't come until he's sure Zeke will be all right. You know how close they are."

The girl looked up at her. "If something happens to his father, part of my husband will die also."

Abbie could not answer. Her throat hurt too much. She picked up her carpetbag and grabbed a cape, heading out the door. With a few quick good-byes she was mounted, leaving with the lieutenant and his eight men, who all watched her sit straight on her horse, an obviously experienced rider. The fact that she was married to a half-breed Indian brought more curiosity than derision; and the rumors some of them had heard that she had lived in this lawless land—even sometimes among the Cheyenne—for over twenty-five years brought respect and admiration as they watched her now. Surely a woman of her obvious beauty and refinement must love her husband and family a great deal to stay on a lonely ranch, with

234

little contact with civilization, no luxuries, and ever-present dangers. Most had expected an Indian woman, not believing the stories that she was white. And all of them were surprised at the air of respectability about her: a woman strong and stubborn, intelligent and brave, they soon surmised as they spent the next three days literally trying to keep up with her. She rode faster than they intended and slept little, refusing to stop more than twice a day for a few minutes rest and a little food. She was as capable of living under the stars as any of the men, and some of them tired before she did. By the time they reached Fort Lyon, they all held her in high regard, and any one of them would have put his life on the line for her.

When they arrived she didn't want to rest at all, demanding to be taken immediately to her husband. She was met in the outer room of the doctor's quarters by Lieutenant-Colonel Petersen.

"Mrs. Monroe," he greeted, nodding his head. "I'm sorry you had to come here, but your husband—"

"Where is he?" she asked anxiously. "You can tell me later what on earth happened. I just want to see him—now."

He sighed deeply and took her arm, leading her into a room where her husband lay in a large bed. A doctor was pulling covers over Zeke's shoulders. She stared at his closed eyes. His face was thin. The doctor turned to her.

"He's out of danger," he told her. "You're his wife?" He looked surprised.

"I am," she answered, chin held proudly. "Will he be all right—truly?"

"As far as I can see. Oh, he'll have a hefty dent in his left side. Part of the flesh was literally blown away. The danger was in loss of blood and a bad infection. He's recovering from both now."

Her eyes teared. "The lieutenant said you had to burn the wound."

He nodded, grasping her arm. "He's a strong man. I could see he drew on some inner strength most men don't have."

She had to smile. "I am not surprised. It's the Indian in him." She looked around the room. "Where is my son?"

The doctor moved away as Abbie went to the bed, sitting down carefully on the edge of it. "He left last night—to be alone and pray, he told us."

She studied Zeke. "I understand." She looked up at the doctor. "Is my son all right?"

"His back was bruised very badly. Said a man hit him with a shovel. He took a bad blow to the head, too. It fractured his skull. There's nothing can be done about that but let time take care of it. How either one of them managed to get here is beyond me."

She looked back at Zeke. "They're stubborn men." She leaned closer, putting a gentle hand on her husband's forehead. The doctor and Petersen left the room, closing the door softly, and Abbie leaned down and lightly kissed Zeke's lips. She pressed her cheek against his then, her tears wetting his own face.

"Don't you dare leave me yet," she whispered. "Don't you dare. You promised it wouldn't be this time."

He stirred slightly and she swallowed back her tears, kissing his forehead, his eyes, his cheek. When she sat up, his eyes were open. He just stared at her a minute, then managed a smile.

"Abbie," he said, his voice weak. "Damn . . . you look good. I . . . could have used you . . . a few days ago . . . when the doc lit a small fire . . . in my side."

She wiped at her eyes, angry with herself for crying in front of him. "Thank God you're alive," she sobbed, smoothing back his hair. "Oh, Zeke, I should have been here!"

"Couldn't . . . be helped. Wolf's Blood . . . can tell you what happened. I don't have the strength." He met her eyes sorrowfully. "I meant . . . to come home to you . . . riding my horse . . . everything fine. We had . . . a small problem with some . . . whiskey traders. I'm sorry, Abbie-girl. Things didn't go . . . quite as planned. And I don't . . . usually let a wound . . . get me down like this. Must be . . . old age."

"Don't be ridiculous," she sniffled. "You were hurt bad. The doctor said he doesn't know how you made it this far—that you survived on an inner strength most men don't have.

236

Now stop talking and get well so we can go home." She sniffed and swallowed, touching his cheek. "You will be . . . all right, won't you? Tell me you'll be all right, Zeke."

He managed to move his arm and reach up and take her hand. "Sure I will, now that my Abbie is here. I told you I wasn't . . . ready yet. Besides . . . when I die, woman . . . it will be more honorably . . . than from the bullet of some no-good . . . whiskey trader. It will be a real . . . Indian battle . . . soldiers and all."

She could not stop the tears then. The last three days had been filled with worry and hard riding and little rest, all the while frightened to death she would get to him too late and find he had died. She lay down carefully beside him and wept. He couldn't move to embrace her, but could only hold her hand.

"It's all right, Abbie-girl. You're stuck . . . with this mean son of a bitch . . . for a while yet."

It was three days later when Sergeant Daniels rode into the fort with his report. He had gone to the Rage ranch as directed, intending to confiscate the supply wagons and arrest Julius Rage, unaware of what had already taken place. Zeke Monroe's bed was soon surrounded by Daniels, Petersen, and Wolf's Blood. Abbie sat in a chair beside the bed, putting down her Bible as the men entered. Wolf's Blood still walked slowly, his back giving him pain. Zeke was propped against pillows half asleep when they entered. He stirred fully awake and rubbed his eyes.

He nodded to the men. "Any more visitors out there?" he asked.

Sergeant Daniels stared at him. He had seen what Zeke Monroe had done to Julius Rage, knowing for certain he'd never do anything to harm Ellen Monroe and have to answer to this man for it.

"Daniels just got back from his investigation of the Rage ranch," Petersen told Zeke.

Zeke glanced at Wolf's Blood, who shrugged and walked to

the other side of the bed, wincing as he sat down in a chair.

"So?" Zeke asked. "Is there a problem?"

Petersen glanced at Abbie. "Maybe we shouldn't talk in front of your wife—about the way you left Julius Rage."

Zeke shifted his position and reached for a pouch of tobacco kept on the table beside him. "My wife is fully aware of what I do to men who hurt my own. Rage fully intended to kill us both, but not before beating the hell out of my son in front of my eyes. They didn't even give him a chance—just snuck up behind him and landed a shovel into his back. They chose not to play fair, so I did the same."

He began rolling a cigarette, and Petersen sighed. "You did a good job for us, Zeke, and thanks to you we know the sources of the problem, at both ends. But I can't fully condone what you did to Rage. Half of Dodge City and the surrounding area are looking for two renegade Indians who murdered Julius Rage and two of his men. They know now that Rage was mixed up in whiskey trade, but they think the Indians that killed him were also mixed up in it—maybe trying to steal the goods back. We're letting them think what they want. They'll never know who the Indians really were, or that they worked for the Army. We've told the townspeople that we will make a search and take care of it. Daniels here says they seem calmed down, and we did at least recover the goods. We sent them on to St. Louis, according to what you told us. As soon as they're claimed at the warehouse there and taken to West Enterprises, more arrests will be made. I thank you for a job well done, and am sorry Rage discovered what you were up to at the last minute like that. The killings you committed were apparently in self-defense, and with so many of Rage's men at the ranch, you couldn't very well just hold the man and try to tell the others the truth. They'd probably not have believed you and might have hung you, so I can't blame you for doing what you had to do." He sighed, grimacing slightly. "But couldn't you have just . . . killed Rage outright . . . without using your knife on him the way you did?"

Zeke took a long drag on his cigarette, his dark eyes frightening in their cold vengeance. "He hurt my son badly.

I've done worse."

Abbie looked at her lap, thinking of Winston Garvey. Yes. He had done worse. Zeke reached out and took her hand, squeezing it, knowing what she was thinking.

"I thank you for keeping me and my son out of the picture," he told Petersen. "And I'm glad I got the information you needed—and equally glad for my pay. I'll be heading home in a couple more days, and if you don't mind I'd like to stay there awhile before taking on any more scouting jobs."

Petersen nodded. "Just don't use your knife like you did on Rage in front of me, or I'll have to arrest you." A faint grin passed over his lips.

"I'll keep that in mind," Zeke answered, his voice and grip on Abbie's hand both noticeably stronger. Petersen nodded and left the room, while Daniels hesitated, nervously fingering his hat. He cleared his throat. "You wanting something, Daniels?" Zeke asked the man.

"Yes, sir. I . . . uh . . . I'd like to keep calling on your daughter . . . soon as I get another leave . . . with your permission."

Zeke studied the man intently. He was strong and stocky, with kind eyes. "I already told you you had my permission for that," he told Daniels.

"Well, I . . . just wanted to be sure."

"You love Ellen?"

The man reddened, feeling uncomfortable under Wolf's Blood's own warning look. He took a deep breath. "Yes, sir, I do."

Zeke just shrugged. "Then go ahead and keep seeing her. I'm not going to do to you what I did to Julius Rage, unless you do wrong by her. She's a good girl. I have another daughter who was badly hurt by a man who promised love and marriage, then used her and left her—just because she had Indian blood in her. You wouldn't have any ideas like that now, would you?"

The man held Zeke's eyes boldly. "No, sir. I wouldn't do that."

Zeke smiled. "I don't think you would either. I'm not holding you to any commitments, Daniels. Just don't take advantage of her or lie to her. I'll not see another daughter hurt the way Margaret was. Understand?''

Daniels put his hat on. "Sir, if I hurt Ellen, you have my permission to carve me up any way you wish."

Zeke laughed lightly, wincing with pain when he did so. "Then you must love her very much."

Daniels smiled, then nodded to Abbie and left. Zeke turned to Abbie, her hand still in his. "You ready to go home, woman?"

"Whenever you think you're strong enough."

He rubbed the back of her hand with his thumb. "I'll be strong enough for more than that before too long." She blushed and he turned to Wolf's Blood. "Sonora will have a fit if you don't get back pretty damned soon," he told the young man. "I expect you're ready to see your wife."

Wolf's Blood grinned and rose, glancing at his mother. "She carries the baby well?"

"She's fine, Wolf's Blood. We'll make up a travois for your father and leave in a couple more days. I know you're anxious to get home."

"I'll not lay on any travois like a shriveling old man," Zeke objected. "I'll ride. I said I'd ride to my dying day and I will. and since I am not ready yet to die, I will ride home. I've had enough of this lying around anyway. The next time I lie in a bed like this it will be with you."

She blushed deeply and Wolf's Blood laughed lightly, walking slowly out of the room. Zeke squeezed Abbie's hand again. "Did you hear anything while I was gone from LeeAnn . . . or maybe Jeremy?" he asked carefully.

"No," she answered. "I wish I could tell you otherwise."

Zeke sighed, remembering the night he'd seen his son, remembering the hurt. He took a deep drag on his cigarette. "Yeah," he said quietly. "So do I." He patted her hand. "Well, Abbie-girl, I'm going to get some shut-eye so I'll be strong enough to ride in a couple of days."

"Zeke, you shouldn't—"

"I'm riding, and that's that." He yanked on her hand. "Come here."

240

She gave him a chiding look, then leaned down. He grasped the back of her neck with more strength in his arm than she expected, pulling her to his lips. He kissed her hungrily, wrapping his fingers in her hair. He released the kiss and studied her brown eyes, so true and loving. "That's the best medicine a man can get," he told her with a wink.

Chapter Fourteen

Charles Garvey paced in his study as LeeAnn nervously brought him his coffee. He'd been gloomy all evening, and she hoped he would not take it out on her later. Often when he was angry, the emotion was expressed in the brutal way he made love to her, as though wanting to hurt her, and she suspected that if she did not cooperate, he would truly beat her. She wondered at how he could have been so charming before marriage, and so cruel afterward. He often bragged that she bored him at times, and that he preferred the whores he often visited to his own wife, unable to understand why she was not more responsive.

LeeAnn didn't care anymore how often he visited the whores. It only meant he would leave her alone, and that was just fine. She had paid a dear price for luxuries and elegance and social importance, and she well knew it. But she had no way out now. She would not disgrace herself and cause a scandal by asking for a divorce, and she told herself that when Charles Garvey was a little older and more settled, when he accomplished all his plans in life, he would mellow. But an inner instinct told her this man would go from bad to worse. There was something maniacal about him, a deep evil that did not often surface but was there nonetheless—something that bordered on insanity.

She handed him the coffee, and he abruptly slammed a hand against the cup, sending it flying. LeeAnn jumped and backed away.

"Bring me some bourbon!" he growled. "I don't want that useless black brew tonight!"

She walked on shaking legs to a table where various liquors were kept. She sniffed at a few, finding the bourbon. Liquor was something she was learning more about. Charles kept much more around than the common whiskey her father drank occasionally. Her husband drank everything—and often. And to soothe her own nerves and shattered romance, LeeAnn had done her own share of drinking lately. She poured his bourbon, then set up a second glass, pouring her own drink.

"What's wrong, Charles?" she asked, handing him his drink. She decided she had best be extra nice to him. Maybe she could calm him down and he would at least not hit her or be cruel to her in bed.

He took the drink, studying her as he swallowed it quickly. "I'll tell you what's wrong!" he growled, tossing the glass into a fireplace. "Somehow the goddamned Army got its nose into West Enterprises and closed the place down!"

She frowned. "What is West Enterprises?"

He walked over to the table, picking up the bourbon and drinking it straight out of the bottle. He lowered the bottle, pacing again, his face dark with rage. "West Enterprises was one of my best sources of income," he fumed. "It's in St. Louis. I owned it, but it's set up so that I am not even directly connected. The government won't get me for this one!" He took another swallow.

"What are you talking about?" she asked, sipping her own drink.

He turned to face her. "I must say, dear wife, that for all your uselessness in bed, you are equally intelligent in other matters. That's the only reason I keep you. I'll not have a bumpkin for a wife, nor an ugly one. It is those two assets, and those only, that keep you in this house with my honored name."

She doubted the honor of the name but said nothing. "What does that have to do with West Enterprises?" she asked.

"I only mean, my love, that I think you're intelligent enough to understand that no man gets rich out of strictly legitimate means. I make more money illegitimately than I do above-board. West Enterprises was one of my sources. But now the Army has arrested Thomas West, my best man."

LeeAnn sighed. "You're confusing me."

He grinned. "It's called 'screw the Indians,' my sweet. You've heard me talk about that game before."

She lowered her glass, feeling the panic in her heart again. What if he found out about her past? He would surely kill her! And every time he talked about his hatred of the Indians her heart broke a little more, her soul filled with more guilt about turning her back on her own heritage.

"Thomas West ran West Enterprises," he continued. "On paper he owned the place. West Enterprises supplies worthless, rotgut whiskey to Indian reservations, as well as guns—outdated, half-worthless guns. The goods, which the Indians want very badly, are hauled to reservations, snuck in by various means, and traded for valuable buffalo robes and government supplies issued on the reservation—blankets, pots and pans, farm tools, furniture, all kinds of things. The stupid, ignorant Indians trade those things for the whiskey and guns, like the fools they are, not even realizing what they're giving away in return for a night of feeling good and hope of arming themselves well enough to fight the Army again."

She looked at her glass, feeling compassion for the Indian. "And the robes and Army supplies are sent back to West Enterprises, the robes sold for a great profit," she added for him.

He nodded, then bowed. "As I said, for a woman you are blessed with unusual intelligence."

"But what happens to the government supplies?"

He smiled. "Simple. They are resold to the Army. In the books, they are newly ordered supplies, but they're really just the same supplies used over again, with a few new things mixed in. West Enterprises spares themselves the cost of ordering new goods, making a profit on the same supplies over and over." His eyes darkened again, the strange evil returning to them. "West Enterprises was the biggest supplier of all. Somehow the Army found out. They've closed the place down, and confiscated all robes and supplies. It will take a long time to get an operation like that underway again. Everything was going so smoothly. Damn!"

She swallowed back tears over the kind of man she had married. How could she have let her own memories of her captivity with the Comanches bring her to this? Had she hated the Indians that much herself then? If only her own father were not one. "How do you think they found out?" she asked quietly.

"Oh, wouldn't I love to know!" he growled.

"What does Tom West have to say? Maybe he knows something."

Her husband's eyes narrowed. "He knows too much. He will be conveniently killed, at my request. I'll not risk anything dragging me into this."

Her eyes widened. "But . . . he worked for you. You said he was your best man. You'd . . . you'd have him killed?"

His eyes ran over her scornfully. "Of course. Some damned Indians killed his source in Dodge City, and our contact at Camp Supply took off for parts unknown to avoid arrest. That leaves only Tom West knowing who really backs this thing. The man has to die. I'll wait a while, then start the operation up all over again, find a new man, make new contacts. It's a lucrative business. It's just another way for me to take advantage of the Indians, and that pleases me greatly." He took another swallow of bourbon. "You know, I kind of hate to see the red man die off, much as that's what I want. I'll have to think of some other way to make my money—find some other poor bastard who's too stupid to know when he's being taken advantage of." He met her eyes, and saw the shock there. He only smiled. "My dear Mrs. Garvey, you must learn to be more callous. You're too sentimental, you know—too soft. That's your biggest flaw. You want gentleness in bed, when it's much more fun to be brutal. And you expect me to help Tom West. I can see it in your eyes. Well, my dear, if he was stupid enough to get caught, he deserves to die. No one is going to get me in hot water and smear my good name."

She studied him sorrowfully. "Does that include me? Would you have me killed if I threatened your reputation—your good name?"

He snickered. "Of course I would. Oh, I'd mourn you. After

all, how many men find something as beautiful and elegant as you for a wife?" He came closer, kneeling down in front of where she sat and unbuttoning the front of her dress. He pulled it open, kissing the deep cleavage of her breasts, and she shuddered with disappointment. She had hoped he would not want her this night. And now he had told her she was dispensable. "Why don't you go upstairs and undress like a good little wife?" he asked then, rising again.

She got up from the chair, glaring at him with eyes as cold as his own. "Certainly," she said coolly. "May I ask, Charles, if a child would make you happier—make you love me just a little more?"

He grinned. "Of course. I'll need a son to keep the Garvey enterprises going."

"Then you will have to stop your monstrous bedroom habits and make love to me the normal way," she told him, almost defiantly. "There is only one way to get a woman pregnant, Charles. I want a baby. And I want to be treated like a normal woman, not like the whores you lay with. Let them be acrobats in your bed. I want only to be a woman and to have a child."

His eyes narrowed again, and he walked up to her, planting a hand around her throat and squeezing until her face reddened. "I will do whatever I want with my own wife in our own bed!" he growled. He shoved her hard then, causing her to fall to the floor. Then he smiled again. "But I must agree with you this time, love. There is only one way to get pregnant. So get yourself upstairs and wait for me." He clenched a fist. "Unless you have found some other man who makes love to you the way you think a man is supposed to?"

Her eyes widened. "Of course not! How can you say such a thing?"

He looked her over as she got to her feet. "Just checking. Maybe you want a man who doesn't limp—or one more handsome."

She blinked back tears. "Don't you understand such things don't matter to me? I only want a little gentleness—to be loved and treated like a normal woman. I loved you, Charles. Why do you seem to try so hard to make me not love you? Why is it so hard for you to accept love, and to give love?"

His eyes glittered. "It does no good to love, my dear LeeAnn. When I was a small boy, I learned about love—and about looking out for yourself. I loved my mother. She was blond and pretty—like you. When I went west with her and the Indians attacked our stagecoach, I wanted to protect her. But I couldn't because I was too little. I'll never forget that, and I've hated the Indians ever since for murdering her—scalping her right in front of me." He slugged some more bourbon. "Yes, I learned that day that it hurts too much to love—not just because I watched my pretty mother die, but because I knew she was going west because my father sent her there for cheating on him." He grinned sarcastically. "I learned many things that day, LeeAnn, things I remembered the rest of my life. I had already learned about cheating wives, but I could forgive her for that. I learned about filthy Indians and how cruel they could be. And I learned that no one, not even a child, can depend on love. You see my . . . uh . . . 'beloved' mother offered me to the Indians, in exchange for her life."

Her eyes softened and she started toward him. "Charles—"

"Forget it, my sweet!" he answered. He drank some more. "You know, I think that's why the Indians killed her—because they held such contempt for her for trying to trade her own son for her life. And maybe that's why they left me there instead of taking me along. I suppose in a way I should thank them for that, but at the time I could only see them as rotten, killing savages. They still are—except now I don't work against them so much because I hate them, but more because they stand in the way of progress, my dear. The land they roam is packed with wealth, and I want that wealth. Every Indian can die for all I care! What good are they?" He set down the bottle. "And don't give me any speeches about love. Just don't you mess around on me like my mother did to my father, understand? If you do, you're dead. Now get upstairs."

"Charles, let me help you. Let me love you."

"Go!" he roared, stepping closer with his fists clenched. She backed up, then turned and fled the room. He picked up the bourbon bottle and smashed it against a wall, following after her then, unbuttoning his shirt on the way. No woman was going to tell him how to behave in bed. His father had taken

248

him to see the whores when he was hardly more than a boy. He knew what women were for, and his own wife was no different.

Abbie lowered the lamp and climbed into bed, wearing only a cotton under slip, for the August night was warm. Zeke watched her quietly. He had been home three weeks now—long enough as far as he was concerned. Abbie gave him a quick kiss and curled up on the cool sheet, her back to him. The house was quiet, Ellen and Jason sleeping outside rather than in the loft because of the heat.

Zeke studied his wife's form, still shapely in spite of all the children, kept firm by hard work. He reached over and ran a hand along her leg and up her thigh, pushing up the slip and exposing bare hips.

"Zeke Monroe you aren't healed enough," she said quietly, her back still to him.

He leaned down and kissed her hip, pushing the slip up more and moving his lips along her back. "I'll be the judge of that," he told her, moving his hand around to her belly and up over her full breasts, while his lips nuzzled her neck. He pressed his hand against her shoulder, turning her onto her back and meeting her lips. He moved one knee between her legs, pushing against private places while his lips moved to her throat.

"Zeke, you shouldn't do this," she protested weakly.

"Of course I should. It's a sure cure. I think the only thing left wrong with me is I haven't had a woman since February. That's a hell of a long time for a man like me, and I've got some love all built up inside of me just dying to be released."

He met her lips again. How could she protest, when she was as hungry for him as he was for her? She returned the kiss with a whimper, reaching her arms around his neck. Her slip was pushed all the way to her neck. The rest was easy, for when it was this hot her husband slept naked. He moved on top of her, shivering at the pleasant feel of her bare breasts against his skin.

Neither of them cared about preliminaries. Nor did they need them. Their passion was instant and powerful, and in moments she welcomed him inside herself, crying out in glorious ecstasy. He moved his hands under her hips, and she was lost in him, her face buried against the broad, strong chest, her body pushed against him by his own strength so that he filled her completely. He pushed in groaning need, not caring that it brought mild pain to his side. The pain was worth it. He was stronger again, making an amazing recovery considering his age. But Zeke Monroe had always had a tremendous capacity for overcoming wounds. It was the disease from within that he could not seem to control. But he would not think about that now. It was summer. The arthritis bothered him little this time of year. He would worry about winter when it was upon them and not before. For now he would enjoy the fact that he was recovering from the gunshot wound, and he was home and with his woman.

His life surged into her, and they lay there breathing heavily, their skin hot with perspiration. But they didn't care about the heat, and he didn't care about his pain. He raised up on his elbows, remaining on top of her, bending down and kissing her hungrily again, searching her mouth with his tongue, enjoying her whimpers and grinning inwardly at how feebly she had argued against doing this. She arched her head back and he kissed her throat.

"Zeke, are you all right?" she whispered.

"What do you think?" he replied in a husky voice.

She could feel his passion returning, and he began moving inside her again. "I think you must be just fine," she whispered back.

She could see him in the lamplight, and he grinned. "I told you this was the only thing left that I needed." Their eyes held, flashing with passion as he moved rhythmically. She gazed at him with haughty, provocative, almost whorelike eyes as he moved inside of her, a look she had given to no other man, for no other man could bring out these things in Abigail Trent Monroe. He in turn took her as though she had no choice, and truly she didn't, for when Zeke Monroe touched her, all resistance vanished, just as it had that first night he took her. He raised up to his knees, grasping her hips and pulling her toward him.

"*Ne-mehotatse,*" he told her softly.

250

She closed her eyes and reached over her head, grasping the brass bars of the headboard, arching up to him and crying out his name when he pushed extra hard and his life throbbed into her once again. In the next moment he came down and enveloped her in his arms, thinking how precious their time was now.

"Abbie, my Abbie," he groaned. "I wish I could hold you forever. Sometimes I wish all life outside of this bed would stop and there would be just you and me and love and this bed, and nothing more."

She swallowed, a lump in her throat making it impossible to reply right away. She could only cling to him, and her chest jerked in a sob. "Zeke," she finally managed to whimper.

"Don't cry, Abbie-girl. I'll always be with you this way—always—even after death. And then some day you'll follow me on *Ekutsihimmiyo*, and we will be together—always and always."

In November of 1873 a daughter was born to Wolf's Blood and Sonora. She was named Iris, for the flower that Abbie loved so much. The ensuing winter was kind to Zeke Monroe. The arthritis flared only mildly, and he wanted to believe that perhaps it was going away. A little voice told him not to be so foolish as to imagine that could happen, but he felt so good that he allowed himself to think the disease would no longer plague him. His side healed, leaving an ugly scar and often flaring with recurring pain that he knew would probably torment him forever. He sometimes wondered how much injury and pain one man could suffer and still survive, and thought perhaps he had more scars and had taken more batttering than any man alive. It was many weeks before Wolf's Blood's back finally stopped bothering him, and even longer before he stopped suffering from recurrent headaches and dizzy spells.

By the spring of 1874 both men were strong again, and the summer was spent mending fences, finishing off the barn, helping in the birth of several new colts, and in branding. Zeke's spirits were high, dashed only late that summer when Sergeant Daniels came calling on Ellen, and brought news telling them that all of Zeke's and Wolf's Blood's efforts at helping route out whiskey peddlers had had little effect. Whiskey trading was rampant again on the reservations, according to Daniels, who had served some time at Camp Supply and had been writing letters to Ellen all that winter and past spring.

"It's bad, Zeke," he told the man, as he sat outside on the porch rail, the entire family gathered around, enjoying the cool night air. "The Indians are getting so much whiskey now they're almost crazy. They're trading everything they can get their hands on for the stuff. The warriors trade needed rations for the whiskey and guns, and then the whiskey keeps them so drunk they don't go out and hunt. The result is their families starve. Women are ashamed of their men, who no longer provide for them in the old ways. The young men are restless, drunk half the time, wanting to go to war again. Whiskey traders dress up like Indians and paint themselves so they can move in and out of the reservation undetected. More and more stray Indians show up, and there's no food for them. I needn't tell you what that will lead to."

Zeke sighed, rubbing at his eyes. "They'll break loose again. There's no way to stop it."

"They are not happy there," Wolf's Blood stewed. "It is no wonder they are drunk all the time. They cannot be men on the reservation. Some are even killing themselves." He stood up, clenching his fists. "The white man has done this to them! Treaty after treaty is broken! They give them land, then take it away again, shoving them someplace new, always to worse places—hot, useless, barren land full of insects and disease! And then they wonder why the Indian is unhappy and drinks himself to death! Don't they understand what it was once like for the Indian? Don't they realize he once rode free—from Canada to Mexico, from the Sierras to the Mississippi River? All of this was theirs! All of it! Now what do they have? Nothing! Nothing but a barren wasteland to which they are confined like prison!"

"Calm down, Wolf's Blood," Margaret told her brother.

Sonora blinked back tears, holding her baby close as it breast-fed. Kicking Boy, now two years old, toddled around at

252

the foot of the steps. She wondered what was happening to her own people. It had been a long time since she had seen the beloved White Mountains, bathed in the Gila River, lived in the land of giant cactuses and red rocks. She missed home, but would not tell her husband so.

"Something else that keeps things stirred up are horse thieves," Daniels told them, often glancing at Ellen, anxious to be alone with her. She watched him lovingly, and he liked feeling important, sitting there in his blue uniform and bringing them news. More than that, though, he liked the Monroes, and was as concerned for the Indians as they were. He knew how they loved the people, and realized the dangers that were mounting with unrest on the reservation. "White men raid the reservation and steal Indian ponies. The Indians are furious about it—claim that if it was the other way around they'd be tried and hung, but when white men do it to them, nothing is done about it."

"Bastards!" Wolf's Blood fumed.

Zeke watched his son, knowing the boy would like nothing better than to rejoin his Indian family and fight again. But he had Sonora now, and two children. And more than that he and Zeke had grown even closer, if that were possible. He would not leave the ranch unless it was with his father to do more scouting, for in spite of the problems, they both still knew that reservations were the Indians' only hope of survival.

"You know what happened at Adobe Walls," Daniels went on. "Renegade Cheyenne made a mess of things there for the buffalo hunters. Sheridan thinks that prompt and swift action against the hostiles is the only solution, with proper punishment, whatever that might be. Colonel Miles has been given full power to attack all Indians who are hostiles. A few renegades surrendered to the agency, but a lot of them are holding out because they don't believe they're protected from the Army. They're not supposed to be punished if they come back to the reservation, but they remember Sand Creek and Washita. It's been a dry summer, and the drought is sapping their ponies' strength, so more and more have been straggling back, according to messages Lieutenant-Colonel Petersen gets. But there's still a lot of trouble out there, Zeke. Too many have

253

broken away. Medicine Water is out there somewhere right now raiding with a war party. And so many Cheyenne have mixed in with warring Kiowas and Comanches that Miles is planning a big offensive: five columns, moving in all directions from Camp Supply to dig out hostiles and send them packing back to Camp Supply where they belong—or suffer the consequences."

The air hung silent and Zeke smoked quietly. "Well, I guess we all know what the consequences are that he refers to," he finally spoke up. He met Daniels's eyes. "Petersen didn't send you here to get me, did he?"

Abbie's chest ached at the words, and Daniels sighed. "Not exactly. He did tell me to let you know what's going on—kind of warn you that he might need you again. Miles is asking for the best scouts, but he said he'd try to leave you be. But if things keep going like they are, I don't see you getting through another year without your services being needed.

Zeke threw down the cigarette and stepped it out. Wolf's Blood looked at the deepening shadows, then jumped over the railing to the ground. "I am going riding," he said sullenly, walking off toward the corral. Zeke watched after him, sighing deeply.

"He's getting as restless as the renegades," he muttered. "He'll not go the rest of his life without making war once more."

"The only thing holding him here right now is you," Abbie spoke up. He met her eyes knowingly. "If he could, he'd take Sonora right now and go fight with the Apaches, and he still might."

"If his father can keep him from making war, then I am glad," Sonora spoke up. "I do not want him to be in such danger even though it is in his heart to join his People again. He speaks often about his uncle, Swift Arrow, and his days in the North with the Sioux."

Zeke frowned, feeling guilty for keeping his son from his heart's desire. Yet Wolf's Blood had returned on his own accord, and he had Sonora now to think about. It was not just for his father that he stayed at the ranch. However, the fact remained that Wolf's Blood all but worshipped his father, and

254

Zeke knew the boy would never leave again until his father rested in death. They heard a horse gallop off in the distance.

Sergeant Daniels cleared his throat. "Not to change the subject, but there is something else I'd like to talk about," he spoke up.

Zeke leaned back, putting one foot up on the railing. "I'm listening."

Ellen reddened and looked at her lap. Daniels looked from Zeke to Abbie, and back to Zeke. "In two years I'll be out of the Army," he told them. "I'm saving up—put some money down on some land east of here, only maybe a day's ride. I intend to settle once I'm out—go into ranching like you've done."

Zeke grinned, rubbing at his sore side. "And you want to settle with our daughter."

Daniels grinned. "Yes, sir, with your permission. We'd like to be married next spring. I've got a long hitch ahead of me and am getting shipped down to Camp Supply till then. I think it's best I wait till I get back to marry, seeing as how there's so much unrest. If I come back all in one piece, we can marry. Then I'll just have a year or so left, mostly right close at Fort Lyon."

Abbie smiled and glanced at Zeke, who studied Daniels intently. "Well, son, I'd say by the look in Ellen's eyes every time she talks about you, you must make her happy. Of course you can marry her. But I'd better not hear from her that you've mistreated her."

Daniels put out his hand. "You'll never hear that," he replied.

Zeke shook his hand firmly. "Why buy land next to mine?" he asked. "Why not settle right here, help run this place?"

Daniels took a deep breath. "Well, sir, Ellen mentioned that. But this place half belongs to Morgan and Margaret, and someday it will pretty much all belong to them. I appreciate the gesture, but I want a place all my own. And we can always help each other out."

Zeke nodded. "I can understand how you feel. Half of me is white. I know a man needs a place to call his own." He rose, walking to the edge of the porch and looking out in the direction in which Wolf's Blood had ridden. "And so does the

255

Indian. The trouble is, the two differ about what can be called their own." He swung his legs over the railing and jumped down, looking back at Daniels. "Marry her and have a good life, Hal. All of you have a good visit. I think I'll go for a ride myself."

He walked off toward the corral, and Abbie shook her head. "Two of a kind," she muttered. "Always have been and always will be."

Chapter Fifteen

It was a hard winter for Zeke, and January of 1875 found him struggling with every step, literally perspiring with pain as he forced himself to ride and do his usual chores. Abbie could do nothing but watch him suffer. It seemed the arthritis attacked every joint this time, not just his back, elbows, and hands, but his shoulders, hips, and legs, so that no position was comfortable. His only deliverance was to be half drunk most of the time. Abbie didn't know whether to be more worried about the arthritis or the fact that whiskey was becoming a needed item. He had always opposed too much whiskey for the Indians, and had deliberately not allowed himself to drink too much of it, knowing the effect it seemed to have on those with Indian blood. But this was a different matter, and too much laudanum was more dangerous than too much whiskey. When she watched him struggle just to get out of bed in the morning, she could not chide him for the whiskey.

What frightened her most was that under these conditions he would surely decide that soon he must find an honorable way to die. She could see him overcoming great pain out of pure stubbornness. He would not let the disease keep him in bed. That was one thing he had promised himself, and he was determined to keep the promise. Abbie could see in his eyes that he did not even want to talk about it. He suffered silently, but his struggling steps and swollen hands told all, and even Ellen and Jason and the rest of the family began asking questions. He could no longer hide his ailment, but the rest of the family had strict instructions from Abbie not to mention it.

It was late January of that winter when the blizzard came, descending upon them from the Rockies with all the force that only nature herself can unleash. Zeke came from the bedroom before light, literally holding onto chairs and walls just to walk. Abbie was already up, knowing by the wind it was a bad storm, and heating the coffee early.

"It came down bad all night," Zeke told her picking up a cup of coffee and slugging it down. "I'm going to get Wolf's Blood and Morgan. We'd best string a rope from the houses to the barn and stables. I've lived out here long enough to know when a week-long blizzard is coming. We'll be buried in another day or two."

She studied the gnarled hands that clung to the back of a chair. "Morgan and Wolf's Blood can take care of it. You'd better stay inside where it's warm, Zeke."

He slammed the cup down and looked at her with dark eyes that flashed with pride. "I'll not stay inside while the others are out there in the cold doing my work for me. I'm just as capable as they are out there in the blizzard, or in bed with you! So quit looking at me like a goddamned cripple!"

She closed her eyes and turned away. The pain had made him snap at her about everything lately. He was not himself at all. Even when he made love to her, it was always almost angrily, as though he thought he had to prove to her that he was still capable of such things. She wondered if perhaps this was another thing of nature—a way of helping her bear losing him some day. Perhaps most people became ornery and bitter when they were dying, making life miserable enough for their loved ones that it was almost a relief when they were gone. She blinked back tears as he put on his winter moccasins and thick, fleece-lined deerskin coat. It had only been the last two weeks that he had been especially difficult, having few kind words for her. But it was so unlike him.

Her heart was suddenly lighter. Yes, it was so unlike him. She knew full well how much Zeke Monroe loved her. It all made sense now. He would never be cruel to her, no matter how much pain he suffered—unless he was trying to do the very thing she had been thinking, trying to make himself obnoxious enough that it would be easier on her when he was dead. Her heart tightened. Did that mean this was the winter he had chosen to die? Surely not! Ellen was to be married in the spring. The spring.

She turned to face him, swallowing back tears. "There is always a spring, Zeke," she said quietly.

He looked at her with a scowl and saw the pleading look in her eyes, the eyes that he loved so dearly. He returned to lacing his moccasins, a difficult job for him now. "Not for fifty-five-year-old men who find pain in every movement," he growled.

"For everyone," she answered. "And I . . . I don't want to face spring . . . without you." Her voice began choking then with the unwanted tears. "And if you think being mean to me . . . will make it any easier . . . that's a stupid thought! I want to remember you the old way . . . the Zeke Monroe I married. I don't give a damn if you're so bad you're carried around in a gunnysack! Just don't . . . don't turn into someone I don't know at all. Don't give me ugly memories, Zeke. I just want my Zeke, whether he . . . crawls across the floor or runs and jumps . . . whether he makes love to me every night . . . or never makes love to me at all. I don't give a damn . . . about any of those things and you know it! It's you I need . . . the person . . . the man . . . my strength and my friend. Don't take those things from me when I might only get to have them for another week, another year. I feel like a woman condemned!" The tears came harder then, her words almost hysterical. "How long do I have, Zeke? How long? One day? One year? Three years?" Her fists clenched and she stepped closer, her face red with anger. "You tell me! You talk about not having much time left! What about me? Have you ever stopped to think that it's the same for me? When you talk about you dying, you're talking about me dying also!"

He stood up and grasped her arms. "Stop it!"

"It's true and you know it! How am I supposed to go on without you—without my Zeke? You're all I've had since I was fifteen years old! I've lived for you—for you and nothing else!"

Their eyes held, his full of bitter sorrow. "That isn't true, Abbie. When I met you, you were a fighter—strong and

259

stubborn. And look at all you've been through. You didn't survive because of Zeke Monroe, Abbie. You survived because of a strength inside yourself that you don't even know you have. When I'm gone, then you'll know. And you'll look at all your children and grandchildren and know why you exist. It isn't just for me, Abbie."

Her eyes were wide with fear. "Don't go—not yet," she whispered. "And until you do . . . don't take my Zeke from me. Let me have him the way he's always been. If you love me, give me that much. Being cruel doesn't make it easier, Zeke. I want every memory . . . to be good . . . like they've always been."

He closed his eyes and sighed, pulling her close and embracing her. "I give up," he told her, kissing her hair. "I never could resist those eyes of yours, or those tears. Much as this thing is killing me, I'll try to hang on, for my Abbie."

She broke into bitter weeping against his chest, wrapped in the still-strong arms and the fleece-lined coat. "And you won't . . . be mean to me?" she sobbed.

He could not help a light laugh, in spite of his pain and the tragedy of the moment. "No. I won't be mean to you." He gave her a squeeze. "I've got to go, Abbie." She pulled back and looked up at him, and he bent down to kiss her gently. "Just don't tell me what I should and shouldn't do, Abbie. I do what I have to do. If you want me to keep going for you, then don't stop me. Agreed?"

She nodded, reminding herself of his tender pride. The Indian in him made him more proud and stubborn than most, and yet that was part of what she loved about him. He gave her a smile and walked to the wall where his hat hung, putting it on and then buttoning his coat. He gave her another quick smile and went out, snow blowing through the door when he opened it.

Outside the wind howled fiercely, and Zeke struggled through already deepening drifts to Margaret's cabin, rousing Morgan awake to the still-dark morning. Then he trudged to the new cabin they had built that past summer for Wolf's Blood and Sonora. The tipi was still erected nearby. There were times when Wolf's Blood preferred the house of skins, especially in the summer. He had never liked a house with walls, nor had Zeke. But some things had to be done for practical purposes.

Wolf's Blood frowned when he came to the door already dressed, also realizing this was going to be a bad storm. But he didn't like the idea of his father being out in it. He knew how much pain the man had been in.

"Father, Morgan and I can—"

"Nonsense! I'm going to the barn to get some rope. And we'd best string it from the cabins to the main house also. I've known men to get lost in a blizzard and found dead ten feet from their own dwelling. I want nothing like that happening on this ranch. Let's go."

The man turned and trudged into the darkness toward the barn, which could not even be seen from Wolf's Blood's cabin. His son quickly planted a beaver hat on his head and went out, not wanting his father to walk to the barn alone. They made their way by literal instinct, lighting a lantern inside the barn. They were soon joined by Morgan. Zeke was already tying a rope to a post just outside the barn doors, while Wolf's Blood watched the gnarled fingers work stiffly, his heart aching at the sight. The boy looked at Morgan with warning eyes. Both men knew better than to offer help or show pity. Zeke stood up then, handing the rope to Morgan.

"Make your way to the house with this. Take some extra and string some from the main house to the cabins." He turned to his son. "Saddle up two horses, Wolf's Blood. We left *Kehilan* and those two mares in the north corral yesterday. We've got to get them back to the barn and we don't dare wait till daylight. This stuff is going to pile up fast and hard!"

"Zeke, it's too dangerous to go out there before light," Morgan objected.

"We have no choice. We'll rope the horses together so we don't lose each other. I can't leave my prime stud out there." He turned and walked back to help Wolf's Blood, and Morgan just shook his head and began walking with the rope toward the house.

"That damned horse!" Zeke was cursing the stud Appaloosa. "Why can't he mate any old place like other horses? Not *Kehilan*. He has to go off alone with his women."

261

"Who would have thought yesterday we would have this problem?" Wolf's Blood answered, putting a bridle on Zeke's horse. "We had that thaw. Yesterday we could see lots of green. It was a nice day. I did not think those dark clouds over the mountains meant something this bad."

Zeke threw a blanket over his horse's back, then put on the flat Indian saddle he always used, wincing with pain as he did so. "It's amazing how fast the weather can change," he grumbled.

Wolf's Blood quickly tightened the cinch for his father. "I could go alone," he said carefully. "I can find anything on this ranch blindfolded."

Zeke put a hand on his shoulder, and Wolf's Blood straightened and met his father's eyes. "Things can get too confusing in a blizzard. I'll go with you and that's that. I'm all right, Wolf's Blood."

The young man looked his father over, then turned and put his own saddle on his mount. Zeke watched him, the loyal son who was staying there out of pure love for his father. Wolf's Blood was almost twenty-eight now. Zeke still thought of him as a boy, but he was most certainly a full-grown man and had been far longer than most. He was replica of his father, as tall and broad and strong, but perhaps even wilder at heart than Zeke.

They were soon mounted, a rope tied between the two horses from cinch ring to cinch ring so they could not lose each other. They headed out of the barn and around toward the north pasture, biting snow whipped by gale winds stinging their faces as they made their way slowly—and for Zeke painfully—toward the north corral, a half-mile ride. In such gales, a half mile could seem like ten miles, and that was how it felt for Zeke and Wolf's Blood.

Morgan literally felt his way to the main house, tying the rope to a porch post. The door opened a crack. "Zeke?" Abbie called out.

Morgan went up the steps to the door. "It's me," he told her. "Zeke and Wolf's Blood went to the north corral to get *Kehilan* and two mares he left there yesterday."

"The north corral! How can they even see to get there!"

"Those two don't need to see to find something," he answered with a wink. But both knew how dangerous it was. "I'm going on to the cabins now, Abbie. We're roping a path between all the houses. You just get a nice breakfast going. We'll all need it by the time Zeke gets back."

He only needed to walk a few feet from the steps before he disappeared again into the blizzard. Abbie shoved the door closed with difficulty and walked to her cook stove, putting in more wood and setting a black frying pan on the hot plate. She dug some bacon from the lard that preserved it and began cooking. She must keep busy. It was the only way to not worry.

Zeke and Wolf's Blood reached the north corral after almost forty-five minutes of urging their mounts through deep drifts, using a cottonwood tree here, a nearly buried berry bush there as landmarks to tell them they were going in the right direction. When Zeke reached the fence he felt a great relief. He whistled for the horses, calling their names, shouting in Cheyenne. He heard nothing but the wind, his heart tightening. He did not want to lose *Kehilan*, but it would not be unlike the nervous animal to become confused in the blizzard and leap the fence. If he did and was lost, he would freeze or starve, whichever came first. He called again, whistled again, and finally there came a whinny. The unpredictable stud loomed into the light of the lantern Zeke waved.

"Here he is!" Zeke called to Wolf's Blood. "Keep calling the mares." He hung the lantern over a fence post, talking softly to *Kehilan* until he managed to get a rope over the horse's neck. He tied it to a post to keep the animal in sight until the mares showed up. Both men kept whistling and calling until finally the mares made their way toward the light of the lantern. Wolf's Blood roped both of them.

"I'll take *Kehilan*," Zeke shouted. "You lead the mares. Let's move slowly along the fence until we get to the gate. Then we'll swing them out and get back to the barn."

"I am ready!" Wolf's Blood shouted back. Zeke lifted the lantern, holding it in his left hand while he held *Kehilan*'s rope in the other hand, not even grasping the reins as he urged his horse forward with gentle Cheyenne commands. The animal obeyed, and they reached the gate. Zeke had to dismount to open the gate, which was stuck against a large drift. He hung the lantern on a post again, then tied his own horse, still hanging on to *Kehilan*.

"I've got to force the gate open," he told Wolf's Blood.

"Be careful! Do you want me to do it?"

"I can do it." He kicked at the snow, clinging to the rope as he bent over to dig away enough so that he could get the gate open. *Kehilan* began getting nervous, and he tugged hard at his rope, yanking Zeke's arm painfully. Zeke cursed and kicked at the gate, opening it enough to go inside. He tied *Kehilan*, then pushed and kicked at the gate more until it opened enough to get the horses through it. He untied *Kehilan* then and the nervous animal began pulling away. Zeke shouted commands in Cheyenne that usually kept the prized stallion under control, although even for Zeke that was not an easy task. The horse seemed especially stubborn, confused by the gale winds and the darkness.

Wolf's Blood could hear his father shouting commands at the screeching and whinnying animal, and knew it must be rearing and tugging. He also knew that Zeke was in great pain. The young man quickly dismounted, tying his own horses and struggling through the snow toward the gate. He ran up to *Kehilan*, grabbing the horse around the neck and shouting his own commands, and both men struggled with the animal until he was through the gate. The stallion tried to run off then, and Zeke hung on for dear life. Wolf's Blood reached around his father and held the rope with him. It took both of them to get the horse close enough to the fence to tie the rope around it and hold him until they could get the two mares out. Wolf's Blood hurriedly got the other two horses out, also tying them outside the fence and then running back to his father, who had sunk into the snow beside the fence, holding his side.

"Father! Are you all right?"

Zeke lay back in the snow, panting. "I . . . can't get up, Wolf's Blood. Not . . . yet."

Wolf's Blood knelt close to him. "Are you hurt?"

"*Kehilan* . . . kicked me . . . in the side where I took that damned buckshot."

Wolf's Blood bent closer and raised Zeke's head. "What can

I do? Should I go for help?"

"No!" Zeke took a deep breath. "I'll be all right . . . in a minute. It isn't so much . . . the kick. It's the damned . . . arthritis." He breathed deeply before continuing. "It's . . . so bad this time, Wolf's Blood. I . . . get down . . . and it takes everything I have . . . to get back up. Just . . . let me lay here a minute."

The young man's eyes teared. He had never seen his father this bad from something besides an injury. And it was the first time he truly realized this thing his father had could cripple and kill him. It was not that he didn't believe his father when he first told him. But he had not envisioned it could really be that bad. He stood back and waited, knowing his father was too proud to ask for help in getting up. Zeke rolled over then, grabbing a fence rail and pulling. Then another rail and another, until he was on his feet, but still clinging to the fence. He threw his head back and breathed deeply before going to his horse and struggling to mount up.

"You . . . take the lantern," he told his son. "I'll tie the stallion to my own horse. That way I won't have to hang on to him myself."

Wolf's Blood nodded, taking the lantern and holding it up to see his father. "Are you sure you can ride?"

Zeke leaned over, untied *Kehilan*, and began tying the animal to his own horse, his swollen fingers having difficulty in making the knot. "I can ride," he replied. "Do me a favor and don't tell Abbie about the kick, will you?"

"But, Father—"

"Don't tell her! And don't tell anyone I couldn't get up out of a lousy snowdrift!"

Wolf's Blood reached up and grasped the man's forearm. "So what if you couldn't!" he shouted at his father. "No one in all this land would ever deny that you are more man than any of them could ever hope to be! You are Lone Eagle, whose knife is great medicine, and whose name is feared by all men who know you, men who would not even think of going against you, even now, because they know nothing can stop you—not even the pain you bear."

Zeke looked down at him from his mount. He knew this son

of his would be as lost without him as Abbie would—at least for a while. He could not speak harshly to his child, who would die in his place if he could. "It's all right, Wolf's Blood. Just do like I say and don't tell Abbie. Promise me."

The boy nodded.

"Now let's get the hell back to the barn before we all freeze out here!" Zeke shouted.

Wolf's Blood ran back to his own mount, untying the horse and the two mares. He held the ropes of the two mares in one hand. They would be easy to lead—much easier than the ornery *Kehilan*. He waved the lantern, signifying he was ready, and they headed back, following traces of the path they had already made but which was fast being covered by new snow.

It turned out to be a harsh winter, both in weather and for Zeke's arthritis. Spring was a most welcome sight, and with the melting snows came relief from the pain that had ravaged Zeke all winter. The swelling diminished. His old nature returned, except that he went through a new kind of suffering— withdrawal from the whiskey and laudanum he had grown dependent upon over the winter. He was determined that whiskey would not turn him into a useless mate, that nothing—not the arthritis or the whiskey or any medicine— would control Zeke Monroe. He spent two weeks in the foothills of the Rockies with Wolf's Blood, doing nothing but praying and renewing his spirit energy, suffering through a mild withdrawal. He returned an almost changed man, his relief over the subsiding arthritis putting him in a good mood, so good that he was again amorous in the gentle, teasing way that Abbie knew him best in bed. Both knew another winter would come, and perhaps he would go through the same thing again. How many more winters he could take that way he wasn't sure himself. But perhaps they would get lucky and the next winter or two would be kind to him.

It was the first of May when Sergeant Daniels came riding in. He was warmly greeted by everyone. Ellen literally ran to him from the garden, hugging him boldly, not caring who saw, for she had not seen her husband-to-be all winter. She was nearly

266

nineteen now, a beautiful young woman, her cheeks flushed with excitement now that he was here.

"Hal! How long do you have?"

He knew she was wondering how soon they would leave for Pueblo to be married. But his smile faded as he quickly kissed her cheek before the others reached them. "I have three weeks, Ellen, but I'm not sure we can use them."

She frowned, her eyes quickly tearing. "What do you mean? What's wrong?"

Zeke came riding up then, looking as strong and hard as ever, wearing only his fringed leggings, for it was a warm day. Daniels thought again what a formidable sight the man made, and it was hard to believe Ellen's letters about how sick her father had been over the winter. Zeke nodded to Daniels and dismounted, and Abbie approached from the house. Daniels stood with his arm around Ellen, not wanting to let go of her just yet. He shook hands with Zeke.

"So when do we all go to Pueblo for the wedding?" Zeke asked with a grin.

Daniels looked from Zeke to Ellen and back to Zeke. "Well, I'd like to go ahead and get married, sir. But I'm afraid Petersen has asked that you go directly to Fort Lyon. You're to go from there up to Fort Robinson and try to talk some hostiles into getting back down to Camp Supply."

Zeke frowned, looking at Abbie, who closed her eyes and turned away. "What's happened?" Zeke asked.

"It's been a bad winter, sir. You know what a hard one it was. Many of the hostiles who had been holding out surrendered: White Horse, Stone Calf, Red Moon. In early March, Gray Beard came in. They all surrendered at Fort Sill. Then instead of sending them on down to the reservation, the military authorities decided certain leaders of the hostiles should be arrested and sent to Fort Marion in Florida."

"Fort Marion!" Zeke exclaimed.

"Dear God," Abbie said quietly.

"I know. It's a hellhole. Few Indians who are sent there ever live long enough to get out again. There isn't a Plains Indian alive who can stand the swamps and heat and mosquitoes of that place." He looked at Wolf's Blood. "If I were you, Wolf's

Blood, I'd forget about ever rejoining in any fighting. Most of the hostiles are sent there now when they're caught. The old ways are just plain gone. Things are getting bad again up north, too. The Sioux and Northern Cheyenne are restless. More and more settlers are coming into Indian territory again, ignoring the treaty. Crazy Horse is in a tuff, that's sure. At any rate, there are a few left up at the Red Cloud Agency wanting to come back down but afraid to. They'd gone there during the winter for shelter. Petersen thought maybe you'd go up there and accompany some of them back south, seeing as how your brother Dan is up there—and Swift Arrow. You might want to see Swift Arrow once more, because I have a feeling there will be more fighting up there, Zeke. General Custer has been sent there. He led the battle at Washita, if you'll remember."

Wolf's Blood clenched his fist. "What about the ones arrested?" he asked.

Daniels shifted uncomfortably. "Well, you know how the Indians feel about arresting male prisoners. They don't understand it at all. The Indian always kills his male prisoners. To be arrested and shackled is a total disgrace, and I don't think there's an Indian alive who understands the white man's form of justice. The authorities picked out Gray Beard, Lean Bear, Medicine Water—even Medicine Water's wife, Calf Woman— and they picked out some just at random. When they started putting leg irons on the men, the women there began singing war chants. Well, you can imagine what happened next, with the men's pride stepped on by being arrested and the women singing war songs."

Wolf's Blood tossed his long hair behind his shoulder. "They broke loose!" he said with a grin.

Daniels nodded. "They did. But the guard opened fire, while men, women, and children began running in a panic for the sand hills about a mile south. They dug in for a fight, so the soldiers brought in reinforcements during the night, but in the darkness most of the Indians—even women and children— slipped right through the troops. In the morning the soldiers prepared for an attack, but found the Indian stronghold deserted."

"Good!" Wolf's Blood hissed. "The white man will never

learn to be as quiet as an Indian can be! That is a good trick they played on the soldiers!"

Daniels grinned a little. "It was. But you know those tiny victories can't really help, Wolf's Blood. And the way the authorities are getting, it wouldn't be wise for you to show too much happiness over any Indian victory. They're liable to arrest you, too. That's how bad things are."

"What happened to the Cheyenne who escaped?" Zeke asked.

"Most finally decided to go back, but they'd run into Little Bull's party, which was on its way in to surrender. News of the arrests at the agency and of some random killing of Cheyennes scared him off, and he turned north. Little Bull is quite a warrior, you know. He stopped to rest at the north fork of Sappa Creek, up in Kansas. A bunch of damned buffalo hunters spotted them and sicked the soldiers that way. A Lieutenant Henely was leading the soldiers who were chasing down the hostiles. He attacked Little Bull's village. You know the method—attack at dawn by surprise. The addition of the buffalo hunters' long guns did the job. A lot of Indians died, I'm afraid, including women and little ones. Little Bull was killed too. The few who escaped went on north and are under the protection of the Sioux at the Red Cloud Agency. Petersen thought maybe you could persuade a few of those to come back to Camp Supply."

Abbie turned around, her eyes wet with tears. "When will it end? When there isn't an Indian left on the face of the earth? Is that what it will take?"

'Daniels sighed deeply. "I think this is the end of it—at least for the Southern Cheyenne, ma'am. There will still be some fighting in the north, that's sure. Your husband would be wise to go up there and try to see Swift Arrow once more. It will even be dangerous for his white brother. He's right in the middle of everything."

Zeke rubbed at his eyes. "I'll ride to Fort Lyon. And I'll go north and see what I can do. But I'll not bring Indians back south to be executed or sent to prison." He looked at a dejected Ellen, then back to Daniels. "You two go on to Pueblo and get married. There's no sense putting that off. You have the time

Daniels. You needn't go back with me. You've waited a long time to make Ellen your wife."

"But Father, you should be there."

He just grinned. "I don't think you need me for what you two have to do. And my presence at the ceremony won't matter much. Besides, I'm uncomfortable around a white preacher."

Ellen reddened deeply and Daniels put out his hand. "Thank you, sir."

Zeke shook his hand again. "She'd better come back with a happy look on her face, that's all. You know what I'm talking about. You'll be gone again by the time I get back, but if my daughter is unhappy, you can bet I'll look you up."

Ellen covered her face bashfully and Daniels held her closer. "She'll be happy."

Zeke looked at Abbie. "Maybe you'd like to go to Pueblo with them," he told her. "It would help keep your mind off things for a while."

"Oh, Mother, would you?" Ellen asked. "I want one of you there. I don't want to get married without any of you around. And it would help keep you from worrying about Father."

Abbie was watching Zeke. "Anything could happen. It takes nothing to trigger the Indians now, and the soldiers. I don't want you getting caught in any cross fire."

"I've been caught in cross fire before, Abbie-girl. This doesn't sound that dangerous, and I would like to see Dan and Swift Arrow again. You go to Pueblo with Ellen. Wolf's Blood and I will be back by July or August."

She turned her eyes to her son. "And what will you do when you get north and see your uncle again? Will you come back?"

Wolf's Blood met his father's eyes. No. He would not leave his father, and he had Sonora. He looked back at his mother. "It will be tempting to stay. But like my father, I know those days are over."

"Do you?" Abbie challenged. "Will I really always have you here at the ranch, Wolf's Blood?"

He sighed and looked at the ground for a moment, then met her eyes again. "I can only promise the present. And I promise I will return with my father from the North."

A soft breeze blew, causing the tiny bells her son wore

braided into his hair to tinkle. For a moment Abbie could hear drums and chants. She knew deep in her heart that the warring would not end without her son getting involved again at some point. And as she had always done with his father, she would have to simply take one day at a time and be grateful for that day's blessings, trying hard not to worry about tomorrow. She turned to Ellen.

"I will go to Pueblo with you. You deserve that much. When we come back, you and Hal can stay in Wolf's Blood and Sonora's cabin until Hal has to leave again. Sonora and the children can stay with me in the house."

Ellen hugged her. "Thank you, Mother!"

Abbie just looked at Zeke. Again he would go away. Again she would wonder if he would come back.

Chapter Sixteen

Abbie watched the ceremony with an ache in her throat. It seemed only yesterday that Ellen was just a baby. All she had was Jason, but even he was no longer a child—not at sixteen.

She buried her resentment at the preacher's questions before he issued the marriage certificate.

"Nationality?"

"American."

"The parents?"

"My father is Ezekiel Monroe. His mother was Cheyenne," Ellen answered proudly, not afraid to tell him. "His father was a white man, from Tennessee."

The minister had frowned and glanced at Abbie. "And you are the mother?"

"I am. Abigail Monroe. My maiden name was Trent, and I have no Indian blood. I came here from Tennessee in 1845."

The man's eyebrows arched. "You must have been just a baby."

She smiled slightly, in spite of the man's obvious disapproval of her marriage to a half-breed. "Thank you. But I was fifteen. I married Ellen's father that same year, at Fort Bridger."

He studied her closely. "You have a certificate of marriage?"

Abbie bristled, reddening slightly. She did not want to spoil Ellen's special day with anger. "I have."

The man cleared his throat and kept writing. "The name of

your husband's parents?" he asked Abbie.

"His father was Hugh Monroe. His mother was called Gentle Woman. They are both dead, as are my parents. My mother Margaret died back in Tennessee. My father was Jason Trent. He died on the trip west."

"Religion?" He met her eyes again.

"I am a Christian. I do not have the pleasure of attending church, as our ranch is too remote from such things. My Bible is my church."

"And is the father a Christian?"

She met his eyes squarely. "My husband has his own religion. His God is called *Maheo,* although he has often mentioned he feels his God is probably my God also. My husband is a deeply religious person, Preacher Nathan, and believes in a Supreme Being. His faith has brought him through danger and pain, things most people could not endure. Because he is a half-breed, he has suffered physically and emotionally since he was a small boy, and I do not see what his faith has to do with my daughter getting married today. She is a good girl, a Christian in every way. Why don't you just get the information you need about her husband's background and let them get married? I have a feeling your questions are more out of curiosity than necessity."

The man reddened slightly and cleared his throat again, glancing at Hal Daniels and continuing his question. Ellen sat in anxious waiting, looking beautiful in a soft yellow dress Abbie had bought new for her in Pueblo, yellow flowers in her hair. The ceremony was finally over. A quiet dinner followed, after which Abbie assured them she was fine and they should go off alone and not worry about her. She would go to her own room, perhaps shop the next day, and gave them orders not to bother about her until they were good and ready. Ellen, her face flushed with love and excitement, gave her a quick kiss, and the two of them left her at the door to her hotel room, going to their own room and closing the door.

Abbie stared at the door for a moment, remembering the first time she had taken a man. How different the situation had been. Yes, they were married—later. But the first time Zeke Monroe made her his woman, she lay in the grass somewhere in

274

the wilds of Wyoming, and as far as she was concerned she was just as much his wife as if they'd seen a preacher first. She gave herself to Zeke Monroe in total love and devotion, heart and soul, not just body. No woman could have loved a man more, whether married in a church or not married at all. Her eyes teared and she turned into her room.

Zeke sat in council, surrounded by several Southern Cheyenne, including his own cousin, Iron Hand, son of Dog Man, Zeke's uncle. Dog Man was dead now, as were so many others, and Iron Hand and Zeke's brother Swift Arrow were the only real family left among the full-blooded Cheyennes. Zeke had gone directly to the Black Hills and into the largest Sioux village there, as directed by Lieutenant-Colonel Petersen. Dan and a company of soldiers had already gone there to talk to the Sioux leaders, among whom sat Red Cloud himself, as well as Young Man Afraid of His Horses, Spotted Tail, and Red Dog. The point of the council was twofold: to convince the Southern Cheyenne to return to their reservation, and to talk to the Sioux about selling a large section of the Black Hills. George Armstrong Custer had discovered the presence of gold in Sioux country, and both Zeke and Dan knew that if the Indians did not agree to changing the territory of their reservation, gold-hungry settlers would come into Indian country anyway, breaking the current treaty and starting yet another war.

The tension was thick. It was difficult for Zeke or Dan to argue with the Sioux, since deep in their hearts they knew the Indians were right. Already miners were streaming in, entrenching themselves along the streams and panning for gold. Dan had labored tirelessly in roaming the hills in search of illegal settlers, routing them out, fully aware that as soon as the soldiers left the miners would come back. The flow could not be stopped. Nothing was harder to halt than gold-seekers. It was impossible—as Dan knew it would be—to stop another war from breaking out, for the Sioux were not in the least interested in giving up more land.

"What promise do we have that we will not be arrested or

shot?" Iron Hand asked Zeke, questioning a return south.

"Just my word, Iron Hand," Zeke replied. "If anything goes wrong, I will turn on the soldiers and fight right by your side. You know I'll do it."

The man nodded. Iron Hand was forty-two now, yet it seemed only yesterday that the man was ten or twelve, and Zeke's father made a special trip to his village to work with the boy and teach him the Indian ways. It was often the custom of the Cheyenne for a boy to be trained by an uncle, just as Swift Arrow had trained Wolf's Blood.

"If you say this, you must be very sure no harm will come to us, Lone Eagle," his cousin replied. "You scout for the bluecoats now, but we know that our brother whose knife is great medicine would not betray his People. He would not track us and bring us back just to be killed or put in chains."

Zeke nodded. "No, I would not. I only want to help, Iron Hand. I know many of my people want to go back home to their families. I am here to assure you it is safe to go, as long as no raiding is done on the way south."

"Many of them will stay with us and prepare to fight for *Paha-Sapa!*" Swift Arrow spoke up angrily. "The Sioux and the Northern Cheyenne will not give in. Not now! Not ever! Let Long Hair Custer come into these hills and see what happens when he tries to force us onto smaller reservations! We have a treaty. The Great White Father in Washington must honor that treaty!"

"He wants to honor it, Swift Arrow," Dan spoke up. "But there are so many whites east of this land, so many you could never count them. And a lot of them are determined to come here and find gold. I do all I can to keep them out, according to the treaty. That's my job, and I work hard at it. But I can't keep up with it, Swift Arrow. I would need thousands of soldiers to keep up with it. You must believe that we are doing out best; but just as you and Red Cloud and the others try to act according to what your people want, so does our own Great White Father. His people are crying out that they should be allowed to come here and look for gold. And there are many more of them than there are of you. In the end, our President will have to give his people what they ask for."

Swift Arrow glared at him. "An Indian dies before he breaks a promise! The white man breaks a promise as easily as he spits tobacco!"

Zeke rubbed at his eyes. Things were much worse than he had thought. He was glad to have found Swift Arrow still doing well—almost too well, for his forty-eight-year-old half brother was still hard and strong. Like many Indian men he looked far younger than he really was—young enough and strong enough to fight, which he fully intended to do if necessary. That was what worried Zeke.

"I have seen the East," Red Cloud spoke up. His standing as a great leader, the man who had beaten the government and the soldiers once before in a fight for the Black Hills and Powder River country, commanded attention and respect. He was a handsome man, and Zeke fully believed the stories that Red Cloud, being such an honored warrior, had slept with many another warrior's wife, causing more than a few marital problems among the Sioux. Yet for the most part, a Sioux warrior would consider it a compliment for such a brave leader to desire his wife. "I have been to the place called Washington, and have spoken to the Great White Father," Red Cloud continued. "I have seen that there truly are many more white men than Indians, and they build great cities and have big guns and all the things they need to destroy the Indian. But they forget that the Indian is not afraid, and that when the Indian knows he is right, he will fight to the death. I have told your President our terms, and he did not accept them. Now we are being told we must go east of here to the Missouri River to accept our supplies. We are against this. We think this is a trick, to get us to go away from this place so that the soldiers and miners can take it over while we are gone." He looked at Dan. "You tell your leaders we do not accept this offer. We will provide for ourselves. We will not go out of this land. If your leaders cannot bring their promised food and goods here to us, then we cannot accept them. This is just one more way the white man has broken the treaty. The treaty says nothing of our leaving these hills and going east for our promised goods."

Wolf's Blood sat next to Zeke, his eyes dark, his attitude sullen. He was sorely tempted to stay with Swift Arrow, and if

277

not for the memory of the agonizing winter his father had had and for his beloved Sonora, he would stay and fight with his uncle. He liked the feeling of imminent war, the thought of again riding down on soldiers and settlers and showing them what happens to those who try to betray the Indian. But he knew as well as his father that if there was another war it would be the last one for the Sioux, and although they might do well for a while, they could never win this time.

Zeke looked at Iron Hand. "Are you going south with me?"

The man looked around him and behind him at the Southern Cheyenne present who had fled Fort Sill and had fought at Sappa Creek. He spoke to them for a moment. Most of them knew Zeke. One asked if he still had whiskey to trade, remembering him from the months he had snuck into Camp Supply to deliver the firewater to them.

Zeke shook his head. "I have told you many times the whiskey is bad for you. It makes you weak like women," he told them, speaking in Cheyenne. "I only brought the firewater because I was trying to help catch the white men who sent the whiskey. The white men who supply you with that whiskey are bad men. They are cheating you. You should not trade robes and needed food supplies for something that will only destroy you."

Iron Hand held his eyes. "Sometimes there is nothing left but to drink the firewater if a man wants to be happy. But even with the firewater, we are not happy being away from our families. We will go back with you."

The dickering over allowing miners into the Black Hills continued until Red Cloud abruptly stood up and said the conversation was finished. There would be no one allowed into their land without a fight, nor would the Sioux go east to the Missouri River for their supplies. He walked off, most of his people following. Swift Arrow stepped closer to Zeke and Wolf's Blood.

"I am glad you could come, my brother," he told Zeke, "even though it was not just to visit as it was the last time you came here. I am sad that it must be this way. I know you are trying to help in your way, and that you would not betray your own. I will be even sadder to see you go again, for this is the last

278

time I will see you. My dreams have told me so."

There were suddenly tears in his eyes. Dan watched curiously, thinking Swift Arrow meant he would probably die in battle. But Zeke knew that the man meant it was the last time he would see Zeke alive. Swift Arrow knew the last time Zeke had visited him that something was very wrong, and both men sensed there was very little time left for Zeke. They had had a chance to visit alone before the pow-wow, and Zeke had finally told Swift Arrow the details of his illness.

They clasped hands. What was there to say? The memories went back many years, to days of riding free, hunting, bringing meat to their mother. They had led very different lives over the years, yet had remained one in spirit, even to both loving the same women, one openly, one secretly.

"We will be together always," Zeke told the man, his throat aching. "One day we will ride the clouds together, Swift Arrow. Our horses will have wings, and there will be none faster. And nothing will separate us. There will be no war and no distance between us."

Dan turned away, sensing an intimacy he should not even be watching, unaware of the real reason the parting was so difficult for the two of them.

"And what of Abbie?" Swift Arrow asked quietly. "You are her life."

Zeke released his hand. "Abbie will always survive."

Swift Arrow nodded. "I suppose. I remember the first day you came riding into our village, Crows chasing you. Her horse fell and she came tumbling toward me, then stood up and shot a Crow warrior." He grinned. "I think of that scene often. I was not very nice to her in the beginning. I did not like a white woman being around. But soon I grew to respect her."

Their eyes held. Zeke knew he wanted to say that he also loved her, but he would not say it aloud, nor would he ever say it in front of Wolf's Blood, even though the two of them had spoken of it once. Swift Arrow had said he would speak of it no more, and he had not.

The man turned his eyes to his beloved nephew. "I am glad you have a woman, Wolf's Blood, and a son and daughter. This is good. It is right that you go back. I can see in your eyes that you want to stay. But do not think I am foolish enough to think we truly can win another war. I know we cannot. But I will fight anyway. For your father's sake, it is good that you go back—for him, for your woman and children, who need you. And one day soon your mother will need you also, for in your eyes she will see your father and will be comforted."

He took out his knife, and Zeke was not surprised when the man quickly slashed the weapon across his own chest. Dan glanced over and stared wide-eyed, unaware of why the man was displaying a sign of grief. He stood back with other soldiers, unable to hear what was being said, but suddenly aware there was more going on than a simple farewell. Swift Arrow pressed his fingers against his wound, then smeared streaks of blood on Zeke's cheeks.

"I show you now only a little of how I will grieve when I know my brother has breathed his last breath."

Zeke's jaw flexed with emotion, his eyes tearing. Wolf's Blood swallowed and turned away, fighting a display of emotion himself.

"*Ne-mehotatse*," Swift Arrow said softly to Zeke.

"Zeke swallowed. "*Ne-mehotatse*," he replied. "*Ciksuya canna śna cantemawaśte yelo*," he added in the Sioux tongue. ("Whenever I remember you, my heart is happy.")

Swift Arrow nodded and turned to Wolf's Blood, touching the young man's shoulder so that he turned to face his uncle. He touched a streak of blood on each of the boy's cheeks. "You are the son I never had. Your father let me have you for a while, and for this I am grateful. You brought light to my life. I will see you again, Wolf's Blood, but there will be much sadness when I do. May the Gods be with you."

"And with you, my uncle," the boy replied. A tear slipped unwantedly down his face and Swift Arrow quickly whisked it away with his thumb, then smiled.

"Do not be ashamed. It is only tears of fear and cowardice that bring shame, not tears of love and sorrow. Go now. Stay with your father and take your people south. This is my home now."

He looked once more at Zeke, then turned abruptly and walked to his horse, mounting up and waving once before riding off. Zeke breathed deeply for self-control before walking back to Dan, who still stood staring.

"What the hell was that all about?" the man asked.

Zeke took some tobacco from a pouch and began rolling a cigarette. He didn't feel like talking about it anymore. What good would it do to tell Dan and Bonnie? They had enough worries of their own. Right now Bonnie waited at Fort Robinson, probably worried to death about her husband riding into hostile Indian country.

"Swift Arrow is just thinking he might be killed fighting," he told Dan. "He felt this was out last good-bye."

"But . . . he cut himself. That's the Cheyenne sign of mourning, as though someone else was going to die."

"He used it to signify himself this time," Zeke lied. "I hope he'll prove to be wrong. I'm worried, Dan, about this whole mess," he continued, trying to veer the conversation in another direction. "Things are going to explode up here."

Dan sighed, lighting a thin cigar. "You're right there, brother. And it's all thanks to Custer. He spotted some flakes of gold in a creek and shouted it all over the East through the newspapers. You know what that means. There are already miners all over these hills. I can't keep up with it, Zeke. Red Cloud and the others are stomping mad, and I don't even blame them."

"And Custer will do everything he can to make matters worse. He's an arrogant cuss. I've heard plenty about him, ever since he attacked the Cheyenne at the Washita. Personally, I'd like to see him surrounded and scalped some day. It would serve him right."

"Well, you just might get your wish. He's the careless sort—takes a lot for granted. He'd better not take these Sioux and Cheyenne for granted, I'll tell you that. There are thousands of them in these hills, and they're damned good fighters. And there can be thousands of them in the hills all around you without your even being aware of it. I wish I could get Bonnie to go east and get out of this mess, but she won't leave my side, which makes me very happy but worries me, too. At least Joshua isn't around."

"How is the boy doing?"

281

Dan frowned, taking a puff on the cigar. "I suppose I ought to tell you, Zeke, that before he went off to college, Bonnie told him the whole truth about his identity."

Zeke glanced at Wolf's Blood, who looked as surprised as Zeke was. "What did he say?" Wolf's Blood asked.

Dan shrugged. "Well, he actually took it quite well. I'd say he's actually happy about it. But he said he wished he was part Cheyenne instead of Arapaho, because you're Cheyenne and he thinks you two are the greatest warriors who ever walked."

They all laughed lightly, the spell broken over the sad parting with Swift Arrow. But there was still a gnawing pain in Zeke's chest. There would be time for weeping later, when he was alone and could smoke his prayer pipe. He sobered again and puffed his cigarette.

"I hope you warned the boy not to tell anyone else his identity—that it could be dangerous," he told Dan.

"We did. But I have to tell you, Zeke, that he deliberately went to a talk given by Charles Garvey himself in Washington. He actually stood up and argued with the man about Indians, without Garvey even realizing who he was talking to. Josh told us in his letter that Garvey was raging mad and they had a hell of an argument. I'd have loved to see it."

Wolf's Blood frowned. "He saw Charles Garvey—face-to-face?"

Dan nodded. "Can you believe it? And Garvey is still half crippled from that fight at Sand Creek—walks with a cane."

Wolf's Blood looked up at Zeke and grinned. Zeke laughed lightly. "Wolf's Blood did that to him," he told Dan. "He recognized Garvey that day—sunk his lance right into his thigh, right through the bone."

Dan folded his arms. "Well, I'll be damned."

Wolf's Blood scowled again. "He is the one who killed the Cheyenne girl I was to marry," he added. "If I was not so badly wounded myself, I would have killed Charles Garvey. But I was only able to get my lance into his leg."

Dan shook his head. "Isn't it strange what a small world it is?" He puffed the cigar again. "At any rate, Josh said Garvey is married now—it's been about two and a half years, I guess. Says the man's wife is real pretty—prettier than Garvey deserves, I'll bet. But then the rich ones always get what they want, I suppose. Garvey is a lawyer in Washington, but still writes a lot of articles about the West in eastern newspapers. Josh is in New York. He's a journalist for *The New York Times*. He also writes articles about the West, but he tells the truth about the Indians and has already won a wide audience. He and Garvey are getting quite a little battle going, so Josh tells me. By the way, what do you hear from LeeAnn?"

Zeke's eyes saddened. "Very little. The last we knew she was working in Washington herself. She doesn't ask for money anymore, and she doesn't even show a return address when she writes. It's very obvious she doesn't want to hear from us and doesn't want us to show up there."

Dan scowled. "I'm sorry, Zeke. And Jeremy?"

Wolf's Blood's face darkened. "Jeremy is a traitor! He works for the railroad. He has a fancy place in Denver, married a fancy woman, and thinks he is too good for us. We never hear from him either, and that is just fine with me!"

"Don't speak so harshly against your brother, Wolf's Blood," Zeke told his son. "He has his life and you have yours."

Dan's blue eyes studied his warrior nephew. "I can't believe how much like your father you are, Wolf's Blood, the way he was at your age—hot-tempered, sure of what's right and wrong, and allowing no deviations. I've seen a lot of sons who looked like their fathers. You not only look like yours, but you're like him in every other way." He stepped closer. "You remember something, Wolf's Blood. Zeke and I were always very different, and for a long time Zeke hated our father while I loved him. I disagreed with him about that, but it never interfered with how I felt about him as a brother. I still loved him. I simply hoped that one day he would realize he really did love his father. You think Jeremy has deserted him, but he hasn't. They're simply too different to be close, just as Zeke was too different from his father to be close to him. And I hope if you run into Jeremy again you'll try to understand him, forgive him, talk to him like a brother and see if you can't patch things up."

Wolf's Blood tossed his hair haughtily, reminding Dan of a

restless stallion. "It works both ways," the young man grumbled.

Dan looked at Zeke, and the two men smiled rather sadly. "Yes, it does," Dan answered. He sighed deeply. "I know a little of how you're feeling, Zeke. Josh is in New York, and my Jennifer is in Denver now. She's eighteen already." He shook his head. "It's hard to believe. She's a teacher, and engaged to a professor. I wish you could see her. She's as pretty as Emily was, only stronger—physically and in character."

Zeke smiled. "If she looks like Emily, she has to be beautiful. I only met your first wife that one time. She was a most beautiful woman, but she reminded me of a piece of china about to break."

Dan puffed the cigar for a moment, turning to look at a campfire in the distance. "She was like that. If I'd had any sense I never would have married her. But when you've been out here in this godforsaken land, and then you go back to a place like St. Louis and set eyes on something like that, it kind of takes away all your common sense. Before I knew it we were married." He seemed to be reflecting on a personal basis, as though no one else was there. "You're right," he said quietly. "She was a piece of china about to break. We were never very happy. God knows we weren't together enough to straighten out our problems. But she gave me Jennifer."

Wolf's Blood tried to picture Jennifer, a full-grown woman now. Was her hair still as red as the sunset? Were her lips still the color of roses and her skin as soft and smooth-looking as the cream his mother skimmed from churned milk? He turned and walked to his horse, suddenly angry with himself for having thought about her, wondered about her. He had seen her only once; that was six years ago, and it was most likely he would never see her again.

"We'll be heading south in the morning," Zeke told Dan. "I'll go tell Iron Hand and the others to be ready. What's next for you, Dan?"

Dan threw down his cigar stub. "Back to Fort Robinson—to wire my superiors and tell them they'll have to come up with some better ideas or get ready for a full-fledged war." He met his brother's eyes and Zeke smoked the last of his cigarette.

"You be careful, Dan. I'd love to see the Indians win this one, but I don't want anything to happen to you."

"It's hell being able to see both sides, isn't it?"

Zeke stepped out the cigarette stub. "Life's been hell for me ever since I can remember, except for Abbie." He put out his hand. "Give our love to Bonnie."

Dan nodded. "You know I will."

"And let us know if anything develops with Josh and Charles Garvey. If Josh decides to spill the truth, we should know, because we'll be involved, too."

"I wouldn't worry—not for a long time anyway. Josh wants the time to be just right—wants to carve his own place in the world first, build his own importance and reputation. He'll have to be very sure of his timing, and ready to defend his stand. If and when Charles Garvey ever finds out who Joshua Lewis is, there's no telling what the man will do."

"That's for certain. The son is worse than the father was, if that's possible."

Dan folded his arms. "It's strange how Winston Garvey just disappeared, isn't it? I wonder if the boy had anything to do with that—maybe wanting to come into his father's money."

Zeke's eyes turned cold. "Charles Garvey had nothing to do with his father's disappearance. That's one thing I'm sure of."

"Well, brother of mine, how do you know—?" Dan didn't finish the sentence. The look in Zeke's eyes frightened even him. "Good God, Zeke . . . you?"

Zeke smiled, but it was an almost evil smile, one a man would give when experiencing a haughty, vengeful victory. "Now, Dan, did I say that?" He put a hand on the other man's shoulder. "Subject closed." Dan stared at him in surprise, wanting to ask questions. But he could see they would not be answered and knew he was probably better off not knowing.

He nodded with understanding eyes. "I hope it isn't another six years before I see you again, Zeke."

Zeke's eyes saddened. He knew it was very likely he would not see this brother again either. Dan had been loyal, coming west to search for him years ago and landing himself in the Army in the process. They had been close, even though separated by miles and years most of the time.

285

"I hope so, too, Dan."

In the distance drums started beating. Red Cloud, Swift Arrow, and the others would hold another pow-wow of their own, without white men, to decide what they should do about the miners who illegally came into their land. There was a treaty. The whites would obey it, or suffer the consequences.

Abbie dug some carrots, trying to keep busy. Ellen pulled some weeds nearby, worried about her own husband now, who had gone back to Fort Lyon. In only a few months he would be through with the Army, and they could settle in the little cabin whose foundation had already been laid before he left. Hal was everything she had imagined he would be, considerate and gentle, but a strong man who she knew would protect and defend her. She was more in love now than the day they married.

Abbie was happy for her daughter, but worried about Zeke. In Pueblo all she heard were stories about gold in the Black Hills, the determination of men to go there in spite of the treaty with the Sioux, and the fact that they might be attacked by Indians. What would happen to Swift Arrow? Surely he would be in the midst of the fighting. She only hoped Zeke had run into no trouble of his own. And poor Dan. Surely Dan would also be heavily involved. It would be hard on him, knowing Swift Arrow was out there—somewhere.

It was late July. Zeke should be back soon if nothing had gone wrong. She laid the carrots in a basket and stood up, turning at the sound of a war whoop on the northern rise, wondering at first if she should get her rifle.

She shaded her eyes as two Indians rode hard toward the ranch, then she set the basket down and smiled. "Ellen, it's your father and Wolf's Blood! Go and get Sonora!"

She began running toward them. Every time her husband returned from danger now she was more relieved than usual. The last winter had been so terrible for him, so full of pain. Surely it would not be long before he found a way to die honorably. But he came back again. She still had her Cheyenne warrior!

His Appaloosa came galloping toward her, and he called out in Cheyenne for his "white woman." She laughed and reached up, and he grabbed her, slowing his mount but not stopping. She gave a little scream as he turned the horse, hoisting her up in front of him and heading for their secret place at the stream.

"Zeke, I'm a mess!" she objected. "I've been digging carrots."

"You look beautiful," he told her, heading toward the place where the grass was thick and soft, and the irises bloomed.

Chapter Seventeen

Abbie brushed out her husband's hair, something she always loved to do. A blanket was wrapped around her naked body, and Zeke sat on the soft grass wearing nothing. No one would bother them here. They all knew better. This was their parents' special place, and having all his gear already on his horse when he returned, Zeke had simply taken his woman to their place by the stream as soon as he returned. They had everything they needed to spend the day there, and they had been apart too long.

Abbie's superficial objections did not last long, for when Zeke Monroe wanted his woman, there was seldom any arguing. It was not long before it didn't seem to matter that she had just been digging carrots. He was back! Zeke was back and she was lying beneath him. The best part was that he seemed so very strong and well. How she prayed he could stay that way!

He had taken her quickly and with great passion. She knew that it would not be enough for him, nor was it for her. They would talk, but they would make love again before he took her back. Now he smoked quietly as she brushed his hair. How she had missed doing this when he was gone. It was something Indian women liked to do for their husbands and so did Abbie. Then she began rebraiding one tiny section at the side, weaving a beaded rawhide strip into the braid.

"In Pueblo all I heard was talk about gold in the Black Hills," she told him as she worked.

He watched the rippling waters of the nearby stream. "It's

there all right. You know what that means?"

"White men in Indian Territory."

"Plenty of them. Too many for poor Dan to keep up with. His job is to kick them back out, but it's an impossible task, Abbie, and I think the government is going to make its own rules and say to hell with the treaty. That's not only illegal, but the Sioux and Northern Cheyenne won't stand for it. It's a real powder keg. I'd like to get my hands on General Custer. He started the whole thing."

She sighed deeply. "If not Custer, it would have been someone else. Did you see Swift Arrow? Is he all right?"

He nodded, taking another drag on his cigarette. He knew she sensed that his brother loved her, but she never spoke of it. "He's as mean and ornery as ever, if that's what you mean. And if there's trouble, he'll be in the thick of it." He threw down his cigarette. "It's such an impossible mess, Abbie. I can see both sides and I don't see an answer. The white man's desire for gold is incredible. Most of the men going there, risking their lives and stirring up trouble, will never find enough gold to make it worth it. Only a few will find the right places. But they all dream of being one of the few, my darling. It happened in California, and then here in Colorado. Now it's happening in the Black Hills. Once there was nothing in Denver. Then someone found gold, and now look.

"Whites everywhere—and nearly all Indians run out of the territory. It has to end someplace, but I don't see where it will. The worst part is they're spreading the rumor that there could be more gold in the Black Hills than any of the other strikes. So the surge will be even worse. It's going to be bad for them, Abbie. The Sioux, Swift Arrow, and the others—they'll never win this one. The gold-hungry miners and the government behind them will sweep through there and that will be the end of it. I see the entire Indian nation in this country slowly crumbling by the wayside, and sometimes I wonder if there will be any left some day—like the buffalo."

She leaned down and kissed his shoulder. "Let's not think about it for today. I'm so glad to have you back, and feeling so well besides."

He put out his cigarette, turning and grabbing her around

the neck, pulling her around in front of him. He bent his legs and she rested her head against his knees, facing him as he traced his fingers over the silky skin of her shoulders and studied her dark eyes.

"You're wanting to tell me something else, Abbie-girl. I can see it in those eyes. Did something happen I should know about?"

She frowned. "Sort of."

He twisted a piece of her hair in his fingers. "And what is that supposed to mean? It isn't Ellen, is it? Is she all right? How did the wedding go? Is she happy? If Hal Daniels harmed her, I'll—"

"Ellen is fine," she told him quickly. "In fact, she wears a happy glow she never had before, and it was on her face the first time I saw her after their wedding night. I'm sure she's very happy, and Hal is good to her, Zeke. He's off to active duty again, but he'll be back in the spring. This will be a long winter for poor Ellen."

He toyed with the piece of twisted hair. "Well, I'll have my own talk with her when we go back. But I'm glad she seems happy, and glad they'll be settling nearby. Hal must have been sent on down to Camp Supply. I didn't see him at Fort Lyon. By the way, I didn't tell you about the odd thing that happened at Fort Lyon, did I?"

She frowned. "What do you mean?"

"That Lieutenant Henely was there—the man who attacked the Cheyenne at Sappa Creek. He was showing off a war bonnet tipped with buffalo horns that had belonged to White Bear. He also had a silver belt he'd taken from a young woman after she'd been killed. There was a Cheyenne woman there watching him show off the articles, bragging about the battle. She recognized the articles, even named the woman from whom the belt had been taken. She looked straight at Henely and predicted the man would come to a violent death for what he'd done." He studied the reddish tint to her lustrous hair. "It was a chilling moment. She seemed so sure."

She ran her hand along his powerful forearm. "Well, you certainly know how the Indians are about those things. You made a prediction once that one day I would stand beside you,

291

although at that time you wouldn't tell me because you were so afraid harm would come to me if you made me your woman."

Their eyes held. "It wasn't Ellen who was on your mind, was it?" he asked.

She swallowed. "No. We . . . received a letter . . . from England."

He studied her eyes, the old jealousy rising, even though he knew it was unnecessary. "Edwin Tynes?"

"Yes."

He let go her the piece of hair and began straightening it by pushing his fingers through it. "He's been gone a good ten years. I didn't figure we'd ever hear from him again."

"He just wanted to write once, to inquire if things were still all right here, and to let us know he's fine, living in his mansion in England. He finally married again. I think he knew we would like to know that. And he sent a copy of an English newspaper, showing one of the many articles he's been writing about the American West, and the strength of its . . . pioneer women."

She saw the mixture of jealousy and sadness in his eyes. Sir Edwin Tynes owned a massive estate next to their land, and the widowed Englishman had watched after Abbie and the children while Zeke had ridden south to search for LeeAnn after the Comanches stole her away. Tynes had fallen deeply in love with Abigail Monroe. He admired her strength and courage, and was fascinated by her beauty in spite of the hardships, her willingness to come to a lawless land with a half-breed husband and put up with all the difficulties that combination can bring to a woman. Tynes had made no effort to hide his love, and had offered Abigail the world on a silver platter, for he was a wealthy, educated, worldly man. Zeke knew the man loved Abbie, and for a while he made life very difficult for his wife, thinking perhaps she would be better off with someone like Tynes after all. Zeke's love for her was so great that he considered bearing the sorrow of letting her go, so that she could live out the rest of her life in luxury and wealth and comfort. For deep inside the brave man lay a little boy who had always felt guilty that he had brought his Abbie to this land and that she had suffered so much for staying with him. He almost rode north after finding LeeAnn and bringing her home, planning to join the Sioux and Red Cloud and let himself be killed. That would free his Abbie to live the life she deserved to have.

But Abbie would have none of it. She had turned down a chance at something most women prayed for. But Abbie didn't want Sir Edwin Tynes's luxuries and comforts. She wanted only her Zeke, accepting whatever hardships might come with that. For what good was a fancy bed and beautiful clothes, a mansion and servants, if she could not have her Zeke? Edwin Tynes could have given her everything, and she turned it down; and though Zeke was tempted to just leave her, for her own good, he also could not go. Though he knew she'd have been better off, he could not bear the thought of another man touching his Abbie.

He smoothed back her hair. "It's pioneer women, hmmm?"

"Yes. It's a beautiful article, Zeke. Very well written."

"That's because he was thinking of you when he wrote it; and all that love he had for you came right through, I'm sure."

"I . . . I thought you'd like to read the letter . . . see the article. But I wasn't quite sure how to tell you. I hope it doesn't upset you. Edwin was very good to us, and it's been ten years since we heard from him after he left. I think he deliberately kept silent, knowing that was best. And now he's married again. I'm glad for him."

Zeke stared in the direction of the Tynes land. Somewhere out there the great stone mansion still sat. Tynes had built it to remind him of England, and Zeke supposed the man had hoped to live in it with Abbie. But that could not be, and Tynes had left, turning the ranch over to a brother and an uncle, who ran it for three years, then sold it to an American rancher from Nebraska. The American preferred a simple log house to the mansion, and now the great castle Edwin Tynes had built sat empty, most of its contents and expensive furnishings and accessories sold off or shipped back to England. It seemed almost haunted—haunted by memories; haunted by things that could have been but never were. That had been a hard time for Zeke and Abbie, the closest they had ever come to parting. But real love bears all things and cannot be denied. Zeke had seen the mansion a time or two in his travels, and it gave him chills. What had ever made him think he could live without his Abbie? Abbie refused to go and see it at all. She did not want to be reminded of those sad times, for in the midst of their troubles, her little Lillian had died and still lay buried on a little knoll on the Tynes property.

He met Abbie's eyes again, then her lips, pulling the blanket from her naked body and laying her back on it. There was nothing to say. The thought of those years brought out a need to make love again, to remind one another who they belonged to, who they loved and could not be without. She broke into tears, remembering how determined he'd been to leave her for her own good, remembering that he had even gone to the harlot Anna Gale in Denver to vent his needs and try to prove to himself he didn't need his Abbie. But it hadn't worked. Some things could not be denied, and this was one of them.

She whispered his name as he moved between her slender thighs, pushing himself inside of her again. There were so many reasons they must do this often, and for a moment the memory of Swift Arrow smearing blood on his cheeks in sorrow flashed into Zeke's mind. He thrust himself hard then and she cried out with the force of it, arching up to him in return. Edwin Tynes had been a handsome, dashing, worldly man that most women would pray to find. But how could he compare to this man who hovered over her now? How could he compare to Zeke Monroe's dark handsomeness; to Zeke Monroe's magnificent build; to this man who had many times risked his life for her, who had protected and defended her, and who loved her beyond all common forces? Could it really be true they had been together thirty years now? Or was it only thirty days? No length of time was long enough, and if she could live to three hundred she would want to stay with this man. Her love, her life! But what if she had only a year left with him, or perhaps two? What would she do? There was no Abigail Monroe. There was only Zeke Monroe's woman, and the thought of being alone brought terror to her heart. No! He must never leave her. Never!

She cried out his name again, pushing, giving, and also taking. Time was growing short. She felt it in her bones. She would take advantage of every moment—every sweet moment—and let her passions flow like the rippling waters of the nearby stream.

While gathering supplies at Fort Lyon in April of 1876, they heard the news. The first spoken words had been heard through a contraption called a telephone, in March of that year. The Indians had thought the talking wires of the telegraph had been magic enough. But a device that could transmit actual voices? All the way home Zeke and Abbie and Ellen talked about it, joking at how handy the telephone would have been during all the times Zeke had had to be away from home.

"Just think of the worry it could have saved me!" Abbie teased.

"Well, maybe they can throw a voice from one room to another, maybe even across the street," Zeke replied. "But they'll never create something that can carry voices over the miles."

They rode on silently for a while, both staring ahead then looking at each other. "Never underestimate the white man's hunger for progress," she told him.

He nodded, frowning. "I was thinking the same thing." He looked back over the horizon again. "It's all changing, isn't it, Abbie? I see all the old ways vanishing. Remember how empty this land was when you and I settled along the river? All we had was a tipi, and there wasn't a soul around but a few trappers at Old Bent's Fort."

"And the Indians," she added.

The wagon clattered on toward home. He nodded. "And the Indians."

In May of that year Hal Daniels came home to stay, much to the great joy of Ellen, and Zeke was kept busy making trips to his son-in-law's property to help finish their cabin. In early July of that same year, Zeke Monroe came home with a face almost gray with dread. He sank into a kitchen chair, ordering an alarmed Abbie to go and get Wolf's Blood.

"Zeke, what is it?" she asked. "Has something happened to Ellen?"

He closed his eyes, putting his head in his hands. "No," he answered quietly, resting his elbows on the table. He rubbed at his eyes for a moment, then faced her again, his eyes red. "About five thousand Sioux and Northern Cheyenne wiped out General Custer and roughly two hundred and twenty-five soldiers under Custer's command a couple of weeks ago. At least those are the figures for now. There might have been even more warriors than that."

She sat down slowly. "Wiped out?"

"Massacred. Every Indian leader we've ever heard of took part: Sitting Bull, Crazy Horse, Gall, Red Horse, White Bull, Dull Knife." He sighed deeply. "I have no doubt Swift Arrow was there, too."

She waited a moment, trying to let it sink in. "Where did it happen?" she asked.

"On the Little Bighorn River. I guess just a few days before that, soldiers had attacked a peaceful Cheyenne village on Rosebud Creek, getting them really riled."

"How did you find out?"

"I rode into Fort Lyon to get some things for Hal and Ellen. Everybody was talking about it there. The stories are wild and mixed up. The only thing that is sure is that Custer and his men were all killed. The Indians were together in great force, and red-hot because their treaty was broken. I guess they'd been ordered onto smaller reservations over the winter and refused to go, so Custer and others were sent into the field to force them to go. No one is sure why or how the man rode right into the middle of such a huge gathering of Indians. They say that including women and children there must have been a good ten thousand Indians in the area. They panicked when they saw Custer coming. The warriors gathered, and that was that. When an Indian is mad, no prisoners are taken. The enemy must die."

Abbie looked at her lap. She wore a tunic that day, and she picked at the rawhide fringes of the dress. "Things will be very bad for them now, won't they? The government won't let this go lightly."

He rose, turning and slamming a fist against the wall. "They had a right! They had a right to kill the bastards! The soldiers shouldn't have been there! The miners shouldn't be there. None of them should be there! There's a treaty! But the goddamned whites are so gold-hungry they're blinded by it! Sure, give the Indians some land, until you find out there's something valuable on it! Then they can't have it any more. Then the government comes and says they're sorry but the poor Indian will have to move on." He turned to face her, his eyes blazing. "And the soldiers have no idea the terror that fills the hearts of the women and children when they see soldiers coming. The Cheyenne especially have memories—of Blue Water Creek and Sand Creek and Washita. They saw Custer and his men and the warriors moved quickly. They weren't about to let that happen again. And it's the Indian way to kill his enemy and spare none, but the government doesn't understand that! Don't you see, Abbie? If they'd just take the time to understand how the Indian thinks, why he behaves as he does, to remember the Indians have memories of unprovoked slaughters of their own women and children; if they would just try to think the way the Indian thinks, they could work with them, be at peace with them. The Indian doesn't understand a man who will make a promise and then break it over and over again. He doesn't understand what the white man wants, why it's so important to go after the gold. Gold doesn't mean a damned thing to them!"

"Zeke, you don't have to explain those things to me. I understand just as much as you do."

His breathing was quick, his eyes teared. "Then you must understand that this is the end, Abbie! It's the end. The government and soldiers won't let up now. Not just the Sioux, but the Apache and the Utes and the Nez Perce—all of them! Already most Indians have been swept under the rug, buried on putrid reservations to rot and die, and none of them give a damn!" His teeth were gritted and he threw his head back, breathing deeply. "They won at the Little Bighorn," he said, his voice husky with emotion. "But they've sentenced themselves to death. I said myself I'd like to see Custer get his due, but this will go badly. They're dying, Abbie, just as surely as if someone were slowly sinking swords into their hearts. They're dying . . . and I'm dying. There is not future now—

not for them . . . and not for me."

He turned and walked out, and her heart shattered at the words. She felt the need to run after him, but knew he did not want her to. She sat frozen in the chair. "Zeke," she whispered. Her heart pounded wildly. She was not foolish enough to think she was his only reason for living, although she meant the world to him. But there was something else that had been important to him, something that was a part of him; and now that something was dying, and part of Zeke Monroe was dying with it.

The government and Army swore revenge. The Black Hills, with their billions in gold, were declared the property of the U.S. government, whether the Indians liked it or not. After a savage campaign against the Sioux and Northern Cheyenne, who had only fought for something they thought belonged to them because the government had promised it would, the Indians were finally severely beaten and surrendered from starvation and broken spirits, signing a new treaty they did not understand, giving up the sacred Black Hills. None knew then that for well over the next hundred years there would continue to be bitter fighting over the legality of that treaty, signed by the Indians because of trickery, false promises, and threats. But the damage was done. Five months after the Little Bighorn, the great Cheyenne chiefs, Dull Knife and Little Wolf, were defeated, many of their people killed, their villages plundered and burned, everything destroyed.

It seemed war had broken out everywhere, and the saddest part was that the soldiers were pitting Indian against Indian, bribing and frightening Indians to turn on their own kind and help the soldiers find and attack hostiles. And after surrendering the Black Hills, the Sioux and Northern Cheyenne were forced into humiliation when their guns and ponies were taken, their tipis searched, the men put under arrest and not even allowed to ride horses. Every place they went they had to walk. There was nothing more important to an Indian warrior than his horses. To walk was to be a woman, and they were broken and disgraced.

And so indeed the battle at the Little Bighorn had brought a reprisal from Washington that cost the Sioux and Northern Cheyenne all that was most important to them, even though they had been right to fight for what was theirs. But the white man wanted the gold, and if not the Little Bighorn, Washington would have found some other excuse to sweep through *Paha-Sapa* and kill and destroy.

In 1877 the great Sioux Chief, Crazy Horse, was bayoneted by a Sioux scout, while peacefully surrendered at Fort Robinson. He was unarmed, a prisoner, yet still a hero to the young warriors. He was killed by another Sioux, one of the many who had allowed themselves to be bought off by the soldiers, who had lost their pride and their fighting spirit.

Not long after, the Northern Cheyenne who had surrendered with Crazy Horse at Fort Robinson were ordered south, to join their relatives on their reservation in Oklahoma. None of them wanted to go. All thought they would be allowed to stay on the Red Cloud reservation with the Sioux, for their leaders, Dull Knife and Little Wolf, had signed the treaty along with the Sioux in 1868, verifying that the Northern Cheyenne could stay in the Black Hills. But the orders came from Washington: They must go south. And so in still another way that treaty of 1868 had been broken, and through the summer of 1877 a thousand Cheyenne made the sad walk south to a land they hated. The trip took three months, and many old people died along the way. A few stubborn warriors slipped quietly through the soldiers and turned back north, refusing to go to the hated new reservation. Among them was Swift Arrow.

In that same year the Nez Perce, a totally cooperative and peaceful tribe in Oregon, were brutally chased from their promised land by whites who simply did not want them there anymore. After a thirteen-hundred-mile struggle, the Nez Perces, under Old Chief Joseph, the eloquent, peace-loving leader who had tried so hard to get along with the whites and abide by their treaty, gave up the fight. But that had not been good enough for the settlers. And in his own poignant words the old chief summed up the way nearly all the old chiefs of all the nations were feeling in their hearts:

"Hear me, my chiefs! I am tired; my heart is sick and sad.

From where the sun now stands, I will fight no more forever."

As predicted by the Cheyenne woman at Fort Lyon, Lieutenant Henely did die. He drowned in Arizona. The woman's prediction had come true; the white soldier paid his price for taking sacred objects from the dead bodies of Indians he had killed.

It seemed during those years of the final demise of the Indian, the very earth and wind were crying out for the People, carrying their mournful wails through the mountains and across the plains. There were death songs in the air, and the rain was their tears. And through it all Abbie saw a restlessness in her husband, and death in his own eyes.

The big black engine belched and hissed as it pulled to a halt. Twenty-five-year-old Jeremy Monroe disembarked, walking to the end of the platform and staring out at Fort Lyon. This was familiar territory—and very close to the ranch. The train whistle blew, and more people came off while others climbed aboard. Soldiers dallied here and there, as well as a few Indians, some apparently working on the loading docks, others just sitting and staring. One looked up at Jeremy, his eyes red from whiskey, droopy bags under them from too many tears. Jeremy felt a pain in his chest. The small amount of Indian he had felt in his blood had disappeared completely. He had been a part of orders to kill Indians who interfered with the railroad, and was also behind much of the slaughtering of the buffalo to feed railroad workers. Now, just as he had predicted, the railroad went all the way to Denver, across the plains of Kansas, through the heart of what was once Indian country.

He straightened his silk vest. At twenty-five, he was extremely successful. His keen mind for business, his loyalty, his eagerness, and his intelligence had brought him a long way fast, and he was proud of himself. He had a fine house in Denver, and a perfect wife. He had a strength of his own, but did not stop to think of where that strength came from; nor did he think about the fact that it was his mother who had taught him so faithfully and so well right at home when he was small, insisting that all her children learn to read and write and do

300

figures. Jeremy had needed little prompting, for he was eager to learn, and now it was paying off.

He walked around the train station, needing to stretch his legs. He had just come all the way from St. Louis, where railroad talks had taken place just as in many other cities. The past year had been one of bitter strikes and physical clashes between railroad workers and soldiers. It seemed that with the Indian problems and the railroad strike, the whole country had been at war. But things were calmer now. The strikes were over, and most of the Indians were on reservations where they belonged. And he had no doubt that because of his own hand in helping solve the strikes, he would move up even faster now, perhaps become a president of the Kansas-Pacific some day. If a man was going to dream, why not dream big?

He gazed out at the horizon again. West of this place lay a ranch—the Monroe ranch. It had been many years since he'd seen it—nearly nine. And it had been that long since he'd seen his mother and brothers and sisters, except . . . was his father still alive? He was afraid to find out. Besides, what did it matter anymore? Surely he would not be welcome there. He had waited too long. It was too late to make amends, and even if he did, he would have to admit to his friends and his wife that he was part Indian.

The whistle blew again and he boarded, taking a seat by a window. He had deliberately taken the Atchison-Topeka line, wanting to check out the competition. A few minutes later the train chugged away, past Colorado plains dotted with snow. It was February of 1878, and there had been a welcome thaw from the harsh winter, but a lot of snow still lay on the ground in patches where it had drifted deeper than other places. Several hours later he spotted a familiar hill, a gnarled old pine sitting alone at the top of it. He pressed his face closer to the window. The ranch! It was part of the ranch! The train rumbled on, and he realized for the first time that a railroad had been built right through the northern section of his father's ranch, something that must have both angered and saddened his parents. He remembered when he was very small, and his mother swore a railroad would never go through their land.

He felt a lump in his throat. He'd been a part of something

301

his parents hated. No. He could not go back. But maybe they wouldn't care. Maybe they would be so glad to see him that it wouldn't matter. But he couldn't take the risk of their chastisement—nor the risk of his friends and new family finding out he was part Indian.

The train rumbled by familiar places. He was too far north to see the house and outbuildings. Perhaps it was just as well. Seeing this much brought more sentiment than he cared to feel. He pressed his lips tightly together as his car lurched and swayed past a herd of beautiful Appaloosas, running free, manes and tails flying in the wind. He stared at them. They were beautiful—perfect—the only kind of horses his father would raise. He watched them for as long as he could before the train rounded a hill and the animals disappeared behind it.

"Good-bye, Father," he whispered. A tear slipped down his cheek, and he quickly wiped it away.

Chapter Eighteen

Charles Garvey stood studying his two-month-old son, Matthew Winston, born in June of 1878. He did not like what he saw lying in the crib, for the child was dark, its skin reddish and it's thick shock of hair straight and black. He toyed with the tiny fist. His son was healthy and strong, something any man should be glad about. But Charles Garvey did not care for people who were too dark. How could his fair wife have had such a child?

He could not stop the unnatural resentment he was feeling for his own son. He had wanted a son—someone to take over the Garvey wealth—someone he could train to be powerful and respected, as he and his own father had been. But this was not the son he had expected, and a suspicion was boiling inside of him that surely his wife had been laying with some other man. After all, she never seemed receptive to her own husband in bed. Perhaps she had found that gentle swooning man she had always seemed to want her husband to be. His own mother had been untrue to his father. Perhaps his wife had been untrue to him.

He didn't want to believe it. LeeAnn was such a meek and proper woman, and he had always thought her true to him, in spite of her coldness in bed and the times he had had to hurt her to make her submit to him. After all, she was his wife, and a man had a right to use his wife however he wished.

She came into the nursery then, rushing to the crib as though she thought her husband might harm her son. "Is something wrong, Charles?'' she asked, checking the sleeping child over.

He studied her, watching her eyes when they met his. "I'm not sure yet," he answered. His own eyes hardened. "Perhaps you can tell me why my son is so dark."

He saw fear in her eyes, and she looked back at the baby. "He's just a baby. You can't tell how a child will look when he is this young. Some children are born with dark hair that turns lighter. And sometimes light hair turns darker. What does it matter? He's your son, and he's healthy and strong. You should be glad of that."

"Is he my son?"

She frowned, meeting his eyes again. "Of course he is."

His eyes scanned her, studying the gentle curves beneath the silk robe she wore. "I am fully aware you don't care for some of my bedroom tactics, my dear. Why, I can't imagine. The whores like it, why shouldn't you?"

She blinked. "I am not a whore, Charles. I cannot accept fully the way you treat me as a wife. But neither have I been untrue to you. Surely you must realize that if I have trouble enjoying sex, I am certainly not the type to go running to some other man to find it." She turned back to the baby. "Frankly, I think I could go the rest of my life without it, unless you want more children."

He grasped her arm then, squeezing it painfully. "No woman goes without it. If you can say that then it only means you've found it someplace else and think you can fool me into believing you don't want it at all, so that I'll stay out of your bed while you share it with someone else!"

She tried to wrench herself away. "You're crazy!" she hissed.

He jerked her close, pressing her tight against him, while holding her hair in a painful grip. "Am I? My mother tried the same thing with my father! She didn't want sex anymore either, but she was spreading her legs for someone else just the same! He told me about her! Told me to never trust any woman! My father never lied to me about anything." He kissed her savagely and her heart pounded with dread. Since the baby was born and before, she'd been able to use that excuse to keep him

304

out of her bed. But she was healed now, and he well knew it.

She turned her face sideways, grimacing at his painful grip and the dread of what he intended to do. "Charles, I've never been untrue to you!" she pleaded.

"That baby isn't mine!" he growled. "I'll give him a few months to start looking like he ought to look. But if he doesn't, you'll never convince me it's mine! What did you do—lay with some nigger? An Indian, maybe? God knows there aren't any around here, but if there were you'd find one just to spite me!"

She pushed at him, starting to cry. "Charles, you're inventing things in your mind. He's yours! He's our baby! Ours!"

He pushed her away then, backhanding her hard and causing her to fall to the floor. He yanked her up before she could get up herself. "Maybe you're telling the truth!" he growled. "I will decide eventually. In the meantime, I will show you who you belong to, LeeAnn Garvey!"

He began dragging her out of the nursery, and the baby started crying from all the shouting. She protested that she should tend to her child.

"Let the bastard cry!" he shouted, shoving her into their own bedroom and slamming the door.

LeeAnn dragged her sore body out of bed, stumbling to the bathroom, where she drew some hot water. She stared at herself in the mirror, her face badly bruised. She would have to come up with excuses for the next week as to why she could not attend planned social functions. She had had to do so before, feigning sickness. She wondered how many of their friends suspected the truth.

She studied her face, the blond hair and blue eyes. She tried to see something of her father there. She looked no more like she belonged to Zeke Monroe than her own son looked like he belonged to her.

She blinked back tears. Her greatest fear had been realized. She had given birth to a child who would look predominantly Indian. She knew the day would come when she could no longer deny her own heritage, and she wondered if her husband would only banish her, or perhaps kill her. Maybe he would kill them both. She felt a cunning defense rising in her blood. Perhaps it was a trace of her Indian senses. She only knew that she would never let Charles Garvey hurt her son. He was hers, and she had never loved anyone more than she loved her son. For now she would simply be careful, and she would never allow Charles to be alone with the baby. She had to think. What should she do? Where could she go? She was too proud and stubborn to ask her father for help now. He had helped her once—risked his life to save her from the Comanches. And for that she had virtually ignored him all these years, turned her back on her heritage and acted ashamed of her own father. How could she go crawling to him now begging for help? After all, she had knowingly married an Indian hater. What bigger hurt could she have brought to her father?

She bathed, glad her husband was gone from the house. The nurse would watch over little Matthew. She would sit in the hot water for hours if she wanted. Then she would have to face the servants again. They all knew what a maniac Charles Garvey was and of the bitter bedroom problems they had, no doubt hearing the beatings and the harsh words, fully aware that the mistress of the house was literally raped periodically.

She sighed, her eyes filling with tears. She had married a crazy man, and he was getting crazier every year. She understood some of the roots of his problem, and if he would just talk to her, if she could just reason with him, if he had one ounce of goodness and mercy in him, she could still love him. But he would not let her love him, nor was he capable of loving someone back. She could see now that he had married her simply to have a pretty wife on his arm. How often he went to the whores she didn't know—and didn't care. It was just as well, for her sake.

She finished her bath and spent the rest of the day sitting beside her son. It suddenly didn't matter anymore that he looked Indian. He was beautiful and healthy, and a good baby. He was her son, and that was all that LeeAnn cared about. And she would make sure no harm came to him, even if she eventually had to leave Charles Garvey. To do so would be a social disgrace to both of them, but her son's welfare was most important.

She heard her husband come home then, and her chest tightened again. How she dreaded hearing him come through the door! She quickly left the nursery, not wanting him to find her there, afraid he would start an argument all over again about the child. She rushed out of the room and to the head of the grand red-carpeted stairway of their mansion. He stood at the foot of the stairs and glanced up at her, studying the bruised face and the hurt in her blue eyes.

"I'm sorry, LeeAnn. I'm just . . . a very jealous man."

She frowned. Every time she was ready to hate him again, he softened. She wondered how much longer she could put up with his dual personality. Something was very wrong with this man and she didn't know how to help him.

"Did you cancel our engagements for the week?" she asked quietly.

He nodded, coming up the stairs. "Are you all right? Shall I get a doctor?"

Her eyes were cold as ice. "You never got one before. Why should you do so now? I'm just fine." She moved past him and down the stairs to the kitchen, and he quickly followed. Somewhere down deep inside he truly did love and desire her. Why did he always end up being cruel to her? If not for the damned baby! Why did the child have to be born so dark? He stood and watched her pour herself some tea.

"I've started a new series of articles about the Indians," he told her, trying to start up a conversation.

She met his eyes. "Have you? What blood-curdling tales do you have to tell about them now?"

He clenched his fists, forcing himself not to get angry again. "Well, now that they are thoroughly whipped, all I can tell my readers is that the agents on the reservations are discovering just what filthy, lice-ridden people they really are. Their habits are deplorable, so I'm told. I think the general public should know that, so that the sympathy that damned Joshua Lewis has aroused will be banished."

She held his eyes squarely. "Perhaps Joshua Lewis is telling the truth, and not the sources you have. Did you ever think

307

of that?"

His eyes flashed and she didn't even care. She wasn't afraid of him anymore, and somehow he sensed it. It threw off his thinking, and she realized that if she were bold and strong with him, it just might actually keep him from beating her. It confused him. He was accustomed to a cringing milksop for a wife. She felt an inner pride building. Was it the same pride her father carried? The same stubbornness of her mother's nature? The same bravery they both carried? Was she more Indian than she realized?

"I . . . my sources are very good," he told her. He sighed and turned away. "I am going to my study. I have a court case to work on for tomorrow."

He walked out without another word, and she smiled. She wondered about this young man called Joshua Lewis, who at twenty-four was already making a name for himself as a journalist. She would like to meet him some day.

The Northern Cheyenne who were now in Oklahoma soon decided they did not want to be there. They longed for the Black Hills, the thick pines and the rushing waters of what they considered their home. In their new and barren reservation, the summer heat was unbearable, and mosquitoes plagued them mercilessly. They choked on dust and the water was stagnant. The government did not issue enough food to go around, and whatever was given out was bad. The flour was nearly black, and almost useless for cooking. The beef was either tough or rotten, usually both. The Indian was accustomed to buffalo meat, a much leaner and more nutritious meat. Their systems could not tolerate the bad meat issued to them, nor was there enough; often the adults did not eat at all, giving what little they had to their children.

It was not long before malaria raged through the reservation, pulling down women, children, and warriors in its ugly death. Their bodies shook with chills, then burned with hot fevers; their bones ached as they wasted away in pain until the life went out of them.

The white doctor was soon out of quinine, which sometimes

helped the sick ones, and he locked his office and left. There was nothing more he could do.

The Northern Cheyenne fell into despair. They had understood, incorrectly, that they were to come south just to see if they would like it there, and that they were free to go back north if they did not. They soon discovered that was a lie, that they were expected to stay in the hot, dusty southern reservation—forever. A keen desire began to build in their hearts to return home—to the Black Hills, to their Sioux friends.

During the winter of 1877-78, their agent finally granted permission for some of the Northern Cheyenne to be given rifles so they could hunt buffalo, but that venture proved to only feed their desires to return home, for all the hunters found were piles of bones scattered over the southern plains, left there by white buffalo hunters. The buffalo were gone. Gone. The hunters ended up killing coyotes for food, and by the spring of 1878 they had even eaten all their dogs. They even considered eating their horses, but this was unacceptable to an Indian; and besides, the horses might be needed—for an escape to the North.

The reservation agent pleaded with Washington for more rations, but Washington was turning a cold shoulder on the original Americans. Let them suffer and die. Everyone would be better off. As spring warmed the land, mosquitoes again swarmed, and the malaria returned to take still more lives, so that it seemed that ultimately every last Cheyenne would die. Then came measles, wiping out many of the precious children, their only hope for the future. Little Wolf and Dull Knife, now old men, decided they must do something. Their first effort was to plead once more with the agent for something to be done to save the children.

The two old chiefs explained that they wished to return to their home in the northern mountains, declaring that they would not stay south another winter, perhaps not even another month. Their wish was, of course, denied. In August those choosing to go north, under Wild Hog, Tangle Hair, Little Wolf, and Dull Knife broke away from those not choosing to go home; the renegades held councils, preparing to escape

Zeke coaxed the young mare out of the corral. He had spent several days gently taming her until he could ride her. He did not agree with the way white men broke horses, considering it stupid and cruel, let alone the fact that sometimes the horse hurt itself. The beautiful Appaloosa pranced gingerly, stepping sideways, still not totally convinced she should allow this, yet trusting her master and wanting now to please him. At his gentle Cheyenne command she calmed down. He had been careful to use the proper bit so as not to harm her tender mouth, and for now he rode her bareback.

Abbie and Ellen watched from the fence. It was good to see Zeke mount up with little pain. The past winter had been the worst ever. The arthritis had gone to his hips, and most men would have been unable to even get up out of bed in his condition. But Zeke Monroe was a stubborn man, and he had refused to stay in bed. There had been days when he could not ride at all, and Abbie knew by his eyes what he was thinking. He had always said he would ride to his dying day—that the disease would not bring him to that point. Her chest ached so badly she wondered sometimes where her next breath would come from, and her nights were sleepless. She knew that he had already made up his mind he would not go through another winter like the last one, no matter how good he felt the next summer.

Zeke Monroe had become a quiet, determined man. He did not become angry and ornery as he had the last time the disease got bad. He had simply resigned himself to what must be, and although they did not discuss it, Abigail Monroe knew her husband well—too well. His determination to die honorably had become a silent topic. She was trying to be strong, trying to think about life without him, but it was impossible. She wondered sometimes what kept her going, for she had become thin and tired over the winter, and her chest hurt constantly. She could not eat or sleep. She was losing him! Losing him! Her life; her love; her whole reason for existing.

He rode the mare in circles for a while, then kicked the

animal's sides and took off for a hard ride. Abbie watched after him, swallowing back tears, wondering if she had ever in her whole life cried as much or as easily as she had the past few months.

Ellen put a hand on her shoulder. "Mother, you don't look well," she told her. "You're too thin and you have circles under your eyes. Why won't you tell me what's wrong? I think you need to see a doctor."

Abbie faced the girl. They had been apart all winter because of the snows that separated the two ranches. But in the summer Hal Daniels often brought his wife to her parents' ranch, for Ellen missed them dearly. Now she had come with the wonderful news that she was three months pregnant. The baby was due in January.

Abbie forced a smile, climbing down from the fence and helping Ellen off. "You shouldn't be climbing around on fences, Ellen," she chastised the girl. "You're pregnant now and must be more careful."

"Oh, Mother, I've been climbing around fences since I was old enough to walk." She put her arm around her mother's shoulders. "And stop avoiding the subject. What is wrong with you?"

Abbie sighed and faced the girl, then could not stop the tears. She suddenly hugged Ellen tightly, crying for several minutes first, unable to speak at all.

"I'm sorry, Ellen," she finally managed to say, pulling away and wiping her eyes and blowing her nose. She held the soggy handkerchief in her fist, watching the horizon where Zeke had ridden. "Your father . . . was very bad this past winter," she told the girl. "Very bad."

The girl frowned. "But he's better now. He looks fine."

Abbie shook her head and turned away. "He's not fine at all. And you know how his Indian heart operates, Ellen. He doesn't want to die a crippled, bedridden man. He . . . wants to die honorably." She turned and faced the girl. "Do you understand what I am saying?"

Ellen studied her mother's sorrowful brown eyes, then her own eyes teared. "You mean . . . he's thinking of . . . dying?"

"He thinks about it all the time now. I can see it . . . feel it.

The only question left is how he will die." She looked back out over the horizon. "He has truly given up this time, Ellen," she said quietly. "It started with the Little Bighorn, and got worse when the railroad came through the north section. And then when those pitiful stragglers came back south, what was left of the once-proud Northern Cheyenne . . ." She swallowed. "It broke his heart, Ellen. The Southern Cheyenne already gave up a long time ago. He goes to see them, and he finds nothing but drunken, broken men . . . men who once rode proud and brave. There used to be no warrior more feared than the fighting Cheyenne, Ellen. They were the bravest fighters, the most daring, the best horsemen. Your father was as good as any of them, and your brother. It's been hard on Wolf's Blood, too, and I still fear he will leave us and go south with Sonora. The Apache are still fighting. God only knows what would happen to Wolf's Blood if he went there. But the only thing keeping him here now is your father. Sonora has talked often lately of going back to her people, and Wolf's Blood would take her if not for Zeke. He's still young and likes new, exciting things. Once Zeke is . . . gone . . ."

Her words were choked off by new tears. Ellen put an arm about her waist and walked her toward the cabin. "Mother, stop this. Nothing has happened yet, and Father looks well. I think you're exaggerating."

Abbie pushed a piece of hair behind her ear. "I wish I was, Ellen. How I wish I was. But I've been with Zeke Monroe for thirty-three years. Your father is fifty-eight, Ellen. And last winter there were days . . . when he couldn't go out and work . . . couldn't ride. To him that is the most humiliating thing that can happen to a Cheyenne warrior."

Ellen spent the next hour trying to comfort her mother, worried now herself. She could not picture life around the ranch without Zeke Monroe. Her father came riding in then, the mare tamer and much more obedient. He dismounted at the house, tying the horse and coming inside, where Abbie had started peeling potatoes, trying to look busy. But she could not hide her eyes, and his heart ached at the sight of her. He looked from her to Ellen, then back at his wife.

"Abbie, if you do much more crying this spring you'll create a whole new creek on this place," he teased, walking to the water bucket and taking a drink. Ellen watched him. Yes. He moved a little slower, although he looked as strong as ever. She hadn't realized it before, but he didn't seem as nimble, and there were tired lines of hard living on his face, new ones that were not there before. He caught her look and scowled at her. "An expectant mother should look happier than that, Ellen. You have life in your belly, which should only remind you that for every life that is lost more than one comes into this world. People go on—life goes on."

He walked to Abbie, taking the small knife from her hands and pulling her out of the chair. "You and I are going to Pueblo for a few days, Abbie-girl. Hal tells me he heard there's a circus there, with those strange animals we've never seen—elephants and tigers and such. I want to see them. Sounds like fun, don't you think?"

She met his eyes as he pulled her close. "Pueblo? But . . . your work here—"

"To hell with it. Morgan and Jason can handle it. You and I are going to have some fun. I want to see if elephants really are bigger than buffalo. And maybe we'll go square dancing. They even have a playhouse, I'm told, where you can go and watch actors put on a real live show. You can buy a new dress or anything else you want."

"But, Zeke—"

He kissed her lightly, then pulled back, and she knew he wanted to do one last nice thing for her. She felt like a condemned person, but he pleaded with his eyes that she not think about it. "It's been a hard winter, Abbie-girl. I want to be alone with you—do something different—show you something exciting. And I want you to see a doctor while we're there. Maybe he can fix you up with some kind of tonic. You haven't looked this way since—" He thought of the time she'd collapsed and seemed to be slowly dying, after Jeremy was born and Zeke had refused to come to her bed anymore, for fear another pregnancy would kill her. She needed him in every way. What was she going to do when he wasn't there at all? Somehow he had to prepare her. "Since Jeremy was born," he finished. "I'm worried about you."

313

Her eyes widened. "You're worried about me? Don't you have things a little backward?"

He grinned and kissed her forehead. "Say you'll go to Pueblo with me. And promise me you'll have a good time."

She rested her head against his chest. "I'll go."

In spite of Abbie's worry over her husband, she had to admit that the trip was a good idea. She doubted that in her whole life she had had a better time than that memorable week. Both of them felt like children at the sight of the strange animals from another land. Zeke was surprised at the size of the elephants. And there were camels with humped backs, as well as striped tigers and men who actually went into cages with them, ordering them around with a whip. Zeke commented that he'd like a job like that, something daring and dangerous. They watched people fly through the air on the trapeze and a man walked on a tightrope, all under a huge tent. They ate popcorn dripping with caramel candy and watched painted clowns walking around on stilts. It was the most unusual thing either of them had ever seen, and Abbie wished Jason and Ellen and the others could see it, deciding that if this thing called a circus came back to Pueblo, the children should come.

They both actually laughed, more than they had laughed in months. Zeke bought her a dress, and they attended a packed barn dance, Zeke wearing a bright blue calico shirt with bloused sleeves that accented his broad shoulders. He wore white man's cotton pants and leather boots, his hair neatly braided to one side, beads decorating it. He was the picture of stunning handsomeness, and Abbie did not miss the fact that many women there stole glances at the tall, dark Indian man; nor was Zeke unaware that several men were appreciating his wife's beauty. At forty-eight, Abbie looked fifteen years younger. She had always been blessed with youthful looks, and even though now she looked like a woman in her thirties, she carried that look with stunning beauty.

Both of them surprised others there when they danced a waltz with smooth flow, laughing inwardly at the surprise in the eyes of some of the people, who did not expect a man like

Zeke Monroe to be able to dance at all. He was proud of his Abbie, as she moved with graceful beauty in the soft green sheathlike, form-fitting dress, its skirt consisting of tier after tier of silk ruffles. The dress was fitted at her small waist, the bodice low enough to reveal the fullness of her bosom and edged in lace. She was still a beautiful woman, and he buried the torture of wondering if and when she would take another man after he was gone. He could not blame her if she did, and knew her well enough to realize she would not settle for anything but the best. If Abigail Trent Monroe gave herself to anyone again, he would be a good man, an honorable man, one who would not disgrace the memory of her first husband.

They danced for hours, mostly square dances, some of the women giving flirting looks to Zeke when they could get away with it, most of them curious about him and his white woman. A few were not allowed to participate in the square dancing because when they had to change partners their husbands did not want them "touching" an Indian. Both Zeke and Abbie were aware of some of the prejudice there, but neither let it bother them. They were here to have fun, and they were having it.

The week went by much too quickly. They had not spoken of sad things or of the future. They had only enjoyed the present, making love every night. All too soon they were on their way back to the ranch, but in no hurry, and one night before getting home Zeke took out his mandolin. She had not asked why he packed it in the first place, and it had been years since he had played it for her. When first she met him on the wagon train, he had surprised everyone when he played the haunting strings and sang Tennessee mountain songs for the travelers. His melodic voice, his ear for the perfect tone, and the beautiful songs he sang enraptured everyone. Most of the songs were his own, made up during all the many hours he had spent alone as a small boy, in the swamps behind his father's house.

A small campfire glowed nearby, and Abbie sat beside him as he strummed the strings of the instrument she loved so much, humming softly. "Thought I'd sing you a few songs, Abbie-girl, like I used to do," he told her quietly.

She smiled. "Will you sing that mountain song I love

315

so much?''

He nodded, then stopped for a moment. "Didn't you miss Tennessee, Abbie, at any time over all these years?''

She picked up a stick and traced it in the sand. "A little—but just at first. After being with you it didn't matter anymore.''

Crickets sang loudly across the plains, and stars shone down on them. They felt like the only two people in the world. But in the distance a train whistle reminded them that they were not. He picked at the strings again for a moment.

"Promise me you'll remember me like this, Abbie,'' he spoke up, meeting her eyes. She just stared at him, her throat constricting. It was the first time he had hinted that this trip had been a last good time together. "Still strong, not too old-looking yet. If ten men came here tonight wanting to take you, I'd fight them all off.''

She managed a smile. "Of course you would,'' she said in a near whisper.

"Remember me this way, Abbie. That's why it has to be. I don't want you to remember me old and broken. I was always strong for you, my back always straight, my skills sharp. All you need is to look at Wolf's Blood to remember me.'' He shook his head. "My God, we've been through a lot, Abbie-girl. Thirty-three years is a long time. I'll never forget how you looked that day I was going to ride out to find your sister and wouldn't let you go along. You actually pointed your pa's old Spencer at me and told me I'd better let you go or else.'' He strummed some more. "'Course, I hadn't put my brand on you yet, but I wanted you more than ever right then.'' He gave her a wink. "And I never thought for a moment you'd pull that trigger.''

She couldn't help but smile. "I'll never forget the winter I waited for you at Fort Bridger after you took the rest of them to Oregon. I was so scared you wouldn't come back, Zeke. The day you rode in was the happiest day of my life.''

He held her eyes. "I'd never have left you there. In all those years, I've always come back to you, haven't I? Have I ever failed you?''

Her eyes teared more and she shook her head.

"You remember that, Abbie. And I'm telling you now that I

make another promise. When I die, I will still come back to you. I will be with you forever, just as alive in your heart and soul as if my body was lying next to you in the night."

"Zeke, don't . . ." she whimpered, looking down then and grasping at her aching chest.

"I have to, Abbie. Someone you love never really dies. You just remember that I will come to you. I will prove to you that I am still with you, even after death. You listen, Abbie. Listen to the voices. Listen to your dreams. I will be there. I will tell you what to do, where to find me. Do you believe that?"

She nodded.

"Don't shame me, Abbie, by being weak and simpering. That's not my Abbie. You be strong, like the little girl I met all those years ago. You take that doctor's tonic for your health. And you let the children and grandchildren be your reason for going on. And you remember that I love you and will always, always be with you. Be strong for me, Abbie. You can do it. And if you love me, you will understand why I will do what I must do. Let me be the man that I am, Abbie. You always have over these years. So do it now."

She met his eyes, her shoulders shaking. "Will you . . . be here in January when Ellen's baby is born?"

He sighed deeply. "I don't think so." He strummed the mandolin again. "If Jeremy or LeeAnn ever come home again, Abbie, you tell them I love them, will you? Tell them I never once stopped loving them and I hold no hard feelings."

She nodded again, tears streaming down her face. He turned his eyes to the fire, strumming a moment before he began the song she loved.

> "See the mist a-risin',
> Out there upon the hill.
> The mornin' sun's a-comin' up,
> And dawn is bright and still.
>
> "I've lived on this here mountain
> Since I was freshly born.
> And there ain't nothin' nicer
> Than a misty mountain morn.

> *"Lord, I know heaven's pretty,*
> *And death I do not fear.*
> *But I hope that heaven's mornin's*
> *Are like the one down here.*
>
> *"I've lived on this here mountain*
> *Since I was freshly born.*
> *And there ain't nothin' nicer*
> *Than a misty mountain morn."*

It had been a long time since he seemed all Tennessee man to her. It was not as important a part of his soul as being Indian was, but for her he would be Tennessee tonight. She knew he would soon enough be Indian again, and he would die Indian. And although this night he sang Tennessee songs about the Smokies and the green hills of that place, she knew she would never go back there, even if he died. She had been in this land too long. To leave it would be to leave Zeke Monroe—Lone Eagle. No! She would stay here in the great West that he loved, and she would die here too. It was only fitting.

With the time it took for travel, Zeke and Abbie were gone over three weeks. It was August when they returned, and Wolf's Blood rode out to greet them, his face solemn. He had been going through his own torture, fully aware of his father's feelings of late. He, too, knew why Zeke had taken his mother to Pueblo. Now his own heart raced, for if ever there was a time to die honorably it was now. But he wondered how he would survive without the father that he worshipped.

He met them on a rise before they even rode down to the ranch. "Soldiers were here," he told Zeke.

Abbie's heart pounded with dread.

"What's wrong?" Zeke asked.

"They need us. The Northern Cheyenne have broken loose and are running north to Red Cloud. They are led by Wild Hog, Tangle Hair, and Little Wolf and Dull Knife. We are to help track them and bring them back. It will be bad for them, Father, if they choose to fight."

Their eyes held. "Yes, it will," Zeke told the boy. "How soon must we go?"

"As soon as we can."

"No, not yet!" Abbie protested. "We just got back!"

"Time is important, Mother. Even as it is, this could take all winter."

Silence hung in the air and Abbie grasped her stomach, hanging her head.

"Do me a favor and spruce things up inside your tipi, Wolf's Blood," Zeke ordered. "It hasn't been used for a long time. I wish to use it tonight."

The boy blinked back tears, understanding. "Yes, Father."

"And bring out *Kehilan*. I want to see him."

The boy nodded. "I want to go with you."

Zeke smiled for him. "And I want you with me. It will be as you predicted, Wolf's Blood. We will be together. But you must be strong."

The boy swallowed. "I am your son. The best man has taught me strength." He turned his horse and galloped down the hill, and in the distance a wolf howled a long, lonely wail. Zeke's long hair blew in the soft breeze. He took hold of the reins to Abbie's horse, realizing she was too stunned to even pick them up herself and ride down the hill.

"We'll sleep in the tipi tonight, Abbie," he told her, his back to her, "like in the old days."

She made no protests. It was fitting. Soon he would leave, perhaps tomorrow. The soldiers would go after the runaways, and Zeke would go with them. The runaways would stand and fight, Abbie was sure. And when they did, Zeke would fight with them. She knew it in her heart. He had his chance and he would take it.

The wolf howled again, followed by a distant train whistle; one a sign of the past, the other a sign of the future. Zeke Monroe had been caught between the two, as well as caught between the two worlds of Indian and white. His mind and soul had been tortured by his two bloods. Perhaps it was good that he would go out of this world and find some peace.

319

Chapter Nineteen

The night was sleepless. How could either of them sleep with the terrible premonition that this was their last night together, after all the years, all the loving, all the hardships, all the sharing and sacrificing? How could he make love to her enough? How did a man say good-bye to such a woman? He had never been able to in all these years. Perhaps he wouldn't be able to now. But the memory of the past winter, the vision of being too crippled to ride or even get out of bed haunted him. He was Zeke Monroe, and he was Lone Eagle, the warrior.

She touched every part of him, and he left no part of her untouched or unexplored. He must remember every curve, every feature, everything about this woman who had been his since she was fifteen. And she in turn wanted to forget nothing. She could not touch him enough or study deeply enough his lustrous black hair, the high cheekbones and straight nose, the perfect lips, the thin scar on his left cheek, the handsome, dark eyes, and the bronze skin. She ran her hands over a still-firm chest and muscular arms, the hard, flat stomach and muscular thighs. Yes, he was scarred, so many scars from so many battles, many of them for her own defense and protection. How did a man survive so many wounds and then be sentenced to die from a hideous disease he could not control? It was not fair. But life had never been fair to Zeke Monroe since he was four years old, and his white father dragged him from his Indian mother's arms, taking him to Tennessee, where he suffered ridicule and rejection. No, life was never fair to a half-breed.

Their whispered words of eternal love were heard by only the nearby crickets and the soft night breeze that slipped through tiny cracks in the weathered tipi. They kept a lantern lit inside, not wanting to lie in darkness, wanting to see, to look upon one another all night.

He moved over her, in the way only he could do, and she was lost in him, this man of men who was her life. It seemed all the years were rushing by her now—memories, memories with every touch and every kiss and every thrust inside of her. She could see mountains and hear rushing waters. She remembered a time when he came to her, after he had left her with Swift Arrow and his people and had to go away. He'd been gone so long she thought he was not going to return. What a beautiful time that was when he came back to her, where she was camped in the land of boiling waters, the place the government now called Yellowstone. She had been bathing beneath a waterfall, and when she emerged he was there, and they made love in the soft grass beside that lovely stream, while the wind moaned through the pines and over mountain peaks. What a wonderful time it was when the Cheyenne could roam such places, hunt at will, live where the air was sweet and the waters fresh and the game plentiful. Why did it have to change? Why? Why did this have to happen to what some called the "Beautiful People"?

Change! Why did there have to be change? Why did life have to be so cruel? Why couldn't anything stay the same. Children stay little? Husbands never grow old? The white man never come to this land?

A distant train whistle reminded her such things must be. For so many years they had fought the idea of a railroad coming through Indian country and through their own land. Now the railroad penetrated every place that was once the Indian's, and the Kansas-Pacific rumbled past their own north pasture. Its whistle brought a terrible ache to her heart—so lonesome. Just as she would be if this man sharing her body now did not return to her.

Surely he would not die! Surely not! He was Zeke, the strongest, bravest man she had ever met. He seemed so indestructible. He was her rock, her strength, her breath. For

322

thirty-three years she had not considered herself as an individual. She was Zeke Monroe's woman. Every movement, every chore, every breath had been for her man.

They did not speak of it. Not that night. They only spoke of love, sometimes talking about the past, mostly making love. When she took him inside of her body she heard drums and chanting, the tinkling of tiny bells and the call of wild things. Did a wolf really howl somewhere on the plains, or was it her imagination? Again came the rushing waters, the moaning wind. The tipi swirled around her, the decorative paintings on its walls coming alive and dancing in a circle, around and around, painted horses and people. All alive. She was with them again, at his village, talking to his beautiful mother, Gentle Woman, and sharing stories with his stepfather, Deer Slayer. His brothers were there: Red Eagle and his sweet wife Yellow Moon and their son Laughing Boy; Black Elk and his wife Blue Bird Woman and their son Bucking Horse. The food was plentiful and the tipis warm, and they shared stories and friendship.

But no. Gentle Woman had died of white man's disease, and Deer Slayer had died of a broken heart. Red Eagle had turned to whiskey, craving it so badly he had sold poor Yellow Moon to outlaws, who killed little Laughing Boy and sold Yellow Moon again and again until she had ended up in the hands of Winston Garvey. Now the only thing left of her was her half-breed son, Joshua. Black Elk and his wife and son had been killed at Sand Creek. And so had Abbie's dear, devoted friend, Tall Grass Woman. She remembered the first time she saw the woman, when she first came to the People as Zeke's wife. Tall Grass Woman had befriended her, and when Abbie had saved the woman's little girl once from drowning, she had become honored and respected by the whole tribe for her bravery in going into the deep waters where monsters lurked. But the little girl had later died of white man's disease. Abbie couldn't even remember anymore if it had been measles or cholera or whooping cough.

How many times had white men's diseases ravaged Indian camps, at times obliterating entire villages? Yes, the future only spelled doom for the few who were left. And now a pitiful handful were trying to make their way north to the land they loved. She was glad Zeke would help track them—glad that he would help them if he could. Perhaps he would die trying. If he did, it was a good and proper way for such a man to die. She could not think of a better way, and yet . . .

She kissed him savagely, and their lovemaking started all over again. Was there a way to keep the night from ending? Why couldn't a person have just one chance at stopping time—just for a little while? But no one except God had that privilege, and He did not choose to do so this night. The moon made its arc over the night sky, still hanging in the heavens when the sun peeped red and large on the eastern horizon the next morning, finding Zeke and Abbie in an exhausted sleep by then, a sleep that could not be avoided after hours of heated passion, followed by quiet tears.

Wolf's Blood was up and had everything packed, horses saddled. He had Margaret start some breakfast, and they waited. He refused to go to the tipi or let anyone else disturb his mother and father. They would come out when they were ready. If he and his father left late, then they would just leave late.

Breakfast cooled, and Wolf's Blood and the others went ahead and ate. Margaret cleared the table. The house was quiet, all of them sensing an impending loss. Even the grandchildren were subdued: Little Zeke, now nine and looking and acting all Indian, much like his uncle, Wolf's Blood. The boy worshipped his grandfather. He felt like crying now, but wasn't sure why. Nathan was seven, a dark, handsome boy, greatly resembling his father, Morgan. Wolf's Blood's own son Kicking Boy was six, and held a proud Indian look about him, often mimicking his father. He was already a good rider, just as Wolf's Blood had been by that age. Little Iris was five, and it was already obvious she would be an exquisite beauty, a grand mixture of her handsome Cheyenne father and her beautiful Apache mother.

They all heard a horse then, and Wolf's Blood went to the door. He turned back to Margaret. "It is Father and Mother. They're riding toward that place they like by the stream, probably to bathe. They will come soon." His eyes were red, and he walked outside to gaze at the very distant purple mountains, praying silently to *Maheo*, feeling death all around him. Somehow his God would have to give him the strength to go on without his father. This would take much more courage and strength than he'd had to conjure up to participate in the grueling Sun Dance ritual. He would go through the Sun Dance ten times over if it would mean he would never lose his father to death. He argued inwardly that nothing would happen, that perhaps he was worrying for no reason. But his deep spiritual senses told him otherwise.

Zeke and Abbie rode to their special place by the stream, into the hideaway where they had shared so much passion. The irises still bloomed all around, mixed with other wildflowers. They had brought a change of clothes and blankets. They would bathe here and put on clean clothes before going back. He removed her tunic, and she removed his leggings and loincloth. Again they touched, wanting to remember, remember. She reached up and he embraced her, pulling her up and letting her wrap her legs around his waist. They kissed again, and again. He knelt down, still holding his tiny wife, and picked up some soap, then walked into the stream with her. They shivered at the touch of the cool water on their heated bodies, then fell into the stream in an embrace. He pushed her and dunked her completely, and she came up shivering and laughing. Yes, he must make her laugh once more. He must remember the laughter and not the tears! And so must she. He ran the soap over her body and she jumped at the tickling sensation, bringing forth his own laughter. He lathered her up, gently washing her, not leaving out any curve or hidden place. He washed her hair then, and held her as he laid her back into the water to rinse her hair.

Then the job turned to her. She washed him, taking her time, running gentle fingers over every hard muscle, over that part of him that had made them one in body, over the strong legs, the broad chest, washing his hair last. She loved his hair and was glad he had never cut it. There had been times he considered it, for her sake, thinking that it would be easier on her when they were in civilized places if his hair did not hang long. But Zeke would not have been Zeke without the long hair that made him more Indian. And she knew that deep inside he had never wanted to cut it. Yes, she had let him be Indian, and she was glad. He'd have been only half a man any other way. Never once in all their years together had she been ashamed of him. She was thoroughly proud of her half-breed husband, proud of his strength and faith, proud of his provocative looks, proud of his skills and bravery.

Too soon they were finished, and he lifted her out of the water and carried her to a blanket, wrapping her in it and gently toweling her hair. He dried himself off while she sat there and watched. Then he dressed and sat down in front of her, letting her comb out his hair. She wondered how she made her arms move and where her breath came from, for she knew he must leave soon now.

He turned to her, gently taking the brush from her hand. He began gently brushing her own hair back from her face, studying her beauty, proud of how few age lines she had on her face, how slim and curved she still was, how smooth was her skin.

"We must go back now," he said softly, setting the brush aside.

Their eyes held and he saw the terror in her own. "One more day?" she asked.

He touched her cheek with the back of his hand. "No, my sweet one. It must be done. I cannot say in certainty that I will not come back, Abbie. But this time . . . I make no promises. I have always before made promises and kept them." His eyes teared. "This time I will not promise, Abbie."

She swallowed. "I can't . . . be without you, Zeke. I . . . can't function without—"

He touched her lips. "Yes you can. You are a strong and brave woman. And I told you before that even in death I will always be with you. Remember to listen to your dreams, Abbie. Watch for the signs, for I will come to you."

She jerked as a sob made its way from the depths of her soul to her throat, and tears overflowed her eyes. He pulled her close, and she rested her head against his chest.

"All we are losing is our physical closeness," he told her gently. "But two people do not have to be together to be one.

Many times when I was away from you, I could close my eyes and I was with you, wrapped in your arms, being one with you. You were not really there, and yet you were. That is the way it will be for you if I should not return, Abbie. You will simply close your eyes and remember these moments we have shared, and I will be there, holding you, kissing you, loving you. And I swear to you, Abigail, that I will still protect you. No harm will come to my Abbie, for I will be watching over her, and she will live to be an old woman, enjoying her children and her grandchildren. And I have dreamed, Abbie, that in old age you were with the People again, helping them, loving them. So you see, you must go on, for I have dreamed it and it must be so. And out of your love for me you will help my People until you are very old and you finally walk *Ekutsihimmiyo* and we are reunited." He kissed her hair. "And when we are, you will be fifteen again, and I will be a young man, and we will ride together on a grand Appaloosa into the clouds, into a land where all is green, and all our loved ones return to us, and the buffalo are plenty, and the children fat and happy, and the People sing again. I see this, Abbie, and it will be so."

She could do nothing but weep. How long they sat there neither was certain. His own tears were silent, mixing into her wet hair. They were beyond making love now, beyond hoping for things that could not be. It was time to accept reality, time to be strong for each other, and each was determined that he and she would leave smiling and not in tears. She finally pulled away from him, blowing her nose and wiping her eyes. No more tears. Why make it more difficult for him? She was empty of tears now. How many had she shed over these years of hardships and worry? But she had chosen this life and this man, knowing full well he would not die an old cripple, but would very likely go down fighting while still in his prime. She did not want to lose him, and yet Abbie knew inwardly that even she would have it no other way for him.

He helped her dress, making her promise to keep taking the doctor's tonic, for she was still too thin. He gathered up their things and lifted her onto the horse, then moved up onto the animal's back with ease behind her. They rode to the house.

He lifted her down, keeping an arm around her and helping

her inside, sensing that her legs did not want to carry her of their own accord. The whole family waited inside: Margaret and Morgan with Little Zeke and Nathan; Wolf's Blood and Sonora with Kicking Boy and Iris; Jason, now nineteen. Ellen and Hal were at their own ranch, unaware of what was taking place. Zeke would stop and see them on his way to Fort Lyon. He scanned his children and grandchildren.

"All of you are a part of Abbie and me," he told them. "If something . . . happens to me, I entrust all of you with her care. I love you, and I am very proud of those of you who stayed on here to help with the ranch and to help your mother. I know that his ranch will keep going. I have taught you well. You know horses; you can all do anything I can do. I'm damned proud of all of you, and I am asking that if LeeAnn or Jeremy ever come back, you will honor my memory by being kind to them and forgiving them, if they ask it."

Abbie turned away, feeling his hurt at the thought of not seeing LeeAnn and Jeremy again. Zeke sighed deeply and put on a smile for them all. "Now, Margaret, if you will heat up something for your mother and me, I want to spend a few minutes with my grandchildren." He turned to Wolf's Blood, sobering at the stricken look on the young man's face. "Is everything ready?" The boy nodded and Zeke held his eyes. *"Ho-shuh,"* he said softly to his son. Wolf's Blood blinked back tears and walked out.

Zeke spent the next several minutes talking to the grandchildren and hugging them. Several minutes later he walked into the bedroom and tried to get Abbie to come out and eat something. She sat on the bed of robes, rather than the brass bed, and in her hand she held the blue crying stones. She looked up at him, her lips trembling.

"I don't think . . . they'll work for me this time," she whimpered.

He walked closer and knelt in front of her, closing her fist into his big hand and pressing her fingers against the stones. "They will work, Abbie-girl. They're magic, remember?"

Could it really have been thirty-three years since she first watched him explain the stones to the little girl who had been bitten by a snake? Surely not! Why, it was only a couple of weeks ago, a couple of months at the most! Not thirty-three years! Time was not supposed to go by that quickly. It wasn't fair.

He leaned forward and kissed her gently. "Come and eat something, Abbie. Do it for me." He helped her up, putting an arm around her shoulders and taking the fist that held the stones, gently pressing it against her heart. "These were my gift to you, Abbie. Way back when I gave them to you I warned you I saw many tears in your life, and I saw you standing alone. You've always known, haven't you?"

She nodded quietly. "I suppose I always did," she said in a near whisper. "I just . . . never would let myself think about it."

He led her into the kitchen and they ate quietly. All too soon he rose from the table, putting on his weapons belt, and the infamous knife. She felt like an old, old woman when she tried to rise, grasping the table, wondering what had happened to her legs. He took her arm and led her outside, saying good-bye again to all the grandchildren, to Margaret, Sonora, and Morgan, and embracing his youngest son. Jason was not all Indian as was Wolf's Blood, but he'd been as loving and loyal, and Zeke was proud of his third son. He looked for a moment toward the western horizon, where on a knoll their little Lillian lay buried. And somewhere out there was Jeremy. He looked toward the east, where his fair daughter lived, his precious LeeAnn, for whom he had risked his life to save her from the Comanches.

Then his eyes rested on Abbie—his Abbie-girl—the woman with whom it all began. What would his life have been like if he had just left her at Fort Bridger that winter of 1845 and not come back for her in the spring? What direction would their lives have taken? And how much control did man have over his own destiny? Perhaps theirs was meant to be savage, a life of hardships, as it had been. People called him a savage, but to Abigail Trent he was not. Yet their lovemaking was sometimes savage, for it was filled with a passion not many people were privileged to enjoy. For some unknown reason their destiny had been carved out for them before they even met on the wagon train. Abigail Trent had come west, and Zeke Monroe had volunteered as a scout for her wagon train. And one night they met, over the light of a campfire. She handed him some coffee, and when he took it their fingers touched. Destiny would have its way.

He walked up and embraced her. *"Ne-mehotatse,"* he told her gently.

"Ne-mehotatse," she whispered. "We will walk together always—always, my beloved. And I will hold you in my arms every night."

He hugged her so tightly she could barely breathe, wishing he would never have to let go of her. He kissed her hair. "Abbie, my Abbie," he whispered. "Forgive me. I don't want to leave you, and yet I must."

Wolf's Blood sat on his horse, facing away from them. Margaret had to turn away herself, resting her head against her husband's chest. The grandchildren stared, Little Zeke crying quietly for a reason he didn't even understand.

"It's all right," Abbie was telling him in a choked voice. "I would have it . . . no other way for you . . . my husband."

He kissed her—a long, almost brutal kiss—then pushed her away. "Remember that whatever you do with your years, even if another man should love you, you belong only to me, Abigail Trent. It is my love that will be with you—forever."

He walked away then. How much longer should he wait? How many ways were there to say good-bye? It must be simply done. He leaped up onto his Appaloosa, then turned, looking down at her proudly, almost haughtily, wanting her to remember him sitting straight, looking like the warrior that he was.

"Nohetto," he said, scanning the rest of them, then looking once more at Abbie. He jerked his horse around to face Wolf's Blood. *"Hai!"* he barked, whipping his horse with the reins and kicking its sides so that his mount went into an immediate gallop. Wolf's Blood turned his horse in a circle, his eyes resting on Sonora, then on his mother.

"This time I make the promise," he told Abbie. "I will return, my mother."

She tried to smile but could not. The man took off after his father, and Abbie watched through tears as they both

330

disappeared over a rise. She swallowed and breathed deeply then, turning to her grandchildren.

"Doesn't your grandfather look grand on a horse?" she said, holding her chin proudly. "You'll not find a better rider in all of Colorado." She looked at Margaret then, walking up and hugging her daughter. "Come, Margaret. We have chores to do."

The Cheyenne flight north became a running battle. The soldiers with whom Zeke and Wolf's Blood rode and for whom they helped track the Cheyenne, were only a fraction of the number of soldiers who were after the fleeing Indians. Soldiers moved out from all directions: from Forts Wallace, Hays, Dodge, Kearney, and others. Soldiers rode the railroads, watching and waiting, ready to charge off the train and follow if the Indians were spotted. Up to thirteen thousand soldiers and volunteers stalked the Indians without letup, so that Little Wolf and Dull Knife and their people had no time to rest.

The Indians were desperate. They must get to their beloved Black Hills. They kept to the roughest country they could find, so that the soldiers could not get to them with their wagons that carried the big guns. Several times the soldiers caught up with them, often picking off the straggling old people and children. But the majority of the fleeing Indians always managed to evade their pursuers, craftily sneaking right through the ignorant bluecoats. Several times Zeke warned the troops he led not to fire—that they should let him talk to the Cheyenne leaders and see if he couldn't get them to surrender. But the soldiers would have none of it, and as they followed the Cheyenne through Kansas and Nebraska, Zeke grew less and less desirous of helping the soldiers. Thousands were tracking a pitiful handful of desperate Cheyenne, who wanted to harm no one, who wanted only to go home. The callousness and lack of understanding on the part of their pursuers was heartbreaking. Zeke knew the job was even more difficult for Wolf's Blood. He had to constantly remind the boy that he must return to his mother, that he must not let her down. If Wolf's Blood turned on the soldiers, he would be killed, and that would be too much for Abbie to bear.

"The time will come when it is a good day for you to die," Zeke told his son one night over a quiet campfire. "You are young. Winter is coming, and already I feel the pain creeping into my bones and joints. This is my time, Wolf's Blood. Let me have my time. You must live and go home to your mother."

They searched through September and October, and the nights grew very cold. Each day Wolf's Blood could see the agony building in his father's body, as he strained just to rise in the mornings, ignoring fierce pain in his hips when he rode.

Zeke knew that the Indians were in a bad way by now. They had not had time to rest, nor even to hunt for food. Surely their clothing was getting ragged, and some were starving. His worries were correct, for among the Indians there was much despair. The old ones were weak, the children suffering from lack of rest and food. By head count, thirty-four were missing, either killed as stragglers, or having run off in confused battles and making their own way north. The two greatest chiefs among them, Dull Knife and Little Wolf, differed in opinion about what they should do. Little Wolf wanted to go all the way into the Montana Territory to the Tongue and Powder Rivers—true Northern Cheyenne country—where they could live like real Indians again. Dull Knife did not think they could make it that far, and suggested they go to Red Cloud's Agency in the Black Hills to see if Red Cloud would help them, give them shelter and food, and convince the government to let them stay there. After all, the Northern Cheyenne had helped the Sioux many times in their fighting. Red Cloud should help them now.

The final decision was to split up. Those who wished to follow Little Wolf all the way north—about fifty men, forty women, and roughly thirty-eight children—would break off from Dull Knife and the one hundred-fifty who would go with him to the Red Cloud Agency. It was a sad parting for the two chiefs and their people. Wild Hog and Left Hand went with Dull Knife.

It was late October when Dull Knife and his followers were caught in a heavy snowstorm that left wet snow clinging to their horses and their own bodies, blinding their eyes and slowing their progress. Then out of the swirling white storm appeared soldiers—all around them. Zeke was among them, having helped track them to this spot in spite of the blizzard, and in spite of a grueling pain that ripped through him now with all its cruel fierceness. The weather had brought forth the worst of the arthritis, and when he dismounted at night he could barely walk. He would cling to the horse's neck until he was able to move his legs, not wanting the other men to see his son helping him, not wanting to look weak in front of any of them. He had fought the pain and kept tracking the Indians, and now they had finally caught up to Dull Knife.

There was nothing for Dull Knife to do but surrender. He begged to be taken to Fort Robinson, where he could be with Red Cloud and the Sioux. The soldiers informed him that Red Cloud was no longer there, that the Sioux had been moved farther north. The leader, Captain John B. Johnson, told Dull Knife he would take him to Fort Robinson, where the Cheyenne could get food and shelter. Dull Knife objected, not trusting the soldiers. Zeke did not fully trust them either, but by nightfall Dull Knife gave in, for his people were freezing and starving. They would go to Fort Robinson, but they made it clear they wanted to keep going north to Red Cloud once they got their strength back. The soldiers promised they could do so.

They headed toward the fort. Zeke lifted three little ones onto his own horse, covering them with blankets and walking himself, in spite of the relentless pain. When they made camp that night, Zeke sensed the uneasiness among the Cheyenne. They did not trust the soldiers, and neither did Zeke or Wolf's Blood. Zeke sat and smoked beside a campfire, unable to sleep. He heard the soft whistle that was his son's signal, and he frowned with concern. The young man wanted to speak alone with him, away from the campfire around which sat a few soldiers. Zeke said nothing, getting to his feet with difficulty and walking toward the sound of the whistle. Wolf's Blood loomed out of the darkness, taking his father's arm and leading him away from the others.

"I think you will get your wish, my father," he told the man.

"What do you mean?"

"I went inside one tipi, to check on some of the children. The woman in there looked up in surprise, for she was pushing a gun barrel under her dress to hide it. I told her not to be afraid, that I was really on their side, and she showed me her necklace, decorated not only with beads, but with gun springs, locks, and pins. She had cartridges tied onto her moccasins like decorations."

Zeke frowned and threw down his cigarette, stepping it out. "They're taking apart guns?"

"Yes. They are hiding them in pieces, wearing them as ornaments to fool the soldiers. They think the soldier leader will tell them to give up all weapons. When they do, they will turn in only a few bows and arrows and a few broken guns. Then later, if they are imprisoned, they will have guns that they can put back together and use against the soldiers."

Zeke grinned a little. "By God I think it could work. If anyone can make it work, the Cheyenne can."

"Of course they can!" The boy sobered. "Father, what do you think will happen? Will they help the Cheyenne, or imprison them?"

Zeke sighed. "I'm afraid I've seen to much abuse to think they'll really help them, Wolf's Blood. They're pissed about the fact that Dull Knife even made it this far, evading so many soldiers all the way. And Little Wolf has apparently still managed to avoid being caught. They might help them at first, but I have my doubts any promises will be kept."

Wolf's Blood put a hand on his father's arm. "And if they choose to fight?"

Zeke put a hand over his son's. "If they fight, I will fight with them, Wolf's Blood. Don't try to help me. Promise me you'll do nothing to help me or to go against the soldiers."

The boy swallowed. "I promise, my father."

Zeke patted his hand. "It's bad this time, Wolf's Blood. As bad as it's ever been. How I'm managing to ride I don't even know myself. But I'll not go on like this. The day is soon coming when I'll never get out of bed again. I won't let that day get here. Every bone and joint in my body screams to be put out of its misery. Understand me, Wolf's Blood. Help me die honorably."

The boy suddenly embraced him in the darkness. "I love you, Father. I will help you. But if you die, part of me also dies."

"It is always so when a loved one dies. But there are other loved ones left behind who need us. My Abbie needs you, Wolf's Blood. You know what to do after I am gone. Go to Dan. He'll help you get permission."

"I will go to him," Wolf's Blood promised. They embraced tightly. The son was to take his father to a very high place in the mountains, where he would build a platform for his final resting place—close to the heavens, where eagles fly.

Zeke left him then, walking painfully slow. Wolf's Blood watched him. Yes, it was a good time. The man he watched now was not the man he had always known, tall and strong and nimble, quick and graceful. The disease raged within him, claiming him slowly and painfully.

The Cheyenne arrived at Fort Robinson, having already been disarmed as they had suspected would be done, but carrying several weapons on their person in the form of jewelry or hidden in clothing. If not for the sadness of the occasion and their starving, frozen bodies, the hidden weapons would have been laughable, a fine joke on the soldiers. But the Cheyenne had no laughter left in them. They were taken to a log barracks built to hold seventy-five men; but all one hundred fifty Indians were crowded into it. The soldiers at Fort Robinson, under Major Caleb Carlton, were friendly toward them, giving them blankets and food and medicine. But Carlton could make no promises about letting them go farther north and join Red Cloud. They were told the soldiers must wait for orders from Washington.

The waiting became difficult, stretching through November, December. The Cheyenne became impatient, and Zeke became almost immobile. He stayed in the log shelter with them, insisting he could help them more, perhaps convince them still to return south and give up their pleadings to go to Red Cloud. But Wolf's Blood knew he only wanted to be near the People, his first love after all.

Wolf's Blood waited with a heavy heart. He asked the soldiers to try to get word to Dan Monroe, his uncle, who had also been moved farther north and was not at Fort Robinson any longer. If only Dan could come and be here with Zeke. The soldiers said they would send word, but Dan was off on patrol scouting for whiskey and gunrunners on the Red Cloud reservation, and would be difficult to locate.

The Cheyenne were given permission to do a little hunting near the fort—a few men at a time—while they waited. But game was scarce, and their hearts were not in it. Once tipis surrounded Fort Robinson. Now the land was barren—of buffalo and Indian alike.

Then Major Carlton left, and things changed. An ominous mood hung over the fort, brought on by the new commander, Captain Henry W. Wessells, a man who cared little for Indians and was nervous and anxious to please Washington. The man constantly watched the Cheyenne, often paying unannounced visits to the log barracks where they were kept, his eyes darting around suspiciously. Finally Red Cloud himself was brought to the fort to talk to the Cheyenne. His words brought great sadness to their hearts, for he could offer no help. He would gladly welcome them to the Sioux villages, but the all-powerful Father in Washington would not allow it. The white people were so numerous that they "filled the whole earth," and the Indian could no longer fight against what the white man told them to do.

Zeke listened with great sadness to the poignant conversation between the Sioux leader and the hopeful Cheyenne. The once-proud and fierce warrior Red Cloud, who had led the Sioux and Northern Cheyenne in victory over the Powder River country just ten years earlier, was now a sad and broken man. It was rumored he was a prisoner on his own reservation. He warned the Cheyenne they must be very careful and do everything the white soldiers told them to do or it would be bad for them. The Sioux leader's words broke Zeke's heart, for the man's pride and power were gone. The soldiers, the miners, the men in power in Washington, the settlers, the railroads, the buffalo hunters—all had worked together to break the Indian's back, to bring the red men of the plains to their knees.

Zeke turned away, unable to even watch Red Cloud, fighting an urge to cry out and charge forward and kill every soldier he could find. But his ravaged body would not even allow him to do that. He rested his hand on the infamous knife, the knife he had wielded against his enemies with such force and skill over the years, often fighting several men at once. It would forever rest in its sheath now, its blade tasting blood no more. Watching Red Cloud was his answer—the finality he needed. They were broken, and his sorrow over that loss was unbearable. He would not live to watch the final remnants be swept up and thrown out like so much trash.

Red Cloud had done all he could do for them. He was taken away, and Dull Knife approached Captain Wessells again with a final plea, telling him that if they were not allowed to go north and join the Sioux, the Cheyenne would butcher one another with their own knives before going back south.

Chapter Twenty

It was early in January in 1879 when the orders finally came from Washington. The Indians must go back south, and immediately. Zeke could barely believe the words, nor could Wolf's Blood. It was the dead of winter. To send the pitiful bunch of Cheyenne back south on a two- to three-month march would be the same as lining them up before a firing squad. Several days after the order was issued, when Wolf's Blood was allowed into the barracks to ask his father what to do, he found Zeke lying in a corner on a blanket, unable to rise.

"Father!" the boy groaned.

Zeke looked at him with bloodshot eyes. "I am . . . only saving my strength, son, for my last . . . battle."

"Father, the soldiers want to send them back—in the dead of winter!"

Zeke took his hand, and Wolf's Blood noticed with great sorrow that his father's hands were so gnarled they looked deformed, the joints swollen to ugly proportions.

"They will not . . . go back," he told his son quietly. "Dull Knife . . . has told them so. They will die first. And so . . . will I, Wolf's Blood. I will not go back to . . . your mother . . . and have her see me this way. She must remember the Zeke she knew . . . not this one. I want you to remember that Zeke also. Go now. Go back with the soldiers, and remember . . . to stay on their side . . . no matter what happens. Promise me, Wolf's Blood."

Tears were suddenly visible in the boy's eyes, spilling down

339

his cheeks. "What . . . shall I do, Father?" he asked in a strained voice. "I am Indian, too."

"You will go home . . . and you will let life take its course, Wolf's Blood. You will go to Sonora . . . and your children . . . and your mother. And you will make me proud. Go now. And remember your promise . . . about taking me to the mountains."

The boy sniffed. "I . . . have tried to find your brother Dan. They say he is coming soon. He is coming from Fort Keogh. He has sent word . . . that it is impossible to bring Swift Arrow . . . for he lives alone in the hills and refuses to come to the Red Cloud reservation. They have . . . given up trying to find him. Dan is not even at the reservation. Fort Keogh is much farther north, in Montana. I fear he will not get here in time, my father."

Zeke closed his eyes. "It doesn't matter any more, Wolf's Blood. Go now. Please go."

The young man cried openly then, unable to stop himself. He bent low and hugged his father. "I love you," he sobbed at the man's ear.

"And I love you, my son," Zeke replied, stroking the boy's hair. "You have been . . . an honorable son . . . and I have loved you as my own life. You are my life . . . and Abbie's. Our seed created the best of both our worlds. I will be with you always, Wolf's Blood, for my blood runs in your veins."

The boy pulled away, choking in a sob, gently touching his father's forehead. "God be with you," he whispered. He rose and ran out of the barracks. He kept running, out into the darkness, where he fell to the ground and wept. There would be no sleep for him that night.

At Dull Knife's refusal to return south, the soldiers came to the barracks the next day and put chains and iron bars over the doors. A constant guard was put around the building. There would be no more food and no more warmth, for no fuel would be provided for the heating stove. Day moved into night, and it was bitterly cold. Women and children shivered, but they helped the men begin to silently put together the many pieces of guns they had managed to hide from the soldiers. One squaw helped Zeke rise. He drew on that special inner strength that

340

his Indian blood gave him, determined he would help these Cheyenne escape and hoping to die in the attempt. The woman rubbed his hands for him, blowing on them to bring warmth. The Indians worked silently and diligently, with only the bright winter moon for light. This would be their last great battle.

Men painted their faces, while women piled anything they could get their hands on under the windows through which they would all make their escape. And in the darkness, they made their move.

Windows were suddenly battered outward, sashes and all. Warriors and women began pouring out, quickly killing or injuring the guards with the guns they had put back together. There was almost instant gunfire from all directions, as soldiers came dashing out of their barracks, leaping onto horses in only their underwear and riding after fleeing Indians.

From somewhere deep inside his soul, Zeke Monroe pulled on incredible strength, leaping through a window with the agility of the others. He would not die crawling on his hands and knees! Zeke let out a war whoop as a soldier headed for him, and he pulled the knife, letting out a blood-curdling scream as he rammed it into the man's heart and ripped downward. He knelt down to take the man's scalp, and that was when he felt the jolt in his back. There was no pain, but he knew.

He turned to see a soldier standing behind him, the man's rifle still smoking. He actually smiled. "It is a good time to die!" he shouted at the soldier, who frowned in confusion, remembering that this man was supposed to be an Army scout. Zeke started to rise, in spite of a gaping hole in the middle of his back; the frightened soldier backed up and fired again, the bullet ripping into Zeke's chest. Zeke fell backward then, the infamous knife still gripped in his hand. He felt the life seeping out of him, but he refused to let go of the knife. He heard someone shouting in the distance.

"I am a scout!" he heard someone say. "Don't shoot! He is my father. I only wish to help him!"

Wolf's Blood! He must hang on, just one more second. He must see his son's face once more. Then the boy was there, kneeling close, groaning the word *father* in Cheyenne. Zeke smiled for him, reaching up and touching his hair.

"Nohahan," he whispered lovingly.

All around them soldiers rode out after fleeing Indians, cutting down nearly half of the Cheyenne warriors. Women and children scattered, but the soldiers found them, killing many of them before they could surrender. One of those killed was Dull Knife's own daughter. Only thirty-two Cheyenne would truly escape to freedom, while a handful hid in the rocks only a few miles from the fort, among them Dull Knife himself, his wife, and surviving son.

None of it mattered now to Wolf's Blood, as he sat holding his father's head in his lap, talking lovingly to the man until suddenly Zeke's hand relaxed and the knife fell from it.

At home on the Arkansas River Abigail Trent Monroe suddenly sat up, wide awake. Someone had called her, she was certain. In her confusion she reached out for Zeke, then remembered he was not there. But surely it had been his voice. . . .

Her heart pounded. She got out of bed, pulling a robe around her. The fire had dwindled and the house was cold from a bitter January night. She had worried so much over how her husband must be suffering in the bitter cold. But now she was made colder by the dread that enveloped her. She hurried to the window and looked out at a full moon. A cloud suddenly swept across it, blotting it out, and the wind blew across the plains with an eerie wail, like women crying.

"Zeke," she whispered. Outside a wolf howled, then another and another, as though the entire ranch was surrounded by them.

For days the soldiers trailed the thirty-two Cheyenne who had managed to get free of the fort and were headed north. The strays were finally surrounded and trapped at Hat Creek Bluffs in a deep buffalo wallow. The soldiers charged the wallow, firing into it, retreating, charging again and firing again, until at last no Indians fired back. Only nine Cheyenne survived, mostly women and children. Dull Knife managed to make his way to Pine Ridge, where he and his family were made prisoners on Red Cloud's reservation.

In the meantime Little Wolf had spent the winter with his own followers living in pits dug into the side of a riverbank. When the weather warmed, they headed for the Tongue River. A lieutenant found them and agreed to talk, convincing Little Wolf finally to surrender, promising he and his people would not be shot. Little Wolf had no choice, his people too weak to fight any longer. They were taken to Fort Keogh, where many of the young men became scouts, just to have something to do, and where many more fell to whiskey and ruin.

After many months, permission was finally granted for the prisoners who had been taken back to Fort Robinson to be united with their Sioux friends on the Red Cloud Agency at Pine Ridge, where they joined Dull Knife. Later Little Wolf's people were given a reservation near Fort Keogh, and Dull Knife and his people were transferred there so that all the Northern Cheyenne who had fled the southern reservation could be together.

Thus the Cheyenne—or what was left of them—would be forever separated; the Southern Cheyenne in Oklahoma, the Northern Cheyenne in Montana, never again to reunite, never again to fight.

A weary Dan Monroe had reached Fort Robinson a week too late, discovering the disaster that had taken place there, and learning that his beloved half brother had been killed. By then Wolf's Blood had left with his father's frozen body wrapped onto a travois, setting out on a journey to the mountains, where he would bury his father alone.

In January, just two days after Zeke's death, Ellen gave birth to a tiny daughter, naming her Lillian Rose after Ellen's dead sister. The weather was too bad for traveling, and it was not until mid-February, when there was a several-day thaw, that Hal and Ellen could bring their new baby to meet her grandmother. But the meeting was a mixture of joy and sorrow, for Hal had been brought a message from Fort Lyon.

Abbie greeted them warmly, but she was thin, her eyes circled. She had told no one about the night she had awakened, thinking Zeke had called to her. Hal and Ellen let her hold her granddaughter for a while. Abbie had always loved babies, ever mourning not being able to have any more after Jason. At twenty-eight she had already had seven children, all by the seed of Zeke Monroe. Finally Ellen took the baby from her arms, and Hal stepped over and put a hand on Abbie's shoulder.

"Abbie, we . . . we got a message from Fort Lyon a few days ago," he told his mother-in-law. Ellen sat down with the baby, burying her face in the infant's neck, unable to look at her mother. Abbie sat rigid, her heart aching so fiercely she wondered if she were dying herself. She looked up at Hal.

"Zeke?"

He frowned and sighed. "There was a damned blood bath up at Fort Robinson. The goddamned government came through with orders that they all be sent back south, in the dead of winter. Dull Knife refused. I guess they'd taken guns apart and hid them, and when they were told they couldn't go south they put them back together in secret and made a break for it. I . . . I don't know the details of Zeke's involvement in the whole thing, but he . . . he was shot, Abbie, by soldiers."

She felt only numbness, as though all her blood had left her body. She could not even cry, nor was she surprised. She rose from the chair, walking to a window while the others watched, not sure what they expected of her. Margaret held her chin proudly, facing Hal.

"Mother and I know the details without having to be told. My father fought with them. He helped them escape. He would have had it no other way." Her voice choked on the last words and she ran outside.

Jason pressed his lips together, not wanting to cry in front of the others. He felt suddenly empty and alone. Abbie turned to Hal. "Tell me, Hal. Was it on the ninth of January?"

He frowned. "How did you know?"

She closed her eyes, putting a hand to her chest. "I marked it . . . on my calendar. He called to me."

Ellen broke into heavy sobbing, and Morgan went out to find Margaret. Jason wept quietly at the table, busily wiping at tears that came too fast for him to hide. Sonora stared wide-eyed at Hal. "What about my husband?" she whispered, so panicked

344

that her voice would not come.

"Wolf's Blood is all right. He'll be a while yet, Sonora. He's taken his father to the mountains to bury him high—on a platform. It was Zeke's wish."

The girl covered her face and wept. Abbie watched them all, and for some strange reason her tears would not come. She knew that the real problem was that she did not dare break down. She was not ready. She could not face the reality of this—not yet. She must be strong for the children, until they were strong again. For the day would come when she could accept this truth, and on that day she would need them more than she had ever needed them.

"Why do you weep?" she said to Ellen and Jason, holding her chin proudly. "Your father died the way he wanted to die—fighting like a true Cheyenne warrior. That was what he was at heart, you know. He died proud and fighting, not a crippled, groaning man in a bed he could not get out of. Now we must all be strong. This is Zeke Monroe's ranch, and we will keep it going just like he did. We will continue to raise fine horses, and we will all make him proud of the family of his seed."

She walked to the bedroom, and Ellen wiped at her eyes, looking at her husband. "This isn't right, Hal," she whispered. "Why isn't she crying? Why isn't she upset?"

He stared at the bedroom doorway for a moment, then turned to her. "I don't like it. She's refusing to let it settle, Ellen. I'm going to go talk to Margaret and Morgan about this."

He walked out, and in the bedroom Abbie went to the window and looked out at a bright blue sky and over a snowy ridge where she had so often watched Zeke approach on horseback. She could see him now, just as vividly as if he really were there. She smiled. Perhaps it was all a mistake after all. Perhaps he had only been wounded, and that was why she felt him calling to her. After all, he had always come back to her. She would not give up or give in—not yet. She would wait—for Wolf's Blood.

It was April when Little Zeke came running to the house to

get his grandmother. "Someone is coming!" the boy told her. "Mother says she thinks it is Wolf's Blood!"

Abbie stared at the doorway. She had slept little over these weeks, trying to convince herself that her invincible husband would be all right after all. She had sat up praying night after night, fighting the torture of reality, telling herself there was a great possibility her Zeke would fool them all and come riding in on his grand Appaloosa, sweeping her up into his arms and taking her to their secret lovenest.

"Is he . . . alone?" she asked her grandson.

"I think he is, but he has another horse with him."

The boy ran out. No! No, he must not be alone! She moved on heavy, unwilling legs toward the door, going through it and standing on the porch. He was coming in from the west, riding slowly, leading a riderless horse. No! She felt the panic building then. All this time she had been strong. She had not wept and carried on. The children and grandchildren had already accepted their father and grandfather's death. All had accepted it but Abbie, and now as Wolf's Blood came closer, Morgan and Margaret hurried to Abbie, both realizing she had still not faced the inevitable, both very worried about what would happen when she did.

Wolf's Blood's eyes were only on his mother. His face was rigid. He was dressed in full Indian regalia, his face painted in mourning, scars on his arms and chest from the slashing he had inflicted upon himself over his father's death. They were still pink and one didn't look fully healed, for he had cut himself deeply.

Abbie watched him. Why, it wasn't Wolf's Blood at all! It was Zeke! Surely it was Zeke, for he looked just like her Zeke, a replica of the strong and beautiful man she had married at fifteen and spent her life with. He came closer, halting his mount in front of the house, while the rest of the family just stared at his haggard face. Sonora did not go to him right away, sensing she must leave her husband alone for the moment, knowing how Wolf's Blood had felt about his father. The boy swung his leg over his horse and slid off, walking up to his mother, who just stared at him.

She reached out and touched his arm. "Zeke! I knew you

346

would come back."

Wolf's Blood frowned and Margaret gasped, turning away. She knew her mother was acting strangely, even mentioning a couple of times that perhaps Zeke would come back after all. But she had not expected this.

Wolf's Blood touched her face gently. "I am not Zeke, Mother. I am Wolf's Blood. I buried Father high on the mountain. It was his wish."

She shook her head. "No. You're Zeke. He always comes back to me."

He grasped her arms and shook her slightly. "Mother, look at me! It's Wolf's Blood!" He felt her trembling, and her eyes were wild-looking as she shook her head again.

"Don't tell me that!" she whispered.

"It's the truth! Didn't you get my message?"

"She got the message," Morgan spoke up quietly. "I think she's been refusing to believe it. She seemed to accept it at first, then started talking about Zeke coming back."

Wolf's Blood searched her eyes. "Mother, it's me—Wolf's Blood," he told her gently, still holding her arms. "Father was killed at Fort Robinson. I buried him in the mountains. Do you understand? You must stop hoping for the impossible. Face it now—right now—before you get any worse!"

She shook her head again. "It's not . . . really true. I . . . thought so at first. You . . . called to me, Zeke . . . in the night. But then I remembered . . . that you always come back, and I knew someone . . . must have got the message wrong."

Wolf's Blood's eyes teared. "Come with me, Mother." He took her arm and led her down the steps, walking her far off and down to the river. She said nothing as they walked, her mind swirling between fantasy and reality. When they reached the river Wolf's Blood turned her, grasping her shoulders. "Mother, you must face the truth. If you don't, it will be bad for you, and your children and grandchildren won't know you anymore. Don't do this to Father. It would break his heart to see you doing this."

She studied him closely. "But . . . you are Zeke."

He sighed deeply, holding her firmly. "All right. If you want to believe that, then listen to me now. Let me go, Abbie. Please

347

let me go now to a place where I will be happy. You've got to let me go so we will both be at peace."

She watched him as the river splashed and danced nearby. She reached up and touched his face. "Must you really go?" she asked, her eyes tearing.

He was glad to see the tears. "Yes. I really must go this time, Abbie. But I will always be with you in spirit, just like I promised."

He waited. For several minutes she stared at him, backing up slightly. She finally blinked and shook her head, putting a hand to her forehead. She stared at him again. "Wolf's Blood?"

He smiled sadly and nodded. "I am the one who promised to return, Mother, remember? Father did not promise this time. He's dead, Mother. You must realize that and accept it. Surely you knew, even the night he called to you."

He watched with an aching heart as several moods seemed to pass through her brown, tired, lonely eyes. An inner force was fighting the truth. An odd groan came through her lips and she grasped her stomach, bending over. "Zeke!" she groaned. "No! No! No!"

Wolf's Blood hurried up to her then, and she grasped his arms so tightly it actually hurt him, her nails cutting into the skin. "Don't . . . let go of me," she begged.

His eyes teared more. "Mother, it will be all right."

"Tell me . . . he didn't suffer!" she groaned.

"He didn't. He died quickly." His voice choked. "I don't think . . . he even felt any pain. It had to be, Mother. He was . . . so crippled. It was his last chance . . . to die honorably. If he hadn't let himself . . . die fighting . . . I'd have had to bring him back here . . . a crippled man on a travois. That would have been so much worse for him."

She gasped for breath, then let out a "no" again in a long scream, hitting him in the chest with her fists. He embraced her and held her tightly against him, his tears mixing into her hair.

"Yes, Mother. You must face it. We're all here for you . . . Margaret, Jason, Sonora and me . . . the grandchildren. We'll survive and be together, like he wanted. He's happy now, Mother. I am convinced he's happier than he ever was in this life."

She wept in gut-wrenching sobs, hardly able to find her breath. He held her, not knowing what else to do, until finally he felt her collapsing. He quickly picked her up. She was limp in his arms as he hurriedly carried her back to the house. He looked at his sister Margaret as he carried their mother onto the porch. "We must watch her closely for a while," he told his sister. "But I think she will be all right."

Margaret touched his arm, where a puffy scar had not healed. "I'm so sorry you had to go through all that alone, Wolf's Blood," she told him. "Are you all right?"

Tears still stained his face. "I don't know yet."

He carried his mother inside and laid her on the brass bed. She groaned and rolled to her side, moaning Zeke's name again. Wolf's Blood frowned and bent to kiss her cheek. "Do not be afraid," he whispered. "Father is with you." He smoothed back her hair, and Margaret came inside with a pan of cool water and a cloth.

"You can leave, Wolf's Blood," she told him. "Sonora and I will get her undressed and in bed. I will bathe her in cool water."

He sighed deeply, wiping at his tears and smearing the mourning paint. He turned to see Sonora standing in the doorway. Wolf's Blood had not even greeted his wife yet. "Forgive me, Sonora," he said softly. He swept her up into his arms, holding her tightly as she cried against his shoulder.

"I was so afraid you also would not return!" she wept.

He kissed her hair. "I had to come back to my Sonora, and my son and daughter, didn't I?"

She looked up at him and he kissed her gently, her lips, her eyes. "I need some time, Sonora. I still have much sorrow inside of me. For a while I cannot be completely yours, for part of me is buried on the mountain."

"I understand, my husband. Just to have you here holding me is enough."

He let go of her, kissing her lightly again. "I will go now and let you help Margaret. I am going riding. But I will return tonight to hold you when you sleep."

They kissed once more, and she went to help Margaret.

Wolf's Blood headed for the door, and Jason called out to him. Wolf's Blood turned to see his young brother standing at the table, looking lost and lonely. "Can I go with you?" he asked. "Please, Wolf's Blood. Don't leave me here. I need . . . to talk."

Wolf's Blood smiled and nodded. "Yes, come with me, my brother. Our father would want it so."

For nearly a month Abbie was bedridden, too devastated and too weak to do much of anything for herself. The children all worried that she would never get up again, for her health seemed to be slipping day by day, her will to live gone. At times she would talk incessantly about Zeke, about the old days, about how it was when they met. She would go on and on, laughing sometimes, but the talking always ended in bitter sobbing. None of them knew what to do for her, and Wolf's Blood reached the point where he was afraid to go and see her, for looking at him only brought more tears. He was a replica of his father, and she could not bear to watch him. She ate less and less, until she was a frail skeleton in the big brass bed.

It was mid-May when she had the dream, as vivid and real as if she were awake and experiencing the beauty of it. Zeke was coming to her on an Appaloosa that had wings. He smiled and waved, and she ran to him. He swept her up onto the horse, and suddenly it all changed and they were flying, the horse gone. She turned to look at him, and he was an eagle, carrying her to the top of a mountain where he gently set her down. He changed back again to Zeke, tall and strong and handsome.

"I am very disappointed in you, Abbie-girl," he told her with a frown.

"But why?" she asked.

"I asked you to be strong, to be the Abbie I always knew. But you have been weak. You have let yourself waste away. You have given up on life, when you have so much to live for. I expected you to care for our children and grandchildren, to be there when they needed you. Now they need you, and you are a weak, weeping woman and of no use to them. Always I bragged that you were as strong as any Indian woman, but now you are acting like the white women who have no strength, no courage. Why do you do this to me?"

"To you?"

"You promised me you would be strong. Now I watch you and my heart is sad when it should be happy. Do not break your promise, Abbie-girl. I never broke a promise to you. You must do the same for me now."

"But how can I be happy, when in a moment you will fly away again and never come back?"

"I told you I would always be with you. Are you saying I lied?"

"No!" she answered in the dream. "You have never lied to me."

"Then believe me when I tell you I am with you always. You will rise in the morning, and you will tell our son that you wish to go to the mountain where my flesh lies in death. You will go to the very top of that mountain, and I will be there waiting for you. I will prove to you that I am with you."

"But . . . how—?"

"Go to the top of that mountain!" he said in a booming voice. Then he softened, bending closer and touching her face. "Go to the mountain," he said in a whisper, his hand brushing her face.

He was suddenly an eagle again, and he picked her up in his talons, holding her gently as he flew away with her. They went through a cloud and then they were on the winged horse again, and he rode her down from the skies and gently placed her on the ground near the house. "To the mountain," he repeated. *"Ne-mehotatse."*

The horse flew off into the clouds and she called after him, but her own voice woke her and she sat up in bed. Sonora came running in from the room where she and Wolf's Blood had been sleeping. They had heard her mumbling in her sleep, and Sonora had already started down the ladder toward the bedroom when Abbie cried out.

"What is it?" the girl asked, going to her mother-in-law to find Abbie sweating fiercely, her breathing short.

Abbie looked at Sonora with a frown. "Go and get Wolf's Blood," she said quietly. "Quickly!"

Sonora went out and called softly to him so as not to wake the children. In moments Wolf's Blood came into the room, and Abbie turned up the oil lamp. Her eyes were lit with excitement and she actually smiled, surprising him. "I must go to the mountain, Wolf's Blood."

He frowned. "What mountain?"

"The mountain where your father is buried. He came to me in a dream and told me to go there."

Wolf's Blood sighed, putting a hand to her forehead. "Mother, you are ill. I cannot take you to any mountain. It was just a dream."

"And no one understands visionary dreams better than the Indian!" she retorted, an unusual strength to her voice, considering how weak she had been. "You have had your own dreams and visions. I am telling you your father came to me in a dream and told me that if I go to that mountain, he will prove that he is with me. He will come to me. I don't know how, but he will come. And if you don't take me, then I will sneak out of this house sometime when everyone is asleep, and I will go alone! But I will go!"

He studied her determined eyes. She was acting more like the fiesty woman his father had married. Zeke had often joked about how stubborn she could be at times. "I think you really would do that," he told her.

"I would!"

The young man sighed. "All right. I will take you. But only if you promise that for the next month you will eat and go for walks and get your strength back. It is too soon to go to the mountains right now. There is still much snow in them, and in the spring there is danger of avalanches and floods. We will go in another month. Even then it will be cold, and I will not risk you getting sick. So you must eat and get your strength back. Then I will take you."

She nodded. "Agreed." She touched his face. "It's been hard for you, hasn't it, my son? I'm so sorry."

He took her hand, squeezing it in his own. "It has been hard on all of us. But if you would be yourself again, it would be easier for the rest of us."

She smiled, blinking back tears. "I know that. You will take me to the mountain, Wolf's Blood. And Zeke will come to me, and I'll be all right then. I know I will. I feel stronger already, just from hearing his voice in the dream. You do believe me, don't you? Zeke told me before he left that he would come to me in a dream and tell me how I could find him again."

The young man nodded. "I believe you, Mother. In another month I will take you to the mountain."

Chapter Twenty-one

There was no arguing with his mother. Wolf's Blood was to take her to the mountain, and that was that. The next disagreement was over how she would go. He wanted to take the wagon. She insisted on riding.

"It will be too hard on you riding that far," her son insisted.

The old spirit that was Abigail Trent rose to the surface. "Look, young man, I have been riding a lot more years than you. You might be able to do fancy tricks and shoot a bow and arrow from under a horse, but when it comes to endurance, I can keep up with you or anyone else. And I will thank you to stop treating me like a feeble, old woman. I am only forty-eight, and I am so excited I feel twenty-eight." She met his sulking eyes and folded her arms. "I am riding, as I always did with your father, and that is that. Besides, would you mind telling me how you expect to get a cumbersome wagon up a mountain?"

He grinned then, leaning back in his chair. "I am beginning to see what father meant."

Her eyebrows arched. "Oh? And just what do you mean?"

"He said sometimes you could be as stubborn as that pack mule we had for a while. I used to pull, and father would push, and neither one of us could make him go if he didn't want to go."

She smiled a little herself. "He said that, did he?"

The boy grinned more. "He also said although you were an obedient wife, he had a feeling he was the one doing the

355

obeying, without even knowing it. He said sometimes an obedient wife can tie a man to her apron strings more tightly than one who is always complaining."

She picked up a potato and began peeling it. "I never once tried to tie him to any apron strings."

"Mother," she raised her eyes to meet his again, "he knew that. He told me such things in a joking manner. He wanted to be tied to you and you know it. And whenever he spoke of you, it was always with much love in his eyes."

Her eyes teared, but she smiled. "Your father used to tease me mercilessly. He was always joking about my old Spencer Carbine, or about how I looked when I sometimes wore a man's clothing to go and hunt with him. Or he'd tell me a tall story, and I would believe him until it suddenly became preposterous and I realized he was fooling me. I'd see that twinkle in his eyes, and he'd say, 'Abbie-girl, when will you ever catch on?' Sometimes I'd get so . . . mad . . ."

Her eyes teared more and she quickly wiped at them with the sleeve of her dress, continuing to peel the potato. She sniffed and swallowed. "My God, I'm so lonely for him, Wolf's Blood," she whispered. "What am I going to do?"

He came to her side, squeezing her shoulder. "You will do just fine, just like Father said you would. He always talked about how strong you are, how you would survive after a time. I will take you to the mountain, Mother, and I think you will find strength and peace there."

She nodded, unable to speak.

They followed the Arkansas River along rich bottomland and thick cottonwoods, where it was cooler. It felt good to Abbie to be out riding again. She had not returned to her normal weight, but she felt much stronger now, part of her energy coming simply from excitement. Zeke had come to her in a dream. She was doing what he had asked her to do.

It was June, the weather pleasant and bright. She was proud, riding beside her handsome Indian son. Surely in looking at the boy, it was obvious Zeke Monroe still lived. Wildflowers bloomed in abundance, and as the land began to rise, Abbie felt her spirits rising. First came the high rolling hills that led to the mountains. Then the terrain became more rocky, the earth harder. They had long passed Pueblo and now were climbing ever higher, into places still wild and untamed, as they made their way toward the *Sangre de Cristo* Mountains, where Zeke Monroe had been laid to rest in a remote, obscure place chosen by his son.

The traveling became slower, as the altitude winded the horses. The river was still below them, but now it surged and rumbled through great canyons. Abbie had never been on this particular route, had never seen this part of the Arkansas River. On the plains where they lived, it was wide and usually calm. Here it tore through canyons and rumbled over rocks, far, far below them. And yet even here there were signs of white man's progress and settlement, for deep in the canyon below, along the very edge of the river, lay the narrow gauge tracks of the Denver & Rio Grande. The railroad would provide the white men with an easier way into the depths of the mountains, so they could bring out the gold that lay in towns like Leadville and Rock Creek. Yes, they must get the gold. Abbie was overwhelmed herself—even though she, too, was white—at the ingenuity of her fellow men when it came to getting to the riches that lay waiting for them in the Rockies. A railroad deep in a raging canyon! How on earth had it gotten there? What compelled men to take such risks? And the saddest part was that even this remote and beautiful place had been marred by white man's greed. Plans were already in the making to take the D & RG all the way to Durango and to Gunnison. And one day in the not-too-distant future it would go all the way across the Rockies to the western side of Colorado. How its builders would accomplish such a feat was beyond Abbie's imagination, for few more formidable obstacles existed than the Rocky Mountains. Some peaks would be impossible to crest. They would surely have to somehow tunnel their way beneath the great granite barriers.

She did not want to think about it. There apparently was no place a white man was not willing to go if he thought he would find riches. They had overrun the Black Hills, shoving the Sioux and Northern Cheyenne aside. They were swarming now

357

in the southwest, creating more havoc for the Apaches. California had long been totally invaded and overrun, some of its Indians already extinct. And there were rumors that they were going to create a reservation for Crow Indians in Montana, right beside the Northern Cheyenne Reservation. Crow! Once they were a bitter enemy of the Cheyenne, and now the white man was going to make them live side by side! She had killed Crow Indians herself!

She decided that she must let nothing surprise her anymore. The extent to which white men would go to invade this land from the Atlantic to the Pacific was apparently endless. She was almost glad Zeke had died, for surely things could only get worse.

They rode on, into ever more beautiful places: hills rich with green pine, its sweet scent filling her nostrils, the clean air bringing new life to her veins. The trees were alive with birds and squirrels. The horses' feet made almost no sound as they walked over ground padded with layers of fallen pine needles. The winter snows had not even totally thawed, and the ground was wet and soft. The pungent smell of rotted logs was mixed with the smell of pine, and hardened snow lay in patches.

They made camp along a rushing stream, and Abbie wondered if she would ever be able to leave this place, where surely few men if any had ever been. They were far from any railroads now, far from any town. They were alone, and all around the woods were alive with life, the hills adorned with wildflowers. The sky was a brilliant blue, the grass deep green, the waters so clear one could see the bottom of the creek and the rainbow-colored fish dashing about. Wolf's Blood speared some for their supper, and it was the most pleasant, peaceful time Abbie had enjoyed in many months.

"I'm glad I came, Wolf's Blood," she told her son. "I can see why you and your father came here whenever you could. A person feels renewed in such a place, more in touch with God. I don't feel so lonely."

"Wait until you see where I left Father. It will be many years before any white men find him—maybe never. It is a good place—high and peaceful."

"How long before we get there, do you think?"

He chewed and swallowed a piece of fish. "Three days perhaps. We must be careful. This is grizzly country, and it is the time of year when the great bear is his meanest, for he is coming out of his long sleep and is very hungry. If we see one, do not move too quickly. And do not go wandering off alone."

She studied him quietly for a moment. "Thank you for bringing me here, Wolf's Blood."

He smiled shyly. "I had no choice. It was Father's wish, or he would not have spoken to you in the dream."

"Then you believe me?"

He set down his tin plate. "Of course I believe you. You and Father were very close in spirit, even though you are white. He loved you as much as any man can love a woman. If you say he came to you in a dream, then I believe it."

Her eyes teared. "I'm sorry to take you away from Sonora. No man likes to be away from his wife."

He began rolling a cigarette, taking up the habit his father had enjoyed. "Sonora understands. She wanted me to bring you." He lit the cigarette and puffed it a moment, then met his mother's eyes cautiously. "She misses her own people, Mother. It is possible I will take her to find some of her relatives."

Abbie frowned. "I would hate to see you leave, Wolf's Blood. I need you." She sighed. "That sounds so selfish. If Sonora wants to find her relatives, you should take her. But the Apaches are in the middle of their own warring, Wolf's Blood. It would be dangerous."

"That does not worry me."

She studied her warrior son. "No, I suppose it doesn't." Her throat tightened. How she needed him! "You won't go soon, will you?"

He studied the cigarette. "No. I would not be so cruel as to leave you for a long time yet. Father would be displeased, and I would worry too much myself. I just wanted to tell you I am thinking about it, so that you also could think about it and not be surprised if I decide to go. Besides, I would come back. You know that."

How familiar the words sounded! How often had Zeke told her the very same thing? And he had always kept his promise, until he could no longer make the promise.

For three more days they made their way through rocks and canyons, great waterfalls and quiet streams. Once a grizzly chased them in a meadow. Wolf's Blood smacked his mother's horse and ordered her to ride hard. He stayed behind her, and they galloped through the green meadow, splashing through a stream and into thicker woods until the grizzly finally wearied and stopped chasing them. They reined their lathered mounts to a halt and turned to watch the animal lumber away, Abbie's heart pounding furiously with fright and excitement. Wolf's Blood shook his fist and shouted at the bear, saying his spirit was stronger than the grizzly's spirit, calling the bear a coward in the Cheyenne tongue. He laughed then as the animal kept lumbering away, its great wide paws splashing through the stream, the hump on its neck wiggling as it moved.

"I did not want to shoot him if I could help it," he told his mother. "I do not like to shoot something without reason. But if he had not given up, I would have had no choice. Now he can go find a mate and make more grizzlies so that they will not die out like is happening to so many other wild things."

His smile faded, and she knew he was thinking of the Indians. He met her eyes. "Come. We will make camp soon, and in the morning we will reach my father's burial place. Remember it is sacred. Do not touch the platform or anything on it."

She nodded. "You forget that I understand these things, Wolf's Blood."

He smiled softly. "Sometimes I do. I am sorry. I should have known I need not tell you."

The next morning found them struggling up a dangerously steep mountain, their horses picking their way over large boulders and fallen trees until they came to what appeared to be a cave. Wolf's Blood led her inside, and she could hear rushing waters. Her heart pounded, for she sensed they were close now—very close. She had to duck her head at times

360

because of the low ceiling of the cave. She could see light at the end of a distant tunnel, and the sound of the rushing water came closer. Soon they emerged from the tunnel, and Abbie found herself in a cove that seemed to her to be a place put there from heaven itself. A thundering waterfall came crashing down from unknown places higher up, roaring into a deep pool that churned with white water and literally disappeared under a rock to more unknown places. Everything was green, and birds and small animals scattered when they entered the cove. Wolf's Blood turned her horse then, nodding toward a high, flat area near the waterfall, where the well-built platform rested.

She went numb. Her son could not have picked a better spot to leave his father. The sun's rays were beaming through pine trees, and at the moment they lit up the place where Zeke rested. She dismounted slowly, but could feel nothing. Were her own feet carrying her toward the platform? She couldn't tell. Wolf's Blood kept hold of her arm, helping her over large boulders and around the pool toward the platform. She could not take her eyes from the spot, not even looking where she was walking.

They came closer. The body still rested on top of the platform, still unmolested, too high for animals to disturb it. It was thoroughly wrapped in heavy buffalo robes and topped with a bright Indian blanket. All sorts of religious articles were hung around the platform: Zeke's prayer pipe, eagle feathers, a bear claw necklace.

"I buried all the things with him that he will need in the hereafter," Wolf's Blood told her, keeping hold of her trembling arm. "I packed pemmican and jerked meat on the platform, nearly all of his gear, his tobacco, his rifle." He swallowed. "The knife . . . is in his hand, Mother."

The knife. No other man would equal Zeke Monroe in the use of a knife. It held great power. Yes, it was good that it was with him. Yet it was difficult to believe that the life had truly gone out of the powerful, virile man who once wielded that knife. So handsome! So sure! So hard and strong!

"I . . . have to sit down," she told her son in a weak voice. He helped her sit on a flat rock, kneeling near her.

"His parfleche of supplies is with him, and his personal medicine bag, with his most sacred possessions. I do not know what was in it. It is forbidden for another to explore a man's medicine bag, or to take anything from it. I do know that once he told me he kept the head of the arrow in it that he took from your body when you were a young girl. He said he kept it as a charm to keep you from ever again being wounded by an arrow."

She covered her face, memories reeling through her tortured mind. How young she had been then! How scared, until Zeke Monroe told her it was he who would remove the arrow, promising her he would stay with her even after she passed out. And when she had opened her eyes again, he was there, just as he had promised. Always he had been there in her greatest hour of need: rescuing her from peril, invading her in the night to satisfy her womanly desire for him, holding her when she needed comfort.

Wolf's Blood put an arm around her shoulders. "Are you all right, Mother?"

She nodded, taking her hands from her face and looking at the platform again. Six months. Six months already since his death. But he had left four months before that. Ten months since that heated night they spent in the tipi, since they splashed and laughed and washed one another in the stream the next morning. They would never do such things again. Yet she knew he was only gone in body.

She stood up, staring at the platform a while longer, then turned to her son. "He isn't really there, you know. That's just a shell on that platform. His spirit is with us right now. He said he would always be with us. And he told me I would find him here, at the top of the mountain. I have to go higher, Wolf's Blood, and I have to go alone."

He frowned and rose, facing her. "That would be dangerous. There are more grizzlies around here, and other dangers. What if you fall? What if—"

"I have to go to the top of this mountain alone, and I'll have no argument about it," she told him flatly. "Zeke told me to go, and I am going. And since he told me, I am not afraid. His spirit will protect me. He will speak to the animals so that they don't

362

harm me, and I will not fall." She looked up past where the waterfall made its appearance from places higher up. The mountain rose higher on that side. It was a gradual rise, but very high. They were already several thousand feet up.

"I can get up there and back down by nightfall," she told her son. "But if I do not come down until morning, do not be afraid. I don't want you coming after me, understand? If a second day goes by, then you can come."

He frowned and shook his head. "I don't like it."

"That makes little difference. I am going higher, and your father will come to me. Don't you see, Wolf's Blood? I don't even care if I die up there. I can't think of a better way to die than high on a mountain, climbing toward the heavens to meet my husband. But I won't die, because he'll be protecting me. And he told me once that I would live to be an old woman, that I would live among the People again and would find a way to help them. Nothing is going to happen to me here. I have too much to do yet."

He sighed deeply, glancing at the rocky ridge high above them, so high that the few pine trees that dotted its top looked tiny. He looked back at his mother, a small but determined woman. He put his hands on his hips. "I can see why Father seldom bothered arguing with you about anything." He looked up again. "I will let you go, but you must take my handgun and plenty of food and a good warm coat. It will be colder up there. Here we are out of the wind and it is warm."

"I'll take whatever you think I should take. Just don't tell me that I can't go."

He scowled, shaking his head. "I don't like it. But if it makes you happy, I will let you." He walked away to prepare some gear for her, and she turned her eyes again to the platform.

"I'm coming, Zeke," she said softly.

It was a difficult climb. She had purposely put on winter moccasins and worn a tunic beneath her buffalo robe coat. The weight of the coat hampered her climb, let alone the supplies Wolf's Blood had packed onto her back. Her hair was blowing long and loose, the way Zeke always liked it, and she wore a leather band around her forehead, Indian-style.

Her breathing was soon labored, and her hands bled from often grasping large boulders while she made sure of her footing. In some places she could walk vertical to the rising mountainside, weaving her way sideways instead of climbing straight up.

The first part of the climb had taken her through thick pine, then through bright green aspen. She grasped their white trunks to help her along. She ran into thick pine again, glancing around constantly to watch for bears. After about two hours of climbing, resting, climbing again, she emerged above the tree line, that invisible barrier where trees suddenly ended and the top part of the mountain was bald, or at least appeared that way from the ground below. Actually it was not bald at all, but was covered with green moss and an array of wildflowers, the colorful rocks decorated with green and orange lichen.

She climbed ever higher, the wind whipping at her now that she had emerged from the trees. The pine trees at the top of the rocky ridge were closer now, sparse, half-dead, and gnarled, for they didn't belong there at all. Somehow they had grown there, but now were dying again, for this was a place where few things survived—God's place and no one else's. There would be no animals up here. Just the wind.

She turned to look out, gasping at the sight. She could see over several ranges of mountains now, peak after peak that stretched north and west. She was awed by the majesty of it. The wind groaned and whined through canyons and cervices, rushing past her with incredible force so that it was difficult to stand. She had never been this high, never seen such splendor. She felt small, so small and insignificant. She wondered if the men greedy for gold had ever stood in places like this and seen how unimportant were all the things they craved.

Memories roamed her mind again. How quickly life passed! What small things humans were! She had passed through forty-eight years of life in what sometimes seemed a day, and someday she would walk the heavens with Zeke and none of it would matter. She opened her arms, wishing she could embrace the mountains, wondering if perhaps she should stay there forever and ever, never going back to life and problems and all the things so silly and unimportant.

Yet she knew she must go back. Her children needed her. Her grandchildren needed her. The Indians needed her. Yes, she would go back. Soon enough she would return to places like this and live forever with Zeke. She turned and kept climbing, and another hour found her at the very top.

She removed her heavy gear and spread out a blanket. Zeke had promised he would come to her here, and she believed him. She sat down on the blanket, and for another hour she simply stared out at the most breathless sight any human could wish to see. If there was a place on earth that resembled heaven at all, this had to be the place. And surely it was close to heaven, for some of the distant peaks were shrouded by clouds, others rising above the clouds. Below her a cloud moved with misty silence, but she was above it, and the sun shone down, bringing little warmth in such high places. The wind howled and whipped at her hair, and she waited. . . .

The afternoon grew late, and the long climb and high altitude took their toll. She lay down on the blanket and was soon asleep. How long she slept she was not sure, but she suddenly awakened when she thought she heard Zeke call to her again. She sat up straight. The sun was lower, shining through two peaks behind her and lighting up the sea of mountains in front of her with splendid colors.

She stood up, her heart pounding. Far in the distance she could see an eagle floating silently on the wind. For some reason she could not remove her eyes from the eagle. She grabbed hold of a gnarled, hardened pine tree with one hand, steadying herself as she watched the great bird come closer to where she stood, circling, dipping, circling, its wings spread majestically, its white crown gleaming in the sunlight.

Her eyes would not leave the bird. It was overhead now, high above her, circling, circling. It dipped lower, and for some reason she was not afraid. Was it coming to attack her? Was she near its nest? No. It didn't seem to be after her, yet it came ever closer. She stood frozen in place as it dipped very near then, circling around where she stood. It called out several times, an eerie screech, as though it were truly trying to talk to her. Shivers went down her spine as it came even closer. She did not budge as it circled so close then that a tip of its wing touched her cheek.

It began circling a wider arc again, and she felt weak. "Zeke!" she whispered.

It called out once more, circling close, a wing tip touching her cheek again. Then it circled away, its great wings floating up and down, then spreading still again, as it let the wind carry it. Tears welled in her eyes, and her throat constricted. "Zeke!" she whispered again.

It was him! Of course it was! His spirit was in the eagle. Wasn't his Indian name Lone Eagle? Didn't he consider the bird his sign, his protector? The bird soared in magnificent form then, and its perfection and beauty reminded her of her perfect and beautiful husband. This was his sign! This was his way of telling her he lived and was with her! His spirit was not dead! Of course not! Men like Zeke Monroe did not die!

"Zeke!" she called out then. Tears streamed down her face. "I love you! I love you, Zeke Monroe!"

The bird called out again, and she watched it circle, around and around, then slowly drift away, circling again, drifting away, finally disappearing into a cloud. She stared at the spot, but the eagle was gone.

She stood transfixed, shivering, but at peace. A glorious feeling came over her that she had never felt before. Fear left her. Sorrow left her. She felt strength warming her blood and bones. She would be what her Zeke had expected of her— strong and brave. She was Abigail Trent Monroe. She had survived things few humans could survive. And she had done it for him. Now she would do this for him.

She smiled and cried at the same time. She was still Zeke Monroe's woman. His death didn't change that. Nothing could change the fact that she belonged to him, and he to her. She had not disappointed him in life, nor would she disappoint him in death.

"I love you!" she cried out again. Her words were carried away in the wind, over the many peaks. Did he hear them? Of course he heard, for the mountains heard, the wind heard, the eagle had heard. He had come to her, just as he had promised before death! He was not dead at all! He was just gone for a while, and some day she would rejoin him. Then they could both soar among the mountains, greet the sun, and walk on the clouds.

She sank to the blanket. The sun was setting. She would bundle up and stay here the night, going down in the morning. Her heart was lighter. She would make it now. She could bear the next few years, for she had her children and grandchildren, and she knew Zeke was with her, wherever she went.

She was suddenly hungry. She chewed on a piece of jerked meat and ate some jam and bread. Moments later she fell into an exhausted and peaceful sleep. And while she slept, the eagle returned, perching on the gnarled pine tree beside her. It made no sound. It only watched her. When she awoke in the morning, it was gone. But a feather was caught in the bark of the tree. She caught sight of it, picking it off the tree with a trembling hand. Her eyes widened and her heart pounded. She looked around, but saw nothing. She looked up into the heavens then.

"Thank you," she whispered. Surely God had been good to her after all. He had brought her Zeke Monroe, in life and in death. She shoved the feather into her dress, next to her heart.

Chapter Twenty-Two

Anna Gale took a quick look in a hall mirror, patting the sides of her upswept hair and fretting again over the gray that was showing around the temples. The once beautiful and notorious prostitute of Denver still had a fine shape to her, although a few pounds heavier. Her eyes were still clear and provocative in their beauty. But she was fifty now, and time was beginning to tell.

The "respectable" boarding house she ran now was quiet, most of its occupants off working or shopping in midday. She walked to the front door, her taffeta dress rustling. She could see the shadows of two figures through the fancy frosted glass of the door, and she opened it with a smile.

Anna's smile quickly faded as she stared at a woman she had not seen in years, and a man who took her breath away. He was a replica of Zeke Monroe, and yet he couldn't be Zeke. Zeke would be much older now. How many years had it been since she had seen him? Fourteen? Fifteen?

"Hello, Anna," Abbie spoke up. "May we come in?"

The woman was speechless. Why on earth would Abigail Monroe come to see her, of all people? She stepped aside without saying a word, her eyes moving from Abbie back to the handsome Indian man with her. Old desires and a long-buried love was stirred in Anna Gale's soul as she stared at the man, closing the door. She looked back at Abbie.

"Abigail Monroe! You . . . you've hardly changed, Abbie."

Abbie studied the woman who at one time would have gladly

stolen Zeke from her. She had aged, but prettily. "Nor have you," she told the woman.

Anna smiled nervously, touching her hair again. "You needn't try to be so kind, Abbie. I am perfectly aware that I have changed a great deal."

Abbie smiled softly, turning to the Indian man, who glanced around the house as though someone had just caged him up. "This is our son Wolf's Blood, Anna. He was just a boy when you last saw him, twelve or so, I think. He's thirty-three now, and I must say he's nervous as a she-cat with new cubs. He hates cities as much as his father did, but I insisted he bring me here. I thought I should see you once more, and I intended to find our son Jeremy, but—"

She stopped talking, noticing Anna paling visibly. The woman grasped the back of a chair, staring at Abbie. "You said . . . as much as his father . . . did?" She accented the word "did," and Abbie's eyes sorrowed.

"I'm sorry. I . . . didn't mean for it to come out quite that way." She swallowed. "Zeke is dead, Anna."

The woman just stared at her. She looked then at Wolf's Blood. Surely Zeke was not dead, for here he stood, in all his masculine splendor! But no. This was the son.

"I'm sorry, Anna. But I thought you would want to know."

The woman swallowed, her eyes quickly filling with tears. "He . . . can't be. Men like Zeke . . . don't die!"

Abbie stepped up and took the woman's arm. "All men die, Anna. We are surrounded by life . . . and death." She patted her arm. "Is there someplace we can go and sit down?"

A tear ran down Anna's face, and she put her hand over Abbie's. "My God, how can you bear it?" she whispered.

"We all have things that we must bear," Abbie replied. "That's the way life is. I had to accept it, or lose my mind."

Anna's lips quivered, and she covered her mouth with her hand, putting an arm around Abbie and leading her to the parlor. How could they be enemies now? Their differences had been many years ago, and though Anna Gale had tried, no woman could take Zeke Monroe from his Abbie, so no real harm had been done.

Anna sat down in a plush velvet chair, hunching over and

crying quietly. She took a handkerchief from a pocket of her dress and blew her nose, while Abbie sat down on a loveseat and Wolf's Blood walked to stare out a window at the busy street. Denver had grown tremendously since he was here once as a young boy. Not even a fire nearly twenty years ago could stop its growth. He remembered his father talking about a time not so long ago when there was nothing at all in this place but wild land, until someone discovered gold along a creek.

"I can't believe it," Anna was saying between sobs. "Such a . . . beautiful man . . . so strong and powerful . . . so skilled . . . so wild and free."

"His spirit still lives," Abbie replied. "I am sure of it, and that helps me go on. And every time I look at Wolf's Blood, I know that Zeke still lives."

Anna blew her nose again, glancing at the tall, broad, muscular young man standing at the window, wearing buckskins, his hair long. She remembered a time when Zeke Monroe had come to her needing information about a sister-in-law and Winston Garvey. How long ago had that happened in Santa Fe? Twenty-five years at least. A ravishing, man-hungry Anna Gale had made Zeke pay dearly for the information— with his body, servicing her like a stud bull because it was the only way she would tell him what he wanted to know. That had been a mistake on Anna's part, for she had not expected to fall in love with the man. After that one night she didn't see him again for years, until he got in trouble once while in Denver and Anna used her wiles with the sheriff to help Zeke. It was then she had met Abbie, for they were in Denver so Abigail could have an operation to prevent her from having any more children.

The two women came to know one another. Abbie forced herself to forgive Anna Gale and befriend the woman, for she had saved Zeke from a hanging. Anna in turn developed a great respect and admiration for the woman Zeke was married to, readily understanding his devotion to his Abbie. How Anna wished she could be like her, but her life of prostitution had been carved out for her when she was an orphaned youngster, before she even came west.

Anna wiped at her eyes. "You're lucky to have your son—to

371

have someone close who is such a fine example that Zeke does live." She blew her nose again. "Oh, Abbie, how? How did it happen?"

"He was scouting for the Army. He was at Fort Robinson, trying to convince some Northern Cheyenne to come back to the reservation in the South. There was a skirmish. The Cheyenne tried to run away, and killed some soldiers. Zeke decided to help his people rather than the Army. He killed a soldier and was shot."

Anna shook her head. "But he's been in so many scrapes, so many battles, Abbie. How did he suddenly get so careless?"

Abbie toyed with the strings of her purse. She had dressed in white woman's fashion for her trip to Denver, wearing a stylish dress of mint green, Zeke's favorite color on her. Her hair was swept upward and covered with a feathered hat. She sighed deeply, struggling to stay in control of herself.

"He . . . wanted to die fighting, Anna. He had a crippling disease—arthritis. It got very bad . . . so he could barely walk and it was torture for him to ride a horse. He had warned me long before that he would not die a crippled old man. He died the only way a man like Zeke can die, Anna."

The woman nodded. "I see. And I agree. It's hard to believe someone like Zeke could get any kind of disease."

Abbie stared at her lap. "It was hard for all of us to believe. But he was riddled with old wounds and scars, Anna. For all any of us know, perhaps that had something to do with it. It's hard to say. He was the worst in the winter time, and in damp weather. He put up with it for several years before finally deciding he could not bear another winter, afraid that the next one would put him in bed to stay. He . . . took his last chance at dying with honor."

Anna sniffed and dabbed at her eyes again. "I can't believe this! It's like a bad dream."

Abbie swallowed. "I know. It is for me, too, but I'm learning to adjust. Wolf's Blood and I have been to the place in the mountains where he left the body—on an Indian platform." She would not tell the woman about her experience on the mountaintop. Only Wolf's Blood knew, and no one else would. It was a personal thing, something no one else would ever believe or understand. And it gave her new strength.

"When did all this happen?" Anna asked in a choked voice.

"It was early last January. It's been nearly seven months now."

Anna breathed deeply and rose, walking over to Wolf's Blood. He studied the woman curiously, aware of the part she had played in his father's life, for in their many talks Zeke had often mentioned Anna Gale. He could see the beauty the woman once carried, for she was still beautiful, even at her age. She looked at him lovingly, and he caught a brief glimpse of the way she must have once gazed at his father, a fiery twinkle in her eye for just a moment, a daring, hungry look. But it lasted only briefly, and her eyes teared again as she looked at him.

"You're a good son, bringing your mother here like this—taking her to the mountains. This must have been very, very hard on you, Wolf's Blood. I know you and your father were very close. He talked about you all the time." She reddened slightly then, wondering if she should have said that. She turned and met Abbie's eyes. "Abbie, about that time a few years ago, when Zeke came here to take Margaret out of that brothel and stayed here at the boarding house—"

"I don't want to even bother talking about it," Abbie interrupted. "We were going through a bad time then. Margaret had run off, LeeAnn had been carried away by Comanches, and our little Lillian died. Zeke was going through a terrible guilt, thinking I would be better off without him. I knew what he would do when he came here—knew he'd do everything he could to prove to himself he could get by without me. But it's all water over the dam now, Anna. And in some ways you helped him a great deal. That's all that matters."

Their eyes held, and Anna's teared more again. "I loved him," she said in a husky voice, holding her chin proudly.

She saw no animosity in Abbie's eyes. "I know that," Abbie replied. She rose from her chair. "Why don't we go and have some tea, Anna? I'll tell you what's happening with the children, and the grandchildren."

The woman breathed deeply and smiled gratefully. Yes, Abigail Monroe was a woman of quality and gentle understanding. "Grandchildren?" she asked. "I never even considered . . . My how time flies! How many do you have?"

"There are five now—at least that we know of. Our daughter LeeAnn went east several years ago, and I am afraid has decided she wants nothing to do with Colorado or her Indian heritage anymore. We have completely lost touch. If she has any children, we wouldn't know."

"Oh, Abbie, that's terrible! How sad! Then the girl doesn't even know her father has died!" She led Abbie toward the kitchen, the two of them still talking. Wolf's Blood stared out the window again at the fancy office building on a distant hill where they had gone to find his brother Jeremy, only to discover the man was in Europe with his high-society wife. They had learned from those who knew him at the office that Jeremy had no children, and that his wife did not want any. When the man they spoke with asked if he could give Jeremy a message, Abbie had simply stared at him with cold eyes.

"Tell him his father is dead," she had said flatly.

The man frowned. "His father? But . . . ma'am . . . he told us his father died a long time ago—some rancher down in Texas."

Never had Wolf's Blood felt more sorry for his mother than at that moment. She had wavered, and he wondered if she would faint. He had taken her arm. "Let's get out of here, Mother."

"But . . . who shall I say was here?" the man asked. "And I'm afraid I'm very confused here."

Abbie managed to stay calm. "Who we are apparently doesn't matter to him," she answered. "You tell him a white woman and an Indian man were here—and that they came to tell him his father is dead. He'll know who it was." She had turned and walked to the door, then stopped, looking back. "And tell him we hope he had a nice time in Europe."

However much the incident had hurt his poor mother, Wolf's Blood couldn't tell. Her only statement was that she was glad Zeke had not lived to know just how badly his own son had deserted him, and she declared that she did not want to speak of Jeremy again.

Wolf's Blood clenched his fists. How he would love to batter his brother's face. He had never told her of the time he and

Zeke had seen Jeremy in Dodge City. Zeke had said not to mention it, wanting to save Abbie the hurt. But she had been hurt anyway.

He gazed beyond the buildings to the mountains that loomed all along the horizon. Out there, far to the South, lay the *Sangre de Cristo's*, and his father's burial place. It was done now. They would probably never go back there again. There was no use in hoping none of it was true, no use in hoping to see Zeke Monroe come riding over a ridge on one of his grand Appaloosas. Going to the site with his mother had helped him realize that himself, even though his father had died in his arms. It was over, and Zeke Monroe rested peacefully in a beautiful green cove deep in the mountains, where only animals dwelled and water thundered and splashed nearby to keep him company. It was time to go home—to Sonora, to the ranch. It was time to go on living. He would have to be strong on his own. There was no Zeke to turn to for strength and advice, no Zeke to talk to over campfires, to smoke the prayer pipe with, to race with. That was the hardest part. There would be no more morning rides. But he had memories—precicus, precious memories—and when he closed his eyes and tried very hard, he could be with his father, could hear his voice, almost talk with him again. And he could remember a man about his own age, riding with a small Indian boy beside him, racing toward the sun.

Charles Garvey rose to greet his visitor, who had refused to give his name to the secretary. His eyes widened when the young man entered, for he looked familiar, and Garvey quickly remembered he was the same person who had argued with him in public over Indians a few years earlier. His eyes hardened, and when Joshua put out his hand Garvey refused to take it.

"What are you doing here?" he asked coldly.

Joshua only smiled. He took a chair, then took a cigar from a box on Garvey's desk and lit it. Garvey reddened with anger, sitting down himself.

"Quite a successful man now, aren't you, Charles?" he commented, puffing the cigar.

Charles closely scrutinized the handsome man before him, perhaps ten years younger than himself, with hazel eyes. The only thing that detracted from his fine looks and build was that he also walked with a limp, only he needed more than a cane to assist him. This young man wore a brace, which showed through at his foot where it wrapped around his shoe.

"State your business, or I'll have you thrown out," Charles spoke up.

Joshua nodded. "You're wondering if I am the young man who argued with you once about Indians," he answered. "The answer is yes. And I never told you my name that day. I will tell you now. It is Joshua Lewis."

Garvey's eyes lit up. "You!" He rose. "Every article you write in the *Times* destroys everything I write about the Indians!" He looked sneeringly at Joshua, his eyes ugly, his lips almost curled with hatred. "You've made quite a name for yourself with your lies about those lice-ridden, stinking, drunken bastards!" he snarled. "And you even admit in your articles that you are part Indian! How can you look people in the eye and say that? You get out of my office, Joshua Lewis! I'll have no half-breed scum in here!"

Joshua just grinned. "Even if you're related to him?" he asked.

Garvey just stared at him, turning a ghastly white. He trembled noticeably and all but fell back into his chair. He gripped the arms of it until his knuckles were white. "You had better have a good reason for speaking such lies!" he growled.

Joshua frowned. "Come now, Garvey. You know a reputable reporter like myself would never lie." He puffed the cigar again. "Yes, sir, when I tell the whole story in the *Times,* you, my dear brother, will be laughed out of Washington. Imagine! After all your hard work at lambasting the Indians—to find out you yourself have a half-breed brother." He clucked his tongue and shook his head. "That will create some gossip that will hang around Washington for a long time."

The look in Charles Garvey's eyes was insane, as their dark, smouldering depths bore into Joshua Lewis, who refused to let the man frighten him. He had planned this sweet moment for too long.

"Tell me, Charles, do I get half the fortune?" He knocked some ashes from the cigar onto the floor. "Oh, no matter. You can have it. The pleasure of the look on your face right now is payment enough for missing out on what was rightfully mine. Besides, I'm a successful man in my own right, and most of your money has been earned illegally, much of it at the expense of the poor Indian. I wouldn't really want to touch such filthy money. And I'm told you're going broke anyway—poor management or something like that."

"Shut up!" Garvey roared. "Shut your stinking mouth!"

Joshua frowned, pursing his lips and putting a finger to them. "Charles, you must keep it down. After all, if you're good about all this, I'll not say a word. Don't make me angry, Charles, and don't get violent. Don't you want to know how we came to be brothers?"

"That's a filthy lie! A lie! Are you insane, Lewis? Coming in here and claiming such nonsense! Explain yourself!" he snarled. "And then I will have you arrested!"

Joshua puffed the cigar for a moment. "All right. But perhaps you'd like to pour yourself a drink first. I know I could use one."

Garvey breathed deeply, his whole body bathed in perspiration. He struggled to control himself as he rose stiffly from his chair and walked to a buffet where he kept liquor. He poured two glasses of whiskey, turning and handing one out to Joshua Lewis, his lips curled in the ugly snarl again. "Enjoy your last drink, Lewis!" he growled.

Joshua took it and nodded a thank you. He leaned forward and put out the cigar, while Garvey sat back behind his desk. "Why are you doing this, Lewis? You can't just walk into a man's office and say he's your brother! You must be a crazy man! What are you after?"

Joshua sipped the drink. "Only one thing, Charles. The truth. I want you to stop cheating Indians, both in your business practices and in your writing."

Charles gripped the glass tightly. "Why?"

"Because if you don't, I'm going public with the truth about you—and your father."

Charles glared at him through hateful slits. "And what is

the truth?"

Joshua leaned back. "Do you remember back many years ago, when you and your father lived in Santa Fe, and your father had a . . . servant? An Indian woman called Yellow Moon?"

Charles's blood began to turn colder. "I remember."

"Good!" Joshua said with a grin. "Perhaps you also remember that a man came to your house one day, an Indian man—quite tall and striking—a powerfully built man who carried a big knife. And he took the Indian woman away."

Charles frowned. This man must be telling the truth. How would he know of things that happened before he could even have been born? "Yes. I never knew who the man was."

Joshua nodded. "Well, I do. He's my uncle—by marriage, not by blood. You see, Yellow Moon was an Arapaho woman who was married to the man's brother, Red Eagle. Red Eagle sold his wife for whiskey and later shot himself. Their small son was murdered by the outlaws who bought the woman. She was then sold to a prostitute named Anna Gale, who in turn gave the woman to your father—to use as he wished. And you can guess that she was more than a servant. Your illustrious, prominent father kept her tied in an attic room and used her to satisfy his sexual fantasies, until she was rescued by Red Eagle's half brother, Zeke Monroe."

Charles frowned, too curious now to go into a tantrum. Zeke Monroe. It was a familiar name, but Charles himself had never known the man, except to now be aware that it was Monroe who had come to his house and taken Yellow Moon away. "Go on," he said quietly.

Joshua sipped more whiskey. "Well, Zeke took his sister-in-law home with him, and gave her to another Cheyenne brother to care for. His name was Swift Arrow. He took her north with him. But when he took her, she was already with child— Winston Garvey's child, a half-breed."

He watched the changes in Charles Garvey's eyes—first curiosity and confusion, then a slow but sure understanding until they widened with dread. "You?"

Joshua nodded. "The same, dear brother."

Charles began shaking again. "It . . . it can't be true!"

"But it is. Yellow Moon was killed in an Indian battle at Blue Water Creek, not long after I was born. I was called Crooked Foot because I had a clubfoot. Swift Arrow could not keep me. He was a Dog Soldier and intended to spend his life fighting for freedom. He could not be burdened with a crippled child that wasn't even his own. So he gave me to Zeke and Abigail Monroe, who in turn took me to a missionary couple they knew—Bonnie and Rodney Lewis. Bonnie's father was a doctor, and Bonnie and Rodney agreed to take me in—adopted me. They saw to it I had several operations that enabled me to walk eventually, although I still wear a brace."

Charles gripped his glass so tightly Joshua wondered if he might break it right in his hand. "If this is all true, why didn't someone come out with it a long time ago?"

Joshua snickered. "The timing was never right. My uncle Zeke and my adoptive parents all feared that if your father found out he had a half-breed son, he'd have me killed, and all those who knew about me. I don't doubt he suspected a time or two, maybe tried in some way to find out. But the secret was well kept, for my safety, and for Zeke's and his family's. After all, your father was a very powerful man. Besides, my parents couldn't even tell me until I was much older, of an age that I would understand all of it." He rose. "But I've had my fill of you, Charles Garvey. And I decided there is only one way to stop you. I am powerful in my own right now. And Zeke Monroe was killed over a year ago at Fort Robinson. There is really no one left you can harm, and if you tried, I would make sure the public knows who was bringing harm to Zeke's family, or to me or mine."

Charles rose himself, glaring at Joshua Lewis, beginning to shake violently. "What do you want, Lewis!" he hissed. "Money?"

Joshua smiled sadly. "No. I want nothing from you but the satisfaction I am getting right now at the look on your face— and to tell you to stop raping the Indians. I want all your articles stopped and all your illegal activities stopped. I know about some of them, too. I am a good investigator, Charles. So put a halt to the whiskey running and reservation cheating, or I will expose you—not just your relationship to me, but the

379

other things you are up to."

The young man turned to leave, when Charles called out to him. "Stop!"

Joshua turned to see the man standing there pointing a handgun at him. "Don't be a fool, Garvey!" he sneered. "I left an envelope and strict instructions with a friend of mine that it be opened and published if I should be found dead. You'd hang."

There were actual tears in Charles Garvey's eyes, as his body shook with rage. "You mother-loving son of a bitch!" he growled. "I'll find a way to get you! I'll find a way!"

Joshua shrugged. "I hope you try, Charles. I'm itching to expose you for what you really are. You should be locked up."

He turned and walked out, closing the door softly. Charles dropped the gun, then whacked the glass of whiskey across the room and fell to his knees, sobbing like a little boy.

It was deep in the night when someone pounded on the door of Joshua's hotel room, where he'd been staying while in Washington on special assignment. He stirred in his sleep, roused more when the pounding came again. He frowned, throwing back the covers of his bed and rubbing his eyes. He glanced at a clock. It was two A.M. He rose, pulling on a robe and stopping to pick up a small handgun. His visitor could be a drunken Charles Garvey. He walked to the door. "Who's there?" he demanded.

"Please . . . let me come in!" came a woman's voice. She was obviously crying.

Joshua opened the door cautiously, and a young woman rushed inside, clinging to a dark-haired child of perhaps two years of age. The woman sank to the floor, weeping, her clothes partially torn. Joshua quickly closed the door and set the gun aside. He knelt beside the blond-haired woman, taking her arm. When she looked up at him, her face was so battered it was difficult to tell what she looked like.

"Good God, woman! Let me get you a doctor!"

"No!" she pleaded, shaking with shock and sorrow. "I . . . I am Mrs. Charles Garvey!"

Joshua's eyes widened in shock, remembering now the pretty young woman he had seen with Garvey a time or two. "What's happened to you?"

"He . . . beat me. I thought he'd . . . kill me . . . but he passed out drunk finally. Thank God . . . I got out with our son. He was . . . going to kill my baby!"

Joshua frowned, totally confused. He looked at the little boy, who sat staring at his mother with wide, innocent eyes. He looked very Indian, a beautiful boy with large brown eyes and straight black hair. But why would Charles Garvey's own son look Indian? He turned his eyes back to the boy's mother, then picked her up in his arms and carried her to his bed, laying her on it gently.

"You calm down, ma'am. Let me get a cool rag to bathe your face."

She grasped his arm. "Is it true? Is my father really dead?" she whimpered.

He frowned and shook his head. "Your father?"

"Zeke Monroe! He was my father! Charles came home with some insane story about . . . about you being his half brother . . . and that your uncle was Zeke Monroe and Zeke Monroe is dead!"

Joshua felt light-headed. He had not known—had not expected this. "My God!" he whispered, sitting down on the bed beside her. "You're . . . you're that LeeAnn? LeeAnn Monroe?"

She clung to him. "Is it true?"

He touched her hair. "I'm afraid so."

She broke into renewed sobbing, nearly hysterical. He pulled her up into his arms, embracing her tightly. So this was the wayward LeeAnn that Zeke and Abbie had not heard from in years. If he was so good at investigating things, why hadn't he figured this one out? That explained the boy looking so Indian. He took after his grandfather. This girl must have never told her husband who she really was, and whatever her reason, she was consumed now with a terrible guilt at finding out in such a cruel way that her father was dead. He rocked her gently as she wept and mumbled about her husband coming home with the story Joshua had brought to him, sobbing that when he mentioned Zeke Monroe being dead she could no longer hide her own identity, finally telling him who she was. He had beaten her severely, and she had fled for her life, taking their son with her. He had declared he would kill the boy, now that he knew for certain the child carried Indian blood. She had remembered someone mentioning that Joshua Lewis was staying at this hotel while in Washington, and she had taken the chance that she could find him here.

"Please . . . help me!" she sobbed. "Don't let him . . . hurt me or my son!"

He stroked her hair, smelling a delightful scent. In spite of her present condition, he knew how beautiful she was. And this was Zeke and Abbie's daughter. Of course he would help her. "Don't you worry about a thing. I'm so sorry, LeeAnn. I had no idea. I . . . I never really knew you . . . and I guess no one ever told you the connection. It was kept such a secret. Only Wolf's Blood knew, besides your parents and mine."

She broke into heavier sobbing, shaking violently. "Oh, God, how can I ever be forgiven for what I've done! I married the son . . . of a man my father must have hated! And I turned my back . . . on my own flesh and blood! Now I'll never see my father again . . . never be able to tell him I love him . . . ask him to forgive me! He . . . risked his life . . . to save me once from Comanches . . . and I threw it all in his face!"

"Hush now," Joshua said softly. "I'm sure that even in death your father knows, LeeAnn. And I'm sure he never stopped loving you. I think he understood."

"I want to go home! I want to see my mother!"

He kissed her hair. Why had he felt compelled to do that? Why did he suddenly feel so protective of her? "Then I will take you myself. It's the least I can do for bringing you this trouble. I'm so very sorry."

He gently laid her back on the pillow. "It would have come out . . . some other way," she sobbed. "Our son . . . looks more and more Indian . . . every day."

Joshua turned to look at the boy, who was toddling toward them. "He's Indian, all right. What is his name?"

"Matthew," she told him. All her words were spoken

painfully through swollen lips. He reached out and set
Matthew on the bed beside his mother, ordering the boy to stay
put. He hurriedly wet down a rag and gently applied it to her
badly bruised face and bleeding lips.

"I'd better get you a doctor."

"No. I'll . . . be all right. I just . . . want to go home. If you
get a doctor, he might . . . recognize me . . . ask questions.
Charles would . . . find me. I don't want him to find me."

He sighed. "All right. But I'm getting you out of these
clothes and giving you a nightshirt to put on. And I'll have no
arguments or bashfulness. I'll not have LeeAnn Garvey dying
in my hotel room. Now how would that look?"

Her body jerked in uncontrolled sobs. She was too weak and
in too much pain to object. He undressed her with gentle hands
and quickly put a nightshirt on her. She could not help but
wonder at his kindness, his sincere sympathy, the respectful
way he did not let his eyes linger on things he should not see.
He was so different. She had known only brutality for years
and had begun to think all men must be that way. But Joshua
Lewis was sweet and gentle, and it reminded her of the way her
father had treated her mother. She had almost forgotten there
was such a thing as kindness, such a thing as men who were
strong but gentle, brave but loving. Joshua Lewis was all those
things. She could tell right away.

"Now you just lie right there and sleep," he told her.
"Here." He poured some whiskey. "Drink a little of this. I'll
get Matthew to sleep. Don't you worry about anything. I'll see
that you get home to Colorado."

Colorado! Why did it suddenly sound so good? Colorado.
Home. Mother. But there was no more father. Would her
mother still love her? Would she forgive her? Who could tell?
But she must take the chance. If Abigail Monroe was the same
woman she had left behind ten years ago, she would welcome
her daughter, no matter what.

Joshua sat down in a big chair with Matthew, who at two in
the morning was droopy-eyed and confused. He held the boy
close and talked softly to him, and in moments the child was
fast asleep in his arms. Joshua stared for several minutes at

LeeAnn Garvey, wondering what kind of hell the woman had been living in. If Zeke Monroe had known, he'd have come to Washington and plowed through the streets, going straight to Charles Garvey and sinking his blade into the man's evil heart, that was sure.

Yes. He would take LeeAnn Garvey home where she belonged.

Chapter Twenty-Three

The train rumbled through Ohio, Indiana, Illinois, and into Kansas. It was May, 1880, and the prairies were alive with wildflowers, except for the vast expanses now farmed. With every mile left behind her, LeeAnn Garvey felt more free. Her heart became lighter. She felt like she was coming out of the pits of the earth into bright sunshine and fresh air, for she was leaving Charles Garvey, and she wondered why she had not had the courage to do so until now. She glanced at Joshua. Perhaps it was because of him that she had the courage. She had always felt so afraid and alone before, not knowing where to turn for help. Why she had run to him in her panic the night Charles beat her she wasn't sure, but she was glad she had done so.

From the way her mother had talked about Bonnie Lewis, now Bonnie Monroe, LeeAnn was not surprised that this adopted son of hers was a gentle and caring person. It was a little unnerving to realize how fate could lead people down unusual pathways. Who would have thought that the little crippled baby her own parents had taken to Bonnie Lewis all those years ago would end up being so important to her own life? And who would have dreamed that LeeAnn Monroe would marry a Garvey? It made her wonder just how much control anyone had over his life. Perhaps everyone's destiny was cut out for them from the day they were born.

She hugged her little Matthew. What would be his destiny? He looked so Indian that even though he was mostly white no

385

one would believe it. She kissed his dark hair. She would protect and defend him. Her son would not suffer for his looks. The thought brought pain to her heart at the realization of how her own father had suffered, and the hurt it must have brought him to die without ever seeing his daughter again. She doubted she would ever get over the guilt of that, but at least if her mother accepted her, it would help a little.

She wished someone had told her all the things she had just learned through Joshua. If only she had known! Surely her parents could not fully blame her for something she didn't know in the first place. She could understand why it was kept secret, and naturally her parents would never dream that somewhere along the way their daughter would meet and marry a Garvey. She wondered now how she could have done such a thing, why she didn't sense the man's evil ruthlessness long before they were wed. But she had been too caught up in Garvey's wealth and prominence. How could she, the daughter of a woman like Abigail Monroe, move so far astray from the way she had been brought up? She remembered her mother mentioning to her that LeeAnn reminded her of her own sister, after whom she was named. Abbie's sister had also wanted a man of wealth, who could put her in fancy clothes and make her socially prominent. She had thought she met such a man on the wagon train, and he had turned out to be a gambler, who stole her away and sold her to outlaws to pay a debt. That LeeAnn was murdered. Now this LeeAnn shivered, realizing how close she had come to being killed herself. Unlike her dead aunt, this LeeAnn was being given a second chance at life.

Joshua stirred and changed positions, his head leaning toward her and touching her shoulder. She felt a faint stirring, but years with Charles Garvey had left their scars, and the thought of being with any man again made her feel nauseous. How she was going to forget the horror of Charles Garvey's touch she was not certain, but somehow she must, and being home on the ranch would help. Still, there most certainly had to be kind men. Look at how her father had always treated her mother. And Dan and Bonnie Monroe were apparently very happy, the way Josh talked about them. And of course there was Josh himself, who had kept her under guard until he could get her out of Washington. Now he was going with her all the way home, refusing to leave her alone. He had taken care of everything: buying her some extra clothes, getting the train tickets, everything. He had even requested a leave from the *Times*. His assignment in Washington was finished anyway. He would take some time off and bring LeeAnn Garvey home, though he told no one. They had slept right on the train for several days, and she ached all over. When they reached Topeka they would get off for a night and stay in a hotel before switching to the Atchison, Topeka & Santa Fe train that would take them to Fort Lyon. It would feel good to sleep in a real bed all night.

She leaned back and watched the Kansas prairie pass by. Yes, she was entering familiar country, and it felt good. She thought about what Josh had told her about the A T & SF tracks going right past the northern section of her father's ranch now. Surely that had made her parents very unhappy. Through Josh, she was seeing the real picture of what had happened to the Indians, and it saddened her. It was probably a good thing her father had died when he did, for things could get worse yet. The days of freedom for the Indian were gone, and she did not doubt that a little of Zeke Monroe had died with them, giving him all the more reason to let his life end. She blinked back tears. Poor father. Through letters from Bonnie, Josh had learned that Zeke Monroe had also been suffering severely from arthritis, something Bonnie and Dan had later learned from Abbie. It all made sense then. Zeke Monroe would not die a crippled man. But the fact remained that he had died without seeing his daughter again, and she could not stop the tears that seemed to come so easily now. She sniffed and stared out the window, and then a hand was closing over her own, squeezing hers reassuringly. She turned to look into Joshua Lewis's gentle hazel eyes, and he smiled.

"Buck up, girl. You're going home," he told her.

She smiled through her tears, and with his other hand he reached up and brushed the tears from her face. "You're looking much better, LeeAnn. The bruises are fading some."

She looked back out the window, and he kept hold of her hand.

By that evening they were in Topeka, and Joshua got her a room of her own, where she enjoyed the luxury of a hot bath and took a nap before he returned to take her to dinner. She ignored the way people stared at her, a blond-haired, blue-eyed woman carrying an Indian baby. The bruises that still showed on her face didn't help any. Was she a captive just recently released? Was the young man with her some kind of government agent? LeeAnn had grown accustomed to the stares and really didn't care anymore. She ate her fill, her appetite returning more with every mile she put between herself and Charles Garvey.

"I am sure he's disinherited me and his son from his will and filed for divorce by now," she told Joshua over dessert. "Not that I care. Knowing what I know, I could never live on Garvey money anyway. It would be an insult to my father."

"Well, I don't think there would have been much anyway, LeeAnn. I'd been doing some investigating of my own, and Charles Garvey was on the verge of bankruptcy. He let too many others handle his business for him, and he was getting cheated right and left by his own men. Serves him right, to say the least, considering the way he cheated people himself. All hell will break loose soon and he'll find himself a nearly broke man, which I doubt he'll be able to handle." He reached across the table and took her hand. "Which leads me to something I am very worried about, LeeAnn."

She met his eyes. "What is that?"

"I want you to be very careful. Stay close to the ranch and Wolf's Blood once you're home. I don't trust Charles Garvey one whit. What he learned about me and about you triggered that strange, almost insane side of him. And once he finds out he's losing his fortune on top of it, he's going to be a desperate, demented man. It would not surprise me at all if he found a way to blame you and probably me, too, for his misfortunes, and now he knows who you really are and where you'll probably go.

388

I'm worried he'll come looking for you—find a way to have you and the boy killed."

She swallowed, her fear of Charles Garvey building all over again. If he got her alone he would make her suffer dearly before he killed her, of that she was certain.

"Look, I don't want you having nightmares over it," Joshua consoled. "I just want you to consider the kind of man he is and be very careful. I think as long as you're on the ranch you'll be safe, until we know for certain what will happen to Charles Garvey. I'll probably go on north from the ranch to see Dan and my mother, then head back east and clean some things up, check out Charles Garvey. Then I'm coming back out here to start my own newspaper, as well as do whatever I can to help the Indians."

She searched the kind eyes. "You're a good man, Joshua Lewis. What would I have done without having you to turn to? Anyone else would have told Charles where I was and let him come for me." She blinked back tears. "Thank you—for all of it."

He smiled softly. "I knew the first time I saw you, before I even knew who you really were, that you didn't belong with that man. And now that I know you're Zeke Monroe's daughter, it's just that much more incentive to help you. Now eat your dessert and let's get you back so you can get a good night's sleep. The train leaves at seven A.M."

They finished their meal, and he walked her to the hotel and to the door to her own room, carrying Matthew on his shoulders, somehow thinking he had to prove to her he was as strong as any other man and the leg brace did not hamper that strength. He lifted the boy down when they got to the door to her room, and the child clung to his mother's skirt as LeeAnn and Joshua stood looking at each other, both suddenly realizing it was possible they were falling in love.

Joshua sighed deeply, leaning against the doorjamb. "LeeAnn, when all this is over, and you're divorced and I'm settled—"

"Don't," she said quickly, looking away.

He reached out and grasped her chin, making her look at

389

him. "Why not? You're beginning to mean very much to me, LeeAnn. We're cousins, but not by blood, only by circumstance. My father was Winston Garvey, much as I hate to admit it. Zeke was my uncle, but only because my Indian mother's husband was Zeke's brother. So we have no blood relation, LeeAnn, and I don't see why we can't . . . I mean . . . damn it, LeeAnn, I think I'm falling in love with you."

She closed her eyes. "You shouldn't. Once I'm free of Charles I want nothing to do with men anymore."

He reached out and grasped her arms. "LeeAnn, you know good and well that not all men are like him. Look at your own parents!"

She hung her head. "You don't understand. You don't know . . . what he was like. It wasn't just . . . the beatings. I could have . . ." He saw a panic building and kept a firm hold of her arms. ". . . could have stood the beatings, if he . . . would have treated me like . . . like a normal woman."

"Don't talk about it now, LeeAnn."

"But you don't know! You don't know! He was . . . demented! Sadistic! I can't . . . think about being with anyone else—ever! I just want to be left alone!"

He forced her to him, embracing her, until she broke into sobbing against his chest and clung to his jacket. "I don't believe that, LeeAnn." He kissed her hair. "And the best way to forget that man is to let a man love you the right way, show you the beauty of it, show you a man can be gentle. That's the only way you'll get over this, LeeAnn. And some day you'll let that happen, and the man will be me. I can't bear the thought of it being anyone else."

She cried for several minutes, while Matthew began running up and down the hallway, oblivious to his mother's problems. Joshua kept kissing her hair, then moved his lips to her temple. "LeeAnn," he whispered. "Don't cry, LeeAnn." He took a handkerchief from his pocket, and keeping his left arm around her he reached up with his right hand and began wiping at her eyes and nose as she leaned back slightly. She finally met his eyes, and then he was leaning closer. She wasn't sure why she let him kiss her. Perhaps she only wanted to know if he could be telling the truth. He met her mouth in the sweetest, most tender kiss she had ever tasted. Charles had never kissed her this way, even before they were married. It made her tremble with feelings totally new to her in spite of being a married woman with a child.

The kiss lingered for several seconds until he finally pulled away, smiling. "See? Was that so terrible?"

She closed her eyes and rested her head against his chest again. "Joshua, I can't promise anything right now."

"You think I don't know that? I just wanted to give you something to think about. I promise not to do that again and not to press you about anything else." He gave her a squeeze. "Now get some sleep."

She pulled away, slightly flushed from the kiss. She unlocked her door, then looked up at him again, realizing he had to be much younger than Charles. "Josh, I don't even know how old you are."

He grinned. "Twenty-six. Is that bad?"

She opened the door, then bent down and picked up Matthew. "I guess not. I just thought of it. I'm twenty-eight. Is that bad?"

His hazel eyes took in her voluptuous beauty. "I hardly call two years a problem. Considering the situation, that's the least of our worries."

She smiled through tears. "I suppose so." She put her fingers to her lips and reddened once more, feeling like a young innocent all over again. "Good-night, Josh."

His smile faded. "Good-night, LeeAnn. I . . . I hope I didn't offend you. I do love you. I know you're in a fix at the moment, but we'll straighten it all out, LeeAnn—together."

She sniffed and held Matthew close. "I'm not offended, Josh. I'm flattered. Thank you for being such a good friend."

He sighed. "I want to be more than a good friend."

Their eyes held. "Bear with me, Josh. Give me some time."

He bowed slightly. "The first thing we'll do is get you home, and you'll be there in just a couple more days. Sleep tight."

He turned and went to his own room, and LeeAnn went into

hers. Both of them slept restlessly that night.

The train ride to Fort Lyon found LeeAnn Garvey more relaxed and happier than she had been in years. Nothing more was said about their feelings. What would be, would be. For now they were at least great friends. It felt good to have a man who really cared about her and intended to protect her. Little Matthew took to Josh well, and that was important, too. But LeeAnn could not bring herself to think any further than friendship for now. For the moment, the most important thing was that she was going home.

They reached Fort Lyon, near the spot of old Bent's Fort. What familiar territory! Her heart pounded with joy and excitement. Josh rented a buggy and horses, and they packed their gear on and headed west, for the Monroe ranch. It was nearly a three-day trip with horses, but LeeAnn didn't mind. It felt good to be in this land again, to ride under the sun and sleep under the stars. Neither she nor Josh cared what anyone would think of their sleeping together in the wagon bed, keeping little Matthew between them for warmth. And LeeAnn found her love and respect for the man grow just because of his own respect and consideration for her. He never made suggestions or touched her wrongly, and did not even mention his love for her again. He would wait, with the care and patience only a man like Joshua Lewis could afford. His friendship was enough for now.

The third day found the wagon clattering over the Monroe property, and LeeAnn's eyes teared at the sight of the grand Appaloosas. She knew through Josh that Morgan ran the ranch now—knew about all the grandchildren and about Wolf's Blood. The only thing she didn't know was how her mother would welcome her. Did Abbie look the same? Did all of them look the same? Her throat ached now, her eyes brimming with tears. Now she could see the barn, noticing that it was not the same one she had left. Josh said he thought he remembered his mother writing him that the old barn had burned a few years back.

She could see the house then. A woman was behind it hoeing

up the ground for a garden. Who else could it be but Abbie, who insisted every year on a vegetable garden, one of the few people in the area who could get vegetables to grow well in ground not meant for much more than potatoes. A horse and rider came toward them now, and LeeAnn straightened and looked toward their approach, shading her eyes with her hand. The rider came closer, and LeeAnn's eyes widened as though she were seeing a ghost. If she didn't know better, she would have greeted him as her father.

"Wolf's Blood!" she said in a near whisper. He reined his mount to a halt and stared at her.

"LeeAnn?"

She nodded, suddenly hardly able to see him for the tears in her eyes. Wolf's Blood looked from her to Joshua in confusion.

"It's a long story, Wolf's Blood," Joshua told him. "For the moment, it's good to see you again. It's been years."

Wolf's Blood nodded. "It is good to see you also. But, how is it that my sister comes home with you?"

"We'll explain later. LeeAnn's only concern now is how you and the family will accept her, after being away so long."

"Wolf's Blood, I just found out about Father!" LeeAnn blurted out. "I didn't know! I'm so sorry! And I've . . . been through so much . . . I just wanted to come home when I heard . . . and be with Mother . . . and stay here! Do you think she'll let me stay?"

He looked at the Indian child. "He is yours?"

She nodded, and Wolf's Blood held out his hand. "Climb up here with me, and keep the boy with you. I will ride you down to her. You know our mother. She will be happy you have come home. It will not matter to her what has happened before. And you bring her another grandchild. This is good for her lonely heart."

LeeAnn stood up and Wolf's Blood sidled his horse up to the wagon, grasping her around the waist and lifting her up in front of him. Joshua handed up the baby and LeeAnn held him in front of her. Their eyes held.

"Go ahead," Josh told her. "I'll give you some time alone. Then we'll all talk."

She sniffed and swallowed. "Thank you, Josh."

Wolf's Blood did not miss the look of love in Joshua's eyes, and he was indeed curious to know what was going on. But for now, the important thing was for LeeAnn to see her mother. He turned his horse and rode down the hill, and LeeAnn could not help but be overwhelmed at how much her brother had turned out to be just like her father. Powerful bronze arms held her on the horse, and she wondered now why she had allowed herself to be ashamed of such strong, good, honest men. She had always been very different from Wolf's Blood, she and Jeremy both so unlike the rest of the children. She wondered what had happened to Jeremy, for Josh had told her he didn't think they had ever heard from him. How sad her father's heart must have been over not seeing either of them before he died.

They came closer, and Abbie's face lit up. She threw down the hoe and ran toward them, shouting LeeAnn's name. In the next moment Wolf's Blood was helping her down and her mother was embracing her, weeping uncontrollably, and LeeAnn wondered why she had doubted that this woman would welcome her or still love her. Abigail Trent Monroe had a tremendous capacity for loving . . . and forgiving.

The group around the table was somber, for Abigail had paled to a sickening white as LeeAnn told her story. Except for Joshua, who stayed to give LeeAnn support, only direct family members were there for the moment: Wolf's Blood, Margaret, Jason, Abbie, and LeeAnn. Abbie's happiness over LeeAnn's return and finding she had another grandson was hampered now by the knowledge that one of Zeke Monroe's own daughters had married a Garvey.

"She can't be fully blamed," Joshua spoke up for her. "None of you told her the whole story, and that isn't her fault. She may have tried to change her life, but she'd not have gone so far as to marry a Garvey if she had known. And she's been through a living hell. She's left the man and wants to stay here with all of you, if you'll let her."

Abbie tried to talk but could not make all the words come out. She sat there trembling, half choking. "It isn't just—" She could not go on. She bent over, covering her face with her hands. Wolf's Blood frowned with concern, coming over and grasping her shoulders, rubbing them gently.

"It is not what you think," he told the rest of them. His eyes rested on LeeAnn. "No one can blame you for something you did not know. The secret was kept for a reason. But none of you know the final truth about Winston Garvey, not even Dan and Bonnie. Only Father and I knew—and Mother." He met Joshua's eyes. "I think you should know now. And perhaps it will only accent more what a demented and dangerous man Charles Garvey could be."

Abbie broke into sobbing. It had been seventeen years, and still she could not forget the horror of it.

"Somehow Winston Garvey figured out Father was the one who could tell him about the half-breed son he wanted to find and kill." He looked at his brother and sisters. "You remember when Father was away during the Civil War, and outlaws came to the ranch and threatened to kill all of us if Mother did not go with them? When Father returned, he and I searched for Mother. We brought her home several weeks later. I think you remember what condition she was in. She almost died. Father and I never told you exactly what had happened to her." He looked at Joshua again. "Winston Garvey had hired those men to take her away—to him. Garvey and two of his men kept her prisoner in an abandoned mine. They . . . tortured her . . . and they raped her . . . trying to get her to tell where you were. She did not tell them."

The room was dead silent, except for Abbie's quiet weeping. LeeAnn paled. "My God!" she finally whispered. "And I married his son!"

Joshua's eyes teared. "Someone should have told us—me, my mother. What can I say, Wolf's Blood? I . . . I owe my life to her."

"No one is to blame but Winston Garvey—for any of it. And we could not tell you because . . ." He looked around at all of them. It had been seventeen years. What could be done now? And who could be trusted more than these people? Besides, Zeke was dead. "Because we wanted no connections between Winston Garvey and myself and my father. That was very important."

LeeAnn frowned. "Charles told me his father disappeared one night, after an Indian raid on his ranch."

Wolf's Blood's dark eyes held hers. "Yes. He disappeared. And so did the two men who helped him hurt my mother. They were left in so many pieces in so many places that they could not possibly be found."

Her eyes widened. "You! And Father!"

He nodded. "And I am the one who wounded Charles Garvey at Sand Creek. He rode with that bastard John Chivington, and he killed the Cheyenne girl I loved, and other women and children."

She put a hand to her head, astounded. Her own father had killed her husband's father! Her husband had killed the girl Wolf's Blood loved, and Wolf's Blood had crippled Charles Garvey. How frightening it was to know how easily fate ruled people's lives. She stood up on shaky legs and walked around the table toward the door. "I . . . I see I can't stay here after all," she said quietly. "I unknowingly . . . betrayed my family in the worst way, especially my parents." She looked at her still-weeping mother. "I'm sorry, Mother. There is nothing else I can say. I'll . . . find a place to go. I'm sure it's difficult for you to even look at me."

She turned to go out.

"LeeAnn!" Abbie called out, raising her head. LeeAnn turned, and Abbie wiped at her eyes. "I waited . . . all these years to see you again," she told her daughter in a strained voice. "Now your father is gone. I want you to stay. Please don't leave again. Not just for me . . . but for Zeke. He would never let you leave again."

LeeAnn's chest ached with love. "Are you sure?"

Abbie nodded. "You're . . . our daughter. We understood why you felt you had to go away . . . after the Comanches. And how were you to know about the other?" She stood up. "Don't leave me, LeeAnn."

The girl looked from her sister Margaret to her brothers. "What about the rest of the family?"

"If we were all kicked out for our mistakes, none of us would be here, except maybe Jason," Margaret spoke up. "He hasn't been out there in the cold, cruel world enough to make any mistakes." She tossled her young brother's hair and he blushed. Then she sobered again. "After what I did in Denver, Father could have told me to go to hell, LeeAnn. But he didn't. He and Mother just wanted me to come home."

LeeAnn nodded, then looked at her mother again, walking up to Abbie and hugging her. "I'm so sorry, Mama," she whispered, feeling like a small girl again.

Abbie patted her back and turned to Wolf's Blood. "Go and fetch Ellen," she told him. "LeeAnn hasn't seen her yet. See if Ellen and Hal can both come and bring the children. We'll have a real family get-together—maybe roast a side of beef."

Wolf's Blood smiled. "I will get them. I can get there today yet."

Moments later Wolf's Blood was riding east to his sister's ranch, his heart lighter. They would all be together—all but Jeremy. But maybe some day Jeremy would come home, too, although he would not be as ready to welcome his wayward brother as he had been to welcome LeeAnn, who at least had a reason for what she had done. But he would not think about that now. They would have a royal feast and all be together, and he knew that someone else would be with them, too. They would all feel him walking among them as they ate and laughed and played with nieces and nephews. The one strength that had kept them a family was gone in body, but not in spirit.

Joshua ended up staying for two weeks. It was a good time for all of them, and Abbie knew it was time to make a decision herself. She had promised Zeke she would do something for the Indians. The children were all settled, and it was obvious that LeeAnn and Joshua would inevitably end up together, once she settled matters with Charles Garvey. Joshua would soon be going north to see Dan and Bonnie. It was time to make the announcement. She stood up as they all sat around campfire: Joshua, LeeAnn, and Matthew; Margaret, Morgan, Little Zeke, and Nathan; Wolf's Blood, Sonora, Kicking Boy, and Iris; Ellen, Hal, and little Lillian Rose; and twenty-year-old Jason. She motioned for all of them to be silent, and they quieted. They studied their mother as she obviously prepared to tell them something. She was still beautiful, still small. Her hair remained a lustrous reddish-brown, with only a hint of gray. Her eyes were still large and clear, and few wrinkles marred her smooth skin. For all the hell she had suffered over the years, she was indeed in marvelous health; and for all her five feet two inches, she was still a pillar of strength to the whole family.

"I have been thinking about something for a long time," she told them, "preparing myself, weighing the facts, remembering some promises I made to your father. I have waited to do what I must do because first I wanted to be strong enough. I had to know I can survive not only without your father, but without Wolf's Blood." Her eyes met her son's. "I am afraid that in your father's absence I moved the share of the burden onto you, my son. I turned to you for my strength, because you are so much like your father. That was unfair. And I think that I can get by on my own strength now, the strength that your father said I always had but didn't know. I guess he was right."

Wolf's Blood frowned. "What are you saying, Mother?"

"I am saying it's time for me to leave here and go north."

There were a few gasps and some whispered objections. Abbie put up her hands. "Hear me out and please don't try to stop me," she told them. "Joshua will be going north soon to see Dan and Bonnie, so there is someone who can take me. Jason has often talked of wanting to be a doctor—one who helps Indians. Dan and Bonnie tell me there is a very good doctor at Fort Keogh who is getting old and who would not mind training someone. Jason would have the added advantage of being part Indian and understanding Cheyenne ways and superstitions. He could go with me and begin learning about doctoring. I in turn could teach, nurse, help some of the Indian women learn to cope with their new way of living—whatever. I made your father a promise, and more than that, he saw in a vision that I would not always stay here—that I would do something to help the People. It's time I started doing it."

She turned to Margaret and Morgan. "You have run this ranch with little help for a long time," she told them. "Zeke told you years ago that when he was gone the place was yours if you wanted it. I am giving it to you. I'll sign over the deed. You two are settled and happy, and Little Zeke is eleven now, old enough to help out. You belong here. And Morgan, you're as good with horses as Zeke was. He taught you many things."

"But, Mother—" Margaret spoke up.

Abbie waved her off. "Let me finish." She turned to Ellen. "Ellen, you and Hal have your own place. And you also are happy and settled." She moved her eyes then to Wolf's Blood. "And you, my very precious son, are free to do whatever your heart tells you to do. I know that for a long time you have wanted to take Sonora south to find some of her people. You have stayed here because of me. Your father has been dead for seventeen months now, and it is time for all of us to get on with our lives. I am sure the other children understand when I say that I would miss you most of all, because when I see you I see Zeke. But perhaps that isn't so good after all. I am sure Margaret and Morgan would tell you that you are free to live here as you always have and be a part of this ranch. Or you can go south—except I want your promise that if you do, you will come back and not stay there."

She scanned the entire circle. "I do not like the thought of leaving any of you, or of leaving my grandchildren. But transportation is easier now. I can ride a train most of the way, and I can visit with Bonnie. I would have Jason with me, and if my intuition is right, LeeAnn will be going along north with us because of Joshua." She looked at the girl, who smiled and took Joshua's hand. "She can wait there until things are settled regarding her marriage, so I will have her with me also."

She looked toward the house, the main part of it being the original cabin she and Zeke Monroe had built together— because her Indian man had decided his white woman must settle in one place. "How can I . . . explain it?" she told them, her voice filling with sorrow. "If I am to . . . go on with my life . . . and rid myself of the terrible grief that still consumes me in the night . . . I must . . . leave this place, difficult as that will be. Here . . . everyplace I look . . . I see your father, standing at the corral, riding over a ridge, walking toward the house from the barn. I . . . seldom sleep in the bedroom anymore. Jason sleeps in there, and I sleep in the loft. I can't bear to lie down on that brass bed . . . or on the bed of robes . . . alone." She swallowed, and a tear slipped down her cheek. "I have to get away from the ranch for a while, children. It's the only way for me to truly be strong again. And I think . . . it would be good for me to go north and see Dan and Bonnie, who I am sure would help me settle there . . . and very good for me to help the Cheyenne all I can now. I choose the North, rather than the South, because of Dan and Bonnie . . . and because your father's only living Indian brother is up there . . . somewhere. Swift Arrow has to be a very lonely and broken man. Dan says he lives alone in the hills and seldom comes down to the agency. To do justice to your father's wishes and memory, I must go north and help the People, and see what I can do for Swift Arrow. Because of that, and because of the memories here that keep piercing my heart like swords, I am leaving the ranch. It just . . . isn't the same for me . . . without Zeke here. Many things . . . have ended . . . for all of us." She swallowed again, fighting not to break down. "And yet all of you are experiencing new beginnings." She turned to Wolf's Blood again. It would be so hard to leave him! "What will you do, Wolf's Blood?"

He frowned, swallowing back his own tears. "I am not certain. But it is the same for me . . . here at the ranch. I see him . . . hear him . . . everyplace I go on this land. I, too, am wondering how strong I truly am. I think perhaps . . . I should leave also . . . for a while. For many years my Sonora has wanted to go to the Apache reservation and find some of her people. Perhaps I will take her there. But we will come back."

There was not a dry eye in their little group. But none of them would try to stop their mother; for not only was she stubborn once she had made a decision, but they also knew she was right to go. She would never be truly strong and free of her grief as long as she stayed at the ranch. Abbie wiped at a tear and nodded.

"It's settled then. And the sooner the better, before I let memories and sentiment make me stay. But I do need some things from Fort Lyon." She looked at Joshua. "Can you wait another week or so?"

He nodded. "If you're sure."

"I am sure." She put on a smile. "Now, let's sing some songs—some of those funny ones Zeke taught us that always

400

made you children laugh when you were little. We'll teach them to the grandchildren." She took a deep breath and belted out the first line of "Big Rock Candy Mountain," and the others forced themselves to sing with her, about busy bees and gumdrop trees. Abbie's eyes wandered as she sang, gazing out across flat land to a spot farther up the creek where overgrowth hid a special place, where the grass was soft and irises bloomed, where once she had lain on the soft grass beneath her man.

Chapter Twenty-Four

Wolf's Blood filled three parfleches with the supplies his mother needed. Fort Lyon was teeming with travelers, soldiers, and settlers, and he had had to stand in line at the supply store, frustrated that this place was getting as bad as a regular city since the railroad went through. He nodded to a few people that he knew, for the Monroes were well known around the fort now. Rarely did Wolf's Blood come here without someone commenting about Zeke—how they missed him, what a respected man he was, sharing a story here and there of how they'd seen Zeke use his knife. The constant questions and reminiscing always brought Wolf's Blood great pain. Yes. Going south was a good idea for now. He must get away from all this. The vision of his father's burial place often haunted him, the memory of lifting the cold, stiff body of what was once a warm, powerful man.

He went into the tavern for a beer before beginning the hot ride back to the ranch. 1880 had brought a hot summer, and he was glad his mother could make most of her trip by train. He had brought back the buggy Joshua had rented, his own horse tied to it, and would return on his mount, loaded down with supplies. He sat down at the bar and ordered a beer from Luke McCabe, the same man who had served drinks there for many years and who knew Zeke well. Wolf's Blood prepared himself for the expected.

Luke shook his head. "Sure do miss you pa, Wolf's Blood," the man said. He made the comment every time Wolf's Blood stopped there. "You know, when he walked in this place, everybody turned and looked." He laughed. "You have the same effect. Not many Indians around as big as you, Wolf's Blood, and you're as good-lookin' as your pa was. I'll never forget that time you and your pa got in them wrestlin' contests and you ended up with that pretty little Apache girl. How's she doin', son?"

Wolf's Blood downed the beer. "Sonora is fine," he replied.

"And your ma?"

"She is well. She is preparing to go north to see my father's brothers and to stay awhile. It is hard for her on the ranch. Too many memories."

Luke nodded. "I can understand that. But this whole area won't be the same without Zeke and Abbie Monroe. It's a shame. Everything is changing, Wolf's Blood. And believe it or not, a lot of white men like myself don't like it any more than the Indians. It's a damned shame, that's what it is."

Wolf's Blood nodded and shoved the glass out for another beer. Luke filled it from a barrel and set it in front of him. "Say," the man said, leaning forward on the bar, "there was a man here earlier this mornin', asking about your place, where it was and all."

Wolf's Blood frowned. "A man? Who?"

"Well, sir, he wouldn't say." The man scratched at his whiskers. "He was kind of an ugly cuss. It wasn't so much his looks as his eyes—kind of crazylike, you know. He was real well-dressed, like a rich man. Asked a bunch of questions about you people—the ranch—asked if your sister LeeAnn had got back. Well, since I'd just seen your brother-in-law Hal here a few days ago and he told me LeeAnn had come home, I had to tell the fella' yes, she was home now. His eyes kind of glittered like he's just won somethin'. I thought that was kind of strange. He asked me which way to the ranch and how long did it take? Seemed to be in quite a hurry all of a sudden."

Wolf's Blood's eyes darkened. "Did you notice if he walked with a limp?" he asked.

Luke frowned, rubbing his chin. "He not only walked with a limp, he used a cane," he replied. "Did I do somethin' wrong, Wolf's Blood?"

Wolf's Blood stood up, leaning closer. "Luke, if it's true that you held my father in high regard and if you were a true friend, which he thought you to be, you will tell no one else what you have told me."

Luke blinked, seeing a warning look in Wolf's Blood's eyes. Like his father, Wolf's Blood had a way of often convincing people with just a look to do what he asked. The man swallowed. "I won't say a word, Wolf's Blood."

"No matter what?"

Luke shook his head. "I never saw the man."

Wolf's Blood grinned. "Did he leave?"

Luke nodded. "Said somethin' about rentin' a horse from here and leavin' soon as he could."

Wolf's Blood reached out and squeezed the man's shoulder. "Thanks, Luke." He turned and quickly left, and Luke watched after him, suspecting bad blood between the Indian and the stranger who had asked about the Monroes.

"I wouldn't want to have that wild Indian after me, no sir," the man mumbled.

Wolf's Blood rode out hard and fast. The path to the fort commonly used by settlers had turned into a hard-packed wagon road. He took it, certain that a pampered man like Charles Garvey would stick to the easiest path. It had to be Garvey. There was no other explanation, and there was no doubt what the man had in mind. He was several hours ahead of Wolf's Blood, but the man couldn't be used to riding. He would tire more easily, take more rest stops along the way. He decided that if he kept up a steady pace, he would catch up to Garvey by nightfall. He coaxed his Appaloosa at a steady pace, first hard, then a little slower, then hard again, hoping the animal would hold out. It was a strong horse, the only kind they raised, but no horse should be run as hard as he was running this one. Yet he had no choice. He could not let Charles Garvey get to the ranch ahead of him. The man was half crazy. The things LeeAnn had told about him only confirmed that, and Wolf's Blood had no doubt the man would come for her because of her betrayal. Why else had he come looking for her alone?

He rode until dusk, then slowed the horse to a trot. He did not want to lose any time. He would ride until it was pitch black and beyond if necessary. He could not let the man get to the ranch. Perhaps Garvey would be friendly and apologetic, convince LeeAnn to go away with him, then kill her and the boy. The thought of anyone harming a child made him seethe with anger, yet LeeAnn seemed to have no doubt that Charles Garvey wanted to kill his own son, just because he looked Indian. He did not believe the child belonged to him.

He kept riding until he saw a small campfire ahead, several feet off the road. He slowed his horse, walking it up to the spot. A man rose, pointing a fancy rifle at him.

Wolf's Blood stared back. He had seen Charles Garvey before: once in Denver when very young, when he beat Garvey up in the street; once when Garvey rode with Colorado Volunteers, who attacked Zeke and the family when they were riding through Kansas to join the Cheyenne for Wolf's Blood's participation in the Sun Dance; and once again, at Sand Creek! Yes. Sand Creek! This man had killed the young girl Wolf's Blood was going to marry. And Wolf's Blood had sunk a lance into this man's leg and made him a cripple. It had been many, many years. But he had not forgotten the face. It had aged, but not changed all that much. He knew now what he must do, even though this man was LeeAnn's husband. It made no difference. He had needed revenge for years. But he must be careful.

"I need to make camp for the night," he told Garvey. "I thought perhaps I could share your fire."

Garvey kept the rifle on him. "I don't share anything with stinking Indians!" he grumbled. He tried to see the Indian better, thinking he looked familiar, but not sure why. It was too dark to see him clearly.

"I can pay you," Wolf's Blood told him.

"Pay me? I don't need your rotten government handout. I have plenty of money. Now get away from here before I shoot you!"

Wolf's Blood backed his lathered horse. "My mount is tired. I cannot ride him any further."

"Then go make your own campfire!" Garvey barked.

Wolf's Blood's eyes glittered with hatred. "You would be wiser to let me share your fire," he said in a threatening voice. "If I leave, you will have to always be watching over your shoulder, wouldn't you? I might come back to rob you. If I stay, you win my friendship and have no worry. If you shoot me, you are in trouble. There are laws in this country now. I am an Army scout. They would investigate."

Garvey frowned, a little confused. Wolf's Blood hoped he would swallow the explanation. He wanted to talk to the man—find out what his intentions were. If not for LeeAnn, he would not hesitate to end the man's life here and now, which he knew he could do even with the rifle pointed at him. Garvey backed up.

"All right, get down," he told Wolf's Blood. "But stay across the fire from me."

Wolf's Blood swung his leg over the horse and walked carefully over to the fire. "I am grateful," he told Garvey.

"Sure, sure! You thieving redskins are all alike—always got your hand out asking for more. Our government hands you everything on a silver platter, and it's not enough. What are you doing off the reservation, anyway?"

Wolf's Blood sat down with a piece of jerky he had taken from his parfleche. He bit into it. "I am a half-breed. They let me be free if I scout for the Army. But there are also other ways to make money."

This seemed to change the light in Garvey's eyes. "Yeah? Like what? Running whiskey, maybe?"

Garvey set the rifle on the ground beside him as he also sat down, picking up a tin cup of coffee.

"Maybe," he answered. He chewed quietly, while Garvey watched him carefully. He was a wild-looking thing, strong and tough, probably one of those restless warriors who had to get free and raise a little hell once in a while. And breeds were sometimes wilder and more vicious than full-blooded Indians, willing to take part in deceitful operations that purebred ignorant savages could not understand. A plan began to formulate in his mind. Why should he take the risk of killing LeeAnn himself? Why not blame it on an Indian?

"Say, half-breed, you wouldn't be looking for something more exciting than scouting at the moment, would you? It pays well. A thousand dollars if you'll do it."

Wolf's Blood stopped chewing, feigning an eager lust for money. "A thousand? I could not make that much in my whole life from scouting."

Garvey's eyes glittered, and he was suddenly smiling and friendly. "I am a rich man. I can pay you that much. Five hundred right now. Five hundred when you're through."

Wolf's Blood scowled. "What is this thing? Would it get me in bad trouble?"

Garvey grinned. "Not if we handle it right. I promise you. Tell me, do you like white women—like to get them naked, maybe?"

Wolf's Blood quelled his killing urges. Not yet. Let this man reveal himself. "I have gotten a few naked," he replied, now grinning wickedly. "Not all of them willing. When I see a pretty white woman, I get excited and want her."

Garvey laughed lightly. "That stands to reason. I've heard about Indians and white women." He leaned closer over the fire. "I'll hand one to you on a silver platter—blond hair, blue eyes, a body that will make you crazy. And I'll pay you to take her. You can do whatever the hell you want with her. But you must promise to kill her when you're through with her. I will bring her to you myself. We can arrange a place to meet. And I want to watch, understand?"

Wolf's Blood frowned. "Why would you do this? I could be hung."

Garvey shook his head. "You won't be. When you're through, you'll hit me a few times, then I'll take her dead body back to Fort Lyon and tell them I was attacked by three renegade Indians, who beat and tied me then raped and murdered my wife before my eyes. I won't name names. In fact, you don't even need to tell me your name. That makes it all the safer for you. And I'll give a description that doesn't fit you."

"You were going to kill her yourself?"

"Yes. But this gives me an out, don't you see? I can have her killed and get away with it. But there's one other catch, Indian, and that's why I'm paying you so much."

Wolf's Blood's eyes narrowed. "What is it?"

"The woman will have a boy with her—a small boy who looks Indian. He must also be killed."

Wolf's Blood's eyes hardened. "Indians do not kill small children. They take them for their own."

Garvey sighed. "What's one kid? Look, I'll pay you fifteen hundred."

Wolf's Blood bit off some more jerky, acting as though he were considering it. He could hardly believe what this man was asking him to do. He was crazier than any of them had thought, and there was only one thing for Wolf's Blood to do. He was glad to have such a fine excuse for doing it, for he had wanted to kill Charles Garvey for many years.

Garvey rubbed his hands together. Why hadn't he thought of this before? It was perfect! He would get rid of LeeAnn and Matthew, and could blame it on Indians besides! It was the perfect way for poor Charles Garvey to lose his beloved wife and son. The papers in the East would eat it up, and he could start a whole new campaign against the Indians.

Wolf's Blood slowly removed his Bowie knife, a fine gift from his father. Zeke would fully approve of Charles Garvey's death, that was certain. He would do this for his father.

"The woman and child—they are your wife and son?" he asked Garvey.

"The woman is my wife. But she was untrue to me. The boy is not mine, so I don't care about him. She ran away from me and I am very angry with her. Hell, you know what it's like to have a squaw cheat on you. I've heard you Indian bucks cut off their noses—something like that. That true?"

Wolf's Blood studied the knife in the firelight. "It is true."

"Well we civilized white men can't do those things. I am very angry with her. She deserves to die. You can earn yourself a lot of money, and get yourself inside a pretty white woman besides. You've got the best part of the deal. I don't even know your name, and you don't know mine, so we're even. What do you say, breed?"

Wolf's Blood smiled wickedly. The road was quiet now. Few people traveled this way at night. It was too dangerous in a land

409

that was still mostly lawless in places like this. He met Charles Garvey's eyes. "I think perhaps we do know each other," he told Garvey.

Garvey frowned. "What do you mean?"

Wolf's Blood placed a finger against the end of the shiny, wicked blade of his knife, twirling it lightly as he held it in his other hand. "I am thinking of another time . . . Denver," he said carefully. "I was sitting on a walkway, a small Indian boy. A bigger white boy came along, kicking a can. He was ugly . . . had a lot of red bumps on his face. He was a little bigger than I—then. He started calling me names. I jumped on him and beat him good, even though I was smaller. He ran away crying."

He met Garvey's eyes. The man studied him with incredulous shock. "How could you . . . know that?" he asked in a near whisper. "That must have been twenty-five years ago—maybe more!"

"I remember my own fights," he answered.

Garvey began to tremble, and Wolf's Blood knew what he would do. Before the man could act, Wolf's Blood reached over and threw his rifle aside, quick as a biting snake. Garvey's eyes widened. "Who . . . are you?"

"I remember another time," he went on. "My family and I were in Kansas, and Colorado Volunteers attacked us. A young man was with them, and I shot at him, then pulled him from his horse. We fought in the water, and I beat him good again."

Garvey tried to think. Yes, he did look familiar. How could he have run into this man more than once and never known who he was? But he still didn't know.

"And still another time," Wolf's Blood continued, enjoying the shocked, confused look on Garvey's face. "I was at Sand Creek. A Volunteer under Chivington rode down the young girl I was to marry. He killed her with his saber. He also wounded me, but I managed to sink my lance . . . deep into his leg . . . so that he was forever a cripple."

Garvey felt a terrible pain in his stomach, and his heart pounded furiously. How could this be? How and why were all these people suddenly emerging from his past to haunt and torture him? What had he done to deserve these things?

"You? You were . . . the one . . . at Sand Creek?"

"Your memory is poor, Charles Garvey. You have made the mistake of thinking all Indians look alike, so you never singled me out any of those times. But I singled you out. I knew who you were, because my father knew your father. My father was Zeke Monroe."

It seemed Garvey's eyes would bulge right out of his head then. He suddenly jumped up and started running, but his game leg prevented speed. A huge Indian was soon at his back, landing hard into him and tackling him to the ground.

"No! Please!" Garvey whimpered. "I'll . . . I'll pay you anyway . . . and just go away! I'll never come back! Honest!"

Wolf's Blood pushed the man's face into the hard gravel. "It is true you will never come back!" he growled. "For you will not live to come back anyplace! You would hire a man to rape and murder your own wife and son—my sister and nephew! You are a wicked, evil man, Charles Garvey, just like your father was! My father killed your father! And now I shall kill you! It is fitting!"

He jerked the man onto his back and quickly slit his larynx—as he had seen his father do a time or two—so that the victim could not scream as he died . . . slowly.

Wolf's Blood finished packing his travois. He would take several horses with him, as gifts to Sonora's people and as an aid in being accepted by them. It was understood that part of the ranch belonged to him, and he could return anytime.

Abbie hurried over with hot bisquits, her heart filled with agony that he was leaving so soon now. But if it must be done, it must be done. Still, she had expected him to wait until she left for the North. Now things were happening almost too quickly, and there was an urgency about Wolf's Blood she did not like. She handed the bag of bisquits to a tearful Sonora, who also looked worried. Wolf's Blood came out of the nearly empty house with more supplies, stopping and staring at his all-knowing mother, who stepped forward to face him.

"What is it you aren't telling me?" she asked.

He looked away and walked to the supply horse, shoving the

411

things into a parfleche. "Nothing. It is difficult for me to go, Mother, to leave you—this place. So I might as well get it over with, that's all."

He came back on the porch and she stood in front of the doorway. "That is not all!" she declared. "I could always tell when your father was hiding something, and I can tell when you are hiding something, too! You're just like him. You might as well tell me. You've been acting strangely ever since you got back from Fort Lyon."

Wolf's Blood glanced at Sonora, who hung her head and went inside to finish getting the children ready. Wolf's Blood sighed, taking his mother's arm and pulling her aside. "I came across Charles Garvey," he told her then.

Her eyes widened. "What did you do, Wolf's Blood!"

His eyes hardened. "I killed him."

She closed her eyes. "Dear God!" She breathed deeply and turned around. "How? And why? Do you know what they do to Indians who kill white men, especially important white men?"

"I had no choice!" he growled. "At Fort Lyon I heard that a fancy man had been there asking about this place and about LeeAnn—a man who used a cane to walk. I knew it had to be him! So I rode out after him before he could get here, and it is a good thing! He intended to kill LeeAnn, and Matthew!"

"How do you know that for sure? They were his family."

"Family means nothing to men like that! They know nothing of love and pity and forgiveness! You should know that well enough!"

She reddened and looked away, and he sighed deeply, leaning against the house. "Mother, I know because when I found him camped I made friends with him first, just to see what he was up to. I got him to talk. And he ended up offering me a thousand dollars to rape and murder his wife and murder his son, so that he could blame their deaths on Indians and his own hands would be clean."

She turned back to meet his eyes, her own wide with shock. "He was going to hire you . . . to murder his own wife and child?"

"Now do you see? He was going to come here and get them, then ride out, where I would attack them all and beat on him

412

some so it would look real. He even said he wanted to watch her being raped! How could I let such an evil man live? If not me, he would have found someone else to kill them! Everyone is better off that he is dead. But I was careful, Mother, just like Father always was. They cannot prove I did it, but they might suspect because they will eventually link him to LeeAnn and find out she was running from him. So I think it is best I head south now. Being with the Apaches in the New Mexico Mountains is a good place for now, until they give up trying to find out who did it."

Her eyes teared, and she reached up and touched his face. "It will be so hard being without you, Wolf's Blood," she told him, her motherly instincts tearing at her heart. It seemed he'd never been a baby, but always a warrior, even when a child. And she had no doubt he'd find a way to get mixed up in the Apache wars. "Promise me you'll be careful. Keep your papers proving your mother is white and your father half white. I have heard bad things about San Carlos."

"We will not go there—not at first. No Apache likes San Carlos, and Victorio still makes war, refusing to go there. And the one called Geronimo lives in Mexico, refusing to go to San Carlos, where the heat and insects kill the Indians. Perhaps we will go all the way to Mexico. I cannot say for now. But Sonora longs to find some of her relatives. I owe her that much. She had been a good wife. We will stay just a while, perhaps a year or two. Then we will come back, and Charles Garvey's death will be long forgotten. If you are still in the North, we will come there and see you."

She hugged him close. "Promise me, Wolf's Blood! Promise me! I don't want to lose you!"

"You will not lose me. I make the promise, just as Father always did."

She pulled away and looked at her handsome son, such a replica of Zeke Monroe. Why was life such an ongoing trail of good-byes? Why did time go so quickly, and babies grow into men and women? She thought of the look on Zeke's face when she gave birth to their first child, this son who looked so Indian and had been trained in the Indian ways. Had it really been thirty-four years? Again she felt the rushing black desperateness of being unable to stop time, of having no control over her destiny or that of her children.

She closed her eyes for a moment, then stepped back. "Go then. But I will see you again, Wolf's Blood, and when I do, you'll never leave again."

He nodded. "This I promise."

Sonora came out then with eight-year-old Kicking Boy and seven-year-old Iris, two beautiful, dark children with wide brown eyes and chubby, round faces. Abbie felt as though someone were wrenching her heart from her body, and she went up to them, hugging each one tightly, unable to speak. She wondered if perhaps a woman loved her grandchildren even more than her children, for it sometimes seemed so, if that were possible.

She stood up, holding Iris, as the rest of the family headed toward Wolf's Blood's and Sonora's little cabin to bid them farewell.

"Do not tell LeeAnn," Wolf's Blood said quietly to his mother before they came closer. "It is best she does not know it was I who killed her husband."

Moments later everything was commotion and tears, everyone hugging and crying. Abbie prayed inwardly that somehow, someday, they would all be together again, all in one place, all these descendents of Zeke Monroe. Somehow she would make that happen. This family would be apart for a while, but not forever.

Abbie emerged from the special place by the stream, where she and Zeke had spent so many hours over the years—talking, making love. She clung to a fistful of purple irises. She had spent the night there—her last night on the ranch for who knew how long. She had wept and wept, until there was nothing but emptiness inside. She knew she must do this, if she were to be truly strong, if she were to learn after all these years who Abigail Trent Monroe really was. Was she really a separate person, capable of surviving, making decisions, having her own personality, her own strength—without him—without Zeke? She had left him in that hidden place in the mountains, met his spirit on top of the mountain and knew he was with her—inside. Now she must stop imagining that he was coming to her physically—stop seeing him on every hillside. There was no other way but to go to new places, until the pain subsided, until she was strong within herself. And she had promised to help the Cheyenne.

She walked straight to the house. She dared not look back. She would wash and change, say good-bye to Ellen and Margaret and the grandchildren, and she would go. At least she would have her precious Jason with her, and LeeAnn and little Matthew would also go.

She breathed a sigh of relief that Wolf's Blood had not been connected with Charles Garvey's murder, thanks to her fast talking. Soldiers had come to the house as a routine, for a man had been found, brutally stabbed to death, along the road that led to the Monroe ranch. Other ranchers had also been questioned. Abbie feigned surprise, and when the soldiers mentioned the identification on the man showed him to be Charles Garvey, LeeAnn had gasped in shock, blurting out that Charles Garvey was her estranged husband. The soldiers questioned her, for they had been told Garvey's wife was LeeAnn Whittaker from New York, and that she had recently left her husband.

"That is true," Abbie answered quickly. "My daughter used a different name while in New York—for personal reasons. She and Charles did not get along, so LeeAnn decided to come home for a while. Charles must have been coming for her."

LeeAnn burst into tears; not that she was mourning Charles Garvey as a person, but he had been her husband and was the father of her child. She cried more over her wasted years, and for the unhappy person she knew Charles Garvey had always been. But it was good that she cried in front of the soldiers.

"Well, for some crazy reason someone murdered Mr. Garvey—for no apparent motive but to butcher a man." The soldier looked around the room. "Where is your son Wolf's Blood, by the way?"

Abbie held his eyes steadily. "He has gone south with his Apache wife," she answered calmly. "He left about two weeks ago."

The soldier held her eyes for a moment, then decided by her bold, sure look that she was telling the truth. And he decided she was not a woman to be argued with. He glanced at LeeAnn then.

"Ma'am, I hate to break the news to you this way about your husband," he told her. "But there's something else you should know."

LeeAnn wiped at her eyes, and Joshua stood near her. "What?" LeeAnn whimpered.

"Well, when we made inquiries back east, we were told your husband had filed for divorce and that he had already . . . uh . . . already disinherited you. Perhaps he was coming to tell you that, or perhaps to patch things up. At any rate, you have some legal matters to straighten out."

"They will be taken care of," Joshua spoke up.

"Who are you?" the soldier asked.

"I am Joshua Lewis, a reporter for *The New York Times* and a good friend of the family. There are some things the authorities should know—about Charles Garvey. I have information to prove he was a disreputable man, a crook, and a traitor, as well as a man going bankrupt. I'll go to Fort Lyon if you wish and make a statement there, and I'll be going back east soon, at which time I'll clear up a few more things. As far as Charles Garvey's murder, I can't imagine how that happened. The man had a lot of enemies and he was very pious. Perhaps he insulted some Indian or trapper at the fort, and they did him in."

The soldiers finally left, and LeeAnn met her mother's eyes squarely. "That was why my brother left so quickly, wasn't it?" she said calmly then. "He killed Charles."

Abbie sat down and took her hand. "The man was coming to kill you, LeeAnn—you and Matthew."

"Dear God!" the girl whispered, putting her head down on the table. "Then it's my fault Wolf's Blood had to go away! He was afraid he'd get caught."

"Partly. Your father always believed in an eye for an eye, LeeAnn, and he managed to get away with a lot of vengeful killings. But things are getting more civilized out here all the time, and men can't live by the old rules anymore. But Wolf's

Blood would have gone south either way, so you are not to blame."

Abbie smiled now as she approached the house. How good it was to have Joshua there—sweet, caring Joshua, who obviously loved LeeAnn devotedly. He had gone to Fort Lyon and straightened everything out. He was so sure of himself, a very strong man inwardly, and even outwardly, in spite of the brace. She hoped the day would soon come when LeeAnn could love again, could allow herself to be with a man again, for she would be very pleased to see her daughter marry Joshua Lewis. For now he waited like a patient friend, loving her quietly, bringing her strength.

Everyone was ready when she arrived, and Abbie ate a breakfast prepared by a tearful Margaret. But Abbie would not worry about Margaret or Ellen. Parting was always sad, but her two daughters had fine, strong men who loved them and were devoted to them. Morgan Brown was a good rancher, a strong man who loved Margaret deeply, who had been a good friend to Zeke, who now knew everything there was to know about raising horses. He would carry on the tradition, producing the most valuable Appaloosas and Thoroughbreds in Colorado. And Ellen had Hal Daniels, whose own ranch was growing, and who was also a strong, devoted husband. Her daughters would be fine until she returned—and she would return.

She washed and changed, then stopped and stared for a moment at the brass bed, her gift from Zeke, the bed on which they had shared bodies and souls during their last years together. Her eyes teared, and she kissed a brass post. The bed would go to Margaret and Morgan now, who would live in the main house. The little trunk of Abbie's special treasures was packed on the wagon. The bed of robes was gone, the robes distributed among the children, two of them rolled and packed into Abbie's belongings.

She came out into the main room, walking up and touching the old, ticking mantle clock that had once sat on a stump inside a tipi. She would leave it here, on the mantle built with Zeke's loving hands. Margaret would take care of it for her—until she returned.

Yes, she must remember she was coming back, for that was

the only way she could bear the leaving. And when she returned she would be a stronger woman. She glanced at the mandolin—the old mandolin, its strings now quiet. It sat in the corner where it would stay, another bit of Zeke Monroe that belonged in this house. She had considered taking both the clock and the mandolin, but she knew it would only make it harder for her to face the fact that her husband was really gone and she must go on alone. She would leave behind those things that only made her long for him with such agony.

It was time for good-byes then, always difficult. She looked around the little house she had shared so many years with Zeke Monroe: the table where they had sat and talked, probably thousands of times; the rocker by the hearth where she sat and knitted, sometimes reading to him; the worn floor where little children had run in and out. She could hear their young voices, hear their laughter. But they were grown now. She must face facts.

She walked outside, glancing at the barn Zeke had helped rebuild while in so much pain—the horses, the glorious horses, that ran in the corral. She must stop looking! She must stop! She hugged Little Zeke, Nathan, and Lillian Rose, who was slightly over a year old now. LeeAnn, Joshua, Matthew, and Jason sat in the back of the wagon, and Abbie climbed into the seat beside a newly hired hand who would drive the wagon back to the ranch after leaving them all off at the train station in Pueblo. They would take the Denver & Rio Grande north to Cheyenne, then a stagecoach farther north into Montana, to Dan and Bonnie and the Northern Cheyenne.

It was finally time to go. The driver whipped the horses into motion, and the wagon lurched forward. Abbie closed her eyes. She would not look to the South, where her precious Wolf's Blood had gone. She would not look to the North, where the special place by the creek remained filled with purple irises. She would not look back—at the horses, the barn, the house. She must not look! She must not even think! She must look forward to new things, new people, new places. How did one stand this terrible ache? Why were people forced to suffer over and over again? Why did something as beautiful as love hurt so badly?

"Good-bye," she whispered.

A shadow passed over them, and she looked up to see an eagle circling over the wagon. She smiled then. He was still with her after all. Yes, she would come back to this place that had belonged to him—when the time was right. The eagle left them then, flying north.

Chapter Twenty-Five

The trip north made Abbie almost glad Zeke was gone, for she realized just how much this land that he had once roamed with the Cheyenne had changed. Now she rode on a train for the first time, amazed at how fast it could go, but watching out the window and visioning riding instead on pretty Appaloosas, side by side with her husband, in a land that was not dotted with civilization or divided by too many fences. And all along the way she caught glimpses of piles of bleached buffalo bones, remnants of the great thundering herds that had once roamed the plains and were already virtually extinct from all regions south of the Dakotas. She had read in one newspaper that in only two years an estimated three million buffalo had been taken from the plains. It was reported that only a few thousand were left, most of those in the northern regions. Abbie did not doubt that those few would also be taken.

"Ten Thousand Buffalo Hides Shipped Today," one headline read. It made her heart ache. Nothing could have been more instrumental in defeating the Indian than wiping out the buffalo. By making use of the hides, the white man had found a way to quietly eliminate not only the greatest beast of North America, but also its native Indians.

When they reached Cheyenne in Wyoming Territory, she disembarked to stretch her legs. She waited with Joshua and the others as their luggage was unloaded, for the rest of their journey would be by stagecoach. Several flatbed wagons, heaped high with white bones, sat waiting at the train station.

Abbie stared at them, grasping Joshua's arm. "What is that?" she asked.

Joshua sighed, knowing how she was hurting. "They're bones, I'm afraid. Buffalo bones. They're picked up by scavengers called 'Bonepickers.' They get paid by the ton for them. The bones are used for fertilizer; the horns and hooves are used in factories back east to make buttons, combs, all sorts of things."

Abbie stared, her eyes tearing. "I see." How ironic that the white men were using the buffalo for the very things the Indians had used them: food, clothing, utensils. Thus, not so much of the buffalo was wasted. But there were many whites greedy for the products gleaned from the animal, and there were not enough buffalo to support that greed.

She felt many chapters of her own life closing: the demise of the Indian; the extinction of the buffalo; the gradual changing of the land from open, wild, and untamed to civilization, towns, and farms; her children grown; her husband . . . gone. No! Not Zeke! Again the rush of depression overwhelmed her. She must not think about it. She must get to Dan and Bonnie— and find Swift Arrow. She fought the sudden desperateness that sometimes grabbed at her when thinking of Wolf's Blood, wondering if he were all right, wondering when she would see her precious son again.

Their baggage was unloaded, and it would be a while before their stage was ready to leave. Joshua treated all of them to lunch. Abbie knew she should be enjoying the trip—seeing Cheyenne, riding a train, going someplace new. But none of it really mattered. She was haunted by the wagons full of bones. She could see them in her mind, and then see Zeke. The two visions kept flashing into her mind—contrasting, haunting.

Somehow she found herself on a stage then, headed north to Fort Keogh, ever farther from the ranch, ever farther from Wolf's Blood, considering the irony of life and fate. She rode with Joshua Lewis, the young man for whom she had suffered torture and rape at the hands of Winston Garvey, and with her daughter, who had married Garvey's son. She wondered how and why people like the Garveys could have gotten involved in their lives when they had lived so remotely from civilization;

how a senator from Washington, D.C. could have ended up being cut to pieces by a half-breed Cheyenne called Zeke Monroe; and how his son could have met a similar fate by Zeke Monroe's own son. And yet her own little grandson was a Garvey. She could not love him less because of it, for he was also a part of herself and Zeke, an offspring of that good seed. With his looks and being raised by a changed LeeAnn and other loving people, Abbie was certain there would be no traces of Winston or Charles Garvey in the boy. She hoped LeeAnn married Joshua soon and that he would adopt Matthew, so that the boy's name could be changed and the name Garvey would never again be mentioned in her presence.

She watched the passing terrain as the stage bounced and jolted over a dirt road toward its destination. Montana and Wyoming were beautiful. The trip through these territories took several days. She did not mind watching the scenery, except for when the coach first left Cheyenne, and she realized they were not far from where her father's wagon train had traveled thirty-five years ago—surely not far from the place where one dark night a scout named Zeke Monroe had lain with her in the grass and made her his woman. And several miles to the west was Fort Bridger, where they had been married, and where she had waited faithfully through the winter for her husband to return from Oregon.

Why oh why did the memories have to keep plaguing her this way? Why was she constantly tortured by the thought of the happiness and fulfillment she had once known? Would she ever really get over his death, ever really know who Abigail Monroe was, ever feel comfortable anyplace but on the ranch along the Arkansas? The ranch! All those years spent working it, loving the man who owned it, the place where she had borne all her children, where she had shared a love greater than any she would ever find again or even cared to find again—greater than most women ever find.

He had been dead for twenty months now. But counting the months since he left to go on that fateful trip . . . why, here it was August! It was two years this month since he left her— since their night in the tipi and the morning they spent bathing at the stream. Two years! How could that be? She looked at her hands. They were wrinkled, but not too badly, for Abbie had faithfully applied the creams Zeke insisted she use. She put her hands to her face. She was fifty. Fifty! But no, she couldn't be! Wasn't it just a year or two ago that she came into this land, a mere fifteen-year-old girl? Now her youngest son, her baby, was older than that! Her first grandchild, Little Zeke, was already eleven. This could not be! Why couldn't she turn back the time to special events in her life when she had been most happy? Why couldn't she just once again experience that first night Zeke Monroe branded her? Oh, the hurt of it! The awful hurt of it! Across from her sat Joshua, a grown man now. But wasn't it just a little while ago when she and Zeke had taken him to Bonnie as a small, crippled baby?

She fought new tears and reasoned with herself that there was one consolation: She was getting older, and in not too many years she, too, would be gone from this earth. That was just fine with her, for when she greeted death she would also greet Zeke Monroe. She would be with him again and nothing and no one could ever, ever separate them. She was as sure at this moment that he was in God's Kingdom as she was sure she was riding in the stage. For in spite of his violent life, Zeke Monroe was an honest man, a good man who would have wanted peace if people would have let him have it. But he had been a man tormented by a sad childhood and by the torture of living in two worlds. The violence he had experienced was not always of his choosing, and the things he had done had been for those he loved. His nature was vengeful and defensive, and he could not control that which came so spontaneously to him. She had never blamed him, but had only understood and loved him. And though some might say the God he worshipped was different from her own, she did not believe it, and she was fully confident that when she met her Maker, Zeke Monroe would be right there.

In the meantime she reminded herself that while she was here on this earth, her husband's spirit was with her wherever she went. She did not have to be on the ranch, where the memories were too fresh and painful. She could be anyplace and still be with him.

She looked out at the Bighorn Mountains to the south and

west. Yes, this was truly beautiful country, and here she would be a little closer to the Rockies. She would like it here, for she would be among the Cheyenne. She wondered what Swift Arrow looked like now. How many years had it been since she saw him last? At least seventeen. The last she had seen him was at the Cheyenne Sun Dance, back in '62, when Wolf's Blood had participated in that great test of manhood. Wolf's Blood was only sixteen then. Now he was thirty-four.

And how old was Swift Arrow now? He was five years younger than Zeke. That would make him fifty-five. But surely not! He couldn't be more than twenty-five, could he? She didn't feel any older than that herself. She was still slim and agile, and everyone told her she looked far younger than her age. She guessed that Swift Arrow also did, for like Zeke his handsome face and strong body had always defied his true age. But perhaps now his spirit was broken. That could do a lot to a man like Swift Arrow. A broken spirit aged a man much faster than years ever could.

She concentrated on him then, feeling excited at the prospect of seeing Zeke's long-lost Cheyenne brother after all these years. And she would be with Dan and Bonnie again. Yes, this would be a pleasant change. It was a necessary thing. They would go to Fort Custer, much as the name felt sour in her mouth. That was where Dan was now. They had found out at the last minute, when Josh sent a wire to Fort Keogh to tell his stepfather they were coming. Fort Custer was much more in the heart of the reservation, and closer to the mountains, which made her happier. Dan had been transferred there, as well as the doctor Jason would work with. And they would be among not just Cheyenne but also Crow Indians, another ironic twist—Crow and Cheyenne together. She was amazed it was working at all. But then circumstances had greatly changed the Indian outlook. It was useless to worry now about old enemies and old hurts. They were one in their situation now—all reservation Indians—all having lost their freedom.

"We'll be at Fort Custer before night," Josh was telling them. "Did I tell you Father plans to retire soon?"

Abbie did not hear. She was remembering a young girl and her new husband riding on horses through the Rockies and

425

toward the Arkansas River, where they would meet her husband's Cheyenne family and live happily ever after.

It did not take long for Abigail Monroe to see she had made the right choice. It was good to be with Dan and Bonnie again; good to see Jason diving into studies and working diligently with the reservation doctor to learn all that he could; good to see the happiness in the eyes of Josh and LeeAnn, and know they would be married as soon as Joshua returned from New York in eight months. But none of that was as important as being among the Cheyenne again, and her services were badly needed.

Her heart ached for them. They were so lost and broken. Alcohol was rampant among the men and even some of the women. Eyes once bright and dancing were dull and lifeless. To help them adjust to their new way of life, try to convince them to send their children to school, and teach them to farm was a momumental task, if not an impossible one. Abbie soon found herself fighting staunchly with the reservation agents and missionaries, the "Friends of the Indians," whose goals and objectives were well-intended but futile. She soon became deeply involved in reservation life, teaching, guiding, helping with births, becoming totally immersed in her work for the People and in her fight with the whites who worked to totally change the Indian into something he was not.

The work was good for her. Her busy days were followed by exhausted sleep at night, so that the painful memories and terrible loneliness were overshadowed by the present and by her work. Through her efforts she began to find herself, her own identity. She had a purpose here now. She could no longer be Zeke Monroe's woman, so she would now be Abigail Monroe, friend of the Cheyenne, teacher, nurse, whatever was required. Her loved ones watched patiently, thinking perhaps she was doing too much, yet knowing it was better than sitting around dwelling on the past.

At first some of the Cheyenne were wary of her, unsure who this new white woman was and why she had come there and seemed so interested in helping them. But her warm love, her sincere eyes, her knowledge of their language, and her efforts in fighting to preserve their ancient customs brought a deep respect and kinship. A few of them remembered her or had at least heard of her. Most of them had known Zeke Monroe, Lone Eagle to them. This was his white woman.

"My own children have Indian names," she told one Cheyenne woman who was afraid to let Abbie help with the birth of her first child. "And I had all my children alone without the help of a doctor, down on the Arkansas River where I lived with my Cheyenne husband."

The girl watched her, panting with pain, wanting to trust her. "This is true? Your children are by a Cheyenne man? They have . . . Cheyenne names?"

Abbie took her hand. "They do. My oldest son is thirty-four, almost thirty-five. He is called Wolf's Blood. My second child, Margaret, was called *Moheya*, Blue Sky. Our third child, LeeAnn, was given the Indian name *Kseé*, Young Girl. Our fourth was a son." She stopped for a moment, feeling a stabbing pain at the memory. Jeremy! Why had he never come, even after she'd left the message of his father's death? She had nearly died giving birth to him. He had been gone nearly twelve years now. Perhaps she would never see him at all.

"His . . . white name is Jeremy," she told the girl. "But he was first called *Ohkumhkákit*, Little Wolf." She swallowed back tears. Jeremy. The Prodigal Son. "Then came number five," she went on. "Ellen—called *Ishiomiists*, Rising Sun. Then our sixth, little Lillian—*Meane-ese*, Summer Moon. She died of pneumonia back in '65." She swallowed, her eyes tearing, and the Indian girl squeezed her hand.

"It is so sad to lose a child. I hope this never happens to me."

Abbie breathed deeply to stay in control, thinking of how rapidly Indian babies died on this reservation. She patted the girl's hand. "I hope it never happens to you, too," she answered.

"Was that all of the children then?"

"No." She smiled, "I had one more—Jason, my baby. He was called *Eoveano*, Yellow Hawk. He is the one who works here on the reservation with the doctor. They'll be along soon, Clay Woman. You must let them help you so that you have a

427

nice strong baby with no complications. It is good to keep some of the old ways—the language, many of the customs. But when it comes to doctoring and your health, the new ways are good. The white doctors have many medicines and much experience, and you should trust them to help you."

The girl kept hold of her hand. "If you gave birth to seven children alone, then surely I can give birth to one, if you will stay with me."

Abbie sponged out a cool rag and wiped her fevered brow. "I will stay with you, until the doctor lays a fine son or daughter on your belly and we hear him or her squalling."

The girl smiled, closing her eyes and preparing for another pain.

In what seemed like only a month or two, a year had passed, and Abigail Monroe became as much a part of the reservation as the Indians themselves. Joshua returned home and married LeeAnn. Never had LeeAnn Monroe thought she could be so happy, as much in love, or as willing in a man's arms. Joshua Lewis brought out all the things in her she had never experienced, taught her what love was supposed to be, and that taking a man was a joy, not a horror. Jason learned quickly, and already took care of some medical needs on his own. Abbie felt happy and fulfilled, but two things loomed in that horizon of fate, reawakening her awareness that perfect happiness was something no one ever found. Bonnie Lewis Monroe became gravely ill with a strange disease that seemed to be eating away at her very flesh, so that she became thinner every day and could barely move because of pain. There was nothing the doctor could do for her, and Dan Monroe, now retired from the Army but remaining to help on the reservation, doing a little ranching on the side, was beside himself with grief. Bonnie had brought him intense happiness since his first wife died. She was practically his whole reason for existing. Abbie well understood his grief, and she remained faithfully by his side, helping all she could with Bonnie, who soon grew totally helpless.

Josh and LeeAnn helped as much as they could. They had

stayed on the reservation after marrying, living in a nearby town where Josh started up his own newspaper and LeeAnn began teaching at a reservation school. There was nothing any of them could do for Bonnie but watch her suffer. It reminded Abbie of the way her own mother had died back in Tennessee, suffering so much that it seemed a blessing to finally bury her. But she felt the old emptiness again at the thought of losing Bonnie—the loneliness that death always brought to the soul. She didn't doubt that it would be relieved somewhat if she could see and talk to Swift Arrow. But he had remained elusive, refusing to come and see her for unexplained reasons. It confused and depressed her. She had so looked forward to seeing Zeke's brother again—the Cheyenne warrior who had taught her the Cheyenne ways all those years ago when Zeke left her to Swift Arrow's watchful care.

She and Swift Arrow had become such close friends, once she won over his trust and admiration. Why would he not come and see her now? Was he ashamed that the Sioux and Cheyenne had been defeated and had to live on a reservation? Or was it that seeing her would remind him of Zeke and bring him too much pain? He lived as a recluse, so she was told, in his own tipi high in the Bitterroots. Soldiers had long given up trying to roust him out. After all, he was just one warrior and bothered no one. He killed his own game and refused any of the handouts at the reservation.

The thought of him living alone tore at her heart, for he had always been such a lonely man, remaining a Dog Soldier and refusing to take a wife, his only family being Wolf's Blood for the few short years the boy lived with him in the North. He was the only full-blooded descendent left of Zeke's Cheyenne mother and stepfather. It was important for Abbie to see him. He was the only remnant from the past and those early years that she spent with the People when freedom was there for the taking. Apparently he was clinging to that freedom now, afraid to come into the reservation for fear of being arrested or sent away. That was the only reason she could think of that would keep him from coming to see her. What other explanation could there be?

As she watched Bonnie Monroe slipping away toward

death's hands, she determined that somehow she must find Swift Arrow. It gave her something to think about, another buffer to ease the pain of the death of a loved one. Yes, somehow she would find her brother-in-law.

It was January of 1882, three years after Zeke's death, when Abbie sat beside a dying Bonnie Monroe, who spoke to her in a whisper. "The top drawer . . . of my bureau," she told Abbie, who had to lean over to hear her. "An . . . Indian necklace. Get it."

Abbie frowned, going to the bureau and opening the drawer. She lifted personal clothing that was Bonnie's, under which an Indian necklace, a bone hairpipe choker that looked familiar to her. She picked it up and carried it over to Bonnie, whose eyes teared when Abbie held it out for her to see.

"It was . . . Zeke's," Bonnie told her, forcing her voice to come through more clearly. "He gave it to me . . . all those years ago . . . after he saved me from those outlaws down in . . . New Mexico . . . when I first met him. I was . . . a young missionary. I . . . loved him, Abbie." The words were sorrowful, as though she thought she had to confess to the sinful feelings she had once had for Zeke Monroe so many years ago. "I think . . . he knew. He gave me the necklace . . . in friendship . . . and told me to always keep it . . . made me promise to always . . . help the Indian in my work. I . . . kept my promise." She reached up with a weak hand and closed it around Abbie's hand that held the necklace. "You . . . keep it now. He said . . . his Cheyenne mother made it. You keep it. And . . . don't hate me . . . for loving him. He behaved as . . . nothing more than a good friend. It was . . . such a long time ago . . . before I even married my first husband."

Abbie's eyes teared and her throat ached. "I've always known," she replied softly, squeezing the woman's hand. "Did you think I didn't, or that if I did I wouldn't understand? What woman who is rescued at the hands of Zeke Monroe, and who is with him alone for several days, is capable of not falling in love with him? He was easy to love . . . so easy to love."

She put her head down against Bonnie's hand, crying

430

quietly. Bonnie smiled, a soft, satisfied glow to her face. "And so was Dan," she answered. "He was . . . so much like Zeke. And he . . . thinks the world of you, Abbie. He'll be . . . so lonely . . . when I'm gone. Stay close to him . . . help him. You . . . understand how he will feel. Promise me . . . you'll watch after Dan. He's been . . . so good to me . . . and to Josh."

"I promise," Abbie whispered. She swallowed, breathing deeply and meeting Bonnie's eyes again. "But don't you worry about Dan. He's a strong man. His Army years made him sure and independent. He'll be fine. But I'll make sure he's never—" She stopped. Bonnie was looking at her but not seeing her. Abbie knew without even checking that the woman was dead.

A terrible blackness filled her entire being. She carefully put down her hand and reached up to close her eyelids. "I love you, Bonnie," she whispered. Another one gone. Too many. She had watched too many die. She looked at the necklace, her hand trembling. Zeke. He had touched so many lives. His strength and spirit seemed to continually permeate the air wherever she went. She held the necklace to her cheek, then kissed it.

How she missed his strength! How she missed the times when she could literally collapse into his strong arms and he would hold her and assure her all was well. And how she missed being a woman in the physical sense. But she only missed it in the sense that she could no longer enjoy the ecstasy of being one with Zeke Monroe. She never even considered such things with any other man, and yet there was a distant, gnawing need that went unfulfilled. How could a woman live all those years with a man who was such an expert at bringing out the passion in her, and then suddenly live with nothing but emptiness beside her in the night? She kissed the necklace again, then dropped it into the pocket of her dress. She took a blanket and covered Bonnie's face, shuddering with sorrow. She must go and tell Dan. That would not be easy, but at least his daughter Jennifer was on her way here from Denver. That would comfort him. Jennifer herself was recently widowed, so for a while they would have one another to cling to. Jennifer was bringing her own daughter, Dan Monroe's only grandchild by blood, whom he had never even seen yet. The timing was perfect. Abbie thanked God they were coming.

April of 1882 brought news that Margaret had given birth to her third child, another son named Lance Clayton after one of Zeke's white brothers. That brother had once lived on the ranch, helping Zeke run it after the Civil War. But Lance had been killed the day the Comanches raided the ranch and rode off with LeeAnn. Abbie was pleased that Margaret named a son after the man. Her count of grandchildren was now up to seven: three boys from Margaret, a boy and girl from Wolf's Blood, a boy from LeeAnn, and a girl from Ellen.

But still there had been no appearance by Swift Arrow. And worse, Abbie had not heard from Wolf's Blood in many months. Dan kept a constant flow of letters and messages going between Fort Custer and Fort Bowie, where an officer was now stationed whom he knew well. All they could discover was that vicious cheating on the Apache reservation was leading to more unrest. Many Apaches had fled to Mexico. In one of these flights, many had been found by soldiers and shot down. White men were doing their best to agitate those who remained on the reservation, deliberately keeping them stirred up so that the Apaches would make trouble, would be removed, and the land belonging to the reservation would be up for grabs to white settlers. Newspapers printed outlandish stories of Apache deprivations, convincing whites that the Indians were as worthless as snakes and should not be entitled to their reservation lands.

General Crook, an experienced Indian fighter and a man who had learned his lessons well when fighting the Sioux and Northern Cheyenne in earlier years, was sent to try to solve the problem with the Apaches. Over the years Crook had developed a respect for red men as human beings, an attitude still not taken readily by most Army men or civilians. He arranged to meet with Geronimo and his renegades in Mexico. Called Gray Wolf by the Apaches, Crook managed a parlay with Geronimo himself, convincing the man to surrender and return to Arizona.

The Apaches were returned, but there was much criticism of Crook for being too easy on them. Abbie and Dan could see the plotting and scheming in messages they received and in local newspapers they read, except for Joshua's paper. The young man tried his best to find out the truth, but all he had to go on was the news coming out of Arizona and New Mexico, much of which they had trouble believing. It was rumored that Crook had made some kind of deal with Geronimo. And Geronimo himself was made out to be some kind of monster, worthy of nothing less than a hanging.

Through all of this, between 1882 and 1884, Abbie could discover no news of anyone called Wolf's Blood. Perhaps when joining the Apaches, her son had changed his name again. Perhaps something had happened to Sonora and her grandchildren, and as a result Wolf's Blood was again on the warpath with Geronimo and the other renegades. If he were coming back as he had originally promised, he should have returned by now. What had happened to her son? What had happened to her precious Wolf's Blood? And what of Swift Arrow, who still had not come to see her?

March of 1883 brought another grandchild, a son to Ellen, called Daniel James. And May of 1884 brought a son to LeeAnn and Joshua, called Lonnie Trent, the first name being that of another of Zeke's white brothers and the second being Abbie's maiden name. Jason was a full-fledged doctor, working on the reservation, and LeeAnn still taught there. Abbie at least had the two of them, plus young Matthew, now six, and the new baby. And Dan's beautiful daughter Jennifer was also with them now, having returned from Denver to stay for good, or at least until she thought her father didn't need her anymore. Her presence, and that of Dan's little four-year-old granddaughter, Emily, named after Dan's first wife and Jennifer's mother, brought the man much comfort and joy. Jennifer was an exquisite beauty, with thick auburn hair and sea-green eyes. She was the image of her mother, Dan's first wife, a beauty by anyone's standards. Her mother had been spoiled and fragile however, unable to cope with frontier life, and the marriage had not been a happy one. But at least one good thing had come of it—Jennifer, as beautiful as her mother but much stronger. She stayed in Montana, teaching at a school for white children, lonely herself for her own dead husband.

The spring of 1885 brought little progress for the Northern Cheyenne, who continued to balk at any kind of assimilation into white society. They did not want to give up their old ways, and Abbie could not help but agree with them. To be the way the agents and teachers wanted them to be was simply too drastically different from the way of life they had always known. Children were taken from homes and sent to distant schools, their hair cut short, their buckskins traded for cotton dresses and pants. Distraught, lonely parents drank and often fought. Nothing was more important to the Cheyenne than closeness to their children, and bringing them up in the Cheyenne way. They felt helpless and empty.

Abbie sometimes tried to forget all of it, for it brought her much pain. And on a warm spring night she agreed to be Dan's company at a dance held for the whites on the reservation and in surrounding areas. She fussed the whole day, wanting to look pretty not for Dan, whom she considered only a close friend and dear brother-in-law, but for that strange "presence" she always felt. She looked in the mirror at dark eyes set in a face that looked perhaps forty, even though she was fifty-five. The gray at her temples seemed to make her prettier, she surmised, or at least that was what Zeke would tell her. And her waist was still small. She stood back and studied her soft yellow dress with its full, ruffled skirt and flowing pagoda sleeves. The bodice was cut just low enough to reveal some of the fullness of her breasts, and her shoulders and neckline were still trim and young-looking. She was pleased with her appearance, considering all she had been through.

But then her throat tightened. Why did it matter? Who cared now? She suddenly realized that she was still taking care of herself for a man who was not even alive anymore. She still dressed for Zeke Monroe. He had been gone for six years, yet she still wondered how he would think of the way she looked. She had been gone from the ranch for a long time now, and it had been closer to seven years since last she lay in her husband's arms. Yet she cared what he would think of how she looked.

Dan was at the door then. Abbie and Jason lived in a small cabin near Dan's house, where he lived with Jennifer and his granddaughter. She swallowed her sorrow and greeted Dan, putting on a shawl and leaving with him, feeling suddenly lonely again.

The dance was the most fun Abbie had had in a long time. It was the first time in seven years she had danced at all or worn an extra pretty dress—not since that lovely week she and Zeke had spent in Pueblo. How could it have been so long ago?

The evening went by almost too quickly. She could tell as Dan walked her back to her cabin that he wanted to talk to her about something. She had suspected for a long time that perhaps he thought he loved her, and she supposed she had tiny womanly feelings toward him. But it was only out of loneliness, and he still seemed more a friend than anything else. She knew he was feeling the same way. It seemed logical they should end up together. And yet somehow it could not be the deep love husbands and wives should share—the kind filled with desire and passion. But then at their ages perhaps desire and passion were no longer necessary ingredients to a marriage. Abbie had known so much of it with Zeke that it was difficult to think of marrying a man that she did not have physical feelings for.

Dan left her at the door with a kiss on the forehead, leaving things still unsaid. Abbie watched him disappear into the darkness, and turned to open the door. It was then she heard someone call her name softly.

She hesitated, her heart pounding. The voice sounded familiar, but she could not quite place it.

"Do not be afraid," she heard then—a man's voice. "Do not run away."

She frowned, looking at the corner of the cabin from where the voice had come. There was a bright moon, and a lantern hung from the porch overhang. A man emerged from the side of the house, his hair long, his movements making no sound at all, for he wore soft moccasins and buckskin clothing. He stepped into the light, taller than she, but not quite as tall as Zeke. Yet it was almost like looking at Zeke. She stared,

435

astounded, bewildered, her heart fluttering like a little girl.

"Swift Arrow!" she whispered.

He looked magnificent—not at all the way she had pictured him, thinking him to be forlorn and ragged, perhaps a drunkard by now, old and disillusioned. He stood straight and strong, a hard look still about him, even though he must be sixty. Surely not! He had always been the most handsome of the three Cheyenne brothers, but age seemed to have been good to him. In an instant she realized he had dressed his best for her, wearing bleached buckskins, brightly beaded and painted, heavily fringed. He wore a bone necklace choker-style around his muscular neck and a gold earring in one ear. His hair was brushed out clean and long, braided at one side with beads wound into it.

He studied her with dark eyes, which were lit up now with a love so obvious it could not be denied. He stepped closer, his eyes falling to the full bosom for a moment, then meeting her own eyes.

She reached out with a shaking hand. It had been so long since she had seen a Cheyenne man stand so proud and handsome. For a moment she was back at the village where Zeke had taken her when only sixteen, where she had first met this man. She touched his arm, and he had to force himself not to grab her then and there. How many years had he loved her? Forty perhaps. However long it had been since first his brother brought her to his village. Did she ever change? She was still so beautiful. He could grab her right now and ride off with her and no one would know—not for a while—not until he had taken her to his dwelling in the mountains and forced her to submit to him. But perhaps it would not take much force. Perhaps he reminded her of Zeke. Still, she was Abigail, a woman he admired above all others, a woman he respected, his brother's widow and a respectable, gentle woman, the mother of his favorite nephew, Wolf's Blood. He had waited all these years to tell her his true feelings, but he could not bring himself to do so even now. The fact remained that she was white, and he was full-blooded Cheyenne. He had just seen Dan leave her. Dan. He was the proper man.

"Why have you waited so long?" she asked, searching

his eyes.

He swallowed, feeling on fire at the touch of her hand on his arm. "I could not come before," he told her in a strained voice. "It was . . . too hard. I knew it would take you many years . . . to get over my brother's death . . . if indeed you ever would. And when I myself heard, I went into deep mourning. I cut myself many times and drank much whiskey and was full of sorrow. My brother was a great man. Such men, it seems, should not die at all."

"It's been so terrible," she answered. "And Wolf's Blood—"

"I know about Wolf's Blood. I have my spies who keep me informed, for I do not like to come here."

"But you should come, Swift Arrow. No harm will come to you. Come and visit with us. Stay here—"

He stepped back as she stepped closer. "No. I have always been alone. I cannot bear to see how my People must live here. So I stay in the mountains alone. But for a long time I have wanted to come . . . just to see you, Abigail . . . to make sure you are well . . . to see if . . ." His eyes roved her lovely form again, and she felt herself reddening under his gaze, felt her heart pounding. She had not had these pleasant feelings since Zeke. ". . . to see if you had changed," he finished. "I see you have not. Do you never age, Abigail?"

Her eyes teared. "Swift Arrow, there is so much to talk about. I have thought about you so often. And to this day I remember with such fondness those days when I was so young and you taught me the Cheyenne way."

"I was not very nice to you then. I did not want you to be there. I even hit you once for looking upon the Sacred Arrows like a foolish child. Always I have regretted that."

"It doesn't matter," she said with a soft smile. "We grew to be great friends, and you learned to accept me. We became sister and brother."

His jaw flexed with repressed desires. "Yes. Brother and sister." His eyes fell to her bosom again. Then he stepped back more, holding his chin high, looking down on her rather haughtily, reminding her of the way Zeke looked sometimes— proud, so proud.

"I . . . cannot stay," he told her. "I only want you to know I am well, and I wanted to be sure that you were. I go now."

"No. Swift Arrow, wait!" she called out desperately. She reached out and grabbed at his arm.

He turned and startled her when he suddenly grabbed her close against him, pressing her breasts against his chest, embracing her in strong arms, his face close to hers.

"I tell you I must go now," he told her in a gruff voice. "What I want cannot be. I only wanted to see you once more, to tell you I am well and you are in my prayers always, Abigail, as you have been for all these many years . . . as any man would pray for his . . . sister."

In the darkness it seemed Zeke himself was holding her. A rush of desire swept through her, but in the next moment he let go of her. "I go. You will not hear from me again, Abigail, but I will remember you always. And do not worry about getting word to me about Wolf's Blood. I will know. I pray for him also."

He turned and disappeared into the darkness. She called after him, but he did not reappear, and moments later she heard a running horse. The sound faded away, and she walked on rubbery legs back onto the porch of the cabin. She clung to a porch post, trembling, feeling on fire. One moment. One brief moment and her mind and heart were whirling! She had not seen him for nearly twenty-three years, and in that one moment it seemed like yesterday, and she had felt sixteen again, had felt close to Zeke again. But it was not Zeke. It was his brother, Swift Arrow.

She pulled her shawl closer around her shoulders, suddenly shivering. Why did she feel this way? She thought about a conversation she and Zeke had had many, many years ago in which he had hinted that Swift Arrow had deep feelings for her. She had ignored the true meaning of what he had been trying to tell her, and had ignored the true reason Swift Arrow had stayed in the north and had never come back south. She had always had Zeke. She would not and could not consider how any other man might feel about her, nor had she had any feelings other than friendly ones toward any other man, not even Sir Edwin Tynes.

She walked to the door. She would not tell anyone she had seen him. He wanted to be left alone and she didn't want to make trouble for him. But she knew she would not soon forget this night, nor how it felt in that brief moment he had wrapped strong, hard arms around her. She touched the doorknob, then stopped when she heard the screech of an eagle. She frowned. An eagle at night? It couldn't be. Yet there was no mistaking the call.

Chapter Twenty-Six

In April of 1886 the news came. Several renegade Apaches had surrendered to General Crook, who had become their friend. But Washington would not abide by Crook's promises to the Apaches, and in fear for their lives Geronimo and Naiche (son of Cochise) had fled with twenty-four warriors back into Mexico. Thousands of soldiers were searching for them—thousands against not quite thirty frightened, desperate men. Because of the breakaway, some of those who had originally surrendered to the hated squalor of Bosque Redondo, the Apache reservation in the deserts of New Mexico, were arrested and shipped to Fort Marion, Florida, to the dreaded, mosquito-ridden, swampy prison that waited there for its Indian "convicts"; waited to claim their lives through despair, heat, deprivation and disease; the place where many red men died of broken hearts, far, far from their beloved homelands.

It was only then, when some thorough roll calls had been taken as Indian men were arrested and questioned, that news came of Wolf's Blood. Dan gave Abbie the news with tragic eyes, his face gray with sorrow. Her heart pounded when she opened the door to see him standing there with a message in his hand.

"What is it?" she asked quickly.

Dan sighed deeply and stepped inside. "I'm afraid Wolf's Blood has been sent to Fort Marion with several Apache men," he told her. He watched her go white. "I'm sorry, Abbie."

She grasped a chair. "How? Why? He's Cheyenne! He

441

should be sent up here!"

"He rode with the renegades, Abbie. From what I can find out Sonora was killed in some soldier attack two or three years ago."

She sank into a chair. "No!" she groaned. "Wolf's Blood! My poor son!" She looked at him with wide, desperate eyes. "What about Kicking Boy and little Iris?"

"I am told two children by that name are at Bosque Redondo. Their ages are, according to record, fourteen and thirteen, and they are listed as descendants of Apache and Cheyenne parents."

She rose, her horror replaced by a stubbornness that was unique to Abigail Monroe. "We must get them out of there! And I will get my son out of Florida!" she declared.

"Abbie, that won't be easy—"

"You can do it!" she interrupted. "You have connections through the Army! You must try, Dan! I want my grandchildren here with me! And I want my son! I am going to Florida right away. I am going to stay at that horrible place with him until he is released or until one of us dies, but he will not stay in that hellhole alone without seeing his mother and children again. We will get Kicking Boy and Iris and we will go to Florida and get their father!"

"Abbie, I don't know if that's possible—"

"We'll make it possible! What do you think Zeke would do if he were alive and heard his son was in that place? He would go and get him, even if he had to fight his way in and take him illegally!"

He grasped her shoulders. "All right. Calm down. I'll see what I can do."

Her eyes filled with tears, her heart screamed with desperate pain. Wolf's Blood! Her precious Wolf's Blood! "Please, Dan!" she said in a near whisper. "Get him out of there! And find a way to let me have my grandchildren!"

He kissed her hair and patted her shoulder. "You sit tight and wait. It might take a few days to get the proper clearances. And it's a long way to Bosque Redondo, let alone a trip all the way across Texas and the south to Florida. Are you up to something like that?"

"For Wolf's Blood? Just the thought of finding my grandchildren and getting him out of there gives me strength."

He sighed and nodded, going to the door.

"Thank you, Dan," she spoke up.

He met her eyes. She would be easy to love, if he let himself think of her as a wife rather than as a sister. But she had been restless for the past year, often mentioning Swift Arrow and commenting on her concern for him. He saw a strange longing in her eyes when she spoke about the man. Between that and knowing there could never again be a man as important to her as Zeke, he had been unable to allow any feelings for her to build into desire. She was, after all, Abigail, and even though Zeke was dead, it didn't really seem so. And he had known her too well over these years, had thought of her only as his brother's wife, a superbly honorable and respected woman. Perhaps in time he would ask her to marry him, out of a sense of duty, out of honor, out of a feeling he should protect and care for his brother's wife. He nodded to her and went out. Yes, he loved her, but not in the way he had loved Emily and Bonnie. Still, what man wouldn't want a woman like Abigail for a wife, in spite of getting older? She had been the finest wife a man could want, just as Bonnie had been to him. He had married Bonnie more out of practicality than love. Her son needed a father and his daughter needed a mother. But that practical marriage had quickly developed into not only a deep, abiding love, but a sexually pleasurable relationship as well. Perhaps it could be that way with Abbie. But something about her remained so untouchable. Was it Zeke Monroe's memory that kept him from thinking of her as anything but a sister? Perhaps it was foolish for him to feel that way. Perhaps he was wasting these years, for Abigail Monroe was exceedingly gracious and beautiful for her age, and there could not be a lot of time left for either of them. Should they live them out alone just because they were not sure what was proper, or because they did not have strong physical urges for one another? Wasn't friendship enough for two such people?

Of course there was Rebecca Moon to consider. She was

perhaps forty-five, a missionary woman who had come to the reservation not long ago to teach the Indians. She was a pleasant person, who had been widowed for many years. Dan found her attractive and knew Rebecca in turn often stole glances at him and seemed to make excuses to talk to him. He liked her very much. But Abbie must come first. She was as lonely as he, as much in need of a mate as he was. He would have to do some deep thinking. But first this thing with Wolf's Blood had to be straightened out. He hurried to the fort's telegraph office.

The train click-clacked over the Southern Pacific tracks, from El Paso across Texas, basically following the Rio Grande, on into Louisiana and through New Orleans, changing trains and going on, through Mississippi, Alabama, and into Florida, toward its eastern coast. It had been a strenuous trip for Abbie, who had first gone to Bosque Redondo, where she had been reunited with her precious grandchildren. Kicking Boy was tall and muscular for his age, looking very much like his father and grandfather, and just as handsome. Iris was exceedingly pretty. Both of them well remembered their grandmother, and the light in their eyes at hearing she was going to try to get their father out of Florida was worth the tiring trip. They were ragged and depressed when first Abbie found them, two lonely children living with a preacher and his family, who did not treat them well. Now the proper papers had been signed. The children would be held at Bosque Redondo and cared for until Abbie returned from Florida to take them north with her.

The emotional reunion with the grandchildren had given Abbie a boost, but still her emotions suffered from all the ups and downs she was experiencing. The next step was to get Wolf's Blood out of Fort Marion, and on the trip there Abbie experienced one of the most painful happenings in her life. She had watched the terrain change as the train rumbled east. She had not been back here since going west at fifteen. She had forgotten how thick were the forests, how tall the hardwood trees. How strange it was to see all of this again—so much green, so much swamp and forest. How odd to feel the humid summer heat that never bothered her as a little girl because she was used to it. But she wasn't anymore. She was used to a drier climate now, and could see why this type of environment was killing the Indians. At one time places like this were home to her. Somewhere north of these tracks lay Tennessee—her old home, her mother's grave. Was it really she who had left Tennessee forty-one years ago? Surely it was someone else, a young girl called Abbie Trent, whose body was not yet developed into a woman's, whose fiesty strength was to help her survive the tragedy that lay ahead for her, and whose heart knew what kind of man she wanted. Then that man had stepped into the light of her father's campfire, and little Abbie Trent was instantly a woman in her desires and in her heart.

She struggled to breathe, feeling as though a pillow were over her face. It was August of 1886, the worst time to be traveling through the South. But she would not wait for better weather. Wolf's Blood could be dying this very moment—desperate and lonely. She glanced at Jennifer, who had insisted on coming along, leaving her daughter behind in Montana for others to care for. Why had the woman been so persistent about coming? She had often asked about Wolf's Blood, frequently mentioning the one and only time she had met him, when she was twelve and Zeke and Abbie had gone to Fort Laramie. Jennifer had often shown Abbie the old war shield and the coup feather Wolf's Blood had given her that day, and her eyes would sparkle. And Abbie sensed that her son had left a lasting impression on Jennifer Monroe, one not just of a warrior cousin, but of a man who easily attracted young women. But they were cousins, and Cheyenne custom forbid marrying into family.

She frowned. Why had such a thought even entered her mind? The two of them had met only once, years ago. And Wolf's Blood had never looked at white women with any desire. What made her think Jennifer had any feelings for him other than as a cousin, or that the very proper, very beautiful young woman would look at any Indian man—even one only part Indian—with any thoughts of marriage? She had simply come along because she wanted to be with Dan, because she was concerned about the long trip and its effects on him, and because she had become a good friend of Abbie and thought she could help her. Still, the look in the girl's eyes when she spoke of Wolf's Blood made Abbie wonder. . . .

To the North lay the Appalachian and Blue Ridge Mountains—home. She could hear Zeke's mandolin and his melodic voice singing mountain songs to her again. When she was a little girl, swinging in her backyard and dreaming of handsome princes and being swept away someday, she had no idea the direction her life would take, or that her prince would be a tall, dark Indian man whose eyes and touch commanded her surrender.

She thought about the ranch. On their way south to the Apache reservation, they had stopped to see Margaret and Morgan and their third boy, already four years old when Abbie saw him for the first time. Little Zeke was seventeen, tall and handsome like his grandfather, a strong young man, loyal to his parents, a big help on the ranch. Nathan was equally handsome, not quite as tall, and fifteen years old by now. Thus Morgan had two fine sons to help him on the ranch, and a third one growing into it.

The ranch looked marvelous, the horses as beautiful as ever. Morgan and the boys had done a fine job with it. But walking there, seeing the house, all brought back memories that made Abbie's heart hurt so badly she felt physical pain. She thought she was over it but that wasn't so, and she could not bring herself to visit the place by the stream where the irises bloomed. Some things were better left to memory and the past. To rekindle them was just too difficult, and she was not certain now that she could ever go back to the ranch to live. It was so much Morgan's and Margaret's now, and that was fitting. To go back would be like trying to make things the way they once were, and that was impossible. She was at least able to face that much now.

Ellen and Hal were happy, and she had seen little Dan, now three, as well as Lillian, already seven, the same age that Abbie's own little Lillian had been when she died. But her granddaughter Lillian was a hardy girl, who could ride a horse and even helped her father on the ranch.

Yes, her children were all doing well. LeeAnn had stayed in Montana with Joshua, for she had just given birth two months earlier to their second child, a little girl named Abigail Iris, a name that brought tears to Abbie's eyes. That made grandchild number ten, as far as she knew. Had Jeremy ever had any children? She had never heard from him. She shook off the sorrow of it. At least he was apparently doing all right. The important thing now was to get Wolf's Blood and take him back with her. Perhaps if she could get him to Montana, his presence would make Swift Arrow come down to the reservation to see his beloved nephew. The thought of it made her heart beat harder again. She had never forgotten that night he had come, the feel of his arms around her. But it had only been for a moment, and that was over a year ago. She had not seen him again, nor did she expect to—unless Wolf's Blood could flush him out.

The heat and squalor of Fort Marion made Abbie shudder. Her son could not be here! Not in this horrible place! Indians died like flies here, if not of disease then of broken hearts. The children of these men had been taken from their mothers back on the reservation and shipped to Carlisle, Pennsylvania, where they were to be firmly schooled in the white man's ways, but where they also quickly died. To the Indian, family was everything, and these families had been split apart by order of the United States government. The old ways had been brutally and forcefully ended, with no thought to a quickly vanishing culture, no thought to the Indian as a human being. Abbie had arrived at Bosque Redondo just in time to keep her own grandchildren from being sent off to Pennsylvania, where she might never have found them.

A guard led Abbie to a squalid fenced-in area, where men sat around just staring, flies and mosquitoes landing on their sweaty skin, biting at them so cruelly that they no longer even brushed them away, for they had become calloused to the bites.

The smell was overwhelming—filth and waste, dirty hair and dirty bodies of men who no longer cared. She had begged Dan to let her come here alone, and against his better judgment he had relented. Papers had been left with the prison master, verifying that the one called Wolf's Blood was not even Apache but Cheyenne and belonged in Montana; also verifying that he was three-quarters white, even though he did not look it.

Men stared but did not move as a guard took her through the gate, watching all of them warily. "Wolf's Blood!" the man called out harshly. "Front and center, wherever you are!"

A moment later a man appeared from behind an outhouse. He was tall, still handsome, but as dirty as the others, his hair nearly to his waist and dusty. Abbie felt an awful pain in her stomach. So thin! He was so thin! The hard muscle was still there, but there seemed to be no extra flesh around it. His face was thin, but the eyes! Everything about him was Zeke, and it took her breath away. It had been so long since she had seen him—so long since she was so cruelly awakened to the memory.

He stared at her in near shock, walking closer to study her. "Mother?" he asked, obvious surprise in his voice. The dark eyes were suddenly angry. "What in God's name are you doing in this stinking place?"

Her eyes teared. "Wolf's Blood!" she whispered. She stepped closer, touching his arm, while the guard watched in near shock himself. He had been told this lovely white woman had a son here, but found it difficult to believe that this wild-looking Indian could be related to her at all.

Wolf's Blood jerked back. "Go away!" he hissed.

Her eyes widened. "What are you saying? I've . . . come to take you out of here, Wolf's Blood."

"And I cannot go!"

Her heart pounded with dread. "Of course you can go! I have papers—"

He stepped closer. "You would have me singled out, just because I carry white blood? No! I will not use my white blood to be treated more special than my friends here! I will not leave them!"

She sucked in her breath, scrambling to think fast. She had not expected this. Wolf's Blood! Her son! He turned to walk away, and she strutted up behind him, grasping his arm and jerking on it, making him turn back to face her.

"How dare you!" she declared, her anger and stubbornness rising then. "Do you know what I've been through trying to find you? Do you know how strenuous this trip was? And have you forgotten your promise to me? You said you would come back! You promised!"

His eyes teared. "That was before Sonora was murdered in front of my eyes, and my son and daughter dragged from our home! I have not seen them in years! For all I know they are dead."

"They are alive!" she retorted. "I have seen them! They are waiting right now at Bosque Redondo, and I will get them when I return and take them north with me—and their father!"

He swallowed. "Kicking Boy—and Iris? They are alive? Well?"

"Yes, my son. Please come home."

His eyes hardened again. "I cannot. I would feel like a traitor using my white blood that way."

"Damn you!" she blurted out in desperate pleading. "You're acting just like your father those times when he suddenly thought I would be better off without him. Why do you have to be so damned much like him?" Tears began slipping down her cheeks. "Look at me, Wolf's Blood! I am your mother. I'm not getting any younger. Don't think of it as being singled out or treated special because of your blood. Think of it as doing something for your mother before she dies. I've spent most of my life always wondering about you—my firstborn, my son, my precious Wolf's Blood! You're the replica of your father, and now he is gone. I need you. I've let you wander and fight and do what you thought was right all these years. All I am asking now is for a few years back—a little time to have my son with me! I've lost so much. I don't think I could bear going back without you! I can't go on losing and losing, Wolf's Blood! Please come back with me, son. Help me pick up the pieces."

He waved his arm around the circle of destitute men. "All of the pieces are here—right here in this prison. Look at them! Helpless! Lost! Alone! Their families murdered, raped, imprisoned, separated! Once these were men—fighting men— strong and brave and powerful! Now they are treated like pigs! They have no strength to go on. And worse than that, they have no pride left!"

"My God, Wolf's Blood, do you think I don't know what's happened? Do you think for one minute I don't understand and sympathize? For much of my life I lived among them! Cheyenne, Apache, what does it matter? The same thing has happened to all of them. And I was married to one! I watched a great part of him die when the People were brought to their knees. When that happened, I knew he would die too. Don't you stand there and preach to me, my son! I already know! And I am tired and beaten. I need you. Please, do this one thing for your mother! If you don't leave with me, I swear to God I'll stay right here! I'll live in the same filth, eat the same slop, and die of disease right beside you! I swear by my God!"

His heart ached for her. He saw a desperate panic in her eyes, and her words were spoken in near hysterics. Mother. His precious mother, whom he had always loved so deeply, in spite of the fact that she was a white woman. This was his father's chosen woman. He knew how she had suffered at the hands of Garvey and his men, knew her strength, knew all she had been through over the years. Perhaps there was not much time left for her, for although she was beautiful and well-preserved, she was still getting on in years. After all, wasn't he forty himself?

He grabbed hold of her, for she looked like she might pass out. The guard shoved a rifle barrel into his side and told him to get his hands off the white woman. Wolf's Blood, always quick to anger, pulled her aside, clenching his fists. "She is my mother!" he growled. "I only thought she might faint!"

The guard's eyes squinted. "Mother or not, she's white, and it's been a long time since you or any of these other bucks have seen a pretty woman!"

The horrible suggestion in the remark brought fury to Abbie's soul, and Wolf's Blood himself had never felt so much anger and hatred. But Abbie's motherly instincts made her act more quickly, for if her son made one move toward the guard he would surely be shot. She darted in front of Wolf's Blood and pushed up on the rifle, then kicked the guard hard in the leg. He let out a yelp of surprise, and Abbie yanked the rifle from his hands while he was momentarily stunned. She walked over to a large rock, holding the rifle by the barrel, and she hit the stock over and over on the rock until the rifle broke. Her anger had brought on a strength and fury she had never felt before.

Abbie turned to face the stunned guard, who just gaped at her. She walked back up to him, her eyes flashing, and handed him the broken rifle.

"If I were not so desirous of getting my son out of here and getting back to my grandchildren, I would have used that rifle on you, you filthy scum!" she growled at him. "How dare you utter such garbage from that foul, stinking mouth! You are not worth all the men sitting here inside this fence, and I highly doubt you have ever come near being the brave and fearless men they once were, you smelly, fat-bellied bastard!"

The man swallowed and stepped back. He didn't take the rifle so she threw it on the ground. A few of the Indian men grinned, making comments among themselves about the spunky white woman who showed no fear.

"Why don't you just leave!" Abbie hissed at the guard. "I'm not afraid of one man here! I would rather stay locked up with all these Indians than be caught alone in a room with you. Don't you touch my son again, and don't you dare touch me!"

The man's eyes moved over her, and he scratched his chin. He had no rifle now, and he did not like the way the Indians stared at him. He could feel them laughing at the fat white man who had been licked by a woman. He wanted very much to insult her severely, for surely she had slept with an Indian or her son would not be one. But he could tell by the eyes that were on him now that he dare not call her a dirty name or touch her. He turned and stalked out, grumbling something about sending in more guards and that she had better get herself out of there. He closed and locked the gate, and Abbie turned back to Wolf's Blood, who stood there grinning. Oh, how he looked like Zeke when he smiled! The same handsome, provocative grin that had won her heart so many years ago.

"So, you have not changed at all," he told her. "I think what Father liked about you was the challenge of conquering you at all, of winning one argument with you."

Her eyes teared again. "How wonderful to see you smile, Wolf's Blood." She stepped closer again. "Please come home. Surely you want to see Kicking Boy and Iris, and they want to be with their father again. You owe it to your son and daughter to come home. And you made me that promise, Wolf's Blood."

He sighed deeply. That he could not deny. His son, and his precious Iris! They had been taken from him so long ago he had long given up ever seeing them again, doubting they even lived. And they were the product of his love for Sonora—precious, beautiful, devoted Sonora, who had died trying to protect her children. Would he ever love a woman again? He placed a hand on her shoulder. No. One did not argue with this mother of his.

"What about the ranch?" he asked. "Is that where you will go?"

She wiped at her eyes. "I don't think so. I visited there, on the way down to New Mexico, and we can stop there so you can see Margaret and Ellen before we go to Montana. But now that I have been away, Wolf's Blood, I know that I cannot go back there to stay. It's still . . . too painful. Too much of him is there, and my life there can never be as it once was. I am certain one day we will all gather there for a nice reunion, in your father's memory. But I can't live there anymore. It's Margaret's and Morgan's now. But you may live there if you wish."

He shook his head. "No. I cannot go back either. There are many things I cannot go back to. I will go with you, Mother, to Montana, closer to the place where once I rode in war with my uncle Swift Arrow. Is he well?"

She blushed slightly. "The last I saw him he was. He visited me only once, after I had been up there several years. For some reason he stays away."

He sighed. "And you do not know why?"

She raised her eyes to meet his. "I'm . . . afraid to know."

452

He studied her eyes and nodded. "But you do know, don't you?"

She looked away. "I don't want to talk about that. Please. Come with me now, Wolf's Blood."

He led her to the gate. "You go and wait at the guardhouse. Who brought you here?"

"Your uncle Dan. Bonnie is dead now, Wolf's Blood. I think this trip has been good for Dan. If not for him, I could not have accomplished any of this. I have him to thank. And his daughter came also."

Wolf's Blood felt a rush of blood to his brain and he actually tingled. "Jennifer?" he asked carefully. "She is . . . here?"

Abbie caught the look and was surprised. "Yes. She lives with Dan now—she and her little girl. She's been widowed for quite some time. When we told her we were coming to get you, she—" She stopped short, seeing the eagerness in his eyes. She was astounded. She had never thought her son had given Jennifer a second thought after meeting her all those years ago at Fort Laramie. He put a hand to his hair.

"Will you do me a favor, Mother? Take her away from here—to the hotel or wherever you are staying. Have Dan stay—with some clothes. He can help me find a place to wash. I . . . I do not want anyone to see me this way. And give me a little time here, with my friends, to say good-bye."

She touched his face. "Thank you, Wolf's Blood." She choked back tears as she turned and quickly left, her heart full of love and gratefullness—and her mind raging with curiosity at his reaction to Jennifer's name. She was well aware that it was only for Jennifer that he wanted to clean up before meeting them.

The trip home found all of them quiet. Much was behind them now, and somehow they must all pick up the shattered pieces of their lives and finish out their years. Wolf's Blood's sullen, silent mood was soon broken by unending questions from Jennifer, who babbled as though she were twelve years old again, her eyes alight whenever they fell on the handsome

Wolf's Blood. He in turn found her amusing, refreshing, beautiful—disturbingly beautiful. Did he dare give in to his amorous thoughts of her—thoughts he had had for years, thoughts that had emerged every once in a while? After all, she was not only a cousin—although not as direct as most cousins—but she was also a white woman. Perhaps because their fathers had had different mothers, there was a way. . . . He shook off the thought and answered her endless questions about Indians, watching her full lips as she spoke, studying the provocative green eyes, taking in her fine shape and seeing in her a woman of substance and devotion.

But he could not help thinking of Sonora, beautiful Sonora. So much was gone. He had hated the railroads as much as any Indian, yet now he rode on a train. At least he was a passenger, rather than riding in the cattle car he had been shoved into when shipped to Florida. He wondered if he could ever be happy again, after seeing what had happened to the Apaches, remembering Sonora's savage killing at the hands of soldiers. How twisted and confused his life had been, moving in and out of his white and Indian worlds. At least he would see his son and daughter again. Somehow he must pick up the pieces, as his mother had said, and at least be a father to his children, although they were already half grown. The first thing he would do was start going for rides with Kicking Boy, as they had done when the child was small, and as Wolf's Blood had done with his own father so many years ago. Riding! Riding on the free wind. Yes, at least the wind was still free.

Jennifer interrupted his thoughts again with still another question, her green eyes dancing. He wondered if she knew how much she disturbed him.

Across from them Abbie sat resting, her eyes closed. Her brief nap was disturbed when she felt a hand close around her own, and she opened her eyes and turned to face Dan, who was watching her closely. "I want to talk to you, Abbie," he told her, "about something I've been putting off."

She felt her face flushing and she looked at her lap. "Yes?"

"Maybe we should get married," he said quietly.

She looked at him in surprise. "Married?" He was so

454

handsome—a good man, strong and sure like Zeke. But still . . . she looked back at her lap. "Dan, I know you have feelings for Rebecca Moon. I've watched how you look at her, seen your eyes light up when you talk to her. I . . . don't want you marrying me . . . out of some kind of duty. Nor could I marry you just because you're lonely and want a wife again."

"But I love you, Abbie. We'd be all right."

She smiled, blushing when she looked at him again. "I am sure we would. And I love you, too. But is our love the kind a man and woman should have for each other when they marry?" He frowned and she squeezed his hand. "Dan, you're a wonderful man, and most certainly a handsome one. I would be honored to be your wife—very honored. But I'm just not sure I want that yet, or that I am ready for it. And I think you should pursue your friendship with Rebecca, to be sure how you feel about her. I'm all right. Really I am. I have my children safe and sound now, and I have my grandchildren. I'm not saying no. I'm just saying we should wait."

He sighed and leaned over to quickly kiss her temple. "The offer is there, Abbie. And I don't think it's just Zeke's memory or any uncertainty you have about me that makes you say no. It's something else, and you'd best get it straight in your heart and mind."

"What do you mean?"

He leaned back and began stuffing a pipe. "Wolf's Blood asked me what I thought of how Swift Arrow was doing. I told him I hadn't seen the man in years." He watched her look away and start to blush. "He told me he was surprised, because you had seen him." He lit a match and sucked on the pipe to light it. "Why didn't you tell me you saw him, Abbie?"

She wrung her hands nervously. "I . . . don't know. I just . . . it was just . . . for a moment . . . after that dance we went to. He was waiting for me in the shadows. He only stayed long enough to be sure I was all right . . . and to let me know he was well. Then he left. I haven't heard from him since."

"Mmm-hmm." He puffed on the pipe and she looked at him.

"What is that supposed to mean?"

"I'm no fool, Abigail. I've suspected for years why Swift

Arrow stayed in the North, away from the only family he had, away from the brother he loved so much, the nephew he worshipped. It takes more than the excuse of making war to make a man do that. And then I began wondering why, when you came to Montana, he would never come to see us. He knew he no longer needed to fear arrest and imprisonment. And the reservation in Montana is better than most. He could have come down. Can you think of a really good reason why he wouldn't?"

She swallowed, looking at her lap. "No," she said quietly.

He puffed the pipe more and put an arm around her. "Well, I can. And when we get back, I can arrange an escort to take you to a place near where we think he might be—roust him out of there for you and bring him to the reservation, if you want. Or . . . we can leave you up there with him . . . to get a few things straight. And I will think about Rebecca Moon, as you say I should. But I have no deep feelings for her at the moment, Abbie. And I am telling you now that after you have spoken with Swift Arrow, if and when you return, I would like you to be my wife. The offer holds. I will love you and be devoted to you and provide for you—defend you. As far as the physical things that go with being man and wife, I'd not touch you unless you wanted me to. I know that your heart and memories are still full of Zeke, even after all these years. But I would also understand if there is someone else who brings out passions in you that have been too long buried."

She blushed deeply, still staring at her lap. "I don't know what you're talking about. And you're embarrassing me."

He grinned and puffed his pipe. "You know good and well what I am talking about. You think about it, Abbie. I'll accept any decision you make, and I'll love you, no matter what that decision is." He gave her a squeeze and patted her arm. "Follow your heart, Abigail, just as you've always done. That's what Zeke would tell you."

She wiped at unwanted tears with nervous fingers. Why had he mentioned Swift Arrow? Why did he think she should see him? It was ridiculous! And yet . . . yes, he was right that she should follow her heart. Zeke would want that. Zeke. What was left in her heart to give after losing him? Was a woman capable of ever loving again after living with such a man?

The train rumbled on, none of them aware that another train was headed back east, carrying more Apaches to Fort Marion, Florida, among them the infamous Geronimo himself as well as faithful scouts who had served the Army well, only to be made prisoners and sent to Florida with their brothers.

Chapter Twenty-Seven

Several Cheyenne men sat in a large circle, not far from the small school for the white children of the reservation. They passed around a bottle of whiskey, laughing and gambling, sharing stories of days when they made war and hunted. Those days were gone, and there was nothing now for them to do but talk about them. Wolf's Blood sat among them, collecting bets on a knife-throwing contest.

"We will see if you are anything like Lone Eagle," one old warrior told him. "Your father could not be matched."

"You forget he is the one who taught me," Wolf's Blood replied.

"You must split an arrow," the old man told him.

Wolf's Blood stood up, his hand on the shiny Bowie knife his father had bought for him nearly twenty-five years ago, when Wolf's Blood participated in the painful ritual of the Sun Dance, now a forbidden practice, although many warriors snuck away each summer to hold their important religious sacrifice anyway. The missionaries on the reservation considered it barbaric, having no understanding of the deep spiritual importance the ritual had for the Indians.

"Somebody shoot an arrow into that tree," Wolf's Blood declared, pointing to a tree near the schoolhouse. "I will be rich when you all pay me."

They all laughed, some of them passing the whiskey bottle again. One warrior stood up with bow in hand, but he was so drunk he could not get the arrow out of its quiver. There was more laughter, and Wolf's Blood took it out for him, taking the bow from the man's hand and shooting the arrow himself.

"At least you can hit a tree with an arrow!" one man hooted.

Wolf's Blood grinned and pulled out the Bowie knife. "Guide my hand, my father," he said quietly. He had tried this many times, coming close but never exact. Zeke Monroe never missed. Wolf's Blood breathed deeply, then flung the shining blade. There was a cracking sound as the arrow shaft split, and the tip of the knife rested just below the tip of the arrow, but not before splitting the entire shaft.

Wolf's Blood let out a war whoop and the others did the same, making a noisy ruckus as they slapped him on the back and began paying him. The door to the schoolhouse opened, and Jennifer appeared at the top of the steps. She marched down them and toward the men, her heart fearful of the drunken Indians, but her anger too great to stop her.

"I would like it quiet!" she announced in a loud voice. They all turned to stare at her. The way some of them looked at her, she felt naked. "I am trying to teach inside that school," she told them. "Perhaps most of you don't care about learning anything, but the children inside do, and I can't teach them when they're all hanging out the windows watching Indians drink and make bets! Now you men go find someplace else to have your fun or I will report you to the agent." She glanced at Wolf's Blood, then blinked back tears and walked back toward the school.

One of the Indian men began mimicking her walk, parading around with a sway to his hips. The others laughed, and when Jennifer caught the game she reddened and hurried inside.

"That white one needs a man," one of the younger warriors commented, taking another slug of whiskey. "Maybe we should give her another kind of education."

The whiskey bottle was suddenly slammed out of his hand, as he was grasped around the throat and shoved to the ground. "Touch her and I will kill you!" Wolf's Blood hissed. He held the man there until his face turned darker and his eyes bulged, then released him, rising and walking to the tree to yank out his knife. He held it out toward them all. "The next one of you who makes a remark about that woman will be bleeding to death!"

460

he warned.

They all quieted and backed away. Wolf's Blood shoved his knife into its sheath. He turned and walked past the school. Jennifer watched him through a window. She hurried out the back door then and called to him. He stopped but did not turn to face her, and she hurried up to him.

"I . . . I heard what you said. Thank you, Wolf's Blood," she told him.

He turned to face her then, his eyes angry. "You do not understand why they are that way. I do! But I am not like them. I was not drinking the whiskey. I visit with them, play games with them, because I feel sorry for them. They have no hope, and they have lost their ways of proving they are men. The whites do not understand what goes on in the heart of an Indian!"

He turned and she grasped his arm. "Don't go yet," she pleaded. He faced her again. "Wolf's Blood, you're such a fine man. I know you don't drink whiskey and such, but if you sit around with them every day, you will become just like them. I . . . I don't want you to be that way . . . sitting around drunk, no purpose to life."

His eyes moved over her body. Since the trip back north, having to look at her every day, answering her endless questions, he could not help but want her. She was the most beautiful creature he'd ever set eyes on. But she was so white, not just in looks, but in nature—so proper and educated. She had been married to a successful man and lived in Denver for many years. She was not the kind of woman for a man like himself.

"And how would you have me be?" he asked.

She blinked and let go of his arm. "You have a son and a daughter. Your father settled into ranching. He lived mostly like a white man, but he didn't abandon his Indian beliefs and spirit.

He snickered sarcastically. "Why should I settle now? My children are half grown, and because of the white man's government and Army, I was deprived of being a father to them for many years. My woman was killed before my eyes. A man needs a woman to settle. That is the only thing that gives him any desire at all to stay in one place and stay off whiskey. A man needs someone who—"

He caught the look in her eyes, and she suddenly blushed and turned away. She put her hand to her face, as though she were wiping at tears. He frowned and moved closer, peeking around at her. "What is wrong with you?" he asked.

She moved away again. "You're so . . . so . . . exasperating!" she whimpered. "Why do you insist on embarrassing me!"

He folded his arms. "How have I embarrassed you?"

She turned, tears on her face and her lovely green eyes angry. "How many ways do I have to show you?" she asked, her fists clenched. "Why do you think I kept that . . . that stupid war shield all these years . . . and the coup feather? Why do you think I came with my father to get you out of prison, and asked you all those questions on the way back?" She began to redden more. "I've . . . I've loved you since I was twelve years old! But then I never thought it was possible for two people like us to ever be together. I married another man, but there were . . . so many times when I thought about you."

He stared at her in surprise, and she turned away again. "I know we're cousins, but our fathers had different mothers, and for years we never even saw each other. It's like . . . like we aren't even related, Wolf's Blood. In a lot of cultures . . . it's all right for cousins to marry. And we aren't even full-blooded cousins. I know I don't understand everything about Indians, but I can learn . . . and I'm strong. If . . . if you wanted to maybe start a ranch . . . like your father did . . . I could help you. I wouldn't mind."

He stepped closer, putting his hands on her shoulders, studying the luster of her red hair in the sunlight as she stood there with her back to him. He reached up and lightly ran his fingers over her hair, and she wondered if she would faint at the touch.

"Since that one time I met you all those years ago, I also thought of you many times," he told her quietly. "But I never thought . . . such a thing could be . . . or that someone like yourself would consider being the woman of a man with Indian blood."

She sniffed and turned, her head hanging. "I don't think

you realize . . . how desirable you are, Wolf's Blood," she said quietly. "And I have talked to your mother many times. I know the kind of son you were. You are a fine man, strong and good. And I am afraid I am so much in love with you I can barely sleep at night."

His heart pounded wildly. She loved and wanted him! He had not considered that she would. He had thought her interest in him was only curiosity, with some feeling only because they were related. He embraced her fully, and she cried quietly against his chest.

"I . . . have money from my share of the ranch in Colorado," he told her. "I can have some of the horses anytime I want them . . . if I choose to start a ranch of my own. Do you like it here in Montana?"

"I wouldn't care where we were," she answered, clinging to him.

He smiled, holding her tighter. "I could start a ranch up here. I think I would like to stay here. Back home in Colorado, it hurts very much to be on the ranch my father built. It is Morgan's ranch now. I think I would like to start something of my own right here."

She looked up at him, her face flushed. "Are you saying . . . you want my help?"

He put a big hand to the side of her face. "You could not stay there and help me unless you were my wife."

She closed her eyes. "I would like to be . . . if you would want it so."

In the next moment warm lips pressed against her own in a tender kiss that made her feel faint with desire. The kiss lingered, turning from gentle to more urgent. Neither of them had satisfied such needs for a very long time. His lips finally moved from her mouth to her cheek, her throat.

"I want it so," he whispered. "Today, if it can be done."

The thought of being one with him sent shivers through her body, and she was sure that if he let go of her this moment her legs would not hold her. "I will be the best wife you could ever want," she told him softly.

The six soldiers with Abbie stopped at the foot of a heavily forested mountain. "He's up there someplace, ma'am."

"Fine. You can all leave. I'll go on by myself."

The men all looked at each other, and their leader pushed back his hat. "Ma'am, I know Dan Monroe told us to leave you be if that's what you asked. But Swift Arrow has been living alone for a lot of years. Some say he's a crazy man. At the least, he's an unsociable hermit, and it's not likely he's seen a woman in a long time. Do you understand what I'm saying?"

Abbie smiled and looked at him. "I've known him for a long time, Captain Eggers. I assure you I'll be all right. And after I have talked to him, he'll bring me down himself and stay with me until we're in sight of the fort. Swift Arrow would never harm me, nor would he allow anything to happen to me. Your only orders were to get me this far. You have no responsibility beyond that. Dan and I both assured you that anything after that was our own responsibility and you would not be blamed. Now please leave with your men. I'll be fine."

The man sighed deeply, resetting his hat. "If you say so, Mrs. Monroe." He turned his horse, waving for his men to follow him, and they headed back to the fort reluctantly. Abbie watched them until they were out of sight, then headed her mount into the trees to begin an ascent up the gradual rise of the mountain. It was so thickly wooded that if a tipi were someplace nearby one would never see it. She could do nothing but keep going, beginning to call Swift Arrow's name.

She had worn her best riding habit, a deep red velvet split skirt and matching short jacket, a velvet hat and high boots. A rifle rested in its boot on the saddle, and she knew how to use it in case she ran into an unsociable animal. But then perhaps the unsociable animal would be Swift Arrow himself. She didn't fear for her person at all, but she hoped he would not be angry that she had come here unannounced.

For over an hour she would her way through the trees, always climbing, calling out his name every few minutes until she began to feel hoarse. She came to a beautiful waterfall and dismounted, letting her horse drink. The place reminded her a little of the lovely cove where Zeke's body rested. The trees were so thick she did not even realize that overhead an eagle circled. She knelt down beside the rushing white water at the base of the fall, wondering if she had been foolish to come here. She leaned over and took a drink herself, and when she raised up again, an Indian man was standing directly across from her, watching her silently.

"Swift Arrow," she said softly. He looked wonderful, wearing beaded buckskins, his hair braided to one side. At his waist he wore a wide leather belt that held a handgun and a knife. In one hand he held a rifle.

She stood up, and Swift Arrow leaped across the stream in one step, then turned and set his rifle aside, turning back to look her over with an appreciative glance. "Why have you come here?" he asked.

She swallowed. "I . . . I'm not sure myself. There was something I wanted to tell you, only now I'm not so certain . . . you would care." She began to redden, wondering herself what had made her think she had to talk to him before deciding about Dan.

He took the reins of her horse and walked the animal to a tree, where he tied it. He removed a blanket from her saddle, coming over to the stream and spreading it out. He sat down on it and motioned for her to do the same. She hesitated.

"Maybe I . . . I shouldn't have come," she told him. "I have no right intruding on your privacy. I have angered you."

He grinned. "You have not angered me. You could never anger me."

Her eyebrows arched. "Not even if I looked upon the Sacred Arrows again?"

He frowned. "Do not remind me of that time I was cruel to you. It was a long time ago. I was a hot-blooded warrior, and you were a stupid young white girl that I did not like so much. We both learned many lessons that year I watched over you while Zeke was away. Now sit. You have come this far, so you might as well tell me whatever it is you wish me to know."

She walked over and sat down on the blanket, facing him. She studied the dark eyes. So much of Zeke shone through. "I guess I . . . I wanted to tell you first how sorry I am . . . about what has happened to the People. I know how it saddens your heart and hurts your pride."

His eyes turned angry, and he looked away, picking up a

465

small rock and tossing it into the water. "It is over now. Sometimes I can hardly bear the pain of it. So much is over."

"But there is much yet to be done, Swift Arrow. Your staying alone up here isn't helping the People. And they need help now more than ever. If we are to save the customs and language and culture, we need to record the stories and language of warriors like yourself, who remember all the old ways—remember what it was like when all the land belonged to the Indian. The little ones need to hear your stories. They need men like you to make it all come alive for them again. I want you to come down to the reservation, Swift Arrow, and help me. I teach little ones reading and writing, but I can't teach them the kind of things you can. I want you to come back with me—help me instill in the young one the language and the old ways. It's our only hope of preserving their heritage, their identity. The missionaries want to make them like white people, want to destroy all that is Indian in them. I won't let that happen. And there is a beautiful spirit inside of them that fights to stay Indian. They need help, Swift Arrow, help from the older ones like yourself who remember. Someday there will be none left who remember, and it will be too late."

He turned to face her, his eyes shining with love again. "There are not many who would try so hard as you. You have always understood, Abigail. I will consider it, if there is a promise I can leave again if I choose, and if I will not be imprisoned."

"You won't be. And you can come back anytime you wish. Oh, please do come, Swift Arrow! Wolf's Blood would be so happy to see you again. With Zeke gone, having you around would be such a blessing to him. He misses his father so, even after all these years. And you were like a second father to him. Surely you long to see Wolf's Blood again, don't you? And his children?"

He sighed. "This is true." He studied her intently. How he wanted her! How he still loved her! He looked away again. "I make no promises." How could he tell her part of the reason he would not come down was because she was there? "You should go now. I will think about all of this," he told her.

The water splashed over shining rocks, and Abbie leaned

over and picked at a wild flower. "There is another reason I came up here," she told him quietly, her face reddening.

He looked at her curiously. "And what is that?"

She swallowed, twirling the flower in her fingers. "Dan . . . has asked me to marry him."

He felt a stabbing pain at his heart, and an irritating possessiveness swept through him. "So?" he replied, trying to sound uncaring. "Marry him."

She met his eyes. "I just thought . . . perhaps you should know . . . you being Zeke's brother and all. I have never really gotten over Zeke, and I'm sure I never will. It makes me feel like I'm being untrue to him." She looked away again. "I really wouldn't be, for no man can ever be to me what Zeke was. I have little to give to any other man but friendship and loyalty. I can't think of Dan as anything but a good friend, but I would like someone strong beside me again, someone to lean on, a companion as I grow old. I . . . I think Zeke would understand that. As far as true . . . passion, mine was spent on Zeke. I have little of that left."

She waited. He said nothing at first, and when she met his eyes he only watched her lovingly. "Do you?" he asked.

She reddened again. "I . . . don't know what you mean."

"I think you know exactly what I mean. You are telling me it will be difficult to marry a man for whom you have no passion. Even in your older years, this is important to you, as it should be. And since you are here, I might as well use this last chance I will have to tell you . . . finally . . . that I love you, Abigail . . . probably as much as my brother loved you . . . and with all the passion you could want."

She looked at him in surprise, then put cool fingers to her crimson face and looked away again. "We're . . . brother and sister—"

"I have only said I look at you as a sister. In my heart you were my woman. But I was a Cheyenne Dog Soldier, and you were in love with my honored brother—a faithful woman, with eyes for no one but Zeke Monroe. Why else do you think I came to the North and never returned? Why else do you think I stayed away as I did, when all that I loved were in the South?"

She put a shaking hand to her face again, somehow deep

inside expecting the words, yet still truly shocked when he spoke them. She smiled nervously, watching the water. "But . . . older Indian men take young wives . . . women who can give them children . . . women who are pleasing to look at in private . . . pleasing to touch . . . young girls who give them pleasure in the night."

He moved closer, touching her cheek with the back of his hand. "And what is pleasure? What is joy and love? Are these things measured by the firmness of a breast or how slim is a woman's waist?" She blushed more and turned her face from him. He moved behind her then, grasping her shoulders. "Can such things comfort a man in his sorrow? Can they relieve the pains of his wounds? Dry his tears?" He gently forced her to turn, and they sat side by side, facing one another. "It is only the beauty of a woman's spirit that gives such comfort to a man. In this kind of beauty, none can match yours. You are the most beautiful woman I have ever known. And I have loved you from a distance for all these many winters, aching with the want of you. Surely you realized why I never took a wife after Yellow Moon died. And even she was my wife only out of duty."

She met his eyes then, hers tearing. "I . . . never thought . . ."

"Yes you did. You only pretended it was not so, because you loved my brother so that you would not allow yourself to acknowledge another man. I am not blind and foolish, Abigail. I know that if you were to lie with Swift Arrow, in your mind and heart you would be with Zeke."

She closed her eyes. "Please don't say it!"

"I must say it! After all these years of lonely suffering I must say it! For now you speak of marrying another, and I may never see or touch you again. I am asking you to be my woman, Abigail, even though you could never love me as you loved Zeke Monroe. My comfort would be simply to call you mine and to lie next to you in the night. In return you can have a little piece of Zeke—through me. The arms that hold you would be dark and strong. The lips that kiss you would be shaped as his. The eyes that behold you would be dark, and in the night it would be like again being with him. Let me do this

468

for you, Abigail, and in return I would at last find happiness in my remaining years."

She covered her face and wept, and he pulled her close. "For you I would go back," he told her. "I would help you teach the little ones, who are the only hope now for the Cheyenne to live on. I would live in a white woman's house and would ask only that you allow me to worship my way, as you allowed Zeke to do; that you would understand if sometimes I rode off for a while to be alone. I would comfort you in the night, Abigail, protect you as he protected you. And I would love you as he loved you. It is what he would want. It would not be a betrayal to his memory, for a man could not be loved more than we loved him." He put a hand under her chin and forced her to look up at him. He studied the beautiful brown eyes of the woman he had always loved and who, in his eyes, had not changed at all from the sixteen-year-old girl Zeke Monroe brought to his village all those years ago. "Tell me, Abigail. Tell me you feel no passion for Swift Arrow."

He met her lips, and she did not resist as he laid her back on the blanket. The water rushed nearby, while her horse nibbled at fresh grass. And an eagle circled overhead. It cried out once, then winged away. *Wagh.* It was good. All was well. The great bird headed south, toward the *Sangre de Cristo* Mountains—to wait. Yes, there was a time to die; but there was also a time to live.

It was the spring of 1887 when Jeremy opened the letter, sitting back in a plush leather chair and puffing on a pipe. He felt nervous, for he had not heard from his mother in years, and he wondered how she had even known where to write him. Would it be some kind of scathing letter, telling him never to return home? He had considered it, after learning his father had died. But he had always been afraid to go, his guilt too strong to allow it. He had finally admitted to his wife years ago that he was part Indian. She had not taken it as badly as he thought she might, and he learned that she really did love him as a person, rather than for his position and money. It actually surprised him, making him wonder if perhaps his own father

469

had also really loved him after all.

He felt a lump in his throat at the sight of his mother's handwriting.

Dear Jeremy,

For many years I have tried to forget about you, angry that you have ignored us for nearly twenty years. But you are my son, the seed of Zeke Monroe, and I must try once more to influence you to come home, and I must tell you for once and for all that you are loved and missed. I can do no more than this.

I live in Montana now, on a Cheyenne reservation. Your uncle, Swift Arrow, is my new husband, and we are very happy, although no man can mean to me what your father meant. I care little whether you approve of what I have done. I needed a man at my side in my aging years, and I can think of none more honorable than Swift Arrow. I feel in my heart Zeke would approve. And, after all, it is the Cheyenne custom that when a warrior dies, his wife comes under the care of a brother.

The real purpose of my letter is to tell you Wolf's Blood, who was imprisoned in Florida for a while, is now with us again and remarried to a white woman, a wonderful young woman who makes him very happy. He is going to start a ranch here in Montana, where your youngest brother Jason is a doctor, and where LeeAnn and her husband also live. We are all going down to the old ranch this summer so that Wolf's Blood can pick out some horses to bring back with him to help him get started. And he must sign over his share of the ranch to Margaret and her husband. We will be spending the month of July there. It will be a real family reunion, with all the children and grandchildren. But it will not be complete if one child is missing. I beg of you to try to come. You will be welcomed, you and your wife, whom we have never had the privilege of meeting. We have all been through so much, Jeremy. It is time, for your father's sake, to all be together and to forget the pain of the past. And there is so much to tell you that I could not possibly get it all in this letter. I will pray everyday that you will come. If you want to do one thing, just one thing, to make up for hurting Zeke, then come to the ranch in July. He will know you have come, and he will be at peace. If you choose not to come, then I must tell you that I love you and that you have a place in my heart always, for you are my son, first and above all. God bless.

Mother

He folded the letter, feeling a sudden urge to cry. He breathed deeply, setting his pipe in an ashtray and rising to leave the study and go to the kitchen, where his wife was preparing tea.

"Mary, what do you think about . . . about meeting my family . . . my mother?"

She looked up at him in surprise. "What should I think? I would be very happy to meet them. Why?"

"I . . . uh . . . I got a letter from my mother, asking me to come to the old ranch this summer. She's planning some kind of family reunion of sorts."

She set down a cup. "I think we should go. You haven't seen your mother in nearly twenty years, and I have never met her at all. And she must be getting on in years. We both know how you suffered when you learned your father was dead, when you finally admitted to me your real heritage." She stepped closer, touching his arm. "Don't let your mother pass away without seeing her again, Jeremy. You could never live with that. This thing over your father was bad enough. I don't want to go through that with you again."

He sighed and blinked back tears, putting on a smile. "I have my brother to consider—the wild one. I think he'd like to pound me into the ground, and I wouldn't blame him if he tried it."

She smiled. "After all this time, and with your mother there? I doubt he'd try it, Jeremy, not if you have a good talk." She squeezed his arm. "It will all work out."

He met her eyes. "Yes. Maybe it would. I'd like to go, Mary."

She nodded. "Then it's settled. And if we are going to go, I want to know all about your family, at least what you know up

471

to twenty years ago. It will help me when I meet them." She sat down to her tea. "Tell me again about your parents—your mother."

He smiled, pouring himself some tea. "My mother." He shook his head, his eyes tearing. "My mother's maiden name was Abigail Trent, and she came out here from Tennessee when she was only fifteen. My father was the scout for her wagon train. We all laugh secretly when she tells us, for the thousandth time, how they met, when he walked into the light of her father's campfire, and she handed him a cup of coffee, and their fingers touched. . . ."

"Don't make me leave you, for I want to go wherever you go, and to live wherever you live; your people shall be my people, and your God shall be my God; I want to die where you die, and be buried there. May the Lord do terrible things to me if I allow anything but death to separate us."

—*Ruth 1:16-17*

Epilogue

It was over for the Cheyenne and other native Americans; at least the old ways were over. Geronimo was to eventually die at Fort Sill, Oklahoma, over twenty years after being taken prisoner and sent to Florida, never again to see the beloved mountains and deserts of his homeland. Most tribes lived in places far removed from what they once called home. And in the Black Hills in 1890, just four days after Christmas, one of the bloodiest skirmishes between Indian and soldier took place—a last battle that started through misunderstanding and panic, as many such battles were instigated. It happened at a place called Wounded Knee, where a handful of defenseless, half-starved Sioux were massacred by soldiers using not only rifles, but bigger Hotchkiss guns that sent flying shrapnel into men, women, and children. When it was over, an estimated three hundred Sioux lay dead, mostly women and children. Others who were only wounded crawled off to die. When the bodies were picked up, some live babies were found beneath the bodies of their dead mothers.

Perhaps the sentiment of many whites at that time is best described in the words of journalist Samuel Bowles *(The Springfield Republican),* who after attending the Fort Laramie Council in 1851 wrote the following words that summed up what was to happen to the Indians over the next forty years:

"We want your hunting grounds to dig gold from; to raise grain on—and you must 'move on.' Here is a home for you;

you must not leave this home we have assigned you. When the march of our empire demands this reservation of yours, we will assign you another—using force, if necessary—but so long as we choose, this is your home, your prison, your playground. . . . Let the Indian die, as die he is doing and die he must, under his changed life. This is the best and all we can do. His game flies before the white man; we cannot restore it to him if we would; we would not if we could; his destiny is to die."

(Taken from the *Wind River Rendezvous*,
St. Stephens Indian Mission Foundation,
Vol. IX, Mar./Apr. 1979 No. 2)

The white man nearly accomplished all that was uttered in that statement, and after the Wounded Knee massacre the following words were spoken by Black Elk, one who was present at that fatal event:

"I did not know then how much was ended. When I look back now from this high hill of my old age, I can still see the butchered women and children lying heaped and scattered all along the crooked gulch as plain as when I saw them with eyes still young. And I can see that something else died there in the bloody mud, and it was buried in the blizzard. A people's dream died there. It was a beautiful dream . . . the nation's hoop is broken and scattered. There is no center any longer, and the sacred tree is dead."

(From *Bury My Heart At Wounded Knee*
by Dee Brown)

Wounded Knee became a symbol of "the end of the end." For many years thereafter the white man did everything in his power to mold the Indian into his own form, to educate him, dress him, give him land, break up the family unit, destroy the culture, wipe out all Indian identity. But to this day his efforts have failed. No race has held more tightly to remaining separate than the American Indian.

And so the fight goes on, and perhaps the true destiny of the American Indian is not yet known. *Otaha!* The song is not yet finished.

Author's Note

This book concludes my **SAVAGE DESTINY** series. I hope all of you have enjoyed reading these stories as much as I have enjoyed writing them for you, and that you will look for the several other novels I have written. Feel free to write me at 6013-A North Coloma Road, Coloma, Michigan 49038. I love hearing from my readers, and I answer all letters. Please include a self-addressed stamped envelope.

SWEET MEDICINE'S PROPHECY
by Karen A. Bale

#1: SUNDANCER'S PASSION   (1778, $3.95)

Stalking Horse was the strongest and most desirable of the tribe, and Sun Dancer surrounded him with her spell-binding radiance. But the innocence of their love gave way to passion—and passion, to betrayal. Would their relationship ever survive the ultimate sin?

#2: LITTLE FLOWER'S DESIRE   (1779, $3.95)

Taken captive by savage Crows, Little Flower fell in love with the enemy, handsome brave Young Eagle. Though their hearts spoke what they could not say, they could only dream of what could never be. . . .

#3: WINTER'S LOVE SONG   (1780, $3.95)

The dark, willowy Anaeva had always desired just one man: the half-breed Trenton Hawkins. But Trenton belonged to two worlds—and was torn between two women. She had never failed on the fields of war; now she was determined to win on the battleground of love!

#4: SAVAGE FURY   (1768, $3.95)

Aeneva's rage knew no bounds when her handsome mate Trent commanded her to tend their tepee as he rode into danger. But under cover of night, she stole away to be with Trent and share whatever perils fate dealt them.

Available wherever paperbacks are sold, or order direct from the Publisher. Send cover price plus 50¢ per·copy for mailing and handling to Zebra Books, Dept. 1811, 475 Park Avenue South, New York, N.Y. 10016. DO NOT SEND CASH.

CAPTIVATING ROMANCE FROM ZEBRA

MIDNIGHT DESIRE   (1573, $3.50)
by Linda Benjamin

Looking into the handsome gunslinger's blazing blue eyes, innocent Kate felt dizzy. His husky voice, so warm and inviting, sent a river of fire cascading through her flesh. But she knew she'd never willingly give her heart to the arrogant rogue!

PASSION'S GAMBLE   (1477, $3.50)
by Linda Benjamin

Jade-eyed Jessica was too shocked to protest when the riverboat cardsharp offered *her* as the stakes in a poker game. Then she met the smouldering glance of his opponent as he stared at her satiny cheeks and the tantalizing fullness of her bodice—and she found herself hoping he would hold the winning hand!

FORBIDDEN FIRES   (1295, $3.50)
by Bobbi Smith

When Ellyn Douglas rescued the handsome Union officer from the raging river, she had no choice but to surrender to the sensuous stranger as he pulled her against his hard muscular body. Forgetting they were enemies in a senseless war, they were destined to share a life of unbridled ecstasy and glorious love!

WANTON SPLENDOR   (1461, $3.50)
by Bobbi Smith

Kathleen had every intention of keeping her distance from Christopher Fletcher. But in the midst of a devastating hurricane, she crept into his arms. As she felt the heat of his lean body pressed against hers, she wondered breathlessly what it would be like to kiss those cynical lips—to turn that cool arrogance to fiery passion!

Available wherever paperbacks are sold, or order direct from the Publisher. Send cover price plus 50¢ per copy for mailing and handling to Zebra Books, Dept. 1811, 475 Park Avenue South, New York, N.Y. 10016. DO NOT SEND CASH.